Praise for Elizabeth Mansfield

"Elizabeth Mansfield is renowned for delighting readers with deliciously different Regency romances."
—*Affaire de Coeur*

"One of the enduring names in romance."
—*The Paperback Forum*

"Readers who have never read a . . . Regency romance could not find a better author to introduce them to the joys of the [genre]."
—*The Romance Reader*

A Christmas Kiss
and
Winter Wonderland

Elizabeth Mansfield

A SIGNET BOOK

SIGNET
Published by New American Library, a division of
Penguin Group (USA) Inc., 375 Hudson Street,
New York, New York 10014, USA
Penguin Group (Canada), 90 Eglinton Avenue East, Suite 700, Toronto,
Ontario M4P 2Y3, Canada (a division of Pearson Penguin Canada Inc.)
Penguin Books Ltd., 80 Strand, London WC2R 0RL, England
Penguin Ireland, 25 St. Stephen's Green, Dublin 2,
Ireland (a division of Penguin Books Ltd.)
Penguin Group (Australia), 250 Camberwell Road, Camberwell, Victoria 3124,
Australia (a division of Pearson Australia Group Pty. Ltd.)
Penguin Books India Pvt. Ltd., 11 Community Centre, Panchsheel Park,
New Delhi - 110 017, India
Penguin Group (NZ), 67 Apollo Drive, Rosedale, North Shore 0632,
New Zealand (a division of Pearson New Zealand Ltd.)
Penguin Books (South Africa) (Pty.) Ltd., 24 Sturdee Avenue,
Rosebank, Johannesburg 2196, South Africa

Penguin Books Ltd., Registered Offices:
80 Strand, London WC2R 0RL, England

Published by Signet, an imprint of New American Library, a division of Penguin
Group (USA) Inc. *A Christmas Kiss* was previously published in Dell and Jove
editions. *Winter Wonderland* was previously published in a Jove edition.

First Signet Printing, November 2005
First Signet Printing ($4.99 Edition), November 2007
10 9 8 7 6 5 4 3 2 1

A Christmas Kiss copyright © Estate of Paula Schwartz, 1978, 1990
Winter Wonderland copyright © Estate of Paula Schwartz, 1993
All rights reserved

REGISTERED TRADEMARK—MARCA REGISTRADA

Printed in the United States of America

PUBLISHER'S NOTE
These are works of fiction. Names, characters, places, and incidents either
are the product of the author's imagination or are used fictitiously, and any
resemblance to actual persons, living or dead, business establishments, events,
or locales is entirely coincidental.

The publisher does not have any control over and does not assume any
responsibility for author or third-party Web sites or their content.

A
Christmas Kiss

· One ·

THE SOUND OF a blow, followed by a sharp cry and the thump-ker-thump of a body rolling down the stairs, did not seem to disturb the two young men seated before the comfortable fire in the library of Carbery Hall, dispiritedly sipping their after-dinner brandies. The imperturbable gentlemen, Reginald Windle, Viscount Farnham, and his friend James Everard, the someday-to-be Earl of Gyllford, were the guests of Geoffrey Carbery, an inattentive and irksome host who was, as usual, not to be found in their company.

"Did you hear thomething?" Reggie asked, his lisp emphasized by the effect of the brandy, which was also beginning to show in the heightened color of his rather chubby cheeks. Though turned out most fashionably in an evening coat cut for him by Mr. Brummell's own tailor, Reggie was a stone-and-a-half too heavy to be considered a Dandy. However, his generous nature and his ever-ready propensity to share with his friends the enormous fortune with which his father had endowed him made him an extremely popular member of that set. Even his inability to disguise his lisp did nothing to diminish his popularity.

Opposite him, deep in a tall, winged chair, his friend Jamie nodded disinterestedly. James Everard, on whose boyishly handsome face no trace of brandy yet showed, was a well-built young man of twenty-two. His curly auburn

hair and shapely legs would have been decided assets had he
aspired to Dandyism, but he cared only for sport. He was
held in high esteem among the Corinthians for his prowess
in boxing and his skill as a horseman. He had little interest
in fashion. As Reggie had pointed out to him earlier in the
evening, his clothes looked positively careless. His neckcloth was tied in a quite commonplace fold, his shirtpoints
were slightly wilted, and his breeches revealed the merest
suggestion of a crease at the hipline. But such were the
depths of despond into which the two friends had fallen that
neither was much disturbed by these solecisms. "Sounds
like someone's fallen," Jamie murmured in answer to
Reggie's question.

"Do you think we ought to have a look?" Reggie
suggested mildly.

Jamie sighed and put down his glass. "Might as well," he
said, getting up and stretching. "There's nothing better to
do."

Reggie took a last sip of brandy as Jamie crossed the
room and opened the door. "Good heavens!" he exclaimed
at the sight that met his eyes.

"It's Geoff!" gasped Reggie, just behind him in the
doorway.

There at the foot of the stairway lay their friend, Geoffrey
Carbery, rubbing his head and blinking his eyes dazedly.
Above him, halfway up the stairs, stood Miss Evalyn
Pennington, the governess of his young sister and brother
and the cause of his shameful neglect of his guests. When
Jamie and Reggie had accepted his invitation to visit
Carbery Hall for some good shooting while the autumn
weather prevailed, they had expected a busy, active fortnight. But Geoff had taken one look at the governess and
had been a useless host from then on. If he wasn't following
her about on her walks with her charges, he was extolling

her charms to his bored and unsympathetic friends. To no avail did Jamie point out to Geoff that his mother would never permit an alliance with a governess; to deaf ears did Reggie repeat the observation that Miss Pennington showed him not the slightest interest or encouragement. Geoffrey was deeply immersed in his first love and, as Jamie remarked to Reggie—with all the authority of complete lack of experience or interest—calf love was not an affliction known to respond to reason or restraint.

"Geoff, are you hurt?" Jamie asked. "Miss Pennington, is he hurt?"

"That is precisely what I intend to ascertain," Miss Pennington answered coolly. She tucked the heavy volume she was carrying under her left arm, smoothed back a stray wisp of dusky hair with her right hand, and then came calmly down the stairs. "Will you be good enough to give me your assistance?" she asked, handing her book to the wide-eyed Reggie and kneeling down beside the fallen youth. Lifting Geoff's head onto her lap, she looked up at Jamie. "A brandy should do very well, I think," she said.

Jamie shook himself into action, raced into the library, and hurried out with his own half-finished drink. He knelt beside his friend and forced the glass between Geoff's lips.

At the first swallow, Geoff shuddered and lifted his head. "What happened?" he asked foggily.

"I hit you with the Atlas," the calm Miss Pennington replied, "and you tumbled down the stairs. I think you have a slight bruise, here behind your left ear, but I'm convinced it is of little consequence. Do get up, sir, and permit me to return to the nursery."

But by this time Geoffrey had noted with appreciation the position in which he was luxuriating and was reluctant to surrender it. "May I lie here for a minute or two, please," he pleaded, "until I feel a little more the thing?"

"Now don't be childish. Here are your friends, waiting to support you into the library where you'll be much more comfortable stretched out on the sofa near the fire," Miss Pennington answered reasonably.

Jamie, filled with a combination of relief and disgust at his friend's words, began to put the pieces together. "Geoff, you devil's brat, don't tell me you accosted poor Miss Pennington right there on the stairs!"

"Well . . ." Geoff shifted in her lap uncomfortably.

"If that don't beat all!" Reggie exclaimed, shocked.

"Get up, you lobcock!" Jamie sputtered. "I wish she hadn't banged your head with that Atlas, so I could have done it properly, with my fists!"

Geoffrey groaned in anguish. "I didn't mean to . . . to . . . But after all, Evalyn, you never let me . . . You won't even listen to anything I have to say to you!"

Miss Pennington sighed. This was not the first household in which she'd been employed where a gentleman had been tempted to behave improperly. Several times in the past there had been gentlemen, young and not-so-young, who'd permitted themselves to embarrass her with improper advances. This unwanted masculine attention was puzzling to her, for she was convinced that her behavior gave them not a jot of encouragement. She was not aware that her dark curls framed a face that—while its features might be considered unexceptional—was made lovely by the serene expression of her mouth and the sparkling brightness of her grey eyes. Nor did she realize that she was slim and shapely and moved with supple grace.

In the past, the directness of her immediate rebuffs had sufficed to quell such amorous advances. This time, however, the smitten Geoffrey would not be discouraged. Even after she was brought to the necessity of defending herself with the Atlas, he still was persisting in his attempts to declare himself. She looked down at his head resting on her lap. "I know what you have to say to me," she said firmly, "and I've told you over and over that it is a subject which needs no further discussion. Now, if you wish to prevent further embarrassment to yourself and to me, please let Mr. Everard and Lord Reginald help you up and take you to—"

A scream from the top of the stairs interrupted her. They all looked up to find Lady Carbery staring down at them aghast. "Geoffrey! Geoffrey, my darling boy, what is it? What has happened to you?" she cried as she hurried down the stairs. Reg and Jamie hastily lifted Geoff to his feet. Miss Pennington rose gracefully and brushed out her skirts.

"It's nothing at all, Mama," Geoffrey muttered uncomfortably, "nothing at all. A little fall. I was a bit dazed, that's all."

Lady Carbery's right eyebrow lifted suspiciously as she looked from one to the other. She was only partially relieved by the assurance that her eldest son had suffered no physical hurt. The presence of Miss Pennington in the midst of all this hugger-mugger made her large bosom swell with indignation. "Miss Pennington," she said in coldly ominous tones, "will you kindly explain your presence here, surrounded by all these . . . er . . . by my son and his guests?"

"I was just excusing myself, ma'am," Miss Pennington replied with her usual aplomb. "I was on my way to return this Atlas to the library. I had entertained little Algie with a bedtime tale of Samarkand, and he wanted to see where it was."

"Never mind fobbing *me* off with bedtime stories, Miss! I distinctly saw you sitting on the floor with my son's head in your lap!"

"Oh, now, I say!" Jamie couldn't help remonstrating.

Lady Carbery looked at him icily. Guest or no guest,

James Everard would not be permitted to interfere in her management of her household. Jamie met her eye, lowered his, and choked back any further comment.

"No need to rip up at Miss Pennington, Mama," Geoff put in heroically. "All she did was try to help me after I fell."

"I see," Lady Carbery muttered. The inappropriateness of chastising Miss Pennington in front of her son and his guests belatedly occurred to her. "Very well. We'll say no more on this matter now. However, Miss Pennington, after you have replaced the Atlas and seen to the children, please come to me in my dressing room." And with those dire words, she majestically turned and mounted the stairs.

Jamie looked at Miss Pennington with sympathy. "I'm afraid Geoff has placed you in a fix," he said.

"Please don't concern yourself about me, sir," Miss Pennington replied. "Lord Reginald, if you would be so kind as to replace that book, I'll return to my duties." With a bow, she turned and made her way up the stairs, the graceful carriage of her head and the unhurried swing of her step giving no hint of her inner agitation.

But later, the three gentlemen, seated round the library fire, could not rid themselves of their feelings of oppression and guilt. "Mama is sure to give her notice. I've really done it this time," Geoff muttered dejectedly.

"I'll say you have," Jamie growled. "If ever I've met a worse gudgeon than you! To accost a girl living in your own home . . . ! It really beats all!"

"I know. But having her so near, and not being able to get her to listen to me—"

"Pleathe! Let'th not hear any more about your thuffering. We've heard nothing elthe for dayth on end!" said the aggrieved Reggie.

"Right!" Jamie seconded. "It's Miss Pennington we're

concerned about, not you. What will the poor girl do if your mother turns her off?"

"I don't know. She's been in service ever since her father died and left her penniless. I suppose she'll have to look for another post. If only she'd consent to marry me . . ."

Jamie and Reggie groaned simultaneously. "Will you stop talking fustian?" Jamie exclaimed impatiently. "Your mother would never permit it."

"That doesn't matter. I'm of age."

Jamie looked at him with scorn. "Huh! You couldn't oppose your mother if you was eighty."

"And anyway," added Reggie, "Mith Pennington don't want any part of you."

"Just so," Jamie agreed, "so let's hear no more on that score. I was wondering . . . how is she to get another post? Won't she need a letter from your mother? What they call a 'character'? A letter of commendation or some such thing?"

"A letter of commendation? Oh, my lord!" groaned Geoff. "If I know my mother, she'll turn her off without so much as a kind word."

"You don't mean it!" Reggie gasped, much shocked. "Why would your mother turn her off without a recommendation? Miss Pennington didn't do anything at all reprehensible. It was you—"

"I know, I know. But mother thinks that Evalyn has been . . . has been . . ."

"Has been what?"

A flush suffused Geoff's bony cheeks. "Has been . . . er . . . setting her cap at me."

"If that doesn't take the cake!" Jamie said with disgust. "As if a beautiful creature like Miss Pennington would chase a scrawny, squint-eyed fool like you!"

"Well," Reggie put in reasonably, "you know what motherth are."

"No, I don't, not having had one since I was a baby. But never mind that. What, tell me, is Miss Pennington to do if she is turned off without a good recommendation?"

Geoff dropped his aching head into his hands. "I'm dashed if I know," he groaned.

Reggie got up and paced about helplessly. "Maybe one of uth could write a recommendation," he ventured.

Jamie glared at him. "That would be just the thing for a woman who wanted a nice, respectable governess for her brats—a recommendation from a *bachelor*!"

"Oh, I thee what you mean. Thorry."

Jamie sipped his brandy thoughtfully. "If only my Aunt Clarissa was here. She'd know what to—" His eyes lit up with sudden inspiration.

"What ith it, Jamie? Have you thought of thomething?" Reggie asked hopefully.

"Wait. Let me think. I may have a plan." The others watched in respectful silence while Jamie sat immobile. Then he looked up. "How does this sound? I'll write to my Aunt Clarissa immediately, asking her and my father to invite Miss Pennington to spend Christmas with us. Then, as soon as the invitation arrives, I'll take Miss Pennington home to Gyllford with me. When Aunt Clarissa gets to know her, I'll warrant she'll take it on herself to get Miss Pennington suitably placed."

"Oh, capital!" exclaimed Reggie, clapping Jamie on the back. "That would be the very thing! And athk your aunt to have Lord Gyllford invite me too, while you're about it."

Geoff jumped up eagerly. "And me, too, Jamie. Perhaps if I were to see Evalyn outside my own home, she'd change her mind about me."

Reggie and Jamie stared at Geoff in disbelief. "You!"

Jamie said scornfully. "You, my boy, can whistle for it! You ain't going to be invited. We don't want you anywhere near that girl."

"Oh, I see how it is," Geoff muttered querulously. "You want her for yourself!"

"Who, me?" asked Jamie in surprise. "Don't be a harebrain. You know I ain't in the petticoat line. Besides, she's much too clever a female for my taste."

"Well, Reggie, then."

In response to that accusation, Reggie simply snorted. His shyness in the presence of females was too notorious to need mentioning.

"If neither of you is interested in her, why are you going to this bother? Why should you be concerned about her?"

Reggie shrugged. "Can't help it. Can't abide theeing anyone in trouble."

"It's only gentlemanly, after all," Jamie explained reasonably. "It wouldn't be at all the thing merely to ignore the poor chit's distress. Especially when the trouble was caused by our own friend and host."

"Very noble, I'm sure," Geoff said with chagrin. "But I don't see why I can't come too."

"Because she'd never agree to come if you made one of the party. Your crackbrained behavior has seen to that."

"And anyway," Reggie put in, "you'd do much better to stay here—at home with your Mama."

Geoff gave Reggie a dagger look and returned sulkily to his chair. "Your aunt and your father might disappoint you," he said with sour satisfaction. "They may not wish to invite a perfectly strange female to spend the holidays with them. Did you ever think of that?"

Reggie and Jamie exchanged glances. For once, Geoff

had scored a home thrust. Inviting a female to his home was not a thing Jamie had ever done.

"What do you think, Jamie?" asked Reggie in concern.

"Don't worry about Father and Aunt Clarissa," Jamie answered with an assurance he was far from feeling. "They'll come through. I know they will."

· Two ·

THE RUTHERFORD BALL was in full swing. The dance floor was crowded with elegantly dressed couples, the card rooms were filling with smoke, the buffet tables were thickly surrounded, and the staircases were thronged with latecomers pushing their way up and early leavers inching their way down. It was obvious already that the Rutherfords were hosting the greatest squeeze of the season.

Philip Everard, the fourth Earl of Gyllford, stood in the immense hallway with his sister, Lady Steele, and surveyed the crush with dismay. "What a mob!" he muttered. "You should have warned me, Clarissa."

"If I had, you'd never have agreed to escort me," she retorted, handing her wrap to a waiting footman. "Now, come along like a dear boy, and don't glower."

"Might I not see you seated and take my leave? I'm sure Gervaise will be delighted to see you home," Philip suggested tentatively.

"Of all the shabby—! And after you promised faithfully that *this once* you would see the evening through! I gave my word to Letitia Rutherford that you would be here, so let's hear no more about scuttling off."

Philip grunted disconsolately. "I do not 'scuttle,' " he said under his breath as he cleared a path for his sister up the stairway with absentminded efficiency. It would have been hard for a stranger to guess that this ill-matched pair had descended from the same parents. Lord Gyllford, tall and spare, his dark hair slightly greying, seemed nevertheless to be younger than his forty-four years. Those observers who knew him even slightly could sense that only his good breeding and his sense of appropriate behavior for men of middle age kept his youthful energy in check. His sister, Clarissa Steele, reached only as high as his shoulder, a plump and placid matron who, though several years his junior, seemed older than he.

They were both widowed. Lord Gyllford had lost his wife after only six years of contented wedlock. Even his sister was not fully aware of the depth of that wound. Something deep within him had walled itself off, and a determination was born in him, somewhere below the surface of his mind, to avoid the possibility of suffering that pain again. None of the many lures set out for him by eligible ladies and designing Mamas had caused the slightest diminution of his determination not to remarry. When, a few years later, Clarissa's kind and good-natured husband, Henry Steele, had succumbed to pneumonia, Philip had invited his sister to return to Gyllford, her childhood home, and run it for him. Happily for him and his son, the rapidly growing Jamie, Clarissa's cheerful warmth had made the absence of a wife and mother less painful, and the years had passed in adequate contentment, marred only by a nagging guilt at the back of Philip's mind that perhaps Clarissa had bypassed her opportunities for remarriage to make a home for him.

This sense of guilt caused him to leave his beloved Gyllford for a month each year to allow his sister to enjoy the excitement of London society. He himself found the entire stay a crushing bore. His active mind could find no satisfaction in the fripperies and pastimes of the London season. At Gyllford Manor he kept enormously busy with the management of his estate and with his writing, his secret vice and joy. He had two books on political theory of a somewhat radical nature published under a *nom de plume* and was proud that not one of his acquaintance had ever guessed he had authored them. He was now busily at work on a third book, and the necessity of escorting Clarissa to London was a most unfortunate interruption.

Well, I'm in for it tonight, he thought, *and I may as well make the best of it. Perhaps Gervaise and some of his circle will gather in one of the card rooms for a little political discus—*

"Philip?" Clarissa's voice cut in. "I insist that you stand up with some of the young ladies for the country dances."

Had the woman been reading his mind? Philip turned and frowned down at her with mock severity. "My dear Clarissa," he said, "I love you dearly and am eternally at your service, but I draw the line at gallanting young ladies on the dance floor. At my age, I think I may be considered exempt." And with that quelling statement, he guided his sister to the door of the ballroom and greeted his hosts with smiling composure. Lady Steele sighed, adjusted her turban, and did likewise.

On the other side of the room, Sally Trevelyan noted their entrance. So adept was she at social intercourse that none of the several young men surrounding her had any notion she'd been watching the door for the past half-hour. Miss Trevelyan had long since acquired the ability to seem to give her attention to several men at once while her mind wandered where it willed. She had been a reigning beauty for several seasons. Her spectacular loveliness, the sophistication and elegance of her manners, and her considerable fortune made her the toast of the polite world. Each season wagers were laid at White's on the likelihood of her succumbing to matrimony, but each season she remained unwed. Sought after as she was, Sally surprised everyone by resisting all suitors. But she loved to create surprises. She enjoyed being the center of attention. She enjoyed knowing her name was on everyone's lips. Why marry while she could attract hordes of admirers? Why marry while each season provided at least a dozen suitors for her hand? Sally flicked a green-eyed glance at the doorway where Philip Everard was being embraced by a simpering Lady Rutherford. Philip was the exception in Sally's mind, the one matrimonial prize she would have liked to win. But Philip had never asked her.

Sally turned to her entourage and dismissed them, saying lightly, "Ah, I see my friend, Mrs. Lanyon. Be off, will you? I wish to be private with her." She crossed the room alone, enjoying the stir her appearance made. Her blond hair was curled in the spectacular new style, *à la grecque*, and her shimmering green gown clung closely to her limbs as she walked. She knew the ladies on the sidelines were watching and gossiping. They suspected that she damped her dresses to make them cling. Well, let them suspect, she thought, tossing her curls arrogantly. They would do it too, had they the figures for it.

She dropped down in a chair next to Mrs. Lanyon with a sigh of relief. Alvina Lanyon was a young matron known to be fast, but the friendship suited Sally well, though she knew that the association was doing no good for her reputation. Alvina had a cool, calculating mind, much like Sally's own, and their intimacy was satisfying to both of them. Alvina was the only woman with whom Sally could be herself.

Alvina looked at Sally knowingly, glanced up at her current *cicisbeo* who was bending over her, and dispatched him for a glass of champagne. "Did you see who just came in?" Sally asked without preamble.

Alvina nodded. "He's finally made an appearance. I saw him being embraced by our hostess," she murmured lazily.

"But now he seems to have disappeared. I wonder where he's gone."

"Into one of the card rooms, I should imagine."

"Yes, to talk the evening away with his cronies, blast the man!" Sally said.

Alvina laughed. "I don't see why you bother about him. The man is past forty, and if you ask me, he's rather frightening. Though I'll admit he's devilishly handsome."

"Don't be a fool. Philip has a brilliant mind, a great deal of address, a sharp wit when he bothers to show it, and a fortune that even I couldn't dissipate. There isn't a female in this room who'd refuse an offer from him."

"I suppose you're right. But of what use is it to get yourself into a sulk? The Earl of Gyllford is obviously not interested in you—or in any romantic involvements. Forget him."

"No," Sally said, her lip curling in an unbecoming line of arrogance. "I don't intend to give up so easily."

Alvina looked at Sally in surprise. "You've not lost your heart to him, have you?"

"I don't know," Sally said thoughtfully. "I'm not at all sure what I feel." She had often asked herself that question. She knew that he attracted her, that she'd set her cap for him and, to her chagrin, he had not responded. The more she had tried to attach him, the thicker had become the wall of cool reserve behind which he'd barricaded himself. Perhaps her feeling for Philip was merely the result of pique at her failure to attract him. But whatever the cause, she was determined to bring him to his knees, and she didn't care a jot if her feeling for him would outlast his capitulation. Her green eyes grew hard and feline as her mind jumped from scheme to scheme. "It would not be so difficult if I had some time alone with him," she said.

"Well, you're not likely to do it this season," Alvina said, leaning back. "I overheard Lady Steele inviting Martha Covington to Gyllford Manor for the Christmas holidays. That probably means they are planning to return to the country next week. You've missed your chance this year."

Sally turned her cat-like eyes on her friend speculatively. "Returning to the country, are they? Well, well, how delightful."

Alvina looked at her friend suspiciously. "What schemes are you concocting now, my dear?" she asked.

"Nothing so very shocking," Sally answered with a mysterious smile. "I was just thinking that a couple of weeks in the country might be the very thing I need. The very thing."

Lord Gyllford's London establishment, Gyllford House, was always quiet on the day following a large ball, for callers were turned aside to permit Lady Steele to remain in bed until well into the afternoon. Lord Gyllford invariably took advantage of the opportunity that the unwonted peacefulness permitted him to closet himself in his study and work at his writing. The day following the Rutherford ball was just such a day. Not until the rays of the December sun became too feeble to light his page did Philip realize that it was time to put his writing aside and join his sister for tea. With a sigh, he thrust the papers into a drawer and leaned back in his chair, stretching and yawning. At that moment, the door opened and Clarissa bustled in, arresting Philip's stretch in mid-air.

"Aha!" she said accusingly, "I've caught you at last."

"Caught me?" her brother asked innocently.

"Yes, my dear, you are caught in the act."

"In what act?"

"In the act of doing nothing. Yawning over an empty desk! It's just as I suspected. You don't do any work in here at all. It's your cowardly plot to hide away from human companionship before tea time."

Philip unfolded his tall frame from his chair and strode over to his sister. Putting his arm affectionately about her shoulders, he smiled down at her. "And why would I want to avoid the company of a woman of your great charm and wit?" he asked lightly.

"And beauty, too, my dear, don't forget that!" declared Clarissa, slipping her arm about his waist as they strolled across the hall toward the sitting room, where a well-laden tea table awaited them.

"How could I forget your beauty when your face is smiling up at me so prettily?" Philip rejoined, looking down at his sister's plump and pleasant countenance. "Of course," he added, "that ridiculous widow's cap which you insist on wearing hides too much of your greatest asset."

"Never you mind about my assets. It's only proper that a widow look like one." Clarissa patted the offending cap lightly and settled herself behind the teapot.

"In that case, I shall find myself obliged to do something to change your widowed state. The world should certainly be permitted to see more of your lovely hair."

"If that's a new way you've found of hinting that I should accept Gervaise, I don't mind telling you that I shall be much obliged if you'd refrain from embarking on an old and long settled subject of dispute."

"What? Give up fighting Gervaise's battle? The poor man would never forgive me. You're a heartless, wanton female to allow Gervaise to waste away in loveless, lonely melancholy."

Clarissa laughed. "Waste away! He can afford to waste away—three stone at least! And as for lonely melancholy, he spends more time at Gyllford than he does at home."

"Exactly so. Perhaps if you'd marry him, I would see a bit less of him."

"I've never been given a better reason for getting married," retorted Clarissa. "It seems you are determined to get rid of me, either by hiding from me in your horrid study or packing me off to marry Gervaise."

"I may be guilty of the second, but acquit me, please, of the first offense. I've really been working all afternoon. I had just finished when you came bursting in. By the way, shall Gervaise be with us at Gyllford for the holidays?"

"Yes, indeed. There's no putting him off, you know. And last evening I invited the Covingtons to come with their entire brood. And . . ." she paused guiltily.

Philip cocked a quizzical eyebrow at her. "And . . . ?"

"And . . . I've asked Sally Trevelyan, too."

"Sally Trevelyan?" asked Philip in surprise. "Why on earth—?"

"I don't know, Philip. She went out of her way to be pleasant to me last evening—you know, she can be quite delightful when she tries—and when she mentioned that she would be quite alone for the holidays, my heart went out to her."

Philip shook his head. "You're much too tenderhearted, my dear. But, Clarissa, I must warn you—if you have any ideas in that direction—that matchmaking is a dangerous business, especially involving me. After all these years, I hope you know that I'm not hanging out for a wife."

Clarissa threw up her hands. "Heavens, Philip, don't eat me. Weren't you doing the same to me not a moment ago? Besides, Sally knows by now that you're a hardened case. She won't be so foolish as to set her cap at you again."

"Well, then, her holiday will be a sad bore, with no one to flirt with. Let's hope Jamie brings home a few friends, so that Sally and the Covingtons' girl may have some game to snare."

"Good heavens!" Clarissa gasped. "I forgot to tell you about Jamie! That's why I burst in on you in the study. We've had a note from him."

"Good. What has that scapegrace son of mine to say?"

"You'll never believe it! He wants you to invite a friend of his for the holidays. A young lady!"

"A young lady? You don't mean it! *Jamie?*"

"That's what he writes." Clarissa pulled a letter from her pocket and handed it to her brother. Philip scanned it quickly.

"It sounds quite mysterious. 'A young lady of my acquaintance.' What are we to make of that?"

"I've no idea, I'm sure. And what sort of young lady would ask to be invited?" Clarissa mused, a bit troubled.

"Do you mean you think she's not quite proper? I hardly think—" Philip read the letter again. "No, I'm quite sure you've misinterpreted. *He* is doing the asking, not she. This Miss Pennington knows nothing about it as yet, I'll wager."

Clarissa took the letter and read it once more. "You may be right. Well, then, shall we invite her?"

"Certainly. I can't wait to see what manner of female has attracted my scamp of a son. I can't believe that Jamie is taken with a girl."

"Why not, Philip? He's twenty-two. He's certain to get, as he calls it, leg-shackled sooner or later."

Philip frowned. "Leg-shackled? There's no question of *that*, surely?"

"No?" teased Clarissa. "Why not? You'd been married for two years by the time you were his age."

"That's true enough. Jamie was born when I was twenty-two. But times were different then. We were more serious at that age. More responsible."

"Perhaps," said Clarissa with a knowing smile, "but boys do grow up, even now. Oh, dear . . . Philip! You may be a grandfather before long."

"A grandfather?" Philip looked at his sister in dismay. "A *grandfather!* Good God!"

· *Three* ·

EVALYN PENNINGTON FOLDED her last garment into a well-worn portmanteau, put the two halves together, and cinched the straps. The work was not laborious; her possessions were meagre, making the traveling bag quite easy to lift and carry. She placed the bag near the door and took a last look at the small, neat room which had been her home for two years. She felt no twinge of sentimentality on leaving it, for it had not been a happy home. Although comfortable and warm (for Lady Carbery had never begrudged her a fire or clean linens), she had never been made to feel part of the family. Lady Carbery had an unyielding and unaffectionate nature, and she made sure that everyone understood that Evalyn was nothing more than a servant at Carbery Hall. Even the children were imbued with that awareness, thus making her position as their mentor and guide all the more difficult.

Among the servants, too, she was a person apart. Her gentle voice and serene disposition endeared her to all of them, but, aware of her superior birth and education, they could not help but treat her with diffidence and constraint. She was a lady, no matter how Lady Carbery tried to demean her, and the servants instinctively knew better than to make her one of their own.

In the five years since she had entered service, Evalyn

had never given any outward indication of her loneliness. She had been reared by her father, Captain Pennington of the —th Foot. Back in '77, at the age of twenty-five, he'd been wounded at Saratoga, had returned to England, retired on a modest pension, married, and set up his small establishment in the quiet of the Devon countryside. For many years, Captain and Mrs. Pennington had yearned to have a child, but by the time one was conceived, they had quite given up hope. Evalyn's mother was past thirty at the time of her birth, and she died shortly after the new-born Evalyn was placed in her arms. Captain Pennington was then forty years old, and although he loved his daughter dearly and gave her the best care and education that his means could provide, he could not change the reserve which his military life had imposed upon his disposition. His wound had left him partially crippled and often in pain, but he had never complained nor asked for sympathy. In fact, any sign of pity from his loved ones or the servants would make him irritable in the extreme. Thus Evalyn grew to maturity without the nourishment of female tenderness, and without acquaintance with feminine tears and vapors. With the spartan behavior of her father as her only model, Evalyn learned to control her emotions, to eschew tears, and to disdain self-pity.

Had she not been her father's daughter, Evalyn might well have given way to self-pity now. Her interview with Lady Carbery had been insulting and humiliating. Lady Carbery's hints that Evalyn had set her cap at the scrawny and unprepossessing Geoffrey would have been laughable if the remarks were not followed by a prompt dismissal from her post, without so much as a character to recommend her to another employer. The only things which stood between her and destitution were the meagre savings in her reticule and the address of a distant cousin whom she had never met.

Her plan, conceived in desperation, was to use her savings to buy passage to London, there to find her cousin and beg for bed and board until she could find a new position. With one last glance round the unloved room, she tied her cloak at the neck, raised her hood, picked up the portmanteau and departed.

Her goodbyes to the household staff having already been said, she was glad the stairs and hallway were deserted. She quietly let herself out the front door and closed it behind her. To her surprise, she found Lord Reginald and James Everard standing on the stone steps leading down to the avenue, almost as if they had been lying in wait for her.

"Good morning, Miss Pennington," said Jamie with a slight bow.

Evalyn answered with a hurried curtsey. "Excuse me, sirs, but I must ask you to let me by. The London stage leaves from the inn in less than an hour, and it is almost a mile's walk from here."

"You're not planning to go to London?" asked Reggie in chagrin.

"Why, yes, sir."

"Did you find a position already, Miss Pennington?" Jamie asked. "Please excuse me for appearing to pry into your affairs, but I have been . . . that is, we both have been concerned about you."

"That is most kind in you, but there's no need for concern. I'm going to visit a cousin for a time, until I can find a new position."

"But, Mith Pennington, will you be able to? I mean, with no letter of commendation . . . ?" Reggie asked worriedly.

Evalyn smiled as bravely as she could. "I'm sure something will turn up. Perhaps my cousin has some connections."

"*Perhaps?* Don't you know?" Jamie asked, puzzled.

"Well, I'm not yet acquainted with her. But please, sirs, I must hurry along. Do excuse me, and thank you for your concern."

Jamie and Reggie stared nonplussed as Miss Pennington started off down the avenue. Then Jamie ran after her and took the portmanteau from her hand. "May we not escort you to the inn? Reggie and I have a matter which we'd like to discuss with you."

Evalyn hesitated. If Lady Carbery were observing her departure from an upstairs window, Evalyn's acceptance of the escort of two young gentlemen would certainly add fuel to the fire of her ladyship's suspicions. *Well*, thought Evalyn, *let her think the worst!* Lady Carbery had done her all the harm she could. Evalyn put her chin up defiantly, nodded her acquiescence to Jamie, and walked off down the avenue with an escort at each side.

It was Reggie who launched into an explanation. "We jutht wanted to apologize for the dithguthting conduct of our friend," he said, "and . . . and . . ." Here his courage faltered.

"It was the most shocking bad taste," Jamie went on, "to say nothing of the disastrous results it has had—making you lose your post through no fault of your own."

"Yes," agreed Miss Pennington, "but since you both have expressed your sympathy several times already, I don't see—?"

Before she could finish, Jamie held out to her a sealed missive which Evalyn saw with surprise was addressed to her. She opened it, and her eyes flew over the words. Lord Gyllford and his sister sent their warmest regards and cordially invited her to spend the Christmas holidays at Gyllford Manor. What did it mean? "I don't understand," she said, looking from Jamie to Reggie questioningly. "I've never had the pleasure of meeting your father and his sister."

"I asked them to invite you," Jamie explained. "You see, it seemed to us that you would find it difficult to acquire a new post without a character."

"Yes, that's true, but I still don't see—"

"My Aunt Clarissa can help you. She has so many friends in Devonshire. Surely one of them must have need of a governess."

"But would she recommend me for such a post without knowing me?" Miss Pennington asked reasonably. "She could scarcely, in good conscience, do such a thing, especially with the knowledge that Lady Carbery has turned me off."

"But that's the beauty of my idea!" Jamie explained eagerly. "She's bound to get to know you if you're our house guest for the holidays. And then I'm sure she won't feel any hesitation in recommending you."

The lane they were following took a turning into the wind. The many capes of Reggie's greatcoat flapped briskly, Jamie turned up his collar and pushed his hands deep into his pockets, but Evalyn didn't even notice the sudden chill. Mr. Everard's kind invitation had thrown her mind in a turmoil. She could not deny the attractiveness of his plan. The possibility of two weeks as a guest in a comfortable home, a Christmas holiday in which she would be treated with civility, even kindness, and the prospect of being assisted to find a new post, all these were infinitely more desirable than the prospect of begging for board from an unknown relative, and searching for employment without aid. But the proposal was too good to be true. She could not accept. There were too many obstacles.

She stopped and turned to Jamie. "Your generosity and concern quite overwhelm me, sir. I can't think why you should have taken this trouble about me. But you must see that I cannot accept."

"No, ma'am, I can't say that I see that at all, can you, Reg?"

"No, indeed," said Reggie earnestly, "it theemth like an exthellent plan to me."

"But surely you both realize that it would be highly improper for me to travel alone in Mr. Everard's company," Miss Pennington explained shyly.

"Oh, but I'll be going along too," Reggie said with pride in having settled a ticklish problem with dispatch.

"Don't be an idiot, Reg," Jamie muttered. "You would scarcely be viewed as a proper chaperone for a young lady. Miss Pennington's right. We need another female with us."

The three of them walked on in silence. Just as the inn came into view, Reggie chortled. "I have it!" he exclaimed. "We'll hire an abigail."

"An abigail?" asked Jamie, his eyes lighting up. "You mean some village girl?"

"There mutht be thome girl at the inn who would be thuitable. What do you think, Mith Pennington?"

"I think you are most generous, but I couldn't dream of allowing you to undertake such an expense in my behalf."

"Nonsense," Jamie put in firmly. "On that score I will not allow you to voice an objection. Reg has so much of the 'ready' in his pockets that he'll not even notice the expenditure. The problem is solved, and you must now agree to come with us to Gyllford."

Evalyn couldn't help but laugh at Jamie's readiness to spend Lord Reginald's money. Her laughter broke the strain and changed their moods completely. They refused to take seriously any one of the number of objections she tried to put forth. Their good spirits couldn't help but affect her own. The deep dejection which her plight had put upon her seemed miraculously to evaporate. A Christmas holiday at Gyllford! The thought of it lightened her heart and lifted her hopes. It was too tempting a prospect to refuse.

Still laughing, they swept her into the inn. Over her much-weakened objections, they looked for a girl to hire to be her abigail. The ridiculousness of the thought that she, a governess, would arrive at Gyllford with her own abigail made her laugh again. Within a very few minutes, the innkeeper's red-cheeked, excited niece had been engaged and had run off to pack her belongings. Then Reggie, in his grandest manner, demanded a private dining room in which Miss Pennington was to wait for them while they returned to Carbery Hall to take their leave.

Alone and breathless, Evalyn went to the window of the dining room. It overlooked the inn yard where, in the midst of much noisy bustle, the London stage was being readied for departure. The passengers were squeezing aboard, the luggage was being tied to the top, the ostlers were running about checking the horses. Evalyn felt a twinge of misgiving. If she had a proper sense of conduct and decorum, she would now be aboard that coach, crowded in among the passengers, heading for a bleak and unknown future. Instead, she was soon to be heading in quite another direction, in a private, luxurious coach, with her own abigail in attendance, and a full fortnight of holiday before her. Undoubtedly her character was not as strong as she had supposed. She was sadly wanting in rectitude. But her awareness of this weakness in her character did nothing to dispel a sense of happy anticipation such as she had never felt before. As she watched the London stage lumber off, there was not a glimmer of regret in her shining eyes.

Jamie and Reg walked back to Carbery Hall to pack their belongings and make their farewells. They were quite satisfied with themselves; they had done a good deed, and they had succeeded in spite of some ticklish problems. "I think we sailed rather neatly over some rough waters," Jamie boasted as they walked briskly down the lane toward Carbery Hall.

"Yeth," agreed Reggie, "but I don't think it will be clear thailing ahead."

"Why not? My Aunt Clarissa will handle things from here on," Jamie assured him airily.

But Reggie shook his head. "Your father and your aunt are bound to wonder why you brought her," he said thoughtfully. "Mith Pennington'th a mighty pretty thing. I'd wager anything you like that they'll think you're enamored of the girl."

Jamie hooted. "What? Me? You're addlebrained. They know me better than that! If you're making yourself uneasy over such nonsense, you're crazy as a coot!"

· Four ·

A *GRANDFATHER!* THE word had burst upon Philip with the effect of a gunshot. Now, two weeks later, back at home at Gyllford, it still had a way of jumping into his mind. He stood at his shaving mirror and stared at his reflection. The hair at his temples had already turned more grey than black. When had it happened? How was it possible he had not noticed it before? Those grey hairs had encroached upon his head as the years had encroached upon his youth, in stealthy stages, bit by bit. He remembered how he'd laughed at the first pale hair that had appeared among the dark, as if that grim reminder of the impending future were a joke of nature. The reality of aging had seemed so far in the future that the warning had appeared ludicrous. But now, before he'd had a chance to accustom himself to the realization, he'd become quite grey, and his youth had disappeared.

A grandfather. Philip shook his head and grinned at himself ruefully. He was not usually given to such mawkish, feminine musings. Besides, Jamie wasn't even married yet! Forty-four years of life did not make one ancient, not by any means. What he needed was a good breakfast, a brisk walk on the grounds of his beloved Gyllford, and a couple of hours at his desk, wrestling with the logic of his antagonist, Burke, to put him in a more sensible frame of mind. But the lift that the thought of his writing always gave him was soon dispelled by the realization that his house was filling with guests. Gervaise and Sally were already in residence, and the whole Covington family was expected to arrive this afternoon. The duties of a host would keep him from his desk all day. He sighed and, his depression returning, he went reluctantly down to breakfast.

Clarissa and Sally were already settled at the table in the breakfast room, drinking their second cups of chocolate. Gervaise was lingering over the sideboard, loading his plate from the generous buffet with cold meats, smoked fish and coddled eggs. The sight of his cheerful countenance did a little to lift Philip's spirit. Gervaise's very appearance occasioned smiles. He always tried valiantly to dress as befitted a man of style and substance, but his girth and his indolent nature were constantly at war with his clothing, and winning. Without warning, a button would come loose here, a seam would split there. His much-harried valet would send him forth tailored and pressed to perfection, but Gervaise would return to the dressing room before long, looking sadly rumpled and shabby. Now, just minutes after leaving his dressing room, his waistcoat buttons already gave the appearance of being strained beyond their strength. Philip was sure the middle one would pop off before Gervaise's breakfast was completely consumed.

All unconcerned, Gervaise's eyes twinkled and his round cheeks creased in a welcoming smile for Philip. "There you are, my boy," he greeted warmly. "We've been wondering if you had overslept this morning."

"I must apologize to you all. I had no idea you would all be so prompt. I dawdled in front of my mirror, I'm afraid."

"Not you, Philip, surely. I've never known you to do so before," Clarissa said in amused surprise.

"That is because you never told me how grey I'm

growing, my dear. I noticed it this morning with quite a shock."

"Nonsense!" Sally laughed. "It makes you look quite attractively distinguished."

Philip bowed his thanks and turned to the sideboard. Was Sally still determined to pursue a useless flirtation with him? Bother the holidays, he thought, bother the guests and bother this whole interruption of his pleasant life's routine! His day was quite cut up.

Sally Trevelyan looked at him musingly. If he had calculated a manner meant to attract her, he couldn't have found a better. As he turned back to the breakfast table with his plate of beef and eggs, she motioned him to the seat beside her. Philip seemed not to notice; he took a seat beside his sister. Sally smiled to herself. Let the man struggle. She had two lovely weeks before her—there was plenty of time.

The Covingtons arrived at mid-afternoon. Hutton, the Gyllfords' imperturbable butler, announced the arrival of the carriage to Lady Steele and managed to throw open the front door, descend the steps and take a magisterial stance at the bottom before the coach had come to a complete stop—and all without hurrying his usual dignified gait. Clarissa and Philip followed soon after, making an impressive welcoming party for the new arrivals.

The six-year-old twins spilled from the carriage first, racing past their hosts and up into the hall with all the abandon that five long hours of suppressed energy can stimulate in little boys. They were followed out of the carriage by their sister Marianne, a seventeen-year-old miss with bouncy curls and warm blue eyes now shining with the excitement caused by this prolonged escape from the schoolroom.

Next came her father, Edward Covington, whose usual,

anxious expression was now replaced by a smile of relief
that the journey had ended without mishap. Twenty years of
marriage to the good-natured but hapless Martha had etched
a number of worried creases into his forehead and a sense of
nervous fearfulness into his spirit. Life with his Martha, he
was wont to remark, was a series of crises and disasters for
which she was neither to blame nor able to resist generating.

Martha herself was the last to be helped from the
carriage. She eagerly hugged and kissed Clarissa and Philip
with effusive warmth. Then she turned to the footmen who
were attempting to unload the great number of boxes and
trunks that the Covingtons found necessary for their sur-
vival away from home. "Be careful with that one, please,"
she urged, "for it contains all the children's gifts for
Christmas morning. And that one has the wine, does it not,
Edward? Clarissa, we've brought you some of that excellent
Madeira Edward discovered on the Continent last year. Oh,
and that one goes to Marianne's room, if you please."

Keeping up a steady stream of warnings and instructions,
Martha moved with the rest of the party to the front hallway.
This large, high-ceilinged room had become a sea of
activity. Old friends were greeting each other with kisses.
Children were being tossed in the air. Wraps were being
removed and carted off up the stairs. Footmen were
weaving their way through the press loaded with boxes and
trunks. Suddenly, one of the twins, having had enough of
the petting and patting of his elders, darted across the stone
floor without heed and collided with a footman who was
staggering toward the stairway under the burden of a large
trunk which he carried on his back. The impact caused the
man to stumble. The trunk fell to the floor with a tremen-
dous crash and burst wide open.

The entire assemblage gasped and turned to stare at the
wreckage. Martha's corsets, stays and undergarments, and

the pots of rouge she had hidden among them, all lay exposed to public view. Martha, aghast, responded as she always did in times of crisis—she swooned. Clarissa and Edward bent over her, administering vinaigrette and soothing murmurs. The guilty twin made loud excuses. The servant stammered his apologies. Lord Gyllford tried to still the hubbub by urging all the other guests into the library where a fire and refreshments were waiting.

In the midst of this confusion, the front door opened to admit Jamie and his party. The little group, rosy-cheeked and in excellent spirits after an invigorating ride through the English winter countryside, stood stock still surveying the chaos, their smiles fading into puzzled concern.

Lord Gyllford came forward to greet them. "Don't look so appalled," he said, smiling reassuringly at his son. "We've had a bit of an accident with a trunk, but it will all be set right in a few minutes. How do you do, Reggie? It's good to have you with us."

"Sir, I'd like you to meet Miss Evalyn Pennington. Miss Pennington, this is my father."

Philip turned, looked down into Miss Pennington's upturned face and felt an unfamiliar lurch somewhere deep in his chest. The serene grey eyes smiling up at him were set in a face whose sweetness of expression struck him with complete surprise. Could this calm, composed, and lovely creature possibly be the choice of his immature, scatterbrained son? He felt quite breathless with shock as, for one frozen moment while he stared at her, the world around him ceased to exist.

Miss Pennington bowed. "How do you do, my lord," she said quietly. "It was most kind of you to invite me. We seem to have arrived inopportunely, I'm afraid."

Philip recovered himself at once. "Not at all," he said, a

reassuring smile lighting his face. "This is quite normal behavior in our household."

Clarissa bustled up in time to hear his words. "Philip, what a dreadful thing to say! How do you do, Miss Pennington? Please forgive this confusion. If you'll bear with us until Mrs. Covington is recovered, we'll be able to see to your comforts as we should. Reggie, my dear, how good to see you! And Jamie, love, it's good to have you home."

With a quick kiss for Jamie and a hug for Reggie, Clarissa turned to go back to the side of the still swooning Martha. A small, involuntary sigh escaped her at the sight before her—the maids hastily gathering up armfuls of lingerie and running up the stairs with them; Gervaise and Sally bending over the prostrate Martha; Edward Covington shaking his head and muttering, "I knew it, I knew something had to happen," under his breath; and the twins, as boisterously as if nothing had happened, chasing each other up and down the staircase.

"I beg your pardon, ma'am," came a soft, calm voice behind her, "but may I be of assistance? I would be glad to take the little boys and settle them in."

Clarissa looked at Miss Pennington with an expression of gratitude and relief. "Oh my, that would be most helpful, and most kind in you. . . ."

"But my dear," Lord Gyllford objected, "it would be unforgivable of us to put a guest to work, like a governess, as soon as she puts her foot in the door. We could not so impose on her."

"If you please, my lord, I would not feel in the least imposed upon. I *am* a governess, after all, and I'd be grateful to be permitted to make myself useful." And without waiting for an answer, Miss Pennington handed her cloak and gloves to a waiting servant and gracefully crossed the floor. Philip and Clarissa stared after her as she spoke a few words to a young woman they took to be her abigail. Then the astounding Miss Pennington took each of the twins firmly in hand and in seconds had disappeared with them around the bend of the stairway.

"Governess? Did she say governess?" Clarissa asked Jamie in surprise.

Jamie grinned down at his puzzled aunt. "Yes, she did. Wonderful, ain't she? Don't worry about it. I'll explain later."

Jamie and Reggie moved into the hall, greeting the others. Martha soon revived, and by slow degrees the whole party made its way to the library, where hot soup and mulled brandy did much to restore order and good spirits. But Philip gave scant attention to the laughter and banter around him. He was staring at his son. Jamie must possess depths beyond his ken. He had brought home a young woman who, although perhaps beneath him in station and wealth, seemed vastly superior in character. Certainly she was not at all the sort of young woman whom Philip would have thought likely to attract a young buck so newly on the town. Philip had to admit that the sight of Jamie's choice had completely surprised him. In the past, he had prided himself on the aplomb with which he had withstood the shocks, disappointments and worries of fatherhood. But this time . . . well, this time Jamie had shaken him profoundly.

· *Five* ·

WHEN GUESTS WERE lodged at Gyllford Manor, the two hours before dinner became the quietest time of day. The ladies were closeted with their abigails, who carefully dressed their hair; the gentlemen either stole a little time for a nap, or discussed with their valets the costume for the evening. Philip availed himself of the temporary lull in the day's activities to visit his son for a *tête à tête*. He found Jamie standing in front of his mirror doing violence to the third neckcloth with which his valet had provided him. Wellstock, the meek and modest manservant who had served Lord Gyllford for years, was always happy when Jamie was at home. Since Lord Gyllford rarely requested his assistance, it was only when young Everard was on the premises that Wellstock could employ his considerable talents as a sartorial expert to the full. Now he hovered about his charge, his face not quite masking the mixed emotions he was experiencing—delight to be assisting a gentleman of fashion again, and dismay at the sight of Jamie mangling his beautifully ironed neckcloths. On Wellstock's arm hung three more freshly pressed cloths which, he was certain, were destined for a similarly tragic fate.

Lord Gyllford surveyed the scene with amusement. "I see you have not yet learned to make a simple fold," he remarked to his son.

Jamie sighed and cast the crushed linen into Wellstock's waiting hand. "I seem to be all thumbs when it comes to tying these cursed things," he grumbled, placing number four around his neck.

"Never mind. I'll show you an easy fold I've developed," Philip reassured him. He smiled at Wellstock's ill-disguised expression of offense. "I know I won't do as well as you, Wellstock, but I think you may safely leave him in my care."

The valet reluctantly took the hint and bowed himself out of the room. Philip, standing behind his son, tied the cloth in a few dexterous movements. "There. That should do."

"It's excellent, father! A capital fold! What do you call it?"

"Call it?" Philip's eyes twinkled. "Well, let's see. Since it's so simple that even you can learn it, why not call it *the Incapable?*"

Jamie grinned back at his father. "Never mind," he said, "I'll call it something modish, like *the Arabesque* or *the Windfall*. That ought to impress Reggie and the other Dandies of my acquaintance." He gave the neckcloth an affectionate pat and turned away from the mirror. "Please sit down, sir. I suppose you've sent Wellstock away because you want to scold me about something. What have I done now?"

"Scold you? What makes you think that?"

"Isn't that what fathers always do when they arrange to speak to their sons privately?"

"Is scolding the only private communication possible between a father and son? What a lowering thought! No, I had no such intention when I sought you out." Philip looked at his son keenly. "Is there something on your conscience that requires a scold?"

"I was afraid you might be put out about Miss Pennington. Do you mind that I brought her here?"

"Mind? Of course not. Why should I?"

"I don't know. Reggie thought you might not like being saddled with a strange female for the holidays. And a governess to boot."

"I admit to being surprised. She's not the sort of person I would have expected you to bring home. But she seems a most well-bred and charming young lady, and we're glad to have her with us."

"I knew it!" Jamie exclaimed in relief. "That's what I told Reg. I assured him that once you and Aunt Clarissa got to know her, there'd be no problem."

"Problem?"

"Yes. Having a governess as a guest. Reggie thought it might be awkward."

"I hope you told Reggie that your aunt and I are not so high in the instep."

"Oh, he didn't think that!" Jamie said hastily. "He only thought that you might not want to concern yourselves—"

"How foolish of Reggie. Surely you both must realize that anything that concerns you concerns us. A fine parent I should be if I failed to be interested in all your concerns."

"I knew you'd feel that way. But I must admit it's a relief to hear you say it. Evalyn—that is, Miss Pennington—deserves a bit of a holiday, you see. Lady Carbery is a real dragon to work for. She treated Evalyn as if she were a . . . a . . . cook maid! Never gave her a kind word. And then, with Geoff accosting the poor girl wherever she went, well, you can imagine what a dreadful time she's had."

"It would certainly seem so," said Philip, trying unsuccessfully to picture Jamie's involvement in that scene of domestic contretemps.

"Not that Miss Pennington ever complained," Jamie went on earnestly. "Not she. She always handled everything with the most remarkable coolness. You should have seen her give Geoff a leveler. Knocked him down the stairs with an Atlas!"

"You don't mean it! That gentle little thing?"

"Word of a gentleman! Knocked him right on his keester. And then came down the stairs as calm as you please and brought him to. And when Lady Carbery appeared, Evalyn was not in the least flustered. Carried it off as if she were serving tea, by God! Really, she's the most redoubtable girl."

Philip couldn't help smiling. What Jamie's description of his beloved lacked in romantic terminology was certainly compensated for in enthusiasm. *Oh, well,* he thought, *literature is full of cases of unlikely matches. Cupid is said to be blindfolded when he shoots his darts.* If his son chose to give his heart to a *redoubtable* girl, Philip had no objection. Jamie could have chosen much less wisely.

"Do you think Aunt Clarissa will like her?" Jamie asked.

"Of course she will. I think she likes her already. The way your Miss Pennington took over the twins this afternoon made a wonderful impression on both of us."

"Good. Then Aunt Clarissa won't have any objection to making the arrangements after the holidays?"

"What!" exclaimed Philip, shocked. "After the holidays? As soon as that?" Surely his son could not be contemplating such a hasty marriage. "There's no cause . . . er . . . there couldn't be any special reason for . . . er . . . urgency, could there?"

Jamie looked puzzled. "Urgency? No, of course not. We just thought that after the holidays might be a good time."

"Do you mean that you and Miss Pennington have already discussed a date?"

Jamie had an uncomfortable feeling for a moment that he had missed something in this conversation. "Well, no," he explained patiently, "I haven't said much to Miss Pennington yet. I wanted to discuss it with you and Aunt Clarissa first."

"You haven't asked Miss Pennington?" Philip was at a loss. Just how far had this affair gone? "I'm afraid, Jamie, that I'm a little confused. Do you and Miss Pennington have . . . an understanding?"

Jamie was shrugging himself into his coat. Now that he knew his actions had the approval of the family, he was finding the subject of Miss Pennington a bit of a bore. "An understanding? Well, yes, I suppose you could say that. She understands why she's here, of course. I told her she was sure to win your approval—and Aunt Clarissa's too—in a week or two."

"But surely you didn't think we could make satisfactory arrangements in so short a time!"

"Well, as to that, it certainly doesn't matter to me how long it takes. We could leave it for Aunt Clarissa and Miss Pennington to decide, couldn't we?"

Philip stared at his son in amazement. Jamie had very easily been persuaded to delay his plans. The switch from loverlike impatience to reasonable indifference was most confusing. The younger generation was quite difficult to understand. Philip sighed and rose. "Well, I'll tell your aunt to give the matter some thought. Miss Pennington seems to be a sensible young lady. Between the two of them, I'm sure they'll know what's to be done."

"That's what I told Reg. Leave it to my aunt, I told him. We won't have to trouble our heads about a thing."

Philip blinked. "What has Reg to do—? No, never mind. I'd better go talk to your aunt before the guests assemble for dinner." And Philip retreated hastily out the door.

A few minutes later, Jamie sat watching Reggie make a final inspection of his attire. Lord Reginald was resplendent in a coat of blue superfine covering a waistcoat of yellow satin embroidered with flower baskets in which each flower was a tiny jewel.

"How do I look?" Reggie asked, turning slowly before the critical eyes of his friend.

"That waistcoat—well, I don't know. Don't you think it's a bit overpowering?"

"Overpowering? How can you think that? You know nothing about thtyle."

"Then why did you ask me? Anyway, I didn't come in here to inspect your waistcoat. I just want to let you know that the Pennington matter is settled. I've told my father the whole story, and he says Aunt Clarissa will take care of everything."

"Oh, capital! I mutht thay, Jamie, it'th very kind of your father and your aunt. I don't think my mother would go to tho much trouble for a mere nobody."

"My father doesn't like to think of people as nobodies. Y'know, I sometimes think my father is a radical thinker. Anyway, we've done our part, and now we can forget it. Let's go downstairs. I want to get another look at that little Marianne Covington. She's grown up to be quite a taking little thing. Did you notice?"

"No, I didn't," responded Reggie flatly, "and I hope, Jamie, that you're not going to turn out ath big a bore ath Geoff."

Meanwhile, Philip was apprising Clarissa of his chat with Jamie. "The long and short of it is," he told her, "that Jamie wants to marry Miss Pennington as soon as the holidays are over."

"As soon as that?" gasped Clarissa. "You can't be serious."

"That's what he told me. But he's perfectly willing to wait as long as you and Miss Pennington think necessary."

"How strange! Does he want us to announce the engagement right away?"

"I didn't think to ask him that. He says they have an understanding. Believe me, Clarissa, that's more than I have. His attitude is completely confusing to me."

Clarissa looked at her brother tenderly. The idea of his having a married son was just too new to him. He needed time to become accustomed to it. "Don't worry, dear," she said consolingly, "we needn't do anything at all until after the holidays. By that time, we shall have grown accustomed to seeing them together, and the whole matter will seem much less shocking. Give it a little time."

"I suppose you're right," Philip agreed.

"We'll go on as usual. There's no need to announce anything until we get to know Miss Pennington better. We won't make any definite plans until after the new year, when all the guests have gone. That seems reasonable, doesn't it?"

"Quite reasonable."

They left Clarissa's room and headed for the stairway. It would not do to be absent while the guests assembled. "At least we may thank our stars that she's such a fine, sensible, imposing girl. Quite lovely, in fact," Clarissa remarked cheerfully.

"Not lovely," Philip said with a sudden grin, "*redoubtable*."

· Six ·

EVALYN SIGHED WITH pleasure as Nancy, her one-day abigail, brushed her hair to a soft glow. Everything in the room glowed. There was a cheerful fire in the grate that lit the hangings of the large four-poster bed with a golden light. The paneling of the walls gleamed. The panes of the tall windows sparkled with reflected firelight. Evalyn had never slept in a room so large and beautiful.

Nancy seemed to read her mind. "Ain't this place fine, Miss Evalyn? Did ever y' see a prettier bedchamber?"

"Never. It's almost too lovely to be true. I keep thinking I'll wake up and find myself back at Carbery Hall."

"Aye, me as well. Not at Carbery 'all, acourse, but back at the inn. Me uncle, 'e knows 'ow t' keep a girl 'oppin'. Bein' with ye in this place . . . well, it's like a dream! Even the room they give me downstairs is finer 'n the best room at 'ome. Ye should see the pitcher on me washstand, Miss Evalyn. Shinin' white it is, wi' blue flowers all over it. I'm almost afeared t' use it, it's so fine! An' the walls is white, an' there's blue curtains an' a blue spread on the bed. An' it's all fer me alone! Y' know, Miss Evalyn, it's the firs' time in me life I've a bedchamber all t' meself!"

"Perhaps you shouldn't become too attached to it, Nancy. After all, you were only hired to accompany me on the coach. You'll probably be sent home tomorrow," Evalyn explained gently.

"I know, Miss Evalyn," said the unquenchable Nancy, "but tonight it's all mine!"

Evalyn smiled at the young girl's unflagging good spirits. Her own were not so consistent. One glance at her worn blue poplin dress, more appropriate for the schoolroom than the dining room, was enough to dampen her joy in her surroundings.

"Do ye 'ave t' wear yer 'air pinned up so, Miss Evalyn?" Nancy asked. "I cin dress it real fine, jus' caught up a bit in the back, so, an' fallin' over yer shoulder like this. I'm real good at fixin' 'air. Real good."

Evalyn let her try, and when, a little while later, she had been buttoned into her blue dress and had thrown her mother's Spanish shawl over her shoulders, the mirror told her she was quite presentable.

The guests had all gathered in the library when Evalyn entered. One glance around the room told her the mirror had been wrong. She looked hopelessly dowdy among the stylish ladies gathered there. Mrs. Covington was looking festive in a green dress of spotted silk. Young Marianne Covington was demurely lovely in a dress of pink sarcenet embroidered all over with white violets. Most breathtaking of all was Miss Trevelyan, whose elegant blond beauty was enhanced by a gown of gold-threaded gauze over mauve silk. Evalyn wanted to run away and hide, but she had learned early how to face an enemy even when hopelessly outnumbered. She put up her chin and advanced.

Lady Steele welcomed her with surprising warmth and insisted that she take a seat right in the center of the company. Accustomed to being kept on the fringes of social gatherings, Evalyn felt uncomfortable in a place of such conspicuous importance. She murmured something innocuous and sank back in her chair, hoping to divert attention from herself. But James Everard was grinning at her approvingly, and Lord Reginald bent over and whispered, "I thay, I do like your hair that way!"

And Lord Gyllford took a glass of wine from the butler and brought it over to her himself. She accepted the wine and looked up to thank him. There was a warm glow in his eyes. Could it be a sign of approval of her appearance? Perhaps her dress wasn't so dowdy after all.

Dinner was announced, and before she rose from her chair, Evalyn's arm was claimed by the host himself. As she crossed the room in that surprising position of honor, she noticed an expression of chagrin cross the face of the lovely Miss Trevelyan. Why she, and not Miss Trevelyan, had been singled out by Lord Gyllford was extremely puzzling.

Dinner at Gyllford Manor was always relaxed and leisurely, often lasting as long as two hours. The guests did not find this wearisome, for, as Mr. Covington was fond of relating, his sister, the fashionable Lady Lofting, had often given dinners lasting five hours. Dinner turned out to be a very merry meal, for Miss Trevelyan, finding herself seated at his lordship's left hand, soon recovered her good spirits and kept Philip's attention with a constant flow of lively conversation. Jamie deftly placed himself at the side of the pretty Marianne and, all through the meal, teased her about her new, grown-up appearance. Marianne fully enjoyed his attentions, giggling and blushing prettily and responding to his compliments with a darting glance from under trembling lashes or a whispered, "Oh, do you really think so?"

Since Philip was only occasionally permitted to turn away from Miss Trevelyan to converse with Evalyn, seated on his right, Evalyn found an opportunity to discuss with her other dinner partner, Lord Reginald, the problem of her abigail. "Forgive me for troubling you about the matter," she said to him quietly, "but Nancy and I were wondering about the arrangements for her return."

"Nancy? Nancy? I don't quite . . . ?" Reggie mumbled, perplexed.

"The innkeeper's niece. The girl you hired to be my abigail. You only engaged her for the trip, you know, and she is expecting to return to the inn tomorrow."

"Good heaventh, I'd forgotten all about her!" Reggie exclaimed.

"I beg your pardon," Lord Gyllford interjected, leaning toward her, "but I couldn't help overhearing what you just said. You are speaking of your abigail, are you not? Has she given satisfactory service?"

Evalyn looked at Lord Gyllford in surprise. "Why, yes, of course. She is a delightful girl, but—"

"Then you should certainly keep her, my dear. Unless she is particularly needed at home just now. Is that the case?"

"No, I don't think she is needed at the inn . . . that is, I'm sure she could be spared . . . but it would be impossible for me to keep her with me, my lord."

Lord Gyllford smiled. "You are quite a decided young woman, Miss Pennington. Tell me, why would it be so impossible?"

"Well, I . . . you see, Lord Reginald has been paying her wages, and I certainly couldn't ask him—"

"No, you certainly could not. Although I fail to understand why Lord Reginald had been required to do so."

"Not required, my lord," Reggie put in. "My privilege, I athure you! Jamie'th pocketh were a bit to let, you thee—"

"Jamie's pockets are always to let, it seems," Lord Gyllford said drily. "I thank you, Reggie, and I will deem it *my* privilege if you will permit me to take the responsibility of the abigail off your hands. With your permission, I shall add her to our household staff."

"Delighted," Reggie agreed promptly.

"But sir, I cannot permit you to go to such expense on my behalf!" Evalyn objected vehemently.

"Miss Pennington," Lord Gyllford said with mock severity, "as much as I admire decided young ladies, I cannot permit them to dictate to me the composition of my household staff. So we'll have no more discussion on this head, if you please."

"But—"

"No buts. You are not eating, Miss Pennington. You must try a little of this ragout of veal and onions. Our cook has a way with ragouts. I think you will find it quite French."

But Evalyn, although overwhelmed with gratitude at the unexpected kindness she was meeting at every turn, felt obliged to voice her objections. She could not accept such generosity. What business had a governess with an abigail? She drew a deep breath and looked up at her host, prepared to do battle. He was looking down at her, the expression on his face daring her to contradict him. She hesitated, but it was not his facial expression that deterred her. It was something far back in his eyes, an expression of such smiling warmth that her words were arrested in her throat. Never had she seen quite such a look in a man's eyes. Her own eyes wavered, and she looked down at her plate. He would have his way. There was no question about it, Lord Gyllford was quite the most disarming man she'd ever encountered.

The gentlemen were left lingering over their brandies, while the ladies repaired to the sitting room. Marianne restlessly wandered from the window to the fire and back again, impatient for Jamie's reappearance. Martha Covington took a seat near Evalyn, thanking her for her kindness to the twins and asking her advice on medication for an inflamed ear which was troubling one of them. Sally took the opportunity to quiz Clarissa about Miss Pennington's identity. "Who on earth is she?" Sally asked, her green eyes watching Evalyn carefully.

"A friend of Jamie's, as I've told you," Clarissa answered.

"Yes, I know. But where did he find her?"

"I believe he met her at the Carberys'."

"Come now, Clarissa, don't be secretive. Did I hear someone say that she was their governess?"

"I believe she was, yes."

"Well, then, why on earth did he bring her here?"

"Sally, don't pry. It doesn't become you. You'll know all in good time. In the meantime, it's enough for you to know that she's here on a little holiday. From what I know of Harriet Carbery, the poor girl deserves one."

"Very well, Clarissa, if that's all you'll tell me, I must be satisfied. But I must say, I don't see why you and Philip treat her as if she were a visiting duchess."

Clarissa laughed. "Dear me, you sound as if your nose is quite out of joint! But console yourself. You'd be just as put out if we were entertaining a *real* duchess. You hate playing second fiddle."

"That's right, I do. I'll say this for you, Clarissa Steele, you are frank to a fault." Sally turned away, leaned back against the sofa, and looked across the room at Miss Pennington. "My dear Miss Pennington," she purred, "do you play the piano?"

"Yes, a little. Would you like me to play?"

"Yes, I would. I imagine you are very accomplished. No, on second thought, I believe I'll do it myself. I have a lowering feeling that your playing will put us all in the shade, and, as Clarissa will tell you, I do not enjoy finding myself in anyone's shade."

Sally sauntered over to the piano, carefully draped her gauze overdress over the stool so that it fell in soft folds to the floor, threw back her head, closed her eyes, and played feelingly. The selection she chose was elegiacally moody. Clarissa watched her for an amused moment and then crossed to Miss Pennington. "Don't be discomposed by Sally's remarks, my dear," she said soothingly. "Sally likes to play the role of an *enfant terrible*. She doesn't really mean what she says."

"I quite understand, Lady Steele, and have not taken the least offense," Miss Pennington assured her. Clarissa was sure she detected a slight twinkle in Miss Pennington's eye. Evalyn leaned forward and whispered, "I think, Lady Steele, that if I put the candelabrum on the piano in front of Miss Trevelyan, *no one* will be able to put her in the shade." And she rose and placed the candelabrum on the piano ledge, leaving the rest of the room in shimmering shadows. Clarissa shook her head and laughed silently. Jamie and Philip certainly had the right of it: Miss Pennington was a most redoubtable girl!

When the gentlemen came in, they found the beautiful Miss Trevelyan at the piano, deep in the mood of her music and bathed in candleglow that set her hair and the golden strands of her dress gleaming. They drifted to the piano, attracted like moths to the light, and applauded her performance with real enthusiasm. Sally laughed and bowed with pleasure, her petulance forgotten. Clarissa glanced at Miss Pennington. Their eyes met, and they grinned at each other. *How delightful she is,* Clarissa thought. *I think I've found a friend.*

Later, with the candles rearranged and the room restored to brightness, the guests were ready for tea and cakes. As Clarissa served and Evalyn passed round the sweets, Gervaise wandered to the window. "Do you think the weather will hold, Philip?" he asked. "I've set my heart on some shooting tomorrow."

"I hope so, for your sake and mine," Philip answered.

"What do you mean? Are you going to join us this time instead of locking yourself away in your study?"

"No, I don't mean that at all. I mean that if you, Edward, Reg and Jamie go out, I shall have a few hours of peace in which to do some work."

"Work indeed! What on earth do you have to do that's so urgent?" Gervaise grumbled.

"Yes, Philip, do tell him," Clarissa said encouragingly. "I've long been curious about what you do when you bury yourself in your study every afternoon." She turned to Gervaise. "I suspect he only hides there to get away from us all."

"That's unfair," said Jamie loyally. "An estate of this size requires a great deal of work if it is to be managed well."

"I'm glad to hear you say so, my boy," Edward Covington said approvingly. "After all, you'll be doing it yourself one day."

But Gervaise would not be put off. "Fiddle. I handle *my* affairs, too; and it doesn't take me nearly as long. He's up to something else, I'm sure."

Philip smiled. "I only disappear into my study to make it seem that my life has more purpose than that of the rest of you."

"Don't let him put you off with that bouncer," Clarissa said knowingly. "He has some secret he's afraid to reveal."

"I agree," Gervaise seconded. "I'll wager he's writing a radical tome."

Martha gasped. "That's not possible! Not Philip!"

"It's a ridiculous idea," said Sally, laughing.

"But that's it, you know," Philip admitted. "How did you guess, you rascal?"

"I haven't spent hours conversing with you on Burke and Bentham and the ills of England without guessing what you're up to," Gervaise chuckled in triumph.

"A radical tome? Really?" asked Jamie in surprise.

"How exciting! About what, Philip? You must tell us," Sally urged.

"I didn't intend it to be a secret. I just don't like to prose on about my interests and make myself a dead bore."

"We won't be bored, I promise," Sally assured him.

"Indeed we won't," Clarissa agreed. "I, for one, won't rest until I know what you're up to."

"Well, briefly, I'm writing a response to a view expressed by Burke, who claimed that the British government represents, and *should* represent, the leisured classes who have education and above menial income—which means only about 400,000 of us. I contend—along with many others, like Bentham—that this is a narrow view. I'm attempting to suggest that all adults living in England make up the 'public' and should be represented."

"Good God!" exclaimed Edward. "Do you mean *everybody*?"

"Exactly so."

"I don't understand this at all," Clarissa sighed. "You mean people who receive wages? And servants and such?"

"Yes, I do."

"Well!" muttered Edward, "I've never heard such nonsense."

"Don't know but what I don't agree with you either, Philip," said Gervaise cheerfully, with keen enjoyment of an old, familiar argument. "I'm not at all opposed to the enfranchisement of tradesmen and householders who pay taxes, but—"

"But, indeed!" Edward nodded with conviction, "but the others—servants, indigents, and so on—well, I draw the line, my dear sir, I draw the line!"

Suddenly the whole room was a babble of voices, Sally, Jamie and Clarissa supporting Lord Gyllford, and the others vociferously against. Lord Gyllford turned his amused eyes to Evalyn, who had taken a seat a little apart from the others and was calmly stirring her tea. "You have not ventured to express your view, Miss Pennington," he said.

The hubbub ceased, and everyone turned to look at Evalyn. "Since I am a member of that class against which Mr. Covington has seen fit to draw the line," she answered with a calm smile, "I had supposed that my views would be obvious. It seems to me, however, that all classes will be represented by the government before very long, whether Lord Gyllford defends them or not."

"Hear, hear!" cried Jamie and Reggie in unison, proud of their protégée.

Sally ignored them and looked at Evalyn with a sneer. "Miss Pennington puts me in mind of a job-horse who bites her master's hand because she thinks the oats he brings her are hers by right. You ought to be a little grateful, Miss Pennington, for Lord Gyllford's support for your class."

Evalyn stared at Sally in surprise and chagrin. How could her simple statement be interpreted as resentment of Lord Gyllford? "I didn't intend—" she began.

"Of course you didn't!" Clarissa defended warmly, and turned to Sally in irritation. "Sally, you are being absurd."

"It was not a fortuitous analogy, certainly," Philip said, amused. "I know you meant to defend me, Sally, but Miss Pennington has really got to the truth of it. All classes *will* be represented in time, regardless of my work."

But Evalyn lowered her eyes, struggling with her feelings of shame, frustration, and resentment. She had not intended to denigrate Lord Gyllford's writing. Yet Miss Trevelyan had deliberately tried to give that impression. What had she done to incur Miss Trevelyan's obvious antagonism? And, of more concern, was Lord Gyllford displeased with what she had said, even though he had spoken up on her behalf? As the conversation picked up around her, she unobtrusively glanced up at Lord Gyllford's face and found, to her surprise, that he was smiling down at her with a look of fond pride. A prickle of unfamiliar excitement ran down her spine, the color rose in her cheeks, and she hastily looked down at her cup. But not before she caught a glimpse—she could not be mistaken—of a barely perceptible flicker of his lordship's right eyelid. Philip Everard, Lord Gyllford, had winked at her!

When, several hours later, the entire household had retired for the night, three people lay awake. Evalyn didn't want to fall asleep. She wanted to relive every moment since her arrival. She wanted to commit to memory Lord Gyllford's every word, every gesture, every expression that she had noted on his face. She would add these, with the other impressions of the people and events of Gyllford, to her small storehouse of happy recollections, to be pulled out and relived on some future evening when, inevitably, the loneliness and drabness of her next post threatened to depress her spirits. In the meantime, she would live each day of this unexpected holiday to the full. She snuggled contentedly into the soft luxuriousness of the bedclothes and smiled into the darkness. She didn't care if sleep never came.

Sally tossed and turned restlessly. Who was that drab little nobody getting so much of Philip's attention? The woman was not a fool, she admitted, but she was only a governess, with no style, no taste, and no real beauty. Sally supposed that some might find the wench somewhat taking, but not in comparison with herself! What did Philip see in her? Sally could find no satisfactory answers. But she was certain of one thing: the irritating little nobody was interfering with her plans to capture Philip. Something would have to be done to get rid of her. And soon. She had not played her hand well tonight, and time was fleeting. She must think of a plan. . . .

Philip could not bring himself to lie down. He paced about his room, vaguely troubled. He knew he would not find sleep until he confronted squarely his feelings of disquiet and guilt. He paused at the window and stared out at the lawn below. The moonlight had turned the frosty grass to a silvered sea. Tomorrow would be a perfect day for Gervaise and the others to ride. Does Miss Pennington ride, he wondered? Miss Pennington. There it was. He was drawn to her as he had not been to a woman in years. Good heavens, he was jealous of his own son!

Disgusted with himself, he stalked across the room and got into bed. How amazing, he thought for the hundredth time, that twenty-two-year-old Jamie should have found in that quiet and unobtrusive girl the same gentle and clear-eyed loveliness that he had seen! But thoughts like this simply would not do. His feelings for his future daughter-in-law must be kept sternly in check and must never be permitted to exceed those of fatherly affection. He put her firmly from his mind, and, forcing himself to concentrate on his next day's writing, he at last drifted into an uneasy sleep.

· Seven ·

THE SUN HAD not yet made an appearance when the men gathered round the breakfast board, already attired in riding clothes. Their host, Lord Gyllford, was the only one not so attired.

"Never thought to call you a spoilsport," Gervaise grumbled when Philip had repeated for the third time his intention to remain behind.

Philip laughed. "You may call me anything you please," he said to his friend, "but I have business that will not wait."

Gervaise grunted. "Your book is the business, I suppose, and, if you ask me, it can wait for years."

"Thank you for the compliment," Philip said drily, "but the business has to do with the comfort of my guests."

Reggie, standing at the window, remarked amicably, "Too bad, Lord Gyllford. It lookth to be a good day for shooting."

They all turned to the window to see a faint light lining the horizon to the east. "We'd better get started, then," said Jamie, downing his last gulp of Jamaica coffee and rising from the table.

Philip walked with them to the stables to make sure they were all suitably mounted and waved goodbye as they rode off noisily. On his return to the house, he was surprised to see young Marianne peeping into the breakfast room. Her hair was already combed and brushed into an entrancing cascade of brown ringlets, and her yellow morning dress was too becoming to have been donned for a solitary breakfast. "Good heavens, Marianne," he greeted her, "what are you doing up and about at this ungodly hour? None of the ladies will be up for hours yet."

"I was hoping to have breakfast with . . . that is, I wanted to see the gentlemen in their riding clothes," she finished lamely.

"You've just missed them, I'm afraid. Or rather they've missed you. They would have enjoyed seeing your pretty face at breakfast. You're looking quite fetching this morning."

The shy blue eyes flickered briefly to meet his, and a small smile brightened her face. "Oh, do you really think so?" she murmured. Philip understood that the question was purely rhetorical—merely a group of meaningless sounds she uttered to cover embarrassment or inadequacy with words. Some friend of hers must have suggested it as a useful cover phrase, to be brought out when needed. He suppressed a smile and said politely, "Is there something I can do for you? Can I get you something to . . . er . . . help you pass the time?"

"Oh, no, thank you," she said, her face crestfallen. "I suppose I'll look into your library and find a book to read." The tone of her voice was so unmistakably gloomy that Philip was left in no doubt as to what she thought of that pastime. She turned, and with hanging head and slow step proceeded toward the library. Philip watched her slow passage across the hall, wondering which of the two young men she had risen so early to see. Reggie had shown no noticeable interest in her the night before. Could Jamie's flirtation at the table the night before have encouraged her interest there? He hoped Jamie had better sense than to encourage a young and innocent female's attentions when he was already—even if secretly—attached to another. He sighed, and something of the gloom expressed by Marianne's retreating back entered into him.

Evalyn opened her eyes to find Nancy pulling aside the curtains. A cold December sun barely brightened the room, but the look on Nancy's face seemed to spread light into every corner. She beamed at Evalyn with an eager smile. "Miss Evalyn, I've such news!" she crowed.

"Good morning, Nancy," Evalyn said sleepily. "What news?"

"Ye'll never credit it, I'm sure. 'is lordship sent fer me this mornin'. Sent fer me in partic'lar!"

Evalyn sat up abruptly. "Do you mean . . . Lord Gyllford?"

"Yes, Miss. Lord Gyllford 'is very self! Mr. 'utton, 'e took me upstairs—'e's the butler, y'know—an' Lord Gyllford, 'e smiles at me an' says 'e'd like fer me t' be in 'is employ, t' serve as Miss Pennington's personal maid, 'e says. To work fer Miss Pennington *exclusive*! Then 'e asks me, ever so kindly, if I think I'd be 'appy workin' ere. Imagine that! An' I says, oh, yes, yer lordship, I'd be very 'appy. Then 'e says I'm t' take orders on'y from you. Then Mr. 'utton, 'e pokes me an' whispers fer me to close me mouth an' make me curtsey, so I makes me prettiest one, an' I say I'd be 'appy t' stay as long as 'e'd like, an' that I'll try t' give good service. An' then 'utton takes me to the 'ousekeeper, an' she gives me this lady's-maid dress an' this lovely cap! Ain't I fine? Don't I look a proper lady's maid?"

Evalyn's head was whirling. Lord Gyllford had surprised her again. Most other men would have forgotten a promise relating to a domestic, made so casually at the dinner table.

His attentions to her were as bewildering as they were pleasing.

She shook her head and tried to concentrate on Nancy, who was gaily pirouetting before her. Nancy did look every inch the lady's maid in her blue bombazine dress, her starched white half-apron and the lace-trimmed mob cap that neatly covered her unruly hair. The cap, threaded through with a blue ribbon that formed a little bow right over her brow, looked charming. "I think you look finer than I do," Evalyn laughed as she climbed out of bed, "and much too fine to be serving a mere governess like me."

"You ain't really a governess, are ye?" Nancy asked, peering at her new mistress curiously.

"But I am a governess, truly."

Nancy's face fell. "But I 'eard 'em whisperin' about ye in the servants' 'all like y' was a fine lady—almos' like ye was one o' the family."

Evalyn looked at her with amused sympathy. "Do you mind very much that I'm not a real lady?"

Nancy considered the question carefully. Then her face brightened. "Well, I s'pose they wouldn't think much o' me below-stairs if they knew, but I don't care. I ain't a real lady's maid neither, so I got nothin' to complain of." She smiled her irrepressible smile. "We'll suit each other fine."

Evalyn hugged the girl warmly. "I think so, too," she said.

Nancy happily set about her new duties. She bustled round the room collecting various articles of clothing for Evalyn to wear. As she opened drawers and chests, however, the brightness again faded from her face. "I wish ye 'ad more clothes t' wear," she sighed. "There ain't enough things 'ere t' keep me busy enough t' earn me wages."

Evalyn shrugged into her least shabby daytime dress and let Nancy struggle with the buttons. "Then perhaps you can help me after breakfast. I mean to see what the twins are up to. If we can keep them quiet and happy, and out of the way of the other guests, we'll have deserved at least some of the unprecedented kindness we've been shown."

But Lord Gyllford had been ahead of her here too. While she and Martha stood side by side at the breakfast buffet, Evalyn asked where the children were to be found. Martha, more relaxed and at ease than she'd been since her arrival, told Evalyn that Lord Gyllford had arranged for Jamie's old nurse, now living in retirement somewhere on the estate, to take charge of the children for the length of their stay.

"But that wasn't necessary," Evalyn said. "I would have been most happy to take charge of them."

"Now, my dear Miss Pennington, that would have been most unsuitable. You are a guest here, as I am. I certainly would not have permitted . . . I could not so impose on you," Martha said.

"It would have been no imposition. I most desire to make myself useful. However, I'll not trouble you further on this matter. Please remember, Mrs. Covington, that I should be glad to be of service to you and the children whenever you have need of me."

The men had left for their day of shooting early, and the house seemed quiet and somnolent. Sally had made no appearance, but Clarissa knew it was her wont to remain in bed until well into the afternoon. Noting that young Marianne was drifting about the corridors aimlessly, Clarissa suggested that the ladies take a drive. Martha and Marianne agreed eagerly, but Evalyn declined, saying that a novel she had started the night before was engrossing her. When the others had left, she found her way up to the nursery. It was not a difficult place to find. Here, as in most of the great houses, the nursery was hidden away on the top floor of one of the wings. There she found the twins happily playing at spillikins on the floor before a cheerful fire. On a rocking chair nearby sat a wizened old lady knitting an already overlong muffler.

"How do you do, ma'am?" Evalyn greeted her. "Are you the lady who had been governess to James Everard?"

"More of a nanny I was," the woman said, looking up with a smile. "And to his father before him." She rose from the rocker with surprising grace and agility and came toward Evalyn with a firm, if slow, step.

"Really?" asked Evalyn in surprise. "To Lord Gyllford himself?"

"Yes, indeed. And a fair handful he was in those days. He kept me hopping, I can tell you. Mrs. Noakes, I be."

"And I'm Evalyn Pennington. I, too, am a governess."

Mrs. Noakes bobbed a curtsey. "And a much better than I, I have no doubt. You're a lady with learning. I could tell that the moment you opened your mouth. As for me, I could only watch over my boys and play with 'em. My boys had tutors enough to teach 'em their Latin and such."

"My charges do not learn much Latin from me either, I'm afraid. Tell me, Mrs. Noakes, do you not find it difficult to take care of two such lively boys as the twins here?"

"Not me," the old woman chortled. "It puts a spring in my step, it does, to be in the company of children again. As I told his lordship this morning, when he rode over to take me up, I'd rather be up and doing than lying about on my bed."

A voice came from the doorway. "What she said was, 'Better to wear out my shoes than my sheets!'" The ladies looked up to find Lord Gyllford smiling at them. "I see you and I have come on the same errand, Miss Pennington."

"And what errand is that, sir?" Mrs. Noakes asked.

"To see how you fare with those young jackanapes," he answered, loud enough for the boys to hear.

"We're fine, Uncle Philip," said one of the twins, not bothering to look up from the game. "We've been very good all day, haven't we, Mrs. Noakes?"

"Like two angels," she answered promptly.

"Since it still lacks an hour to midday, it won't do to praise you yet," Philip told the boys. "I'll expect a full report at your bedtime." Then, turning to Evalyn, he asked quietly, "Well, my dear, are you satisfied?"

She flushed and turned to Mrs. Noakes. "Good day to you, ma'am. I hope you'll not hesitate to call on me if you should have any need of my assistance."

She turned, and, finding Lord Gyllford holding the door for her, she left the nursery, her cheeks burning in embarrassment. Lord Gyllford walked beside her down the hall. She glanced up at him timidly. "I'm sorry, Lord Gyllford, if I seemed to be concerning myself unduly in the affairs of your household, but I had so hoped to make myself useful."

"There's no need at all for you to feel embarrassment, my dear. I quite understand your feelings. However, Jamie has invited you here for a holiday, and a holiday you shall have. You may as well resign yourself to it."

"Jamie is . . . I mean, your son is very kind, but I have no wish for him to put you in a position of such . . . inconvenience in my behalf—"

Lord Gyllford stopped her with a gesture of impatience and grasped her firmly by the shoulders, turning her so that they faced each other squarely. "Try to understand, Miss Pennington, that Jamie's wishes exactly match mine in this. We both of us, and my sister, too—have invited you to be a guest in this house. A *guest*. It is, and will continue to be, a pleasure for us to make you happy during your stay. Do you understand? Can you not accept the trifling steps we've taken to make you comfortable?"

Evalyn shook her head. "I am more grateful than I can say, but—"

"You 'but' me too many 'buts,' young lady. Just say yes."

Evalyn looked up at him. His face was close above hers, his eyes looking compellingly into her own. Again, something she saw back in his eyes made her words stick in her throat. Her heart pounded and her chest heaved with emotions completely new to her. She nodded. "Y-yes, my lord," she managed, and dropped her eyes.

"Thank you," he said quietly, and his hands fell from her shoulders. They turned and walked down the corridor without speaking. At the top of the staircase he turned to her again. "My guests all call me Philip," he said pointedly, "and I hope you will permit me to call you by your Christian name. Evalyn is a lovely name. It suits you."

"Of course you may, my lord," she said.

"Not 'my lord,' " he corrected. "Philip."

She looked up at him, her cheeks crimson. "Oh, I don't think I . . ."

"Yes, you can. Say it. Philip."

His eyes still held that look. She took a breath, gasped, "Philip," and fled like a schoolgirl down the stairs.

Philip looked after her until she disappeared. Then he went down to his study and pulled the door shut behind him. As he crossed to his desk, he caught a glimpse of his face in the mirror over the mantlepiece. A smile—a rather foolish one, he thought—still lingered on his face. He stared at his reflection as the memory of his misgivings of the night before flooded into his mind. He had promised himself to avoid her, to keep his feelings fatherly and cool! "Oh, that was well done, Philip," he said aloud, in a tone of sardonic self-disgust, "very well done indeed!"

Evalyn forced herself to walk down the hallway toward

her room slowly and with, she hoped, one last shred of dignity. She had behaved like the silliest chit of a schoolgirl, and how she was to face Lord Gyllford again she didn't in the least know. Yet something inside her was bubbling with suppressed joy, and a smile hovered at the corners of her mouth. If she were sure no one would see, she would have liked to waltz down the length of the hall. She could almost hear the music—*Philip-tah-tum, tah-tum, Philip-tah-tum.* Heavens, what was wrong with her? She'd never waltzed in her life!

But fortunately, before she made a complete fool of herself, she noticed two figures at the far end of the corridor near her room. One was Miss Trevelyan, wearing a diaphanous robe over her nightclothes, her hair still dishevelled by sleep. The other—goodness, it was Nancy!

Evalyn hurried down the passageway, to be greeted by Miss Trevelyan. "Ah, there you are, Miss Pennington. You must really speak to your abigail, you know. She's kept me out here in the hallway arguing for at least five minutes. She has no idea how a maid should go on!"

"I'm sorry if she's done something out of the way. What seems to be the problem?"

Nancy sniffed in a decidedly truculent way and spoke up quickly. "She asked me to do 'er 'air, and I won't," she said, sticking out her chin stubbornly. "Lord Gyllford said I was to work for you ex-clu-sive, didn't 'e?"

Evalyn suppressed a smile. "Yes, indeed he did, Nancy, and you were quite right to wait to ask my permission," she said tactfully, trying to smooth things over.

"Well, I ain't asking yer permission, Miss Evalyn. She's got 'er own maid to do for 'er."

"Did you ever hear the like?" said the scandalized Miss Trevelyan. "How can you put up with such insubordination? I only asked her because my Annette is nowhere to be found. How dare this impertinent minx refuse me? If I were you, Miss Pennington, I'd pack her off this instant!"

"I think you must leave the handling of Nancy to me, Miss Trevelyan. Nancy, dear, you have been rude, and I think you must tell Miss Trevelyan how sorry you are for speaking so."

Two large tears welled up in Nancy's eyes. "I d-didn't mean to be rude, t-truly. But 'er m-maid, Annette, would explode l-like a firecracker at me if I was to go n-near 'er m-mistress's 'air! And me bein' the n-newest on staff, it'd be for sure a slap at 'er pride! And the m-master did say I was to work for you ex-clu-sive, didn't 'e? 'Tain't right to go disobeying him on me very f-first day! So what'm I t-to do?" And she wiped her eyes with her sleeve.

"There, there, Nancy," said Evalyn soothingly, putting an arm around the girl's shoulder and putting a handkerchief into her hand. "Wipe your eyes and go down to the hall to see if you can find Miss Trevelyan's maid—what's her name? Annette? Yes, tell Annette she's wanted right away."

Nancy wiped her eyes. "Are ye goin' to pack me off, Miss Evalyn?" she asked, her underlip quivering.

"No, of course not. Now go along."

Nancy cast her a thankful look. "Yes'm. I'll run right down and do me best to find 'er." And she ran off down the hall.

"It seems to me, Miss Pennington, that you have much to learn about the handling of servants," Sally Trevelyan said coldly.

A pointed retort to the effect that Miss Trevelyan herself had something to learn in that regard—seeing that her Annette was nowhere to be seen when she was needed—occurred to Evalyn, but she did not express it. It would not be pleasant for Lord Gyllford and Lady Steele if their guests were at each other's throats. So she bit back the retort and said politely, "Would you, perhaps, like *me* to do your hair?"

Sally, expecting an angry retort, was disarmed by the gentle reply. "Oh," she said in surprise, "do you think you could?"

"I could try," Evalyn answered. Sally smiled and led the way to her room. It was panelled and furnished in a manner quite similar to Evalyn's, but she noticed with some surprise that it was smaller than hers and the bed hangings not as rich. Why, she wondered, would the Everards give a governess a more elegant bedroom than they gave to Miss Trevelyan? The Everards certainly had strange ways of doing things.

Sally sat down at her dressing table and handed Evalyn her brush with a conciliatory smile. Evalyn began to brush the long, golden hair with trepidation. She knew nothing of hairstyles or the proper way of dressing a lady's hair. But before she had to admit her inexperience, a knock at the door stayed her hand.

"Yes?" called Miss Trevelyan.

"It's Clarissa, Sally. May I come in?"

There was a moment's hesitation, and Evalyn noticed an uneasy flicker in Sally's eyes. "Yes, do come in, Clarissa dear," Sally sang out in a tone of false eagerness.

Clarissa came directly to the dressing room but stopped in surprise at seeing Evalyn—and with a brush in her hand. She looked from Evalyn to Sally with a puzzled, almost troubled, expression. Then she smiled politely. "Oh, Miss Pennington, here you are! I tapped at your door not a moment ago and wondered where you'd gone. But Sally, what on earth is going on? Surely you haven't asked our Miss Pennington to do your hair?"

"Well, I didn't exactly . . . that is, I . . ." Sally began.

"Her Annette seems to have disappeared, and I volunteered," Evalyn put in quickly.

"Oh, I see," Clarissa said, but it was clear that she was not pleased. Fortunately for Evalyn's peace of mind, a breathless and contrite Annette made an appearance at that moment. Evalyn excused herself and made her escape.

"Will you wait outside a moment?" Clarissa said to Annette after Evalyn had left. Annette closed the dressing-room door behind her. Clarissa looked at Sally in the mirror of the dressing table. "I must ask you, Sally, not to play any of your . . . tricks . . . while you are here."

"Tricks?" Sally asked, all innocence.

"She may have been a governess, but all that is at an end, as you will learn in due course. While she is here and under my roof, I expect you to treat Miss Pennington like a member of the family. I trust I'll not have to speak to you on this head again." And she walked from the room, leaving Sally staring at her retreating back in both anger and embarrassment.

Annette came back into the dressing room in considerable trepidation. The petite French maid knew her mistress well, and her expression as she sat staring at the mirror boded no good. Miss Trevelyan was obviously seething with suppressed fury. "I'm so sorry to be late, Ma'm'selle, and not to have been here when you awoke, but it is so early still. I did not expect you to call until two or three. Please do not look so angry at me."

But all Annette got for her pains was a box on the ear.

Clarissa tapped again at Evalyn's door, several gowns thrown over her arm. "Come in," Evalyn called, and looked up in surprise as Clarissa entered with some hesitation.

"I . . . I'm not disturbing you, am I?" Clarissa asked a little nervously.

"Oh, no, of course not. I was just staring out the window at your lovely grounds."

"You shall see them in the spring, when all the shrubs are blooming. It's quite lovely then."

"I hope I may be invited back some day to—but what is that you carry, ma'am?"

Clarissa felt the color rise in her face. "My dear," she said haltingly, "I hope you won't take this amiss. I know you can't have much to wear, given your circumstances, and I have so many gowns that were purchased when I was much slimmer than I am now. No, please, Miss Pennington, don't refuse until you've heard me out. Believe me, my dear, when I say that I don't care what you wear. But all these lovely things are going to waste and taking up room in my chests and cupboards, and it would give me such pleasure to see you wear them."

"Oh, Lady Steele, how can I? You and Lord Gyllford have given me so much already."

"Please don't call me Lady Steele. I feel we've already become friends. And, as a friend, won't you just try one of these, to see if there is any chance that it can be altered to suit you? Please, Miss Pennington. I'd be so obliged to you."

"Well, if you agree to call me Evalyn . . ."

A delightful hour was spent among the silks and muslins and poplins. At least three gowns were found to be immediately useful, with the help of a sash here or a button there. All the rest would be suitable with only a small amount of alteration, and Clarissa assured Evalyn that she had just the woman to do it. Evalyn, standing in front of a mirror, stared with pleasure at her reflection. She was wearing a dress of lilac twilled silk, trimmed along the hem with a row of delicate white embroidery. "Oh, Clarissa," she breathed, "I don't know how to thank you. I've never worn anything so exquisite!"

Clarissa sighed with pleasure. "And I'm sure I never looked so lovely in it as you do."

Evalyn sank into a chair, quite overwhelmed. "I can't quite believe all this," she said, shaking her head as if to wake herself from a dream. "If anyone had told me, a week ago, that I would be spending a fortnight in a room like this, and wearing a dress like this, and finding friends like this . . . Oh, Clarissa, you are giving me a holiday I shall remember all my life!"

· Eight ·

SALLY CURLED UP on the luxurious divan in her bedroom, but left her book unopened on her lap. She had more than an hour to wait before she would begin to dress for dinner. In the meantime, she had a great deal to think about. She was not doing well in her attack on the fortress of Philip's reserve. She had not been able to spend one moment alone with him since she'd arrived. It was clear that he was avoiding her, but he had always seemed to do so. She hoped that his motive was fear of her attractiveness. Many men she had known had exhibited that fear. It was as if they could sense that, if they fell under her spell, they would somehow lose control over their lives. If that was the problem with Philip, she was sure she could handle it, once she overcame this initial resistance.

But now another problem had come between her and her goal. Miss Evalyn Pennington. That Philip was attracted to her was clear. But the small and inchoate attraction did not explain Miss Pennington's position of importance in the household. That was the puzzle Sally had to solve if she were to make this dreadful fortnight of rustication pay off.

The primary question to answer was why Clarissa and Philip seemed so eager to make a to-do over a nobody of a governess. Clarissa had clearly hinted, in her scolding earlier today, that Evalyn's days as a governess were over.

Why? The obvious answer was marriage. Evalyn was to be married, thus alleviating the necessity for her to earn her own living. But whom was she to marry? If she were about to marry an Everard, that would explain why Clarissa and Philip were going to such pains to make her feel at home. But which Everard? It could not be Philip, of that she was sure. Although he was obviously attracted to her, he could not be the man; he had just met her! Sally had been present at Miss Pennington's arrival and it had been obvious that they had not met before. And their conversation at the dinner table last evening indicated that no intimacy as yet existed between them.

Jamie, of course, was the logical one. Sally had the distinct impression that the governess had been invited by Jamie. They had arrived together, and had obviously met some time before. Yet he had seemed quite indifferent to her last evening and had even flirted with the Covington girl. Of course, if the announcement were to be withheld—if the engagement were to be kept secret for some reason— Jamie's behavior might have been carefully calculated to throw observers off the scent. But Sally was not the average observer. If Jamie really were attached to her, it would not escape Sally's keen eye. She would watch and see.

Of course, Reggie was a possibility. He had arrived with Jamie and Miss Pennington and had evidently been staying with Jamie at Carbery Hall. And if it were Reggie who was Miss Pennington's betrothed, there would be an obvious reason for keeping the alliance secret: Reginald Windle, Lord Farnham, would have great difficulties explaining to his family that he wanted to wed a governess. The Windles, if she knew anything of the matter, were not nearly as openminded as the Everards. On the other hand, Reggie had already succeeded to his titles and wealth, and he was in no danger of losing them no matter whom he married. No, no.

She was on shaky ground with Reggie. Besides, why would Clarissa be so protective of Miss Pennington if she were *Reggie's* intended? Surely Reggie's betrothed would not have such importance in this house, would she? Well, it would be an interesting evening. If she watched closely, she might well have some answers before she went to bed that night.

The evening proved to be a complete disappointment to Sally. Not only did she fail to advance her own cause, but by the end of it she was bored, disgruntled, and as much in the dark about Miss Pennington's position as she had been earlier.

Philip took Martha on his arm when the guests went in to dinner, and Sally, though she watched her host and the governess with catlike intensity, could catch no covert glances passing between them. Philip seemed to take no special notice of Miss Pennington, even though Sally had to admit that the mousey creature looked quite lovely in a well-cut lilac gown that must have cost her a year's wages.

After dinner, Sally expected to be asked to play and sing. Instead, she was compelled to join Clarissa and Martha at the card table, and there she was trapped all evening. Gervaise joined the card players when the men rejoined the ladies, and Edward and Philip huddled over a chess board. Whenever she was able to look up from her cards, Sally studied the others, but she was unable to find any signs of a liaison between Miss Pennington and any one of the eligible men. Jamie, having exchanged the merest pleasantries with Miss Pennington, spent the evening teasing Marianne, to that young lady's obvious delight. Reggie spent most of the evening in Miss Pennington's company, but they seemed on such an easy, friendly footing with each other that Sally was convinced only a fool could read into their light badinage any signs of romance.

A light supper was served at ten-thirty, and the guests rose from their various pursuits to gather for refreshments. Now was the time Sally hoped to catch a glimpse of the truth. After supper, the goodnights would be said, and everyone would be off to bed. It was the last chance of the day for lovers to communicate with each other. Secret messages could be passed by the warmth of a glance, the twitch of a smile, the surreptitious touching of hands. Sally was determined to miss nothing. Miss Pennington was the first to say goodnight. She included the entire company in the smile she gave, and left the room without a backward glance. Reggie bore Jamie off with him, saying he wanted to show his friend the new riding coat he intended to wear on the morrow. Before he left the room, Jamie stopped at Marianne's side and whispered something to her. Sally moved a little closer.

"But you must wear something warm if we're to go driving in the curricle," he was saying. "The wind can cut right through you, riding in the open like that."

"But I hate my old pelisse," Marianne answered with a pout.

"Nonsense," Jamie said. "I'm sure it's most becoming. Anything you wear will look just the thing."

Marianne blushed with pleasure. "Oh, do you really think so?" she breathed ecstatically.

From this snatch of conversation, it was hard for Sally to believe that Jamie's heart was occupied by an entirely different young woman. Jamie's words were the words of a carefree boy. The entire matter remained very much of a puzzle.

Jamie, completely unaware of having been the object of Sally's scrutiny, entered his friend's bedroom and dropped down on the chaise, putting his feet up comfortably, folding his hands behind his head and leaning back, the very picture of a sultan surveying his *hareem*. "Well, let's see that riding coat of yours," he said to Reg cheerfully.

"Don't be tho harebrained! Do you really think I want to have your opinion of my coat? Your opinionth have no conthequenth when it cometh to matterth of thtyle."

"If that's so, why did you say you wanted to show it to me?"

"I jutht wanted a word in private with you. I haven't had an opportunity to talk to you thith evening. There'th thomething on my mind."

"Well, out with it, man. What's the matter?"

"Dash it, it ain't an eathy thing to tell one'th betht friend."

Jamie sat up abruptly. It wasn't like Reg to hold back his words, unless there was something seriously amiss. "Good God, Reg! Is there something wrong? You ain't sick or anything?"

"No, no nothing like that. It'th only . . . well, remember the joke I made latht evening . . . about you . . . ?"

"What joke? I don't remember."

"You dropped in here before dinner and were talking about Marianne. . . ."

"Oh, yes, I remember now. You said something about me turning out to be as big a bore as Geoff."

"Yeth. Well, you are."

Jamie gave his friend a dagger look. "That's not funny, Reg."

"I'm not trying to be funny. I mean it," Reg said, looking down at his shoes in some embarrassment.

"Are you trying to tell me I'm making a cake of myself over Marianne?"

"Not exactly making a cake of yourthelf. But you may very well be turning into ath much of a bore ath Geoff if you don't watch it. You thpent the whole evening in her pocket, and you intend taking her driving tomorrow. I thought we'd be out hunting!"

"I have every intention of going hunting tomorrow," Jamie said, getting to his feet and speaking belligerently. "I only promised to take her out for a short spin in the curricle after we return."

"Well, I know how thingth can develop. You begin by taking her driving for an hour, then you take her walking for an afternoon, then you kith her in the shrubbery, and before you know it, you're betrothed!"

"Me? Betrothed? To a mere chit out of the schoolroom? You must have dipped too deep in the brandy—you're foxed."

"I'm ath thober ath you are, and I'll tell you thith, Jameth Everard—I will not remain here at Gyllford to hear you go on and on about Marianne ath Geoff did about Mith Pennington."

"Confound it! I never expected to hear such humbug from you, Reg Windle! If you think there's any similarity between me and that idiot Geoff Carbery, you're no friend of mine! Have you ever heard *me* prose on about some female? Have I ever accosted an unwilling wench on the stairs? If you don't beat all!"

Undaunted, Reggie looked at his friend calmly. "No, I ain't ever known you to behave like Geoff. But I ain't never known you to be taken with a female before, either. I've found, though, that when love attackth 'em, all men act like foolth."

Jamie glared at Reggie in irritation, until it occurred to him that he had observed the very same thing himself. His tension eased, and a laugh escaped him. "Oh, come off your high ropes, Reg! You're right about lovesick fools, of course, but I ain't one of 'em. There's a big difference between a harmless flirtation to pass the time and losing one's head over a girl, you know."

"Mmmmph," grunted Reggie, unconvinced. "I only wanted to drop a word of warning. Only a word to warn you that you're getting near deep water, that'th all."

"Don't brew up a storm about nothing. Come along with Marianne and me tomorrow, and you'll see there's no deep water."

"No, thank you. That'th not nethethary. When we get back from shooting, I intend to thpend the time with my valet. I have to dethide which waithcoat to wear for dinner."

"If you spent any time deciding about the waistcoat you're wearing now, it was time ill-spent," Jamie said mockingly.

"What'th the matter with it?" Reggie demanded.

"Striped satin? How can you ask? It makes you look like an upholstered chair."

Reggie looked at Jamie with scorn. "Thtriped thatin ith all the rage, you ignoramuth," he said with disdain. Then he glanced down at his chest, grinned, and added, "Though I did think, mythelf, that I look a bit like a chair."

Jamie roared with laughter and fell back on the chaise. Reggie broke out in laughter, too, and it was several minutes before the two of them could catch their breaths. Finally, Jamie sobered and said, "Now, this is more like it. I was afraid for a few moments that you were going to leave."

"And I would, too, if our vithit here at Gyllford turnth out like the one at Carbery Hall."

"No chance of that, I assure you. And you will come with Marianne and me in the curricle tomorrow, won't you?"

"No, of courthe not. Whatever for?"

"For the practice. A little flirtation is good experience, so that when we meet someone who really matters, we won't make cakes of ourselves."

"Not I. I won't make a cake of mythelf. I intend to remain a bachelor all my life."

"It ain't likely. You're too good a catch. You may as well agree to come along, for I don't intend to take no for an answer."

"Very well, I'll come, but only to thee that you don't get carried away."

Unfortunately for the hunters, the morning sky showed a heavy covering of clouds. By the time the breakfasters peered out of the windows, they saw a dense fog and a cold-looking drizzle. It soon became obvious that the weather was not likely to clear in time for the day's sport. Gervaise promptly announced that he, for one, was returning to bed. Edward declared his intention of spending the morning catching up on some correspondence, and Philip headed, as usual, for his study. Jamie and Reggie looked at each other glumly. Young, energetic and eager for sport or adventure, they found the prospect of the day ahead of them filled only with boredom and gloom. With a wordless sigh, Reggie looked down into his cup and stirred his tea aimlessly. Jamie propped his elbows on the table, put his chin in his hands, and stared resignedly into space.

The brisk entrance of Miss Pennington into the breakfast room roused them both. Her expression was lively and purposeful, her morning dress of flowered muslin had an air of spring about it, and the lilt of her voice when she greeted them seemed to brighten the room. They jumped to their feet.

"Good morning, Miss Pennington. You're up and about early," Jamie remarked.

"Please sit down. Don't disturb yourself on my account," Evalyn urged. "I shall just help myself to some of this delicious-looking smoked fish and a cup of coffee and join you, if I may."

Reggie held her chair for her, and Jamie poured her coffee. She looked from one to the other in gratitude. "How pleasant to be gallanted by two gentlemen at once," she said.

Reggie rather ungallantly muttered, "Well, there ain't much elthe to do." Then, recollecting himself, he quickly added, "Oh, I beg your pardon. I did not mean—"

Evalyn laughed. "I quite understand," she assured him. "The weather is so dreadful, and you've been cheated of a day of sport."

"Exactly so," Jamie sighed. "And what we're to do with ourselves all morning we just don't know."

"I should think two such intelligent and ingenious gentlemen as you are—and you certainly proved yourselves so in your handling of *my* problem—would have no trouble in inventing some amusements."

"I doubt that we're as intelligent and ingenious as you think," Jamie said ruefully. "We outdid ourselves with your problem."

"Quite right," Reggie agreed. "Our brainth are back to their accuthtomed lethargy."

"You'll think of something, I'm sure," Evalyn said and sipped her coffee unperturbed.

"You seem to have some purpose for the morning, don't you? What are you about, Miss Pennington?" Jamie asked.

"Nothing that would interest you, I'm afraid. I think that on a day like this, Mrs. Noakes will have her hands full amusing the twins. I intend to make myself useful to her."

Jamie's face brightened. "I say, Reggie, would you like to come up and see the nursery? I remember I had quite a good collection of toy soldiers in all kinds of battle regalia, from the Normans to Marlborough."

Reggie made a face. "How exhilarating," he said drily.

"I know it doesn't sound very appealing to you, Lord Reginald, but only think how exciting it would be for the twins!" Evalyn suggested with a gleam in her eyes. "It would be the very thing for a rainy morning like this. Would you mind very much coming along with me? The boys would so enjoy seeing Mr. Everard's soldiers—they are the very things boys like."

Reggie let himself be persuaded, and the trio made their way upstairs to the nursery. As they approached, they heard the sounds of a commotion and came to the door to find the twins on the floor, pommelling each other, with poor Mrs. Noakes standing over them wringing her hands and squeaking remonstrances in a quite ineffectual manner. Reg and Jamie rushed to the rescue, Reg lifting one of them and holding him in firm restraint while Jamie lifted the other and stood him on his feet.

"All right, young man," Jamie said to the boy who, by the tears running down his face, made clear that he had been getting the worst of it, "what's amiss here?" And he wiped away the tears as unobtrusively as possible.

"Freddie kicked me," the boy answered truculently.

"I did not!" shouted the other, twisting powerlessly in Reggie's grip.

"So your brother's name is Freddie," Jamie said to his charge. "What's yours?"

"T-Ted—Theodore."

"Oh, I thay!" Reggie said, exchanging amused looks with Jamie. "Freddie and Teddie!"

"That was Mama's idea, not ours!" said Freddie, still struggling to free himself of Reggie's grip.

"Be quiet!" Reggie said sternly. "A boy who kickth hith brother ith not worthy of lithening to."

The boy twisted around and looked at Reggie with interest. "You said that wrong," he accused. "You sound strange."

Reggie nodded matter-of-factly. "It'th a lithp."

The boy giggled. "What's a lithp?"

Jamie frowned at him. "A lisp. That means he doesn't pronounce the letter 's.' But bigger men than you have learned not to make sport of this gentleman's way with words. There's nothing wrong with the way he uses his fists, you see."

The boy's eyes grew round. "Oh, are you a boxer, sir?" he asked Reg with dawning respect.

Reggie grinned. "I've thtepped into the ring a few timeth," he said.

"He has a punishing right, that I can tell you," Jamie added, rubbing his jaw for emphasis.

"Can you show us how to box?" the twin called Teddy asked eagerly.

Evalyn, who had been standing with Mrs. Noakes and watching the proceedings with amused interest, felt it was time to step forward. "Not here, I'm afraid. But these two gentlemen have come upstairs purposely to show you some wonderful toy soldiers and to tell you about the battles their uniforms represent. Isn't that kind of them?"

"Tell them *what*?" Reggie asked with an air of a man who had been unwittingly trapped. He met Jamie's pleading look with a grimace, and then shrugged. "Oh, very well. Go ahead and find the thilly thingth. We haven't anything better to do."

Lord Gyllford, when he chanced to look into the nursery

an hour later, was startled to find a number of his guests gathered there. A table had been set up in the middle of the room, and lined up upon it were several dozen little painted toy soldiers. On the far side of the table, Reggie and Jamie were acting out the Battle of Crécy. On the near side sat Evalyn, Clarissa, Martha and Marianne, and the twins, watching the display in rapt fascination. And in her rocker, contentedly knitting, sat Mrs. Noakes. His lordship listened for a moment, smiling over the liberties his son and Reggie were taking with history, then tiptoed stealthily away.

By the time the Battle of Blenheim had been won, the clouds had lifted and the day had brightened considerably. After a late luncheon, Jamie reminded Reg of his promise to ride out in the curricle. Reggie demurred. "Three will be a crush," he said.

"Rubbish. Marianne will take only a small space. I won't have you backing out now."

Marianne, positively glowing at the thought of two escorts, was quite ready. Her pelisse was serviceable rather than becoming, but her bonnet, with its high poke and bright red bow captivatingly tied under her left ear, more than made up for it. Jamie helped her up and tucked a blanket around her legs, the two friends climbed up and took their places on either side of her, and they set off.

Their destination was the nearby town of Ashwater, about ten miles to the northwest. Jamie chatted happily about the points of interest along the way—the neat cottage belonging to the bailiff of the Gyllford estates, the home woods where, in season, the quail and pheasant were plentiful, and the notorious "hanging tree" where once, before Jamie was born, a highwayman had met his end—to which Marianne responded with her eager "Really?"

Reggie was silent except for a few negative comments on

Jamie's way with the horses. "Took that turn a bit too fatht, didn't you?" or "Watch out for that rut! You'll dump uth in the ditch!"

Jamie blithely ignored the warnings until a wheel chanced to catch in a deep rut just as he was rounding a turn at a good clip. There was the sound of a crack, the curricle lurched wildly to the right and came to a sudden stop, the horses plunging and rearing frighteningly. One of the horses broke from the reins and galloped off into the underbrush and out of sight. Jamie jumped out of the carriage with a shout and ran to calm the remaining animal. Reggie glanced worriedly at Marianne, who sat stunned. "You're not hurt, are you?" he asked.

She shook her head.

"It ain't anything but a broken wheel, I expect. Don't worry." Reg patted her hand awkwardly and climbed down gingerly from the lopsided vehicle. Hurrying to Jamie's side, he helped his friend get the horse under control.

Jamie looked at Reg shamefacedly. "It was the damned road. I hope you're not thinking that I let the horses get away from me, are you?" he asked belligerently.

"Of courthe not. Don't be a gudgeon."

They walked to the side of the curricle and surveyed the damage. The wheel had broken from the axle and lay useless and crushed under the weight of the carriage. "Well, what now?" asked Reg.

"There's only one thing for it. I must get to the village and rent us another conveyance. This wheel will not be repaired in a day."

"I'll go, Jamie. I can ride the horthe. You remain here with Marianne."

"No, that won't work. The road has so many turnings and forks, you'd never find the way."

Reggie stared at him in horror. "You're not thuggethting that *I* remain here with her!"

"Come now, Reg, don't be a saphead. It will only be for an hour or two."

"An hour or two! It may ath well be a month! No, no, I couldn't."

"But Reggie, you must!"

"No, wait," Reggie said, thinking desperately for a way out. "Why don't you take her up on the horthe with you, and I'll walk alongthide?"

"That would slow me up too much. Besides, I'll have enough trouble riding without a saddle to worry about having anyone else up with me."

But Reg was adamant. "Thorry, old man, but you'll have to think of thomething elthe. I told you that girlth, particularly young oneth, are not in my line. I wouldn't know what to thay to her for two minuteth, let alone two hourth."

"Be reasonable, man! I must be the one to go, for I know the way and I am known at the stable in the village, so I won't have any trouble procuring a conveyance. Someone must stay here with Marianne. We cannot leave her alone, can we? Even *you* must see that!"

Though he cast about urgently in his mind for another solution to the problem, poor Reggie could find none. He glumly shrugged his acquiescence. Jamie grinned, clapped him on the shoulder, and hurried to face the shivering, frightened Marianne. With Reggie's help, they lifted her down from the tilted curricle and set her on the ground. Jamie expressed his regrets for the accident in the briefest terms possible. Then he unfastened the reins from the horse, jumped on its back, and galloped off down the road.

Reggie looked down at his charge with trepidation. "You are shivering, Mith Covington," he said with concern. "Pleathe let me give you my coat."

Marianne looked up at him gratefully, but shook her head. "Oh, no, Lord Farnham. I'm not c-cold. Only f-frightened."

"No need to be frightened. No real harm done," Reggie assured her. "Jamie will be back before you know it with a hired hack."

There. That was the extent of his conversation. What else was he to say to her? He took a quick glance at her face. She was peeping at him from under the brim of her ridiculously grown-up bonnet with an air of expectation. Heaven help him, how was he to fill the two hours looming up formidably before him?

· Nine ·

PHILIP LOOKED UP from his desk at the sound of a knock at his study door. "Come in," he called.

Clarissa peeped in hesitantly. "May I come in?" she asked. "I don't want to disturb you."

"What is this unwonted timidity?" Philip asked, cocking an amused eyebrow at her. "You've always come in without the slightest qualm."

"That was before I realized what important work you do here, my dear. I'm much more respectful now that I realize you're an author."

"And very proper, too. But now that you've demonstrated this admirable humility, you may stop being a peagoose and come in."

Clarissa laughed and entered, closing the door carefully behind her. When she saw his desk, covered with closely written pages, her expression changed. "Oh, dear," she said regretfully, "I *am* disturbing you. Perhaps I should wait until later to talk to you."

"Nonsense. I am not writing another New Testament. The world can wait indefinitely for these words of mine. Come now, sit down and tell me what's on your mind."

"Are you sure you don't mind?"

"Quite sure. I was about to clear my desk and join our guests anyway."

"Oh, I'm so glad of that. That's what I've come to ask you to do. I find myself in a bit of an embarrassment. . . ."

"Embarrassment?"

"Yes, and it's your son's fault."

"Jamie? What's he done?"

"He's gone off in the curricle with Marianne and Reggie and left poor Evalyn here to her own devices. Not that she's shown the least sign of being upset, but still—"

"Do you mean to say he's gone off without even asking her to join the party? Surely he couldn't have done that! He *must* have asked her. Perhaps she didn't want to go and told him she preferred to remain at home."

"No, Philip, he didn't even ask her. She knew nothing about the expedition until Martha mentioned to me, in Evalyn's presence, that Marianne and Jamie had gone off together. Martha had a decided matchmaker's gleam in her eye. I think she's beginning to believe that Jamie and her Marianne may make a match of it."

"Oh, my Lord!" Philip exclaimed in disgust.

"Just so," his sister sighed. "Knowing that Evalyn had overheard all this had me ready to *sink!*"

"I could wring Jamie's neck."

"So could I. Except, of course, that Evalyn was not in the least discomposed. She's been helping me weave the Christmas wreaths, and there she sat working as calmly as you please, as if it were the most natural thing in the world for one's betrothed to go off with another girl."

Philip got up and paced about, musing. "I've noticed this strange behavior myself. Jamie neglects Miss Pennington shamefully. But I've never seen her look in the least constrained. Do you think it's something they've decided between them?"

"I don't know what you mean," Clarissa said, puzzled.

"Well, we told them that we'd make no announcement until after the new year. Perhaps they've decided that we wanted them to keep their feelings secret from our guests, and so they pretend not to notice each other."

"But how foolish! I never intended for them to dissemble in that way. In fact, it is quite the worst way to prepare society for the news of their betrothal."

"Now I don't know what *you* mean," Philip said.

"It will be a shock enough when society learns that James Everard is betrothed to some girl unknown to the polite world. If they have been seen together—seen to be taken with each other—there will have been at least some . . . oh, what shall I call it? . . . preparatory gossip."

Philip made an impatient gesture. "I don't care a fig for the gossip of what you call the polite world. It's Miss Pennington I care about." He suddenly stood stock-still, realizing he had said more than he'd meant to. "Miss Pennington's feelings, I mean," he added lamely.

"If what you surmise is true—that they are behaving this way to keep their relationship secret—we need not worry about her feelings," Clarissa said sensibly. "However, I do not credit it. It's too foolish a plan."

"Then how do you account for Jamie's behavior?"

"I don't know. I only know that I cannot like having poor Evalyn so neglected."

"Neither can I. You may be sure I shall speak to Jamie at the first opportunity. Meanwhile, one would think that Sally could keep her company."

"Sally is a—! Never mind. I don't want to tell you what I think of Sally. You will only think me small-minded, and remind me that you told me not to invite her. It's enough to say that I don't think she and Evalyn have quite taken to each other. Besides, she's gone riding with Edward and

Gervaise, and I don't expect to see them again until almost tea time."

"I see. Well, what can we do?"

"I was hoping that you could squire Evalyn about a bit. It would please her, I know, to have Jamie's father's attention and approval."

Philip was silent. Clarissa looked at him curiously. He was staring out into the middle distance, as if his mind were on something else. "Philip?" she asked, "is there something wrong? It cannot be that—? Don't tell me that you don't *like* Evalyn."

Philip stared at his sister. "Of course I like her," he said, "but I . . . I am rather busy, you know, with our guests and the book, and I've been thinking that I ought to start planning for Boxing Day and the rest. . . ."

"If I didn't know you better," said the puzzled Clarissa, "I would take you for the worst of curmudgeons. This rationalization is not at all the sort of thing you have ever before indulged in. What's come over you?"

Philip sighed. "You're right. I *am* behaving like a curmudgeon. Come, let's go into the sitting room. I shall be delighted to rescue Miss Pennington from the boredom and neglect she is no doubt suffering in your company."

Miss Pennington did not look in the least as if she needed rescuing. She and Martha were seated at a large table which was completely covered with greens and ribbons. There were evergreen branches, shoots of holly boasting bright clumps of red berries, strands of ivy, sprigs of mistletoe, and a profusion of ribbons and candles. The ladies were happily fashioning a number of "kissing boughs." These were gaily-decorated baskets made by shaping evergreen boughs and tying them in place with ribbons. Within the baskets would be placed a few apples and candles, and each would be hung from a doorway, with the lively, white-berried mistletoe hanging like a tassel underneath. While they worked, Martha and Evalyn were pursuing a lively discussion about the possible dangers to the morals of a young lady like Marianne of reading novels like Miss Burney's *Evalina*. Philip and Clarissa entered the room in time to hear Martha stating earnestly, "I am convinced that such reading weakens a young lady's moral fiber."

Philip nodded to the ladies and sat down at the table, looking at Evalyn with interest to hear what her response to this would be.

"I don't think so, Martha," she said in her straightforward, unaffected way. "A young girl has so much to learn about life. The reading of novels provides her with experiences without the necessity of living through these experiences in actuality. Thus she may be spared the dangers and pain of real experiences, while gaining wisdom from the vicarious ones."

"Is that how *you* became so wise, Miss Pennington?" Philip couldn't resist asking. "Have all your experiences been from books?"

Evalyn blushed and answered laughingly, "What other experiences should a lady in my circumstances have had, my lord?"

"That's tipping me a leveler for my impertinence!" Philip acknowledged with a grin. "I humbly apologize, Miss Pennington. But if a mere man may give his views on novel reading—"

"By all means, Philip," Martha urged. "I should love to hear them."

"You may not, when you learn that I won't give you much support. I don't see any danger to a young woman's morals in such reading. However, I do see a danger in Miss Pennington's view. It would be too bad, Miss Pennington, if a young woman used novels to substitute for life's experiences. Vicarious living is not a proper substitute for reality. Joys can never be as fulfilling in books as they are in life, and even dangers and pains are more meaningful when they are real."

"I have to agree with you about the joys," Evalyn admitted, "but I think that life brings enough dangers and pains without our seeking them. Just reading about them would be enough for me."

Philip's grin widened. "What? *Cowardly*, Miss Pennington?"

"Merely cautious," she returned promptly.

Clarissa was pleased to see how well they got on. Whatever maggot had got into his head earlier seemed to have disappeared. "Evalyn was asking earlier about the portraits in the gallery, Philip," she said. "You must take her through one day and tell her about the rogues in our family's past."

"I'd be delighted," Philip agreed cheerfully. Turning to Miss Pennington he suggested, "Would you like to go now?"

"If you have the time," Evalyn said, "and Clarissa can spare me . . ."

"Of course," Clarissa agreed. "Go along, both of you."

Philip rose. "How about joining us, Martha? Or have you already made the acquaintance of our illustrious ancestors?"

"More than I want to, thank you. Clarissa and I will be quite content to stay here and have a good gossip while we finish these wreaths."

The gallery, which was really a long corridor connecting two wings of the manor house, was designed cleverly. The wall which faced west was lined with windows, thus letting in the very last of the setting sun. The east wall was unbroken by any windows or doorways, and was completely lined with portraits. They were of a wide assortment of sizes and styles, from tiny, gay miniatures to enormous canvasses of gloomy pomposity. Philip pointed out an impressive, though distant, relation who had sailed with Drake; a sweet-faced, grossly overweight matron surrounded by seven children who was his great-grandmother; a slim, dark-eyed beauty who was his great-aunt and who, he said, had openly claimed to have been a mistress of George the Second; and his grandfather, the second Earl of Gyllford, whose grizzled hair and humorous eyes seemed to Evalyn to be very like the man who now stood beside her. "He's quite the handsomest man in the collection," Evalyn said impulsively.

"Do you think so?" Philip asked. "I'm not surprised, of course. They say that Jamie is very like him."

"Jamie? Oh, I thought rather that . . ." She stopped in confusion. "That is . . . I mean . . . I hadn't noticed that."

Philip looked at her curiously. If she and Jamie had agreed to keep their alliance hidden, they surely needn't play the game with *him*! Was she embarrassed to acknowledge to Jamie's own father that she thought Jamie handsome? Blast the pair of them, he thought. They were certainly puzzling.

Evalyn moved quickly to another portrait. "I've been wondering about this gentleman," she said, pointing to a painting of a thin, sharp-nosed old man with a completely unsuitable, heavily powdered, many-curled wig, and a great number of rings on his fingers.

"Why did you single out Uncle Joshua? You are looking at the late and unlamented Joshua Alexander Sebastian Selkirk Gyllford, known far and wide for taking more than six hours to dress for dinner. Sir Joshua reputedly spent twelve of the sixteen hours of his waking day in his dressing room. I have it on excellent authority that he employed three valets at once, since no one valet could stand the strain."

Evalyn laughed. "I singled him out because I have the perfect mate for him. She hangs in my bedroom. She has a nose every bit as . . . er . . . important as his, a wig as high as an urn and hung with all sorts of pins and jewels and fripperies, and wears at least three rings on each finger."

"They sound a good match, though I can't say I recall the painting. I wonder if it could be his wife, Aunt Caroline."

"Would you like to come and see her?" Evalyn asked.

"Yes, indeed. It would be a great joke for the family to know that Uncle Joshua had been so suitably matched. If it is indeed Aunt Caroline, I may hang them side by side."

"But how will you know? Will you recognize her?"

"I met her only once or twice, when she was quite old, but it is possible that I may recognize her."

They started back through the gallery. Suddenly Evalyn stopped. "Oh!" she said softly.

"What is it?" Philip asked in concern.

"Something silly. I . . . I'm afraid you will think me miss-ish. . . ."

"I already think you miss-ish," Philip teased, "so don't hold back on that score."

She laughed. "I'm afraid I am. You see, I'm not always certain about just what is proper in your circles. Is it . . . perhaps . . . not the thing for me to take you to my . . . ?"

"Your bedroom?" Philip gave a snort of laughter. "Haven't your novels taught you that? It will be quite proper, my dear, I promise you. We need only leave the door ajar, and you will not be compromised." And he tucked her arm under his and proceeded down the corridor.

The lady in question hung on the wall opposite Evalyn's bed. Philip needed only a moment to recognize her. "It is Aunt Caroline to the life! I don't remember seeing this painting before, but if I had, I would never have consigned it to hang in a guest room. What a dreadful sight she is, to be sure. When I think of all the guests who have slept in this room, and who must have suffered untold nightmares from the sight of her, I'm quite contrite. I shall have her removed instant—"

At that moment, his lordship was interrupted by the precipitate entrance of a dishevelled, wild-looking Nancy, Evalyn's unconventional abigail, plainly agitated in the extreme. She rushed across the room to the window, the words spilling out of her as she ran. "Oh, thank the good Lord y're here, Miss Evalyn. Only take a look out the window! It's Joseph, the under-footman, got 'isself stuck on the ledge outside, and so terrified that 'e'll not move a 'air to get 'isself off!"

"Nancy, I don't understand a word of what you're saying. Are you telling me there's a *man* out there on the ledge?" Evalyn asked.

"Yes'm," cried Nancy, almost jumping out of her skin in impatience. "Come, look for yer—" Turning as she spoke, she caught her first glimpse of Lord Gyllford. Her mouth dropped open, and she gasped in horror. "Oh, no!" she groaned.

"Please don't trouble yourself about my presence, girl," Lord Gyllford assured her, "but I'm sure you must be mistaken. There couldn't be a man out there—we're three stories above ground!"

"B-b-begging your pardon, me lord, but there *is*. It's Joseph, y'see. Standing right out there too scared to move."

"Then stand aside, please, and let me see to him," said Philip firmly.

"Oh, no, me lord, not you!" Nancy almost shrieked, and, like the intrepid girl she was, she stretched out her arms across the window to bar the way.

"But, Nancy," Evalyn said reasonably, "surely his lordship is the only one of us strong enough to handle a fully grown man. Step aside, as he's asked you, and let us have the man in before he falls."

Nancy, though shaking and tearful, refused to budge. "Ye don't understand. 'e can't move because 'e's so scared. If 'e sees 'is lordship, that'll send 'im over the edge fer sure!"

"The girl may be right," Evalyn said to Philip. She turned to the window without another word, opened the casement and peered out. When she turned back, her face was pale and her mouth tense. "He's out there, all right," she told Philip tensely, "frozen to the spot and trembling in every limb."

"How far from the window?" Philip asked.

"About ten feet, I'd say."

"Too far to reach. I'd better get some men organized down below, and he can jump into a blanket," Philip said and started for the door.

"Oh, no, please!" Nancy begged. She ran to Philip, dropped down on her knees in front of him and grasped his hand. "Annette asked me *partic'lar* not to say anything to anyone but Miss Evalyn. It'd be the end of 'er if anyone else learns of this! Oh, please sir! Once ye go out o' this room, there won't be no way to keep it quiet."

"Don't be a fool, girl," Philip said, his voice gently at variance with his words as he lifted her to her feet. "You don't want the man to die, do you?"

"There may be another way," Evalyn ventured.

"I knew ye'd think o' something," Nancy said, looking at Evalyn with adoration and relief.

"What do you suggest?" Philip asked.

"Let me try to coax him to move. He'll have no reason to be frightened of me. And if you stand behind the casement, right alongside me, you can be ready to grasp him as soon as he gets close enough."

Philip nodded his agreement and came across the room in three strides. Evalyn opened the casement and looked out again. A stone ledge ran the length of the outside wall, extending from the wall about a foot, except under the windows where the ledge curved outward to form small, circular balconies. The balconies were edged with low, wrought-iron grilles which permitted the inhabitants of the rooms, should they desire to do so, to step outside in safety. The footman, however, stood on the narrow part of the ledge, halfway between Evalyn's balcony and the one belonging to Sally's room. He stood immobile, his back against the wall, his shirtsleeves flapping in the wind, his hands clutching the coat of his livery, pressing it in a crushed bundle against his chest. His eyes, wide with terror, were fixed on the ground three stories below.

Philip put his hands on Evalyn's waist and lifted her over the sill, and she stepped out on the tiny balcony. Philip climbed up after her, but remained hidden by the casement.

"Good afternoon," Evalyn said to the footman in so calm and ordinary a voice that Philip stared at her in amazement. "You are Joseph, are you not?"

Joseph's head remained fixed, but the pupils of his terrified eyes slid to the corners in his attempt to see who was speaking to him.

"You needn't turn to look at me," Evalyn continued in her calm way. "I'm only Miss Pennington. You've gotten yourself into a fix, haven't you? Well, don't be concerned—

we shall soon get you out of it." Without a pause, she continued to speak in her everyday, softly modulated voice. "I think—don't you?—that it would be best not to turn your head or look round, but perhaps you had best not look at the ground either. Looking straight ahead should serve us best, I think. Yes, just like that. Very good. Now, then, it seems to me that all you need do is slide your right foot toward the right a very little way. There's no danger, you know; the ledge is very firm. I'm standing on it myself. Just a little way to the right. Yes, just so. Good. Now you need only to slide your left leg to meet it. There! Very good indeed. All we need are a few more movements just like that, and we shall have you safe. A bit to the right again. Good. Now the left . . ."

Thus, bit by bit, Evalyn coaxed him closer to the balcony. The moment he was close to the railing, Philip caught him under the arms and pulled him over the grille onto the balcony. Evalyn caught the footman's coat as it dropped from his hands, and she and Philip gently helped the shaking man over the sill and into the bedroom.

Nancy embraced Joseph in her enthusiastic relief. "Oh, thank goodness," she exclaimed ecstatically. "Thank goodness!"

Joseph, beginning to get his color back, turned to thank his benefactress, and for the first time saw Philip. His face turned ashen, and he fell to the ground in a dead faint.

"Confound it!" Philip muttered in disgust. "My presence seems to do nothing but add complications."

Evalyn's lips twitched. "Not at all, my lord. You were indispensible. How could we have hauled him over the railing of the balcony without you?"

Philip frowned at her. "Throw me no sops, my girl. I have the most lowering feeling that, had I not been here, you and your intrepid abigail would have managed very well, and I'd never have heard a word of this entire affair. But never mind that now. What shall we do to bring the fellow round?"

"Nancy, go to Annette and see if she can give you a bottle of vinaigrette."

Nancy returned shortly, but it was Annette herself who carried the restorative. She bobbed a quick curtsey to Philip and Evalyn, and promptly knelt at Joseph's side, holding the vinaigrette under his nose, and murmuring endearments in her native tongue. Joseph shivered, groaned, and opened his eyes. He looked at Philip, winced, and struggled to get to his feet. But Annette held him back. "No, no, *mon cher*, you are not to get up yet," she said tenderly.

Joseph pushed her arm aside and got to his feet awkwardly. "M-m-my lord," he stammered.

Annette jumped up and took a heroic stance in front of him. "You'll not scold my Joseph, milord," she said bravely. "It is all my fault. To me must come all the blame."

"Annette, be still," Joseph whispered fiercely. "His lordship's business is wi' me, not you! Be off to your lady, do y'hear me?"

"I'm glad to see you've got your courage back," Philip remarked drily. "For a while I was very much afraid I had a jellyfish in my employ."

"It was only the height, my lord," Joseph said earnestly. "Ever since I been a tot I been terrified o' heights. Even if my mum stood me on a table I'd yell like a screech owl."

"If you're so afraid of heights, how is it we found you outside a third-story window?"

Joseph stiffened. "Can't tell you that, my lord."

"I can tell him! Me, Annette! I have to be ashamed of nothing, *moi!*"

"Be quiet, girl," Joseph hissed at her. "Do y'want to get

us both sacked? Get back to y'r lady before she misses you."

"If you don't mind, Joseph," Philip said with some asperity, "I'll decide who goes or stays. Now, I don't care to pry into your private doings, but I can't allow my guests to be troubled with incidents like this. Unless I learn, and quickly, why you were outside Miss Pennington's window, I'll sack the lot of you."

"No, no m'sieur! I deserve it only! You are a good, kind man—so everyone says downstairs. I will explain it to you. . . ."

Joseph began to interrupt. Philip stayed him with a glare. Annette said to Joseph softly, "Do not be angry with me, *mon cher*. Someone must explain. It is *amour*, milord. Joseph and I . . . we are for many months . . . how you say? . . . betrothed. But we cannot marry. Joseph supports his *maman* and has not yet enough savings for me to leave the employ of Miss Trevelyan. And Miss Trevelyan does not like for her dresser to be married. So we must wait, and wait . . . *comprenez?*"

Philip said impatiently, "Yes, of course, but what has this to do with being outside the window?"

Annette hung her head. "The rest, it is more . . . *difficile* . . . difficult to say. . . ."

Joseph stepped forward. "I'll tell him. Y'see, sir, gossip spreads real quick in the servants' hall, and if Miss Trevelyan ever should get word that Annette and me is planning to be wed, well, you can be sure that'd be the end of Annette's position. So we ain't ever told nobody about it. Well, you can see that it would gall a man . . . never being able to walk out with his girl or nothing . . . so, when Annette tells me that Miss Trevelyan is out riding for the afternoon—and I not needed this afternoon neither— well, then, I fair jumped at the chance to see Annette alone.

I slipped up to Miss Trevelyan's room and Annette let me in—"

"Yes, yes, enough!" Philip cut in, with an embarrassed glance at Evalyn. "There's no need to explain further. I take it that Miss Trevelyan returned from her outing a bit earlier than expected, is that it?"

"Yes, sir, that she did. And there was no place for me to go but out the window. I knew I'd never make it to the next room, but there was just nowheres else to go!"

"But there's something I don't understand," Evalyn said. "What had my Nancy to do with all this?"

"I was passin' by, on me way to check yer clothes for this evening," Nancy said, "when Annette comes out o' Miss Trevelyan's room looking so white and desp'rate-like, it fair pulled me heart out o' me. She was 'alf crazy with fright. She told me what happened, so I ran to find ye."

"I see. But Nancy, I thought you and Annette were at swords' points."

Nancy shrugged. "That's true enough. But if she was that desp'rate, I 'ad to help her, didn't I?"

"Yes, of course. You did the right thing," Evalyn assured her.

Annette embraced Nancy warmly. "And I never forget, Nancy. Annette never forgets a kindness. For you, and you, Miss Evalyn, I will prove someday my gratitude," she said with feeling.

All eyes turned to Philip, who was staring at them nonplussed. "I suppose you're all hoping that I will excuse you and forget the whole sorry incident," he said glowering at them. "Very well, I will." He turned to the footman and thrust his coat into his arms. "Here, go along. But see that there are no more clandestine meetings, and that you never again go climbing walls."

A chorus of thank-yous greeted this announcement, but

Philip only glared. Nancy and Annette curtseyed hurriedly and ran out. But Joseph would not be put off. "I don't know how to thank you proper, my lord," he said with real gratitude.

"Joseph," said Philip softly, "I will speak to Hutton about raising your wages." Joseph stared at Philip openmouthed. "Well, we must see what we can do to get you married without too much delay," he added gruffly. "Now, go along, man, go along." Joseph made an attempt at a bow and almost ran to the door, shrugging himself into his coat at the same time. "And walk with some dignity," Philip said in disgust, "some dignity, if you please. We don't want to set the whole house talking!"

At the door, Joseph made another attempt to express his thanks, but Philip waved him out. When he had left, Evalyn smiled at Philip warmly. "That was very kind in you, my lord," she said.

"My lord again? I thought we had agreed on Philip. May I say, *Miss Pennington*, that Jamie was right when he said that you were a most redoubtable girl?"

"Did he say that of me? I must thank him, if it is indeed a compliment."

"Can it be otherwise? Of course it is a compliment. Your calm and composure out there on the balcony were quite remarkable in a woman. Most ladies would have fainted or had hysterics."

"You're not being very kind to my sex. As for me, I couldn't have behaved otherwise. My father was a soldier and would not have permitted fainting or hysterics in anyone living in his house."

Philip, standing close to her, lifted her chin and looked down at her with sympathy. "Poor Evalyn," he said softly, "were you not permitted even tears?"

"Oh, no! Tears would have been considered the worst weakness."

"It must have been a difficult childhood. I most sincerely feel for you."

A twinkle appeared in Evalyn's eyes. "Don't feel regret for my *childhood*, my lord," she said, "but rather feel it for me *now*."

"Now?" Philip asked.

"Yes. You see, I am being compromised."

Philip recognized the twinkle. "Compromised, my girl? By me?"

"Yes, I'm afraid so," she said in her almost perfectly serious way. He dropped his hand from her chin.

"And how am I compromising you?" he asked in a tone of almost perfect severity.

"You see, I am alone with you in my bedroom."

"Yes, but I explained earlier how that fact need not be compromising."

"Yes, I remember," Evalyn assured him, "but I'm afraid your Joseph has closed the door."

Philip gave a shout of laughter. "Vixen!" he said. "You have garrotted me again! Very well, Miss, I'll go. And I shall take Aunt Caroline with me." He lifted the portrait from the wall and strode to the door. There he paused and looked back at her. "But I shall retaliate, never fear. I shall replace this portrait with the one of my great-aunt Lucy Gyllford Axminster. She is the lady who murdered her husband in cold blood, convinced the magistrates that the deed was done by a highwayman, and attended the funeral as calmly as you please, without troubling herself to shed a single tear. I think you and she should deal extremely well together!"

· Ten ·

REGGIE'S NOSE WAS red and his fingers frozen. The sun had already sunk below the horizon and would very soon take with it the last of the light. To make matters worse, a sharp wind was whipping up. No matter how often he looked down the lane he could see no sign of Jamie or the carriage he was supposed to hire. He glanced at Marianne trudging along doggedly beside him as they tried to keep warm by pacing back and forth along the road. She appeared to be extremely cold and uncomfortable, but he had to admit that the girl had made no complaint in the almost two hours since Jamie had left them. It had been a dreadful time. Reggie had wracked his brain for topics to discuss so that the time would pass comfortably. He had tried to discuss horses, but Marianne admitted to being afraid of them. He had brought up the subject of travel, but Marianne had never been anywhere. He broached the subject of the London season, but Marianne was not yet out and had no knowledge of it. Her monosyllabic answers to his questions were dampening in the extreme, and his head ached from casting about for a subject on which he could draw her out. For a while, he was quite ready to strangle her with the ribbons of her ridiculous bonnet. But now, looking down at her rosy-tipped nose and blue-tinged lips, he found himself touched with sympathy for her plight which, he belatedly realized, might be even worse than his own.

"Pleathe let me give you my coat," he pleaded for the twentieth time. "You mutht be freezing."

"No, I assure you," she said with a pathetic little smile. "I'm doing quite well, really. It's only—"

"Only what?" asked Reggie in consternation.

"My fingers. They're stinging me so. If only I had thought to bring my muff. It's lined with fur and would have been such a comfort."

"I have an idea," ventured Reggie bravely, feeling suddenly imbued with a sense of gallantry toward the poor creature. "Why don't we thit down on that tree thtump, and I'll rub your handth. That'll warm them up a bit."

"T-thank you," she said in a quavery voice, and sat down on the stump. Reggie sat down beside her, took her hands, and rubbed them vigorously. When he looked up to see if she were feeling any better, he found that she had turned her face away from him, and that her shoulders were heaving gently.

"My word!" he exclaimed in real agony. "Mith Covington, you're not crying, are you?"

She nodded, and a sob escaped her. Reggie felt sick. He was absolutely incapable of dealing with a sobbing female. He glanced quickly down the road in a desperate hope that he might see a sign of Jamie, but there was none. He felt an overpowering urge to run down the road as fast as his legs could carry him, but he resisted—he was born and bred a gentleman, after all. With real courage he turned to her again and asked, "What ith it? Your fingerth? Did I hurt you? Pleathe, you muthtn't cry!"

The shoulders heaved more violently, and the sobs became louder as Marianne shook her head. "N-no, of c-course n-not!" she managed. "It's n-nothing *you've* done. It's m-me!"

"I don't understand," Reggie groaned in mounting desperation. "Ith there anything I can do? Here, take my coat."

"Don't you d-dare take your coat off!" Marianne cried, hastily turning to him. "I w-won't have you c-contracting an inflammation of the l-lungs because of m-me!" And her tears resumed.

"Ith *that* what'th worrying you?" Reggie asked amazed. "What a goothe you are! I am wearing a coat and a waithtcoat under thith greatcoat. I'll be fine." He stripped off his greatcoat and put it around her shoulders.

"I know I'm a goose," she sniffed. "You've been so p-patient with me, and s-so g-good and k-kind, and I've been such a b-bore!"

"A bore! How can you think thuch a thing! I've never heard thuch thtuff and nonthenthe," Reggie exclaimed with perfect sincerity. "It'th all my fault. I never know what to thay to young ladieth."

"It's you who are talking stuff and nonsense now," Marianne sniffed. "You've been a perfect gentleman, and you t-tried so hard to c-converse with me. But I can n-never think of things to say. And I so wanted to be interesting!" And with a fresh flood of tears, she dropped her head on Reggie's shoulder.

It seemed only natural for Reggie to support her by slipping his arm about her waist, and patting her back sympathetically with his free hand. If Marianne were not wearing that terrible bonnet, he would have put his cheek against her soft brown ringlets. An unfamiliar feeling of warmth and strength flowed through him, and he found himself hoping that Jamie would not turn up just yet. "There, there, Marianne, don't cry," he heard himself murmuring over and over. Without quite realizing what he was doing, he lifted her chin and, with the exquisite, lace-edged handkerchief he pulled from his pocket, he tenderly wiped her cheeks.

"I'm s-sorry to b-be acting like s-such a b-baby," Marianne said, her voice still quivering with tears, her wet lashes fluttering enticingly over melting blue eyes. Entranced, Reggie bent closer. She lifted her face to his and, to his utter surprise, their lips met. For a few seconds, neither of them moved. Reggie felt dizzy, as if his head were flying off into the air. Then he realized what he was doing. He was kissing a girl! *Jamie's* girl.

"Oh, Lord!" he groaned and jumped to his feet. Marianne stared up at him in trusting and innocent surprise. "Marianne!" he said in a choked voice, "I mean, Mith Covington . . . I'm very thorry. I don't know what to . . . I don't know what came over me! It wath unforgivable, I know, but I give you my word it will not happen again."

"Oh," Marianne said in a tiny voice, and a tear started down her cheek again.

"Good God, you're not going to cry again!" said Reggie in despair. "I know what I've done can be very upthetting to a young girl, but it wath not tho very bad, really. Pleathe, Marianne," he begged, sitting down beside her and grasping her hands. "Truly, you can trutht me. I've given you my word. I won't break it."

"I don't w-want your w-word!" she said between sobs.

"Marianne! What can you mean? You cannot *want* me to kith you!"

"Why not?" she asked, sniffing into his handkerchief.

"Becauthe . . . becauthe . . . well, for one thing, everyone knowth I've no way with the ladieth. I'm much too fat, and I lithp—"

Marianne's usually limpid eyes flashed. "You have a way with *me*! And you are *not* fat! Everybody says you always look in the height of fashion. Jamie says you're top-of-the-trees! I heard him! And as for your lisp, well—"

"Well—?"

"I think it's . . . lovable!"

Reggie gaped at her in astonishment. "Lovable? I don't want to be rude, Marianne, but are you thure you're not touched in your upper workth?"

Marianne was forced to giggle. "Oh, Reggie, you're so droll!"

A distant sound of horses' hooves brought a sense of urgency to Reggie's next words. "That'th all very well, Marianne, but you mutht promithe me to forget what . . . what'th happened here today."

"But why?"

"I haven't time to explain. Jamie'th coming. You do like Jamie, don't you?"

"Oh, yes, but—"

"And he liketh you. Therefore, you mutht promithe me—"

Marianne looked dangerously close to tears again. "I don't understand. Don't *you* like me?"

Reggie looked toward the approaching vehicle in desperation. Jamie was practically upon them. "It don't matter whether I like you or not," he explained hastily. "He liked you firtht, you thee?" A rather shabby phaeton was drawing up in front of them. Reggie pulled Marianne to her feet. "You do underthtand, don't you? And you won't cry, will you? That'th a good girl!"

Jamie, cheerful and self-satisfied at having rescued his party from a nasty fix, was full of the adventures he'd encountered. He'd found, on his arrival at Ashwater, that the livery stable where he was known had no one in attendance, and that he had not a penny in his pockets. His account of his attempts to establish credit made for a lengthy and humorous monologue, which occupied him through the entire trip home. If his passengers were somewhat preoccupied and unusually quiet, Jamie seemed to take no notice at all.

Clarissa knew that the evening would not go well. All the signs of trouble were apparent even before nightfall. First, one of the horses that Jamie had taken appeared at the stable wild-eyed and riderless. When she had finally found Philip, who had unaccountably disappeared for over an hour, he calmly told her not to worry, that Jamie was quite capable of handling any emergency on the road. His reassurances fell on deaf ears, for she knew that Martha would fall into hysterics if she got wind of the news that something had happened to the curricle in which her daughter was riding. By the time Jamie and his party finally appeared, looking cold and exhausted, it lacked only half an hour to dinner time. The rest of the household had already gathered in the drawing room, and the necessity of keeping them amused for an additional half-hour while Jamie, Reggie, and Marianne dressed, severely taxed her nerves.

The second trouble sign was the news that Martha imparted to her. Freddie, one of the twins, was complaining of an earache. Clarissa tried to make light of it to Martha, assuring and reassuring her that children often have complaints in the evening which disappear magically by morning. But earaches were often symptoms of severe infection, as Clarissa well knew, and the fear of a serious illness invading her household hung over her like a cloud.

But the trouble that most depressed Clarissa was her relationship with Gervaise which, he had made clear this afternoon, was approaching some sort of climax. He wanted her to marry him. He had always, as long as she could remember, wanted her to marry him. He'd been an admirer in her youth, and she knew that he'd never married because of a strong sense of loyalty to her, although she found it hard to believe—his protestations to the contrary—that his love for her could persist into middle age. She believed that it was simply a habit with him to think of himself in love with her. Nevertheless, his unwavering devotion had been a source of comfort to her through many years. He had been a trusted adviser, an escort, a gentle and cheerful friend. She counted on his support, enjoyed his company, and found his comfortable companionship one of the necessities of her life.

But now he was threatening to withdraw these from her. He had made it clear that he wanted a wife, not a friend. He had told her quite firmly this afternoon that he wanted some time alone with her as soon as she could arrange it. She knew what he would say. And she knew what her answer had to be. She had other obligations. She could not marry. But she did not want to lose his friendship. Why, oh why, had he chosen this time to force this dilemma upon her?

He ought to have realized that the Christmas season was the worst time of year for additional pressures. She had so much to see to and to organize. Christmas eve was only two days off. There were the Christmas baskets still to get ready for distribution among the tenants, the Yule log ceremony, and the transportation to midnight mass to arrange, to say nothing of the late supper they would have afterwards. Then the enormous Christmas dinner for the next day had to be planned—a particular problem since she never knew how many neighbors would be dropping in. Then there was Boxing Day following, when it would be their turn to prepare the feast and entertainment for the servants' special day, and give them their Christmas boxes. Trust Gervaise to muddle her at such a time!

Sitting at the foot of the dining table, Clarissa surveyed her guests carefully. The snatches of conversation she heard sounded cheerful, the food was delectable and abundant, the candlelight gave the faces a warm, lively glow. But Martha looked strained and seemed to have her mind elsewhere. Sally, flirting with Philip outrageously, nevertheless seemed to be watching everyone with those cat's eyes of hers, as if she were a French spy trying to ferret out some dreadful secret. And Reggie was a little silent tonight—not like himself at all. Jamie, however, was persisting in his attentions to little Marianne, who was in high color tonight and looking very lovely. Evidently Philip had had no chance to speak to his son and was endeavoring to make up for it by keeping up a lively conversation with Evalyn. Well, things could be worse, she thought. We might brush through this evening after all. She stole a glance at Gervaise, seated at her right. He was regarding her with his apple-cheeked smile. "So," he said teasingly, "now that you've checked all your other guests, you finally give me a glance."

"Oh, pooh," she laughed and patted his arm affectionately. "I don't trouble about you. You're quite one of the family."

His smile faded. "I suppose I have been so," he said, looking down into his plate, "but you must take no one for granted."

Hutton, the butler, came up behind her at that moment and leaned over her, asking for instructions on serving the second course, so Clarissa didn't have to give Gervaise an answer.

While waiting for the men to finish their port, the ladies sat in the drawing room somewhat dispiritedly, Sally playing the piano without her usual enthusiasm, Marianne pacing about the room in obvious boredom, and Clarissa staring at the fire abstractedly. Evalyn, noticing the worried frown on Martha's brow, approached her and said, "You seem to be a little troubled this evening, Mrs. Covington. I hope there's nothing wrong with the twins."

Martha looked up eagerly and made room for Evalyn on the settee. "I *am* a bit troubled," she admitted. "Freddie's complained of an earache. Clarissa thinks it will go away by morning, and of course she's probably right. But it's my nature to fear the worst. If it should turn out to be an infection, I'm sure I shall suffer a *collapse*, for I don't know what I can do for him. Our doctor at home is quite capable and knows the twins so well, but he is too far away to be brought here, and I have no confidence at all in strange doctors."

"I'm sure that, if a doctor were needed, Clarissa will know of a capable one," Evalyn said comfortingly.

"Yes, but strangers are strangers, no matter how well recommended they may be. And a strange doctor would not know Freddie as he should."

"But he need not be familiar with his patient if you or Mr. Covington can give him an accurate history of Freddie's past illnesses."

"Oh, Mr. Covington is no help at all in these matters. He always says that I make fuss enough for two and retires to his study. Tell me, Evalyn, do you think I should give the boy some medication? I've brought some James's Powders with me, and some mint water, too. And I've heard that putting a roasted onion in the ear can be quite beneficial."

Evalyn looked dubious. "Why don't we go upstairs and see if he is sleeping comfortably? Perhaps he has already gotten over his pain, and your mind would be at ease."

"Oh, *would* you go with me? I know I shan't relax until I am convinced that the dear child is not suffering."

The two women left the drawing room and did not return for over an hour. When they came back, they found that Philip, Gervaise, Edward, and Jamie were enjoying a lively game of silver-loo. Sally was still at the piano, Reggie turning the pages for her, and Clarissa listening to the music with all the attention she could muster. And Marianne was gazing moodily out of the window at the moon. Martha took a seat beside Clarissa, who leaned over and whispered, "How is Freddie? Is he sleeping comfortably?"

"He is now," sighed Martha with relief. "Your Evalyn is a gem, truly she is. We found Freddie cross and uncomfortable, and quite unable to sleep. But Evalyn soothed him, and had her Nancy make him some herb tea and heat up some oil which she dropped in his ear. And before I knew it, he had dropped off to sleep. We stayed and watched over him for quite a while, but he seems to be sleeping so contentedly that we came away."

"Oh, I'm so glad," Clarissa said, relieved.

"Yes. You can imagine how grateful I am. Do you think, Clarissa, that Evalyn would consider taking a position as governess with us? I know she is a guest here, and I wouldn't dream of asking her without your permission, but do you know anything of her plans for after the holidays? Does she return to the Carberys, or has she another post?"

Clarissa smiled enigmatically. "I'm delighted that you found her so helpful. She is truly a remarkable young woman. But I'm quite sure that after the holidays, she will be . . . er . . . otherwise engaged."

Evalyn, meanwhile, had joined Marianne at the window. "What a lovely moon," she remarked.

Marianne looked downcast, and sighed feelingly. "Yes, very lovely," she said.

"I suppose you are thinking that it is a night on which to be gazing at the moon with an interesting young man, rather than to be making polite conversation with a prosy, chattering female," Evalyn said with an understanding smile.

Marianne looked stricken. "Oh, no, Miss Pennington,

not at all! I hope I didn't . . . that is, I never intended . . . I didn't mean to offend—"

"Of course you didn't. You haven't given me any reason to be offended. It's only that I know I would have felt, when I was your age, that a night like this is wasted if it isn't shared with a young man."

"I don't feel that way. I find young men quite confusing and difficult, and I wouldn't care in the least if I never spoke to any of them again."

"Oh, how cruel! There is at least one gentleman in this very room who would be very sorry to hear you say so."

"No, there isn't. If you mean Jamie, you can see that he sits across the room laughing over his silly card game and has not exchanged a word with me all evening. And as for Reginald Windle, he has been languishing over Miss Trevelyan in the most odiously deferential way, just as if nothing whatever had happened between—" And here she stopped and blushed in embarrassment.

"I don't wish to pry, of course," Evalyn assured the girl gently, "but Lord Reginald is a particular friend of mine, and I'm sure he would never have offended you knowingly."

"Oh, he didn't offend me, exactly," Marianne hastened to reassure Evalyn, and before she was aware, she had confided to Evalyn the whole story of her adventures of the afternoon. "So you see, Miss Pennington," she concluded, "that is why I am so confused. How can a gentleman kiss a girl one minute and ignore her the next?"

"It certainly is a puzzle," Evalyn agreed, "but it seems clear that Lord Reginald feels honor-bound to leave the field to Jamie."

"Do you really think so?" Marianne asked hopefully. "You do not think he has forgotten me already?"

"I don't believe he could have done so. But honor is

important to gentlemen, you know. More important than love, I think. So you must not blame him too much for putting his honor before his heart."

"Oh, Miss Pennington, you make him sound quite romantic! Do you think I should put him out of my heart, too?"

"I'm sure I don't know. Are you certain that he's really there? I was under the impression that Jamie is the one who attracts you."

Marianne sighed again. "Oh, dear, I wish you hadn't said that. I don't know which of them I prefer. Do you think that means I'm . . . flighty?"

Evalyn bit back a smile. "No, of course not. I think it means that you are not acquainted with them for a long enough time. In due course, your instincts will tell you which one you love."

"Are you sure, Miss Pennington? Do you think I will ever be certain?"

"Oh, yes. When you are truly in love, your instincts will point him out to you, just as the needle of a compass points north."

Marianne gazed at her with something like adoration. But even as she spoke, Evalyn was uncomfortably aware that, instinctively, her own eyes were about to turn toward the gaming table. It was only by a physical effort—not unlike the effort of keeping the needle of a compass from pointing north—that she was able to restrain herself from turning to look at Philip's face.

· Eleven ·

SALLY BID EVERYONE goodnight with her brightest smile, floated off gracefully to her room like a blond goddess on a cloud of mauve silk, closed the door gently behind her, and kicked over the nearest chair with a vicious swing of her foot. "What an idiot I am!" she said aloud. She paced the room, her hips swaying angrily. What was she doing in this rustic backwater? She belonged in London, in a whirl of balls and soirées, gambling games and masquerades, intrigues and flirtations, and the thousand other diversions with which she was accustomed to give excitement to her daily existence. She was so bored here she wanted to scream! She had known, in maneuvering her invitation, that she was condemning herself to a fortnight of quiet evenings and lazy days, but she had not expected to be humiliated, to be forced to take a back seat to a nobody of a governess. Why, even that seventeen-year-old chit, Marianne, was arousing more interest among the men than she! What was the matter with these men? Were they blind?

She picked up a taper with shaking fingers and lit all the candles of a large candelabrum. She carried it to her dressing room and set it on the dressing table in front of the mirror. In the strong reflected light, she studied her face with intense concern. Her green eyes glinted back at her as brightly as ever, subtly accented by the blacking with which she darkened her lashes. Her skin was smooth and un-marked by a wrinkle, freckle, or blemish, and the soft pink color of her cheekbones was due as much to nature as to art. Her tear-drop diamond earrings made glittering highlights on her cheeks and emphasized their smoothness. Her neck was long and graceful, her shoulders smooth as ivory. The only fault she could find with the picture in the mirror was in the arrangement of her hair. She had felt, earlier this evening, that Annette's suggestion for her coiffure was very becoming, with its part down the center and a cascade of tight curls falling over her ears. But now, in contrast to the insufferable Miss Pennington's simple style, it looked ornate and artificial.

There was a light scratching at the door, and Annette entered diffidently. "You have come up to bed early, Ma'm'selle," she ventured.

"You are late!" Sally countered angrily. "I expect you to be here waiting for me when I come up to bed!"

"But, Ma'm'selle, how am I to know—?"

"I'll brook no arguments, girl!" Sally cut in. "Stop jabbering and take down my hair. And by the way, don't fix it in this style again. It's dreadful."

"*Zut!* Did you not say to me earlier that—?"

Sally narrowed her eyes threateningly. "Are you going to talk back to me about everything? Watch your step, Annette. You can be replaced quite easily, you know. I don't know why I've put up with you this long."

Annette had heard these threats many times before and was unmoved. "You did not have much amusement down-stairs tonight, eh?" she asked impertinently, pulling the pins from her mistress's hair.

"Amusement! It was the greatest bore I've ever been forced to endure. I don't think I can stand much more. I'm tempted to pack up this very night. I'd get to London if I had to travel on the public stage!"

Annette drew in her breath and opened her mouth to object. The possibility of being forced to leave Joseph so soon came as a shock. Although Lord Gyllford had been true to his word and had arranged for a promotion for Joseph, the pair had not yet had time to benefit from the new arrangement. It would be terrible to be forced to leave him now, when she had been expecting to spend another ten days in his company. But she knew that she could not hope to sway her mistress by argument. Perhaps she could soothe her out of the sullens. A better mood might make the idea of rushing back to London less appealing. "Perhaps Ma'm'selle is only a little tired," she suggested amicably.

"Ma'm'selle is not in the least tired. How can I be tired? I haven't been dancing, have I? I haven't done anything that would tire a dowager in her eighties!"

Annette, having taken down Ma'm'selle's hair, now undertook to unhook her gown. She remained silent, trying desperately to think of some way to make the stay at Gyllford appear more attractive to her willful employer, but nothing occurred to her. She helped her Ma'm'selle into her filmy nightdress, a costly trifle made of layers of gauze, each layer a different shade of blue, and picked up the garments Miss Trevelyan had discarded. Ordinarily, she would have departed with them, but tonight she lingered in the dressing room, pretending to be busy putting things in order, hoping that she would learn more of Miss Trevelyan's plans.

Sally, not in the least sleepy, stretched herself luxuriously on the chaise and mulled things over. Philip had been unapproachable ever since her arrival, but she had seen nothing to make her think that he had designs in other quarters. While Miss Pennington's position in the household still remained a mystery, she was almost convinced that Philip was not involved in it. There was no reason to feel that her campaign was lost. She might win him still, if she could get near to him. She would have to make him more approachable. She would have to waylay him in his study, or surprise him by appearing early at breakfast. . . . She was clever—she would find ways. As for Miss Pennington, if her presence should become a threat to her plans, Sally would find a way to discredit her.

Annette made a noise in the dressing room. "Are you still here?" Sally asked. "I don't want you any more tonight. Go to bed."

"I only wish to put away your things. Look, you have left your diamond earrings lying here. Do you not want to lock them away in your jewel box?"

"Oh, bother. Just leave them there and go away."

"But how foolish, Ma'm'selle! It is not at all proper to leave such things lying about for anyone to pick up."

"There's no one here who would—" Sally stopped and rose slowly from the chaise. She walked to the door of the dressing room and leaned against the frame. "Perhaps you're right," she said to Annette, a strange smile turning up the corners of her mouth, her eyes showing a calculating gleam. "One should never be too careless with valuables, no matter where one is, don't you agree? You are very right to caution me. Here, I'll put them in the box, Annette, and you must make sure I lock it carefully. You must be sure we do this every night, all the time we stay here. Will you remember to remind me, *chère* Annette?"

Annette ogled her mistress in suspicion. What was the meaning of this sudden emphasis on the safety of her jewels? And the sudden affection with which she was speaking? Annette didn't like the glitter of those green eyes.

Ma'm'selle was planning some devilment, of that Annette was sure. "As you say, Ma'm'selle," she said carefully.

"Every night, for as long as we stay here, we must remember to do this, *n'est-ce pas?* It is your own suggestion, after all."

"But, yes. It is of all things the most sensible," Annette said, watching her mistress carefully. "Does this mean we are to remain here?"

Ma'm'selle Trevelyan smiled enigmatically, locked the jewel case, and tucked the key under a powder puff in a glass dish on the dressing table. "Yes," she said thoughtfully, "I think we'll remain for a little while. This rustication may prove to be somewhat enjoyable after all."

Reggie woke early the next morning and drew aside the window curtains to find the ground covered with a light sprinkling of snow, and the sky heavy with the threat of further precipitation. Blast! he thought, another day of enforced inactivity. Another day in which he would be obliged to linger about the house, making polite conversation and playing silly card games. And worst of all, he would have to see Marianne and pretend to indifference and distance, while all the while he would remember their warmth and intimacy. He climbed back into bed and tried to go back to sleep. There was no point in dressing now. No one would be down to breakfast before ten on a day like this. He closed his eyes and tried to will sleep to return to him again, but he felt obstinately wide awake. His mind returned, as it had done repeatedly the night before, to the little patch of woods where he had spent the previous afternoon. He could see the tree stump, the fading sunlight lighting the bare treetops, the wet lashes of Marianne's eyes flickering tremulously against her cheeks. He could see her lift her eyes, and then her face, close to his. And he could feel again the surprising warmth and softness of her lips against his own.

He sat up, leaned back against the pillow, his eyes wide open. Of all the men in his wide circle, he was the last expected to lose his head over a girl. Reggie was the one to whom the others came with their problems in matters of the heart. Old Reg would be sure to take it all as a great joke and a bore, and tease them out of the doldrums. Anyone could have predicted what Reggie's future would be: a rich and fat old bachelor, riding to the hounds, organizing shooting parties and elaborate and well-attended dinners. Not that he was at all averse to keeping a ladybird or two for amusement. But ladies of the muslin company did not count in this regard. They never affected one's emotions. One did not become involved with them in any serious way.

But a naive, innocent girl like Marianne—one whose birth and station in life were similar to his own—well, that was quite a different case. One kiss and he could have been a doomed man. Fortunately, Jamie had staked the first claim. Reggie had no intention of altering his plans for the future for any girl, and certainly not for a chit just out of the schoolroom, not yet "out," with no *savoire-faire* or address. She could barely make civilized conversation!

He sighed. All that was far from the truth, and he knew it. Why, when they had sat together on the tree stump, her conversation had been utterly charming. Where, oh, where could he ever again find a girl who would describe his lisp as "lovable"?

But he mustn't dwell on it. He must discipline himself to put her out of his thoughts. He must find some other way to occupy his mind. He cast his eyes around the room. There on the mantle was the very thing. He hadn't spent any of his time in such pursuits since his days at Cambridge, and even then he had avoided it as much as possible. But there was nothing else he could think of. Yes, there was nothing for it but to get out of bed, get that book from the mantlepiece and spend the morning reading. He sighed. Love can get a man into preposterous situations. He crossed the room bare-footed and lifted the book from the shelf. It was somewhat yellowed and covered with dust. He blew it clean and looked at the title—*The Life of Mr. Jonathan Wild the Great*. Well, it sounded as good as any. Reggie pattered back to bed and propped himself up among the pillows. To what ignominy had he fallen! As he turned stoically to the first page, he hoped fervently that word of this activity would not leak out to his friends. He would never be able to live it down!

Evalyn was also spending the morning in a novel way. She had been trying to find a solution to a problem that had been disturbing her since her arrival at Gyllford; she wanted to express her thanks to her hostess in some sort of tangible way, but she had nothing in her portmanteau that would make a suitable gift. Her Spanish shawl was the only one of her personal effects which might answer, but Clarissa had in her possession several shawls much more beautiful. Yester-day, however, in a chance conversation with Joseph, she had come upon a solution. She'd met the footman in the hallway and had entered into polite conversation with him. During this, she learned that he had once been employed in Birmingham in a factory owned by a Mr. Henry Clay, who had patented a process for making *papier-mâché*. This material had become very popular throughout England, and was used for things as diverse as buttons, paper cases, tea trays, and coach panels.

The material was very easy to make at home, Joseph said in response to her questions, needing only strips of paper soaked in glue or size. The wet paper could then be shaped on a mold or any solid surface. When dry, it had the consistency of thin wood and could be varnished, lacquered, painted, or decorated in any number of ways. Evalyn, who had seen many objects made from this material, immediately decided that she would try to make a button box for Clarissa out of this ingenious material.

This morning she, Nancy, and Joseph had paid a visit to the kitchens, where she had procured some flour, a large bowl of water, and some heavy paper. This they took to Evalyn's room where, under Joseph's supervision, they tore the paper into strips, soaked it in the ready-made glue, and shaped the strips around a porcelain box which Evalyn had found on her dressing table. Joseph assured her that when the paper had dried it could easily be lifted off the porcelain, which could then be returned to its original condition simply by washing it.

When the makeshift mold had been covered, Joseph returned to his duties, and Nancy and Evalyn washed up. Evalyn looked at the morning's work with a pleased smile. The box and the lid had been neatly set to dry on a table before the window. Tomorrow, she would remove the mold and begin the process of varnishing and decorating. It would not be a valuable gift, but it would be delicate and colorful, and she was sure Clarissa would be pleased with something made with such loving care.

This morning was an important one for Gervaise, too. Rather carefully attired in a rose-colored coat with slightly rolled lapels, and a pair of blue pantaloons fitting tightly from waist to ankle in the new Parisian style and trimmed with a row of buttons down the outside of each leg, he entered the library nervously. He looked around with a sigh of relief to see that the large room was unoccupied. He had insisted on a meeting with Clarissa and now was beset with doubts and misgivings. It was not at all his style to force her hand, although he had long felt that his dog-like devotion to her all these years was somewhat demeaning to his sense of his own manhood. Middle-aged and corpulent as he undoubtedly was, he was still a man of some stature and dignity, and to be forever dangling after a woman who could not make up her mind did not seem to him to be appropriate behavior. The time had come to ca'l a halt.

He was sure that his instincts in this matter were sound and rational, yet misgivings crowded in on him. After today's interview with Clarissa, his life would not be the same. If she agreed to marry him, he would, of course, be obliged to give up some of the comforts of a bachelor's existence—the freedom to come and go as he pleased, to run his house to suit himself, to plan his amusements, his meals, and his wardrobe without interference. This he was more than willing to do, to dispel the gloom with which his frequently recurring periods of loneliness enveloped him. If, on the other hand, she refused him, he would be cut off from his hitherto easy access to the one place where he felt at home and happy, Gyllford Manor, and from the sense of exhilaration and contentment which her companionship had provided all these years.

The high, starched points of his shirt collar cut into his full cheeks uncomfortably, and his coat felt annoyingly tight over his abdomen as he walked stiffly to and fro across the Oriental rug covering part of the library floor. Why had he let his man trick him out in so formal a style? His pantaloons, which earlier today had seemed to him the height of fashionable elegance, now seemed singularly inappropriate for country wear. His coat, which Weston had cut himself, and which had fit him quite admirably when he had first tried it on, now seemed positively ill-fitting. And finally, to his chagrin, he discovered that he'd been nervously twisting a waistcoat button and it had come off in his hand.

Staring down at the irritating button, he came to a decision. He would immediately return to his room and send his man to Clarissa, informing her he was not feeling up to snuff this morning. He started for the door and, true to his luck, came face-to-face with her. "Of course, you would arrive at this moment!" he muttered.

"Oh, dear," said Clarissa, confused, "have I misunderstood the time?"

"Not at all," Gervaise answered. "You are as precise and punctual as a tax collector."

"What a charming simile," she murmured drily.

"No offense meant, dear lady, I assure you. It's only that I am not quite dressed this morning, it seems." And he held out the button sheepishly for her inspection. "I was about to leave for repairs."

Clarissa laughed. "No need to run away," she assured him. "Often and often I've seen you with a button missing. I'm not at all put off by it."

Seating herself on a sofa before the fire, she patted the place next to her and urged him to sit down. He shook his head. "I'm afraid to chance it. If I sit, I fear that more of these blasted buttons may come loose."

"Poor Gervaise. Then why do you choose clothing with such an inordinate number of buttons? Look at those pantaloons! There must be at least sixty buttons on them!"

He looked down at the pantaloons awkwardly, his cheeks reddening in embarrassment. "I thought these pantaloons would make me look quite up to snuff—the complete man of fashion," he said, crestfallen.

"And so they do. Truly. Even without the button, you look complete to a shade," she assured him, regretting her hasty criticism.

He cocked a knowing eye at her. "No need to flummer me, my girl. But perhaps this is a good moment to point out that when we are married, you may, if you please, take complete charge of my wardrobe."

"And thus we come to the point," she said with a sigh.

"Yes, we do. Clarissa, I can no longer be put off. I cannot stomach this life any longer. I have a big empty house which depresses my spirit every time I set foot in it, because you are not there to greet me. I have a steady stream of invitations which I refuse, because I do not like to go alone. I have a French cook who overfeeds me, because I have no one to supervise and curtail his excesses. I have an overweening valet who dresses me like a counter-coxcomb, because I have no wife to select my wardrobe. I have—"

"Enough, enough!" Clarissa cut in with a voice tinged half with amusement and half with annoyance. "I shall provide you with a housekeeper of taste and character who will be happy to handle most of your problems in return for an extortionate wage, which I know you can well afford, and which shall be much less costly than providing yourself with a wife."

"That is unworthy of you, Clarissa. I don't think our problem can be solved with levity."

"Yes, you're right," she said, chastised. "I'm sorry, my dear."

"Well, then, what have you to say to me?"

"What can I say, Gervaise? I value your friendship more than I can say."

"Friendship, *faugh!*"

"Don't sneer at it so unkindly. I will admit to you that your friendship has sustained me through many years that might otherwise have been unbearably lonely."

"Do you admit that? Then you must know that I feel it,

too." Heedless of his buttons, he sat down beside her and grasped her hands. "But Clarissa, my dear, I've not made a secret of the fact that your friendship has never been enough for me. When you were married to Steele, I had no choice but to keep you my friend. But it was always your love I wanted. After his death, I hoped . . . But you know all this. Why should you keep me waiting now? We have not so many years ahead—"

She waved him to silence and turned her head away. "Please, no more. I shall weep and disgrace myself. We mustn't talk like this. You know my situation. I cannot marry and ignore my obligations."

Gervaise sighed and rose awkwardly from his seat. "I can no longer accept that excuse," he said, leaning against the mantlepiece and staring down into the fire. "It had some validity when Jamie was a child. A woman was badly needed here then, and you were the only one who could fill the void. I understood and accepted it. But Jamie is twenty-two! He'll be married himself before long. There's no reason any longer for you to postpone your own life—your own happiness. Unless—"

"Unless?"

He turned to face her. "Unless you don't believe that marriage to me will make you happy," he said, looking at her levelly.

She dropped her eyes. "I think . . . I *do* believe that I would be happy with you, Gervaise. . . ."

He was beside her in an instant, kissing her hand tenderly. "Oh, my dear!" he said, moved.

"But, dearest, I cannot marry you. Not because of Jamie, but Philip. He is accustomed to my presence. He has never coped with the running of a household, as you have. He would be in a terrible muddle. I could not desert him, I could not!"

Gervaise raised his head, and eyed her with anger. "Nonsense! You don't do the man justice. He is quite capable of looking after himself. He would be the first to tell you not to make such a sacrifice of yourself."

"Yes, so we must never tell him. Never. I insist upon that, Gervaise."

He stood up and drew himself up to his full height. "There is no need to tell me that, Clarissa. You know better than to think I would run to him for aid behind your back!"

"I know. I'm sorry to have offended you, my dear."

"Offended me! What a peagoose you are. You have severed our relationship without a qualm, and you worry about trifles."

"I have many a qualm, I assure you. Must our relationship be severed?"

"Yes, I've determined on it," he said stubbornly.

"But why, my dear? Why can't we go on as before?"

"No, I can no longer abide it. I must have a wife. I'm too dashed lonely without one. If it can't be you, then I must cast about for someone else." He gave her a quick, shrewd look from the corners of his eyes. "I may be a fat old clown, but I'm still able to attract a few good-natured females. One of them will agree to share my life and wealth."

Clarissa snorted. "Don't be so damned humble with *me*, sir. I'm well aware of the lures that Gussie Monks has been casting in your direction these ten years, and she with a fortune that quite dwarfs yours. She's good-natured enough for anyone, if one doesn't mind the addled brain that goes with it. And you needn't think," she added, getting up and walking quickly to the door, "that you can weaken my resistance by making me jealous, because it won't wash!" And she slammed the door behind her.

"Is that so?" he shouted at the closed door. "Well, we'll see how you feel when you're a guest at my wedding!"

The door opened, and Clarissa stood on the threshold, looking contrite. "Did you say something?" she asked innocently. She stepped inside and carefully closed the door behind her.

"Never mind. What did you come back for?"

"To ask if you intend to remain or to leave in a huff."

"Under the circumstances, I certainly can't remain, can I?"

"You certainly can and you certainly should. I'm counting on your support through the Christmas festivities, Boxing Day and the rest. You would be a malignant churl if you deserted me now."

"A malignant churl?" he repeated, a smile forcing its way to the corners of his mouth. "I scarcely find that an accurate or fair description of my character."

Clarissa's mouth also showed signs of a smile. "I suppose not. But if you agree to remain, I promise to give some more thought to our . . . difficulty."

"More thought? I was under the impression that you'd been doing that these past ten years!"

"So I have," she answered pertly. "I'm a very slow thinker."

"Oh, go along, you nodcock, and leave me to my misery."

"But you will remain, won't you?"

"Yes, fool that I am. That gives you ten days to think. Ten days. Not a moment longer."

"Good," she said. She blew him a kiss and left the room. He looked after her with an expression of amusement mixed with disgust. She had deftly managed to keep him dangling by offering him just enough encouragement to keep his hopes alive. Well, he thought as he left the room, she did say she loved me, didn't she? If memory served, she had *almost* said it. Absorbed in interpreting her remembered words, he didn't notice Reggie coming down the hall until they almost collided.

"Sorry," said Gervaise. "Wasn't looking where I was going."

"No harm done," Reggie assured him. "If you're on your way to breakfatht, I'll join you. There wath no one in the breakfatht room a moment ago, and I hate to eat alone."

"Don't blame you a bit, my boy," said Gervaise feelingly. "Don't blame you a bit. I hate to eat alone myself. I was going to change my clothes, but I'll keep you company at breakfast first."

"Much obliged," Reggie said. "But I would change after breakfatht, if I wath you. Thothe pantaloonth are not at all the thing. However did you perthuade yourthelf to wear them?"

· Twelve ·

THE SNOW STARTED again before noon and fell heavily and steadily for the next three hours, covering the landscape with a thick blanket of fluffy whiteness. The sight pleased everyone, with the possible exception of the twins, who were unconditionally refused permission to go out and play in the drifts. Freddie, whose earache had disappeared, leaving him with only a mild case of the sniffles, was still considered "under the weather" and had to stay indoors. Teddy, though exhibiting no signs of sickness, was similarly imprisoned until, his mother said, she could be sure that he had not caught the illness from his brother.

But Clarissa could not help noting that the rest of the household was surprisingly and delightfully cheerful. Even Sally, who yesterday had shown unmistakable signs of boredom, was vivacious and utterly charming. She had broken in on Philip in his study and had managed to coax him out to join the party for luncheon. It had been a very merry meal, with Jamie making jokes, Marianne in such good spirits as to actually have uttered several full sentences to the group at large, and Sally teasing and flirting shamelessly.

Even the house had an air of cheerfulness. Holly wreaths had already been placed on all the mantlepieces, and delicious smells were emanating from the nether regions, where all sorts of delicacies were being prepared for a splendid Christmas dinner. Clarissa herself felt more cheerful, now that she and Gervaise had had it out. Nothing was solved, and the problem still loomed before her, but she had managed him so far and, with a little luck, she felt confident she could do so again.

After luncheon, Philip and Edward had ridden out on horseback through the snow to find a tree from which they would cut a huge Yule log for this year's festivities. They would choose a tree of appropriate height and width, cut it down, trim it, tie a rope around it, and bring it back to the house by dragging it along the ground between them. It would be kindled on Christmas Eve by first lighting a piece of last year's log, which had been saved for this purpose. It was a ritual the whole family enjoyed. Clarissa was afraid that Jamie had felt a bit of resentment when he was asked to surrender to Edward his place in the search for the tree. But Jamie didn't seem to mind. Instead, he had offered to teach Marianne how to play billiards, and that pastime seemed now to be occupying them quite happily. Clarissa was therefore free to spend the afternoon in making plans with the housekeeper and cook. Her guests were doing very well without her.

Clarissa was unaware that one guest at least was less than happy. Reggie had put a good face on it, but things were going hard with him. After luncheon Jamie had asked him to help teach Marianne to play billiards. Reggie refused. Jamie couldn't understand it. "Why not?" he demanded. "What else do you have to do?"

"I . . . er . . . have thomething to do in my room," Reggie told him, and turned to go.

But Jamie restrained him. "What on earth have you to do

there?" he asked. "It's too early to pick out your waistcoat for dinner."

"I have other wayth to thpend my time," Reggie declared proudly. "I don't need to uthe all my time to confer with my valet."

Jamie eyed him suspiciously. "Well, then, what will you do?"

"Private buthineth."

"Private business? Do you take me for a flat? What private business?"

"If I tell you, it will not be private."

"Since when do you have private business you can't tell me about? You're doing it much too brown, Reggie. Something's amiss, and I'm going to get to the bottom of it."

Reggie capitulated. Jamie was his best friend, after all. "I doubt you'll believe me, but I'm going to my room to read."

Jamie gaped. "To what?"

"You heard me. To read."

"To read? A book?"

Reggie glared at him. "What elthe would I read? A recipe for mushroom and kidney pie?"

"Cut line, Reggie! Do you expect me to swallow a whisker like that? I've never seen you read a book in all my life!"

"I'm reading one now."

"Then tell me the name of it!" Jamie challenged.

"*The Life of Jonathan Wild* or thome thuch title. Very interethting, really. About a magithtrate who ith thtcccpcd in corruption. . . ."

"Spare me, please. I've heard enough for one day. Reading a book!" Jamie shook his head, unbelieving. "You must be *sick*!"

"Take a damper, Jamie," Reggie said threateningly. "Remember that I can flatten you when I've a mind to. And you are not to tell anybody about thith. If you breathe a word, you'll have to anthwer to me, even if you *are* my betht friend."

"Do you think I have windmills in my head? No one would believe me anyway."

"Good. Then we have nothing to worry about." And he turned and walked off down the hall.

Jamie went to the billiard room much shaken. That Reggie should have turned bookish was an occurrence a man could not take lightly. He would have to look into this problem, and soon.

Evalyn had spent the early part of the afternoon telling the twins a story while spooning hot soup down Freddie's throat. Now, with everybody in the household busy at various amusements and occupations, she found a few hours before her to spend as she wished. She put a last coat of lacquer on her *papier-mâché* box, and as she looked up from that completed task, the sight of the fresh snow on the gardens below made her yearn for the outdoors. She donned her thickest boots and her one sturdy cloak, and made for the front door. As she crossed the wide front hallway, Philip and Edward clumped in, laughing and shaking the snow from their boots and hats.

"Good afternoon, Miss Pennington," Edward greeted her. "Come out and see the enormous log we've prepared for the Christmas fire."

Before Evalyn could reply, the library doors opened and Gervaise emerged, yawning. Philip pointed to him and laughed. "Look at what you've done, Edward. For shame! Your crowing has awakened our lazy friend from his afternoon nap."

"Not at all," Gervaise declared, unperturbed. "I had already awakened when you two burst in the door."

"A likely tale. Many's the afternoon I've had to rouse you and send you on your way with barely enough time to dress for dinner," Philip teased.

"Balderdash. Don't listen to him, Miss Pennington. He has a hidden, nasty streak, which makes him enjoy cutting up the reputations of even his oldest and dearest friends."

Evalyn laughed, but couldn't resist coming to Philip's defense. "It must be a well-hidden streak," she said, "for I've never seen the least sign of it."

"Oh, well said," purred a female voice behind her, and all eyes turned to find Sally poised gracefully on the stairway, a vision in wine-colored kerseymere. Clarissa stood just behind her, smiling benignly at everyone.

"Ah, there you are, Edward," Clarissa said. "I hoped you had returned. Your wife has been asking for you. She has developed a crick in the back of her neck and claims that only you know the trick of setting it right."

Edward sighed a patient, long-suffering sigh. "Yes, I do. After all these years of matrimony, there's scarcely a problem which I've not developed the trick of solving." He handed his coat to a waiting footman and, making a little bow, hurried off up the stairs.

"Philip, my dear," Sally said invitingly, "I've come for *you*. We are organizing a game of billiards, and I need a partner."

"Thank you, but I should not be an asset to you. It's been years since I handled a billiard cue."

"Never mind that. I am expert enough for both of us," she countered smoothly.

"You must excuse me, I'm afraid," Philip said, unbudgeable. "I have some rather pressing matters which need attending to."

The color rose in Sally's cheeks and her eyes glinted; nevertheless, she managed to smile. "Very well, then, I'll have to persuade Gervaise . . ."

"A much better choice than Philip, if I do say so myself," Gervaise said with aplomb. "I'm a far better billiard player than anyone you're likely to find within a hundred miles."

"Spoken with truth and appropriate modesty," Philip said smiling.

Gervaise climbed the stairs, took Sally's arm, and tucked it under his own. "Come, my dear, let's go and defeat the enemy." And he led her up the stairs, giving Clarissa a saucy glance as he passed her by. Clarissa favored Philip and Evalyn with an amused shrug, then followed the billiard players up the stairs.

Evalyn tied the strings of her cloak, lifted her hood, and started toward the door. Philip, shrugging out of his coat, looked at her in surprise. "Do you mean to go out, Miss Pennington?"

"Why, yes."

"But not alone, surely?"

Evalyn smiled. "I'm not a schoolroom miss, Lord Gyllford. Surely I'm old enough to take a little walk unattended."

"I see you have relapsed into formality and are calling me Lord Gyllford again."

"But did you not, a moment ago, call me Miss Pennington?"

"Did I? I apologize, but I will not be put from the point. Why is Jamie not keeping you company?"

"Jamie?" she asked in surprise. "Why on earth should he?"

"Surely he cannot like to see you spending so much time alone. If you will postpone your walk for a minute or two,

I'll find him. I'm sure he'll be delighted to keep you company on your outing."

"I won't hear of such a thing," Evalyn said, shocked. "Disturb Jamie merely to accompany me on a little walk? I'll not go at all, if you think my walking alone is improper, but I wouldn't for the world have Jamie's billiard game disturbed."

"You young people are indeed a puzzle to me," Philip said, shaking his head in perplexity. "But of course, there is nothing improper in your taking a little walk by yourself, if you're sure you want to."

"Yes, I do. I love fresh-fallen snow. I've been wanting to get out in it all afternoon."

"Then of course I won't prevent you," Philip said. Evalyn made a quick curtsey and turned to the door. "Wait, Miss Pennington," he called after her. "I wonder . . . would you object to *my* company?"

"Of course I wouldn't, if I had not just heard you say that you have pressing business to attend to."

Philip grinned guiltily. "You listen to me too carefully, my dear. I admit to you, on the expectation that you'll not give me away, that I have pressing business only when asked to play billiards."

Evalyn smiled, but shook her head. "You are being kind, I think. I cannot feel easy thinking that my silly walk is taking you away from more urgent matters. Please, sir, if my walking out alone troubles you, I shall gladly stay indoors and think no more about it. I'd be very grateful if you can do the same." And she quickly untied the ribbons of her cloak.

Philip went to her, took her hands from her cloak, and tied its ribbons again. "We are both being overzealous and foolish, I think. You shall certainly have your walk, and alone if you wish it so. I only ask you to believe that I would truly enjoy joining you, if you will have me. You're not the only lover of new-fallen snow, you know."

He was looking down at her earnestly, with the glow of warmth in the back of his eyes that had, at least twice before, caused her heart to lurch and her spine to turn to jelly. She said nothing, her throat suddenly too constricted to permit her to speak. "Well, Evalyn," he asked with his endearing grin, "may I come?"

She nodded shyly, and he turned and signalled to the footman who had retired discreetly to the stairway while they spoke. Before she'd caught her breath, he had put on his many-caped greatcoat and, leaving it unbuttoned, with his muffler hanging untied from under its collar, he had taken her hand and led her out the door. The air was crisp, and a light wind blew the powdery snow into their faces. They came down the steps and walked along the curved avenue. Philip glanced down at her. "Are you sure that light cloak is enough?" he asked.

Evalyn cocked her head and looked at him askance. "I begin to think, Lord Gyllford, that you would make a better governess than I. Your overwhelming solicitude quite befits the profession."

Philip threw back his head with a shout of laughter. "I do sound like a clucking old hen, don't I? Very well, Miss Acid-Tongue, not another solicitous word will you hear from me."

"Good, my lord. It will be an immeasurable aid to our future conversation."

"There it is—'my lord' again. Why do you suppose, Miss Penn—Evalyn, that we find it so difficult to call each other by our Christian names?"

"I'm not sure," Evalyn answered slowly, giving the question more serious attention than Philip had intended, "but I think it may be that our inequality of rank makes it difficult for us to be comfortable together as friends."

His smile faded, and he turned to her almost angrily. "What nonsense! Do you think I see a *governess* before me every time I look at you? What a pompous fool you must think me!"

"Not at all," Evalyn answered in the calm, reasonable voice he so much admired. "But you can scarcely expect us to forget completely the very great gulf that our so-different stations in life have built between us."

"I would forget your so-called 'station' completely, if you didn't keep reminding me," he stated flatly. "You must try to be a little less belligerently *poor*, my girl, and try to accept the truth of what you really are."

"What am I but a governess, and an unemployed one at that?"

He grasped her by the shoulders angrily. "I could shake you! Can you truly believe that the word 'governess' has anything to do with the you that I—that anybody with eyes—must see when we look at you?"

Evalyn stared up at him. "I have no idea wh-what you see when you look at me," she said breathlessly.

His anger was instantly dissipated by the ingenuous look in her eyes. "A lovely girl," he said quietly, "a warm, witty, serene, kind, lovely girl. Will you remember that?"

She nodded wordlessly, and he dropped his hands from her shoulders. They walked on through the deepening shadows. "I suppose it is too much to hope that you can see anything but 'his lordship' when you look at me," he remarked somewhat ruefully.

"You must know," she answered in her forthrightly way, "that I see a great deal more than that."

He grinned down at her. "I see a great deal more than that, *Philip*."

She smiled back. "I see a great deal more than that, Philip," she repeated obediently.

"Where did you get this overly strong sense of class differences, I wonder? Was it your family?"

She told him, hesitantly at first, but more comfortably after a while, about her father and their life together. "It was not he who ingrained my sense of my 'place' into me," she said at last. "It was, I suppose, a result of holding the post of governess in three rather noble households."

Philip frowned. "Treated you shabbily, did they? I could wring their necks."

"Not at all. They were very kind, really. It's just . . . how can I explain? You like to deny its existence, but there is an invisible sort of barrier set up between the classes. When one inadvertently moves to pass through it, the disapproval is unmistakable. One learns to recognize the lines of demarcation rather quickly."

"Well, my dear, you shall never feel that disapproval again," he said fervently, "and that I promise you."

"In your own home, perhaps," she corrected gently.

"Anywhere! Ev—" he began, but a gust of wind shook the trees above them, and a small avalanche of snow fell on top of them. Philip's tall hat was knocked to the ground. Laughing, he shook the snow out of his hair and brushed it from his shoulders. Then he turned to Evalyn and brushed it from her hood and cape. "There, that's better. Are you all right?"

"Yes, of course."

"I know I promised not to be old-henish, but I can't help noticing how very thin your cloak is. You must be frozen." He pulled the muffler from his neck and wound it twice around her throat. The daylight was fading rapidly, but in the dim glow he could see her face quite clearly. His hands, still holding the ends of the muffler, were stayed, his breath arrested. Her eyes were smiling up at him gratefully. A few snowflakes, which had clung to her cheeks and caught in her lashes, gave her face an enticing sparkle. For a moment neither of them moved. Then, as if impelled by some irresistible instinct long dormant in him, he pulled her to him. She lay against him unmoving, her face tilted up. His heart was pounding so loudly that he knew she must hear.

Evalyn heard. She couldn't think—she couldn't analyze the meaning of any of this. He was holding her in his arms, his heart pounding against her. That was enough for her now. She would think later. Now she could only feel an enveloping sense of joy unfolding like a flower inside her. She recognized on his face, so close above her own, the look she had seen before, lurking deep behind his eyes. Now it seemed to be shining from his whole being. She waited, breathless, for the kiss she knew was coming. But suddenly, shockingly, before her startled gaze, the warmth in his face faded, instantaneously replaced by an expression she could only describe as horror. His body stiffened, and he abruptly thrust her from him. "Oh, my God!" he groaned. "What am I doing?"

She did not ask for an explanation—she couldn't have uttered a word. And he gave none. Instead, he dropped his eyes from her face and said in a constricted voice, "It grows dark. We'd better go back."

Evalyn bent down and picked up his hat. She held it out to him, her eyes searching his face. He looked at her briefly, a look of chagrin and shame, took the hat from her and turned away. They walked back to the house in silence.

A waiting footman sprang to attention when they entered the dimly lit hallway. Philip waved him away and turned to Evalyn. "I must apologize for my unaccountable behavior," he said in a distant voice. "I've never before heard of a case of midsummer madness striking anyone in the dead of winter, but it is the only explanation I can offer—"

"Please, Philip, don't joke. I don't underst—" Evalyn began.

He went on as if she hadn't spoken. "I can only thank you for permitting me to accompany you," he said, "and to assure you, Miss Pennington, that I shall not so offend you again."

She gasped. *"Miss Penning—?"*

But he had turned away and was striding across the hallway. He took the stairs two at a time and was gone, leaving Evalyn staring after him, the snowflakes melting on her cloak and dripping down to form little puddles on the floor around her.

· *Thirteen* ·

WELLSTOCK SAID LATER to his cronies below stairs that he'd been sure that his master had been digging deep in the bottle when he looked into the bedroom that evening. There Lord Gyllford sat, one boot on, the other in his hand, staring ahead of him at nothing. Wellstock had stood in the doorway for at least five minutes, waiting to be recognized, and his lordship did not move the whole time. Finally, Wellstock had coughed discreetly, walked in, and pulled off the other boot. Still his lordship did not seem to notice him at all!

"Are you all right, my lord?" Wellstock had asked in deep concern. He had never known his master to make indentures. Not at all a drinking man.

Lord Gyllford had slowly focused his eyes on Wellstock's face. "Oh, it's you, Wellstock," he'd said in a dead—but not a drunken—voice. "Go away, man. I'll not be needing you."

"But you're not dressed, my lord, and dinner is scarcely a half-hour off," Wellstock had remonstrated.

"Look in on Jamie, will you? I can dress myself tonight," Lord Gyllford had said shortly.

Wellstock had taken himself off, but he'd looked back before he left, and there was his lordship in his stockinged feet, sitting exactly as he had been when the valet arrived.

Philip knew very well that he had to dress for dinner. He just couldn't seem to rouse himself. A deep depression had taken hold of him and seemed to weigh him down like lead. The prospect of facing everyone at dinner time and making cheerful conversation only added to his misery. He felt an urge to hide away somewhere, in a corner of the cellar or the attic, as he had done when he was a little boy and had been severely reprimanded by his usually adoring and adored mother. What humiliating feelings these were for a man with a son of his own, a son whom—heaven help him!—he'd been on the verge of betraying. How could he so have forgotten himself?

His only excuse—though he knew his behavior had been inexcusable—was a strong sense (a feeling he'd not before put into words) that Jamie and Evalyn did not suit. She seemed older than Jamie, more mature, more—how could he describe it?—more at peace with herself. Jamie seemed still to be a boy, still playing games with life and flirting with adulthood. But Philip realized that he might well be rationalizing. His analysis of the situation could no longer be trusted. His objectivity had been hopelessly impaired ever since he'd laid eyes on the girl his son had chosen to marry. There was only one realization he could accept as truth: that he loved her. He could no longer fool himself about that. For almost twenty years he'd guarded himself against this emotion, only to tumble into it with the one person he should most have avoided. What evil fate had decreed that his son should attach himself to the one girl whose nature, face and voice seemed especially designed to penetrate the strong defenses behind which he had walled himself for so long?

But was he mistaken about Evalyn's nature? This question was more painful to face than the awareness of his own weakness. Her true character could be other than what it appeared. He accepted fully the entire blame for what had happened this afternoon in the snow, but Evalyn's behavior, too, had not been above reproach. He had lived too many years and was too experienced to have misinterpreted what he'd read in her face as he held her in his arms. She had accepted his embrace with eagerness, even joy. Could she have forgotten Jamie as completely as he had? Yet he alone had shown signs of guilt. And afterwards, how could she have stared at him with those eyes so full of painful and complete innocence?

If he didn't know Evalyn—if this had happened to a pair of strangers and the story had come to him—he would have been able to explain the situation well enough. He would have said the girl was an adventuress, trying to see if she could permanently attach the richer father before letting go of the bird-in-hand son. But he couldn't, knowing Evalyn, believe it of her for a moment. Perhaps he was completely besotted, but he would swear that there was not a trace of deceit or avarice in her.

Yet he could think of no other explanation for her behavior. The expression in her eyes when she looked at him had been no more daughterly than his had been fatherly. *Could* she be an adventuress, making a game of him and Jamie both? An adventuress could be successful only if she didn't behave or look like one. Was her straightforward manner, her completely convincing air of innocence, the polished performance of an artful dissembler? The mere suspicion made him feel sick. He could not—would not—believe it of her.

These nagging questions could not now be answered. But his overriding sense of guilt could be dealt with. He could not again allow himself to be alone in her company, not until she had married Jamie and he had learned to contain his feelings for her within strict bounds. In time he would

rebuild the protective walls behind which he had successfully barricaded himself in the past. In the meantime, he
must find some outward means by which to separate himself
from her. Sally! How fortunate that she was present for the
holidays. Sally had made it quite clear that she would enjoy
his attentions. Well, she would have them. He knew it ill
became him to use her in this way, but he trusted himself to
keep his attentions well within the bounds of gay companionship. Sally was quite up to the mark and would recognize
easily the difference between a sincere courtship and a
harmless flirtation.

Philip hurried down and entered the drawing room,
meeting Clarissa's frown with an apologetic smile for his
extraordinary lateness. He scanned the room quickly, helpless to keep himself from searching out Evalyn's face
among the others looking up at him. He did not immediately
see her, and he wondered if she had been too upset by his
behavior to make an appearance this evening. But she was
there, sitting a little apart from the others, and looking pale
and strained. He ached to go and comfort her, but he forced
himself to look away. It was Jamie's place—not his—to
soothe the worried lines from her forehead, to coax the
color back into her cheeks. Philip could only hope fervently
that Jamie was aware of what his duty was.

He turned and greeted his guests, apologizing profusely
for keeping them waiting. The butler, who had had to tell
the cook twice to return the succulent chops to the fire,
announced dinner in a tone of voice that scarcely revealed
his relief. Philip went directly to Sally and bowed. "You
are a vision tonight, my dear," he said, "all draped in
velvet. What do you call that splendid color you're wearing?"

Sally looked up at him with a cautious glint. "I believe
my *modiste* calls it Venetian red."

"Yes, it does put one in mind of an Italian painting. But perhaps you should have waited until tomorrow evening to wear it. What a perfect color for Christmas eve."

"If it pleases you, your lordship," Sally said with coy smoothness, "it is appropriate at any time."

"It does indeed please me. So much so that I have an unquenchable desire to escort such Venetian loveliness in to dinner. May I have your arm?"

The cautious look was still in her eye as she glanced up at him, but he favored her with the most disarming smile he could muster. "Thank you, my lord," she said, pleased with herself, and gave him her arm. As she swept past Evalyn, she did not neglect to cast the governess a look of triumph.

Sally had had a busy afternoon. From the window of the billiard room, she had seen Philip and Evalyn walk down the avenue together. Even from that distance, Sally could discern their complete absorption in one another. She saw Philip stop and turn to Evalyn, speaking to her with an intensity that Sally could almost feel. She had to recognize at last that the attraction between Philip and the governess, however inexplicable, was quite real. The time had come for her to put her plan into action.

As soon as she could, she had escaped from the billiard room and hurried to her bedroom. She closed the door behind her and locked it against any chance intruder. A commotion behind her, coming from her dressing room, made her jump. "Who's there?" she called sharply.

"Only me, Ma'm'selle," came Annette's voice, and the maid came hurriedly from the dressing room, smoothing back her hair and adjusting her cap with nervous fingers. It occurred to Sally that Annette had been up to some mischief.

"What are you doing here?" Sally demanded.

"I make ready the things for you to wear tonight," Annette said with a shrug. "Are you not early, Ma'm'selle?"

"I'm a bit tired. You may go for an hour or so, Annette. I want to rest."

Annette cast a hurried glance over her shoulder into the dressing room. "But, Ma'm'selle," she objected, "I must brush the velvet most careful, to make the nap to shine. I will close the door to the dressing room. Annette will be quiet like a mouse. You will not be disturb', I promise."

Sally clenched her teeth. "Must you argue about everything I say to you? I want to be alone. Get out. I don't want to see your face for an hour."

Annette bit her lip, bobbed a quick curtsey and went to the door. She cast another glance back at the dressing room, unlocked the door and went out. Sally locked it again and went to the dressing room. She took her jewel-case key from beneath the powder puff, unlocked the case and removed her diamond drop earrings. With a satisfied smile, she held them up so that the light from the window shone through them. They were large, many-faceted stones, the most expensive of all the valuables in her possession. She dropped the jewel-case key on the dressing table and crossed to the dressing room door. There she paused. It wouldn't do, she decided, to leave the key lying on the dressing table. Annette would notice the theft too soon. She went back, locked the case and replaced the key in its hiding place. Then she went swiftly from the dressing room.

She dropped the gems into the bosom of her dress, unlocked the door and looked out into the hallway. It was empty. She closed her door quietly behind her and walked silently down the hall to Evalyn's room. She scratched at the door. There was no answer. Stealthily she turned the knob. The door was open. She entered, closed the door behind her, and looked about her in surprise. The room was unmistakably larger than hers! The governess had been given a grander room than her own! Her green eyes flashed angrily. To think that she had been made to take second place to a mouse of a female without station, breeding, or beauty! But Evalyn's favored position in this house would be short-lived. Sally's lips curled as she reached into her gown and took out the diamonds.

Her eyes roamed the room for a suitable place to hide them. The hiding place must be carefully chosen. Evalyn must not discover the jewels. They must be discovered— and only after careful search—by a magistrate or by Philip himself. Hiding them among Evalyn's articles of clothing would not serve—Evalyn or her obnoxious little abigail would be sure to come upon them. Under the mattress was too obvious and unimaginative. Dropping them in a jar of face powder or a pot of rouge might do, but Evalyn's dressing table held no such objects.

Sally's eye fell on Evalyn's work table near the window. On it sat a little *papier-mâché* box which Evalyn had obviously just made. It had been charmingly lacquered and set out to dry. Sally touched it gingerly. Fortunately, it had dried completely. She opened the lid. A satin lining, stuffed with cotton wadding, had been glued inside. Sally smiled. She had found the place. She pulled a corner of the lining loose and slipped the diamonds in behind the padding. Then, confident that it would come loose again at the slightest touch, she pressed the corner back into place. She was satisfied that a careful searcher would feel the sharp outlines of the diamonds through the padding. She replaced the lid, and swiftly left the room.

Now, sitting at the dining table, basking in the glow of Philip's rather marked attentions, she wondered if perhaps she'd been hasty. Perhaps the whole thing had not been necessary—perhaps she had overestimated the extent of Philip's interest in the governess. Her green eyes flicked to Evalyn's face. The girl was pale and looked to be under a strain. Philip, too, had a look of strain, and she noticed that he rubbed the bridge of his nose from time to time, as if he had a headache. Something had passed between them, Sally was certain of that. No, she had not made a mistake; she would let the diamonds play their part.

For Evalyn, the dinner was a continuation of the nightmare that had begun when Philip left her, cold and trembling, in the empty hallway. She had gone to her room and knelt before the fire when Nancy had found her—she didn't know how much later—still wearing her wet cloak. Nancy had immediately embarked on a tirade of scolding until she glimpsed Evalyn's face.

"Miss Evalyn," she gasped, "what's 'appened to ye?"

Evalyn looked at the girl's honest face, and its expression of warm and sincere concern was too much for her to bear. Unaccustomed tears began to roll down her cheeks.

Nancy was aghast. "Oh, my lady," she whispered, awed, "I ain't never seen you cry!" The girl lifted Evalyn to her feet and led her to the bed. Evalyn put her face into the pillow and sobbed until her body felt wracked and empty. It was as if all the tears she hadn't shed since her childhood had been stored up inside her and had finally broken loose. When the flood subsided, and she looked up, she found Nancy still regarding her, wringing her hands in helpless and agonized concern. Evalyn tried to smile and reassure the girl. "I don't know what's come over me," she said in a tremulous, unrecognizable voice. "It's really nothing, Nancy. I'm just a bit blue-devilled, that's all."

Nancy didn't believe a word of it. "Blue-devilled!" she exclaimed. "Do ye take me for a clodpole? It's plain as pikestaff someone's 'urt ye bad. It ain't me place to know yer business, Miss Evalyn, and it's just as well ye don't tell me, because if I was to learn who upset ye like this, I'd wring 'er neck for sure!"

Evalyn gave a hiccup of a laugh and tried to pull herself together. "I must make myself presentable and go down to dinner," she said helplessly. Nancy rose to the task, bathing her mistress's swollen eyes and reddened nose until she looked more like herself, and helping her into her clothes, as if Evalyn were a baby. All the while, Nancy kept up a stream of talk about nothing at all, hoping to divert Evalyn from brooding about whatever had so disturbed her. But Evalyn could not be diverted. Philip's face, with its shocking expression of horror and self-disgust, could not be blotted from her mind.

Evalyn had no one to blame but herself. She had been enjoying her few days of luxury and attention and had not wanted to think about the consequences or the future. She had responded with instinctive naturalness to the warmth in Philip's eyes and to the obvious pleasure he had found in her company. She'd been aware that she was drawn to him as she had never been to a man before, but she had not let herself analyze or identify her feelings. Then he'd taken her in his arms, and the truth became blindingly clear. She had fallen heedlessly and headlong in love with a man who was completely beyond her sphere.

She was not a fool. She knew that he had been attracted to her almost as strongly as she to him. Perhaps he had drifted into it as thoughtlessly as she had done, only to realize suddenly that the attraction led to a dead end. "What am I doing?" he'd said in that horrified voice. There, on the verge of kissing her, he had realized how impossible a situation he was in. For all his kindness to her, for all his courageous words about his disregard for her "station" in life, a man in his position could not marry an impoverished governess with no family. He must have realized, too, from what she'd told him about her upbringing, that she was too properly reared to accept a *carte blanche*. He'd awakened himself with that dreadful look of horror and had uttered, "What am I doing?" in the nick of time.

She wasn't angry. She shouldn't even feel hurt. She understood perfectly. All she had to do now was to pick up the pieces of her heart and paste herself back together again. All it took was a little courage and the ability to withstand some pain. She was her father's daughter; those were the things she had learned early.

But here at dinner she began to realize how difficult the job of putting herself together would be. Every time Philip laughed into Sally's face, which he was doing with repulsive frequency, she felt he was dealing her a dagger blow. Every time he turned his eyes away from her, a pain cut through her chest. Every time she had to smile and make rational remarks to one or another of the people around her, it required an effort of will she was not sure she was strong enough to make. She could only hope that her courage would hold until enough time had passed to allow her to say her goodnights and make her escape.

After dinner, Sally was asked to entertain, and she played and sang with great enthusiasm for almost an hour. "We must have some carols tomorrow evening," Clarissa requested when Sally at last rose from the pianoforte. "Carols are what I most enjoy about the Christmas festivities."

"Really?" Jamie asked in surprise. "I could name a dozen things I enjoy as much, or more."

"Pooh," challenged his loving aunt, "name one thing that captures the spirit of Christmas festivities half as well."

"You are altering the point, aunt. You were speaking at first of enjoyment. If it is *spirit* we are speaking of, then the answer must be the Christmas Mass. But if it is the festivities we are discussing, then my enjoyment lies in many other things besides the singing of carols."

"Well, what then?" his aunt persisted. Everyone looked at Jamie with amused interest.

"Do you want the shocking truth?" he asked his aunt with a twinkle.

"The truth, of course."

"Then I would choose, without hesitation, the Christmas mistletoe!" His answer was greeted with a loud laugh, and he glanced at Marianne and winked broadly at her. "All the ladies be warned," he said. "I shall be lurking behind every doorway as soon as my aunt has hung the kissing boughs."

"A good choice," chortled Gervaise, "but, as much as I enjoy kissing the ladies, there is something I would choose even ahead of mistletoe."

"It's not hard to guess what that is," Clarissa teased. "The Christmas goose!"

"I was going to say plum pudding, but in truth it is hard to choose between them," Gervaise said laughing.

"What?" asked Martha. "And you call yourself English? How can you have overlooked our good roast beef?"

"Shall we combine all of them and agree that it's the entire Christmas dinner that is the crowning glory of the festivities?" suggested Edward, ever the compromiser.

"I'll agree to that," Gervaise said.

"You look dissatisfied, Reggie," Clarissa said. "I hope that you will support me in my feeling that there are things more important than food and kissing."

Reggie roused himself from the gloom in which Jamie's wink at Marianne had sunk him, and he smiled politely at his hostess. "I don't know if you will think thith ith thupport, but nobody hath mentioned what I find to be motht enjoyable: the wathail bowl."

"Hear, hear!" Edward cheered. "The wassail bowl by all means! What would Christmas be without it?"

Sally leaned forward. "Let's not forget the dancing. When all the neighbors gather and the musicians break into a lively tune, I do love to dance with a handsome partner. Don't you agree, Philip?"

"I would not forego any of it," Philip answered, "the mince pie and the plum pudding, the turkey and the goose, the wassail and the home-brew, the songs and the dancing, they all have my support. But if I had to choose only one thing—the one indispensable festivity of the day—I think I would choose the Yule log. I love to see the great blazing fire. Have you noticed how everybody is, sooner or later, attracted to it? It becomes the heart, the visible center of the room, and all the faces gathered in a semicircle around it seem to shine in the dancing glow of the flames."

"Oh, Philip, how right you are!" sighed Martha, much moved.

"Yes, I'll have to agree," Gervaise said reflectively. "How perfect it is on Christmas Day to sit round the fire, listening to the hiss of the roasting pears, smelling the chestnuts, while the wind howls away outside the windows. What are those lines of Milton—something about a storm outside—?"

"I know the ones you mean," said Philip. " 'And out of doors, a something storm o'erwhelms . . .' No, I'm afraid I've forgotten them."

Evalyn's voice came softly from somewhere behind him.

" 'And out of doors, a washing storm o'erwhelms/Nature pitch-dark, and rides the thundering elms.' "

Philip turned to look at her, unable to keep from his eyes the look of appreciative pleasure she'd roused in him. Their eyes met and held, and it was several seconds before either of them could look away.

· Fourteen ·

SNOW FELL AGAIN during the night, and the dawn of the day before Christmas was barely perceptible behind the heavy clouds which gave a sullen look to the sky. A gusty wind had blown up, rattling the windows and blowing the snow into drifts. Clarissa forced herself out of bed before her abigail appeared to waken her. She pattered across the icy floor quickly, knowing that the day held too few hours for the completion of all the tasks she had left herself to do. She had to see to the hanging of the rest of the Christmas greens—the holly wreaths and the kissing boughs which she, Martha, and Evalyn had wrought so painstakingly throughout the week. She had to speak to Hutton about preparing the things needed for the Christmas eve games, like Jamie's favorite, snapdragon. And, most difficult and time-consuming, she had to arrange for the tenants' baskets (after she filled them with sugar cakes, pails of her special Christmas punch, plump Christmas birds, and trinkets for the children) to be labelled, each with a personal note, and loaded into a carriage so that Philip could deliver them that afternoon.

She dressed quickly and left her bedroom, closing the door quietly so as not to disturb the sleeping household. To her surprise, she found that Evalyn, fully dressed, was emerging from her room.

"Evalyn, my dear," she whispered, "why have you risen so early? I doubt that even the servants are up and about."

"I knew this would be a very busy day for you, and I hoped you would permit me to help."

"Of course, my dear. But this is supposed to be a holiday for you. I don't wish you to give up your rest on any account, even mine."

"I am not accustomed to sleeping late," Evalyn assured her. "It was no sacrifice to get up early."

"Then I thank you most sincerely. I'll enjoy both your assistance and your company. But, Evalyn, you do look a little fagged. There are shadows beneath your eyes. You must promise me that you'll lie down for a rest later today."

A few minutes later, wrapped in huge white aprons, they stood ladling the punch into pails, and carefully wrapping the sugar cakes to keep them from crumbling in the baskets. Neither one took notice of the fact that they were strangely silent until they both sighed at once. Clarissa looked up in surprise, caught Evalyn's eye, and laughed. "Dear me," she said, "we neither of us seem to have captured the holiday spirit. Such heartfelt sighs! How do you account for our mutual depression?"

"I certainly can't account for mine," Evalyn said with what she hoped was a reassuring smile. "I'm having the most wonderful holiday of my life. It must be the weather that has lowered my spirits."

"I can't blame the weather for mine," Clarissa admitted. "I rather like the snow at Christmas time."

"Then it must be something more serious that is troubling you," Evalyn suggested, not wanting to pry but offering a sympathetic ear.

"Yes, I find it serious, although you may think it foolish in a woman of my years to be troubled by such a thing."

"I'm sure I couldn't think lightly of anything that troubles you," Evalyn said earnestly.

"But you will think me foolish when you learn that I'm fretting over a proposal of marriage. Imagine! At my age, to carry on in my head like the veriest schoolgirl!"

"A marriage proposal! But Clarissa, how wonderful! Is it . . . I hope you'll not think me forward to ask . . . is it Gervaise?"

Clarissa looked at her in surprise. "However did you guess, Evalyn?"

Evalyn smiled. "It was not at all hard to guess. I've noticed many times that often, even when he is speaking to someone else, his eyes seek you out."

Clarissa blushed with pleasure. "Do they? I was not aware . . ."

"Oh, yes. And when you're not in the room, he seems to be watching for you to come in the door."

"Oh, dear. That *is* touching, when you think how many years we—Evalyn, I almost wish you hadn't told me. How can I face him and tell him I cannot accept him when you have painted this tenderhearted picture of him?"

"But why must you refuse him? It cannot be that you don't care for him."

Clarissa cocked her head and looked at Evalyn with a twinkle. "Why do you say that with such assurance? Have you caught *my* eyes searching *his* out?"

Evalyn laughed. "Perhaps not. But you tease him so affectionately, and . . . I don't know. I felt sure—"

Clarissa sighed. "I don't deny you're right. But I cannot marry him. And I cannot bear to tell him so."

Evalyn's smiled faded. "I'm so sorry, Clarissa," she said softly. "It is dreadful when 'impediments' prevent 'the marriage of true minds.'"

Clarissa's eyes misted over and, to her embarrassment,

two tears rolled down her cheeks. She quickly brushed them aside with the back of her hand and laughed tremulously. "Isn't it amazing how Mr. Shakespeare has something appropriate to say for every occasion?"

"Yes, but even his words don't really help," Evalyn said regretfully. "I wish *someone* could help you, Clarissa."

"Someone could, if only he realized . . ." Clarissa began. "But no. I am not being fair. I cannot expect Philip to marry just to please me."

Evalyn caught her breath. "Philip . . . ? Marry?" she asked.

"Well, yes. You see, he's the impediment, the poor dear. I cannot leave him alone in this great house, especially now with Jamie about to set up his own establishment." And she gave Evalyn an arch smile. "To leave him at this time would be unthinkable," she went on. "Philip would be in a complete domestic muddle within a month if he were left to manage by himself."

"Perhaps you underestimate him," Evalyn ventured.

Clarissa regarded her with some surprise. "That's what Gervaise says, too. But I don't agree. You see, Gervaise has managed his household beautifully all these years and thinks it quite easy. But Philip is the sort of man who is always preoccupied with serious concerns. He wouldn't pay attention to the thousands of domestic details that must be attended to. That's why I cannot marry Gervaise. He doesn't need me as much as Philip does."

"I see. That's why you hope Philip will marry?"

"Yes. I've been pushing him to do it for years and years! Not only for myself and Gervaise, of course—I'm not as selfish as that—but for Philip's own happiness. The lengths I've gone to to put eligible females in his way! The ruses and excuses I've devised to lure him to social events! I've been positively shameless, but to no avail. The man is quite immune."

Evalyn, her eyes fastened on the package she was wrapping, said hesitantly, "Perhaps he will surprise you one day . . . soon . . ."

Clarissa shook her head. "You are thinking of Sally, are you not? No, there's not a chance of that. Philip dislikes her, I think, even though his attitude did seem to be softening last evening. But I myself don't wish them to make a match of it. I don't like her above half. Evalyn, I'm at my wits' end! He'll soon be too old to attract a proper female—"

"Old?" Evalyn said in genuine surprise. "How can you say so?"

Clarissa smiled at her fondly. "There are not many girls your age who would *not* say so, my dear. Forty-four is a far cry from youth."

"Forty-four is a perfect—! I mean, a very good age for a husband," Evalyn said, her eyes lowered and her cheeks revealing a flush. "There must be hundreds of girls even younger than I am who would think themselves lucky to . . . to marry a man like Lord Gyllford."

"You are a darling," Clarissa said warmly, and patted her hand with affection. "Just talking to you has lifted my spirits immeasurably. You can have no idea how happy I am that Jamie has brought you to us!"

Later that morning, Jamie peered into the breakfast room to find only Marianne present. She looked charming in a morning dress with ruffles of lace at the neck. But she sat stirring her tea in a decidedly listless manner. "Good morning," Jamie greeted her cheerfully. "Am I the last to come down?"

"No, not quite," Marianne said in a small voice. "Everyone's been here but . . . your friend."

"Reggie? Is he still abed? That's not like him."

"He has not seemed . . . that is, does it seem to you that he . . . ?"

"That he what, Marianne?"

"That he has been . . . avoiding companionship these last few days?"

"Now you mention it, yes, I have," Jamie answered, his brow wrinkling. "He's been acting dashed queer, as if he's in some sort of hank. Been meaning to look into it. If you'll excuse me, Marianne, I'll do so right now."

Determined to get to the bottom of the mystery of Reggie's strange behavior, Jamie marched firmly up the stairs and into Reggie's bedroom without so much as a knock on the door. Reggie was sitting up among the pillows, his nose deep in a book he'd evidently more than half finished.

"Good God!" Jamie exclaimed. "Not reading again!"

Reggie started. "Well! of all . . . ! What'th the idea of thneaking up on me like thith? You didn't even knock!"

"You can get down off your high ropes, Reggie Windle, and don't try to tip me a rise. I came in without knocking to catch you unaware. Something has pitched you into a bumble bath, and I mean to find out what it is."

"Nothing to find out," Reggie said flatly, sticking his nose back in the book.

"You'll tell me," Jamie threatened, "or you'll feel my fists. Spending your time reading! Why, it ain't even *healthy*! And you've been avoiding me . . . don't deny it. Even Marianne noticed it."

"Oh, she did, did she?" asked the voice behind the book. "Well, it ain't any of her conthern."

"Stop hiding your face behind that book and look at me,"

Jamie demanded. "Something has put you out of frame, and I want to know what it is." His voice lowered, and he asked in a troubled voice, "Have I said or done anything to offend you, Reg? You know I'd rather cut my tongue out than hurt your feelings."

"Don't be a beetle-headed flat," Reggie said, laying the book aside and looking up at Jamie with a troubled frown. "Maybe I'm homethick. I've been thinking that I might go home to Farnham tomorrow . . ."

"Farnham?" Jamie exclaimed impatiently. "Whatever for? There's no one there except the servants!"

"To my thithter, then. She athked me to come for the holidayth."

"Yes, I remember. And you said you'd rather spend a month in prison than a week with your sister. Damn it, man, I'm your best friend! Can't you tell me?"

Reggie twisted the edges of his comforter with nervous fingers. "Hard to talk about it," he said slowly. "Dathed embarrathing."

Jamie perched at the foot of the bed. "Embarrassing or not, you'd better get to it, because I'm not moving until you do."

"Damned babblemonger," Reggie muttered. Then, after a pause, he sighed and plunged in. "It ain't anything you've done. It'th me! I've gone and done the motht addlepated thing. I've been an even greater lobcock than Geoff Carbery."

"Geoff Carbery?" Jamie asked in complete bewilderment. "Whatever can you . . . ? You don't mean you've done something stupid in the petticoat line?"

Reggie nodded glumly.

"I don't believe it! You?" A thought struck him like a lightning bolt. "You don't mean that *you've* accosted Miss Pennington?"

"No, of courthe not!" said Reggie, outraged.

"Well then, who?"

Reggie glanced at his friend with an expression ridden with guilt. "Marianne," he said tragically.

Jamie blinked. "Marianne? That child? You couldn't have behaved improperly to such an innocent! I'll not believe it of you."

"Well, it wouldn't have happened at all, if you hadn't made me remain with her on the road the other day. I mean, what would *you* have done if she'd been crying, and she looked up at you with thothe big eyeth of herth, and thaid that *you* were handthome and kind and . . ."

Jamie, beginning to understand, felt an irresistible urge to laugh. Struggling to keep his expression serious, he asked, "Said you were handsome and kind, did she?"

"Yeth, and . . . and . . . that my lithp was lovable . . ."

"L-lovable? She said your lisp was love—*lovable* . . . ?"

"Yeth, she did! I mean, *any* man would have kithed her . . . !"

It was too much for Jamie. He put his head back and roared with laughter. The more he thought of Reggie's lovable lisp, the more he laughed. Reggie stared at him in mounting vexation. "I don't thee what there ith to laugh about," he said coldly. "She ith *your* young lady, after all."

"Y-you're doing it much t-too brown, Reg," Jamie gasped, wiping his streaming eyes with his sleeve. "I'll believe the h-handsome and k-kind part, but a l-lovable lisp—!" But Reggie's words reached him at last, and his laughter faded away. "W-what did you say?" he asked.

"I thaid there ith nothing to laugh about," Reggie repeated rigidly.

"No, no, the other part. About Marianne being my young lady."

"Well, what about it?"

Jamie stared at Reggie in sudden understanding. "Is that it? Have you been hiding away behind a book because you thought that Marianne and I—?"

Reggie glared at him angrily. "You're not going to pretend that you're not attracted to her, are you? You told me you were, the very firtht night we arrived!"

"Reggie, you gudgeon! You cannot have thought I was serious! I like her, of course, but nothing beyond the ordinary. There aren't any other females here to flirt with, and I wanted to pass the time . . ."

"Do you mean it, Jamie?" Reggie asked urgently. "You really don't care for her?"

"Of course I mean it. How many times do I have to tell you I ain't in the petticoat line? Besides, now that I think about it, it seems plain that she's liked you better from the first. If you ask me, she's been looking blue-devilled ever since you began avoiding us."

A gleam of hope lit Reggie's face. "Do you really think tho?" he asked.

Jamie had to laugh again.

"Now what'th tho funny?" Reggie demanded.

"You," Jamie said between gasps. "The way you said, 'Do you really think so?'—well, you sounded just like Marianne!" And Jamie roared again. Reggie blinked, tried to look severe, and then slowly collapsed into helpless laughter.

"Of course," Jamie added, when he could manage to speak, "she doesn't have your l-lovable lisp!"

Reggie's response was a well-aimed barrage of pillows flung at Jamie's head.

The snow had stopped falling and the sky had lightened by the afternoon, and over luncheon several eager voices joined to beg Philip to permit them to accompany him on his rounds of the tenants. Sally, whose vivacious quality was blooming under the warmth of Philip's attention, spoke feelingly of the pleasure of riding through the snow. Reggie, happily restored to the society of his friend and Marianne (the story of *Jonathan Wild* forgotten), seconded Sally's views and immediately claimed two seats in the carriage—one for him and one for Marianne. Jamie promptly demanded a seat next to them.

"Mutht you came along?" Reg had asked, *sotto voce*.

"Yes, I must," Jamie had answered decidedly. "Just because you've won the fair lady, don't think you'll get *me* to retire with a book!"

The group gathering in the front hallway that afternoon made a gay assemblage. There was much laughter, the clump of heavy boots, the commotion of several footmen helping the men into their greatcoats. Mufflers were wound around throats, muffs and mittens found for eager hands. In the midst of the turmoil, Philip noticed Evalyn walking quietly up the stairs. He nudged his son. "I think you should ask Miss Pennington to join us, Jamie. It seems to me that you've become neglectful of including her in your activities."

"Oh?" Jamie asked, puzzled. "I didn't realize that I was expected to—of course, I'll ask her." He ran up a few steps and caught her arm. "Miss Pennington," he said, "we're all about to go riding in the snow. Why don't you join us?"

"Do come!" called Sally from below. Her watchful eye had missed nothing of this byplay. "It promises to be a most amusing outing." She took Philip's arm possessively and laughed up at him.

"Thank you," Evalyn said, "but I prefer the warmth of the indoors."

"Come now, Miss Pennington," Philip said in his most

avuncular manner, "I heard you say not long ago that you loved new-fallen snow."

Evalyn lifted her chin and regarded him with her disconcertingly direct stare. "You must have mistaken me, my lord," she said. "The sight of it brings back associations that are not at all pleasant to me. I'm afraid I'm not in the least tempted." With a little curtsey, she turned and walked purposefully up the stairs and out of sight.

Jamie looked at his father curiously. "If I didn't know better, sir, I would think you'd been given a very decided set-down."

"It certainly seems so," Philip said gruffly, his ears a little red.

"The girl acts more like a duchess than a governess," Sally murmured, half to herself, with reluctant admiration.

"I told you," Jamie said, "that she's a very—"

"Yes, we know," Philip cut him off drily. "A very redoubtable girl."

Evalyn closed the door of her room behind her and leaned against it, trembling. She considered throwing herself on the bed and sobbing her heart out, but without Nancy's restraining presence, she might not be able to stop. Sobbing, as she had discovered yesterday, did very little good. It was a momentary relief at best, and it reddened the eyes, caused the lips to swell, and left one utterly drained and numb. No, she had better keep her wits about her and decide what to do. She could not continue in this fashion, that was clear. She could not pull herself out of this dejection if she were obliged to see Philip every day, to watch him dance attendance on Sally, to hear his voice, to see his face in the firelight, to catch the glances he threw at her occasionally, and store them up to feed on later, like a starving bird in the snow. The look he had given her last night, when she had recited those lines of Milton's, had sustained her all night long. No, she must go away. It would be foolish to subject herself to more of this feeling of hopelessness and pain.

She still had the money in her reticule which she had saved from her wages. With careful management, it would see her to London. And she still had the address of the unknown cousin who might provide her with a place to stay until she could find work. Quickly, before she allowed the warmth and luxury of the room and the kindness of the people in this house to change her mind, she pulled the battered portmanteau from under the bed and began to pack.

When Nancy found her, she was almost finished. The girl gaped at her openmouthed. "Miss Evalyn! What're ye *doin'*?" she squeaked. "Y're not *leavin'*?"

"Hush, Nancy. I want no one to know about this. Quickly now, I shall need your help."

"Well, ye ain't goin' to get it! Ye was supposed to stay 'ere till the new year. Where're ye goin'? An' why?"

"Don't ask questions, Nancy. I must go today. You know that I wouldn't be doing this if it weren't necessary. Don't make this harder for me than it is already."

"Oh, Miss! Y're breakin' me 'eart, fer certain! This 'as somethin' to do with yesterday, don't it?"

Evalyn merely nodded.

"I knew it! Ye ain't been the same since. It was somethin' bad, I know. Miss Evalyn, I ain't askin' ye to tell me what it was, but if ye could see yer way clear to speakin' to 'is lordship about it—"

"His *lordship*?"

"Yes, Miss. 'E 'as a good 'ead an' a kind 'eart. Everyone says so. An' 'e likes ye. I could tell that when ye was both 'elpin' to get Joseph out of trouble. 'Is lordship could 'elp ye, I know 'e could!"

"He couldn't help me, Nancy."

"Are you sure? Positive sure?"

"Yes, dear, I'm positively sure," Evalyn said with a small smile.

Nancy's lip quivered. "Miss Clarissa then. *She* might be able to . . ."

"Nancy, don't. There's no one to help. Please don't look at me so, or I shall start to sob again." But it was Nancy who sobbed. Evalyn put her arms about the girl's shoulders and tried to soothe her, but Nancy was inconsolable.

"N-nobody was ever s-so g-good to m-me b-before," she cried. "It ain't r-right for someone l-like ye to 'ave to g-go away. And on C-Christmas eve, too. It ain't right."

When Nancy's tears had ceased, Evalyn rose and said in a firm, steady voice, "You must help me now, Nancy. Do you think you can?"

Nancy sniffed and nodded.

"Good. Now, listen. You must find Joseph for me and ask him if he can take the curricle without anyone knowing and drive me into Ashwater. Tell him we can do it when everyone is dressing for dinner—in about half an hour. Then, Nancy, you must stay in here for the night. If anyone knocks and asks why I haven't come down to dinner, tell them I'm not feeling well and have gone to bed."

"B-but they'll be bound to find out sooner or later," Nancy said.

"Yes. Tomorrow you're to find Miss Clarissa and give her this letter. I also want you to give her this box I've made for her. If you can find some silver paper, we can wrap it up before Joseph comes for me. And give her these gloves that I've knitted for the twins. Tell them they're from Father Christmas."

"Oh, Miss Evalyn . . ." Nancy whimpered.

"And Nancy, this is for you. It's my Spanish shawl. It

was my mother's. It would make me so happy to know you have it."

"Oh, no, Miss Evalyn, I couldn't. It's too pretty fer me. . . ."

But Evalyn put it around her shoulders. Nancy burst into fresh tears, and the two embraced. "Oh, Miss Evalyn, what's to become of me without ye?"

"I've written about you in my note. I'm sure Miss Clarissa can find a place for you, if you want it. Now, go along, Nancy dear, and get Joseph for me."

Half an hour later, Evalyn put on her cloak, picked up her portmanteau, and looked around the room. The portrait of Philip's aunt gazed at her coldly. She could hear Philip's voice. . . . "You and she should deal extremely well together." She could see through the window the outlines of the balcony railing over which she and Philip had pulled Joseph to safety. She looked at the dressing table where she had left the few packages that were all she had to express her thanks. And thanks she owed in full measure to all the people in this house. Despite the pain she carried with her, a pain for which no one was to blame but herself, she realized that she had experienced more of the emotions of living, had felt more of the pleasures, the joys, the excitements and—yes—the sufferings, than in all of her days before. Yet, as she crept stealthily down the back stairs to where Joseph sat waiting in the curricle, she realized with a shock that, since the day she had left the house of Lady Carbery, less than one week had elapsed.

· Fifteen ·

SALLY LOOKED WITH pleasure at the dress laid out for her on the bed. She had chosen it especially to wear tonight—Christmas eve. It was of the loveliest Florentine silk in a green that exactly matched her eyes and was cunningly designed to drape across the bosom in the most flattering way. The tiny puffed sleeves could be pulled back off the shoulders, and the high waist admirably suited her figure. It was a deceptively simple creation, the only trimmings to be found in a wide band across the bottom, where a classic design had been intricately woven into the material and edged with seed pearls.

Annette had already dressed her hair. It was brushed back into a knot at the back of her head, with only a small part of the front escaping into little curls that surrounded her face. A jewelled band circled her head, and later she would thrust a tall ostrich plume into the center of it.

A gasp from Annette in the dressing room widened her smile. "Ma'm'selle! Come quick!" the girl cried.

"What is it, Annette?" Sally asked in a voice that was calculatedly casual.

"Your diamond earrings, Ma'm'selle! I cannot find them!"

"I don't want to wear the diamonds tonight, I told you. I want the pearl drops."

Annette appeared in the dressing room doorway, looking distraught. "*Mais, non! Vous ne comprenez pas!* They are gone!"

"What do you mean, gone?"

"I mean gone! Disappeared! *Perdu!*"

Sally strode quickly to the dressing room and surveyed the open jewel box. "Are you sure?" she asked, looking through the contents hurriedly.

"But of course I am sure. Did you not put them here yourself, in this very compartment?"

Sally carefully emptied every compartment and every tiny drawer, while Annette watched nervously at her elbow. "How strange. . . ." mused Sally. "Only you and I know where I keep the key. . . ."

Annette straightened up and spoke haughtily. "You are not suggesting, Ma'm'selle, that I am responsible for such a thing! You cannot believe that I—! I am no thief, *moi*!"

"Oh, be still, Annette! I'm not accusing you. It would be stupid for you to have done so, and you are not stupid. Irritating and disrespectful, yes, but not stupid."

"For that, I suppose, I should make thanks. But why do you think it would be stupid of me to have done it?"

"You would be the first one suspected, as you well know. No, you are not the culprit. I think you had better go and bring Lady Steele to me. She must be informed at once."

A moment later Clarissa, wearing a loose wrapper, her hair only half dressed, hurried into the room. "What is it, Sally? Annette says you've something to tell me. Of the greatest moment, to use her words."

"Well, it is of some moment, I'm afraid. I hate to trouble you with this matter, my dear, but I don't see what else there is to do. My diamond drops have disappeared."

"Diamond drops? You mean those magnificent diamond earrings?" Clarissa gasped. "Are you sure?"

"Oh, but yes, *Madame*. We have looked most carefully," Annette said earnestly. "They have assuredly disappeared."

"You see," Sally explained, "Annette has instructions that she's to stand by me and make sure I lock them away in my jewel box after every time I wear them. I'm inclined to be somewhat careless, so we devised this system between us, didn't we, Annette?"

Annette eyed her employer curiously. Something in Ma'm'selle's voice put Annette on the alert. She knew her Ma'm'selle very well. The "system" was devised only two nights ago, and at the time, Annette had not been comfortable about the manner of its devising. She had felt then that Miss Trevelyan was up to some trick. Now she was sure of it, but what it could be she did not know. There was nothing she could do but answer the question. "Yes, we did," she said reluctantly. She would have liked to add "two nights ago," but decided to hold her tongue.

"I see," said Clarissa, who looked quite pale, her brow furrowed in worried lines. "You think that someone in this house may have stolen them?"

"I don't see what else I can think," Sally said.

"There are other possibilities. When was the last time you saw them?"

"The night I wore the mauve silk, isn't that so, Annette?"

"Yes, Ma'm'selle. Two nights ago. Then we put the earrings away here in the box."

"Are you sure you haven't worn them since?" Clarissa persisted.

"Quite sure. Last night I wore the Venetian velvet and decided not to wear any jewels with it. We did not even open the box."

"Oh, dear. I don't know what to say. A thing like this has never happened before. Sally, do you think we might wait a day or two before we do anything about this? It is so awkward, especially on Christmas eve, to start questioning servants and so on. . . . Perhaps if we wait, the earrings will turn up."

"I don't see how they possibly can," Sally said, masking her impatience for her plan to unfold, "but I wouldn't dream of upsetting your holiday festivities. I'm sure I can rely on you to handle the matter tactfully. Do just as you think you should, Clarissa. I leave it entirely in your hands."

"Thank you, my dear," Clarissa said. "I regret that such an occurrence should have taken place in my home, but I'm sure the earrings will be restored to you before long." But her worried frown did not disappear as she retreated, much disturbed, to her own bedroom.

The kissing boughs had been hung over the doorways of several of the downstairs rooms, and Jamie and Reggie, coming down to dinner early, had placed themselves on either side of the drawing room doorway. As each lady made her entrance, the two young men bent and kissed her cheeks simultaneously. First, Martha arrived, bearing a twin by each hand. The boys, dressed in long trousers, white shirts with turned-down collars trimmed with lace, and blue coats exactly like their father's, had been permitted to join the adults for dinner for this occasion. When they saw their mother caught under the mistletoe by two gentlemen at once, they went off in a fit of giggles. Their sister followed. Marianne, her brown ringlets shining from an hour of energetic brushing, looked—to one man at least— the very essence of feminine loveliness in her demure evening gown of ruby-colored lustring. When she was kissed, her brothers giggled again, louder and longer. It became infectious, setting off the entire room when Clarissa entered, and climaxing in a paroxysm of merriment when Sally at last came in.

Almost an hour later, the guests had still not left the drawing room to go in to dine. Hutton had twice put in his head to see if he could enter and announce dinner and had twice withdrawn, because one of the company had not yet put in an appearance. Finally, Clarissa beckoned to him and whispered instructions to dispatch a footman to see what had detained Miss Pennington. Philip watched the interchange and quietly and unobtrusively left the drawing room. The returning footman found his lordship pacing the hall. "Well, where is Miss Pennington?" he demanded abruptly.

"She begs to be excused, my lord. She is not feeling well."

"Did she say what was wrong?" his lordship asked in concern.

"No, my lord. I did not speak to the young lady. Her abigail informed me she had retired."

"I see. Very well, you may tell Hutton to announce dinner. I'll inform Lady Steele."

He returned to the drawing room and told the assemblage that Evalyn had retired early. He informed Clarissa in a low voice that Evalyn was not feeling well. Clarissa shook her head. "I told the girl she was looking fagged. I'm glad she decided to go to bed, though I'm sorry she will miss the Christmas eve celebrations. Don't look so worried, Philip. I'm sure she'll be right as rain after a good night's sleep."

After an excellent dinner, the guests gathered in the drawing room for an evening of Christmas games. First they played hunt-the-slipper, as a favor to the twins. Then forfeits, by popular demand, with Marianne unanimously chosen as the crier of the forfeits. She surprised the entire group by devising forfeits of great ingenuity, and announcing them in a voice that could be heard at least by those who were close by or listening with attention. And, at last, Jamie's favorite, snap-dragon, was announced.

Hutton entered with great ceremony, bearing a broad, shallow bowl filled with brandy. He was followed by two footmen, one carrying a tray of raisins and the other a table, which was placed in the middle of the room. The bowl was set on the table, the raisins dropped into the brandy, and then Jamie lit a long stick and ignited the brandy, to a chorus of oohs and aahs. The blue flame jumped merrily. The guests were requested to pull the flaming raisins from the bowl and pop them into their mouths. This was to be done to the accompaniment of the snapdragon song and, if the experience of the past gave any clue, much clapping of hands and derisive laughter.

"Here he comes with flaming bowl,
Don't he mean to take his toll,
Snip! Snap! Dragon!"

they sang as Edward gingerly put his fingers into the flame and hastily withdrew them, empty.

"No, no," Jamie cautioned him. "You must be very quick about it, like this." And he thrust his hand into the brandy with a darting motion and had popped three flaming raisins in his mouth in the wink of an eye.

"Doesn't it hurt?" asked Teddy, awed.

"Not a bit, if you're quick. Here, you try." And he lifted the boy over the bowl.

"With his blue and lapping tongue
Many of you will be stung,
Snip! Snap! Dragon!"

The boys were quick learners and popped the raisins in

their mouths with amusing bravado. Sally, graceful and quick, took her turn to prolonged applause. Marianne was too timid to try, so Reggie fed her with the raisins he'd procured. Everyone managed to take a turn before the flame died out, and, to the twins' disappointment, the game ended as they all sang the final stanza:

> "Don't 'ee fear him, but be bold,
> Out he goes, his flames are cold,
> Snip! Snap! Dragon!"

The game was such a success that nobody, not even Sally, noticed that Philip had quietly slipped out of the room. He ran up the stairs and knocked softly at Evalyn's door. A wary, frightened Nancy opened it a crack and peeped out. "Good evenin', ye lordship," she said in a quivering voice.

"Good evening, Nancy. I've come to see your mistress. May I come in?"

"Oh, no, me lord," she exclaimed. "She's fast asleep."

"I see. Is she very ill? What did she say was troubling her?"

"Only a 'eadache, me lord. Nothin' to worry over."

"But perhaps I should send Clarissa up—just to see if she's feverish . . ."

"Oh, she ain't feverish, me lord, I promise ye that. There ain't no use disturbin' 'er now."

Philip scanned the girl's face closely. "Very well. But you will stay with her all night, won't you? And be sure to send for me if she should wake and need anything. Will you do that?"

"Most certainly, me lord. I won't leave this room all night. Ye 'ave me word on it."

"Yes. Well, goodnight then," he said, and reluctantly turned away.

Philip found the rest of the evening very nearly unendurable, but he played the part of host so well that nobody suspected it. One thing beyond his control was the weather which, it was soon discovered, had become so bad that the plans for the evening were adversely affected. The snow fell so heavily that attendance at the midnight service was not possible. Instead, Edward was asked to conduct a brief family service, carols were sung with gusto, and the little group gathered for the late supper in a happy Christmas spirit. Philip, however, could not help giving a sigh of relief when the company finally disbanded and headed for their beds.

Edward Covington had had a memorable evening. Not only was he proud of being asked to conduct the service, but he had had a talk with Reggie that had induced in him a most unaccustomed, fatherly glow. A brief talk with Marianne, just before she retired, had increased his sense of exhilaration, and it was with a pleased, self-satisfied smile that he readied himself for bed. His man dismissed, he put on his frogged dressing gown and tapped at the door which connected his bedroom with his wife's.

"Come in," Martha called. As he entered, Martha's abigail, who had been administering nosedrops to her mistress, glanced at Edward's dressing gown, replaced the bottle of medication, and hastily withdrew.

"What is it, my dear?" asked Edward with a suppressed sigh. "Another cold?"

"Oh, no," his spouse reassured him, sitting up among the pillows and patting the space beside her invitingly, "it's only a preventive measure. You know how I am in such weather."

Edward sat down on the bed and took her hand. "Yes, my dear, I know how you are. But I don't know if it's altogether wise to take medication before it is needed."

"Why would it be unwise?" she asked him reasonably. "If the medicine is beneficial when one is sick, why should it be harmful when one is well?"

Edward opened his mouth to respond, found himself nonplussed, and shut it again. He shrugged. "Never mind that now. I have some news that will surprise you, I think."

"News? You surprise me already. What news can you possibly have? We left each other scarcely an hour ago."

"Did you notice tonight that, during the games, Reggie took me aside? He asked me to step into the library to have a word with him."

"No, I can't say I noticed. What on earth did he want with you?"

"Prepare yourself for a shock, my dear. He asked my permission to pay his addresses to Marianne!"

Martha's mouth dropped open, and she stared at her husband, speechless. She felt for a moment as if she were in a dream. She could not have heard him properly.

"Did you say Marianne? He wants to court *our* Marianne?"

"So it would seem."

"You cannot have understood him! You've made a mistake. Marianne is only a child! She'll not have her come-out until next year!"

"So I told him," said her laconic husband with irritating calm.

Martha caught her breath and clutched at his arm. "What did you tell him? Edward!" she almost screamed. "You didn't *refuse* him!"

"Hush, my dear, don't get so excited. One minute you say she's too young, and the next you say you don't want me to refuse him. You must try to be calm and compose your mind."

"Compose my mind! How can I compose my mind when you tell me you whistled the Farnham fortune down the wind!"

"I didn't do any such thing. Do you take me for a fool?"

"Well, then, what *did* you do? Will you stop talking and tell me what you said?"

"I can scarcely stop talking and tell you anything," Edward responded with asperity.

"What?" asked Martha. "Sometimes, Edward, I find it extremely difficult to follow you."

Edward sighed. "Very well, my dear, suppose we start all over again from the beginning."

"Yes," agreed his wife, leaning back against the pillows, pressing her hands against her breasts and taking deep breaths to calm herself, "that"—she breathed—"would be a very good"—she breathed again—"idea."

"Well then, I repeat. I accompanied Reggie to the library where he told me, in an excellent, succinct style, that he had grown attached to our daughter—"

"How remarkable," exclaimed his wife in gratification. "In less than a week! I must say I would not have believed she had it in her."

"You are not to interrupt with irrelevancies, ma'am. As I was saying, Reggie said he had grown attached to our daughter and would like my permission to pay his addresses to her."

"Yes, yes. Well?"

"Whereupon, after I had gotten over my surprise, I pointed out to him that she was only seventeen and had not yet been presented—"

"Very true. Just what you ought to have said."

"Thank you. Then Reggie said he was aware of that, and

that he was willing to give her a chance to have her come-out and see a little more of the world before extracting a firm commitment from her."

Martha clapped her hands together gleefully. "Did he say that? How considerate of him! I must say, I'm thoroughly delighted with the boy. I think that should serve very well, don't you? It will give me plenty of time to persuade Marianne that putting up with a little lisp is nothing but a trifle when compared with the Farnham fortune and the right to be called a viscountess."

"I don't think you'll need that time. When I told Marianne what had transpired—"

"You told her?"

"Yes, of course. I stopped in at her bedroom before coming here. She threw her arms about my neck and said she was the happiest girl in the world!"

"Oh, Edward, I can scarcely believe it! Our daughter . . . to be a viscountess, the lady of a great house in the country, a London residence, all the horses and carriages she could want, the servants, the gowns, the pin-money . . . Edward, I think I'm going to faint . . . !"

Edward stood up abruptly and frowned down at her. "If you do," he said severely, "I'll march out of here and leave you where you fall. It's bad enough to have you fainting when trouble occurs, but if you begin to do it when *good* things happen, you'll get no help from me!"

Philip lay in his bed that night, staring up at the shadows cast on the ceiling by the flickering firelight. For the fourth night in succession, it was Evalyn who had caused his insomnia. Tonight it was an uneasy feeling of guilt that was keeping him awake. He feared that she had taken to her bed because of the treatment she had received at his hands. And at Jamie's hands, too. His irritation at his irresponsible son was chaffing him severely. What sort of man had his son become? The beetlehead had not shown a moment's concern over Evalyn's absence this evening. He had enjoyed his Christmas eve completely and had indulged in his silly games with the light-hearted enthusiasm of a child without a care in the world.

Two days ago, Philip had promised Clarissa to take Jamie to task, but he'd not yet been able to bring himself to deliver that much-needed lecture on the duties of a prospective bridegroom to his bride. Obviously, he could put it off no longer. Tomorrow he would have it out with Jamie. He went over in his mind the various instances of neglect of which Jamie had been guilty. Yet it would not be advisable to throw a recital of Jamie's thoughtless acts at his head. Perhaps it would be better to encourage Jamie to announce his betrothal immediately, so that he and Evalyn could feel free to exhibit publicly their attachment to each other. But Philip would not neglect to point out to his rackety son the necessity of giving his bride his undivided affection and attention. Philip rehearsed several speeches in his mind and imagined the scene with Jamie in several different ways. Somehow, though, no matter how calmly and reasonably each scene started, Philip found himself concluding each imaginary encounter by firmly wringing his blasted son's neck.

· Sixteen ·

THE TEN-MILE drive to Ashwater took more than two hours, for although the curricle was light, the passage through the snow was difficult. The open carriage did not afford much protection from the elements, and Evalyn and Joseph were chilled to the bone by the time they drove into the inn yard. Joseph shook his head worriedly as he helped Evalyn down from the carriage. "I hope you know what you're about," he said, voicing his disapproval for the fourth time that hour. "You'll never get a hack on a night like this, and even if you do, you'll not make it to Launceston. And if you do get to Launceston, you'll not see the Exeter stage 'til this snow clears."

Evalyn looked at the snow swirling about the inn yard. It seemed to be coming down more heavily than before, and the wind was growing stronger. Drifts were beginning to form around the gateposts and along the walls of the inn. "Perhaps you're right, Joseph," she said, a worried frown creasing her forehead, "but I shall contrive somehow. Meanwhile, come in and get warm before you set off for home."

The Bull at Ashwater was a small, cheerful inn, with a taproom that was usually filled with lively activity at this time of evening. On this night, however, a solitary drinker sat in one corner, and Mrs. Fern, the landlord's wife, knelt before the fireplace adding wood to an already lively blaze. Otherwise, the place was deserted. Hearing footsteps, Mrs. Fern looked up to see Evalyn and Joseph standing in the doorway. "Bless me," she exclaimed, "where'd you come from? I ain't heard no carriage."

She bustled over to Evalyn and took her cloak. "Here now, Missy, sit you down near the fire. You're shivering something fierce."

"Get the lady something hot to drink," Joseph said, putting down the portmanteau. "She's chilled to the bone."

"And you, too, by the look of you." She hurried off, muttering to herself on the peculiarities of folk who would venture out on a night like this, and Christmas eve, too. She returned in a moment with a pot of hot tea and two steaming mugs of mulled wine. Joseph took the wine and drank as quickly as he could swallow the hot brew. "I'd best be getting back, Miss Evalyn, before the drifts get too deep," he said.

"Yes, I'm worried about that, Joseph. What will happen if you get stuck in a drift?"

"I'll dig myself out, don't you worry none about me. It's you what's got me concerned."

"You're so kind to worry about me when I may have gotten you in a devil of a hobble."

"Not me," he assured her with a grin. "If I been missed, I'll tell 'em that I took the curricle to see my sick mum in Bridestowe. I ain't never seen you tonight, Miss Evalyn, and that's a fact." He winked at her broadly and wrapped his muffler tightly around his neck. "Well, I best be off. You take good care o' yourself. Good luck to you, ma'am. I hope you get some good o' this night's work."

Evalyn watched through the taproom window as Joseph drove off in the snow. Then she returned to the fire, sat down and sipped her tea slowly. The enormity of her predicament slowly overwhelmed her. Perhaps she had been foolish and hasty. The trip to London would be long and costly, even in the best weather. She had to get to Launceston to pick up the stage to Exeter, the last stop of the London-Exeter stage. Each change would require additional funds for tipping the ostlers who handled her luggage, for accommodations if a long wait was required between connections, and for goodness-knew-what other exigencies which might arise. She had no idea of the cost of a hack to Launceston, but her meagre funds would certainly not provide for more than one or two nights' lodging while waiting out the storm.

There was one consolation. The snow would surely prevent anyone at Gyllford from coming after her, if they were inclined to do so. Not that she expected anyone to follow her. She was a stranger to them, after all. Kind as they had been to her, they had known her for only a week and had no obligation to be concerned for her welfare, especially after they learned that she had chosen to run away from them. She sighed. Would Philip miss her? she wondered. What would he think of her foolish disappearance? She remembered the warm gleam in his eyes, his slight, teasing smile when he had taken the portrait from her bedroom wall. How amazingly close they had been at that moment, as if each one could read the other's thoughts. It was too painful now to think about. What would there be in his revealing blue eyes when he learned that she had gone? Would they be scornful of her foolishness? Angry at her thoughtlessness? Or would they be completely indifferent? Would he dismiss the news with a shrug and turn his eyes to the beautiful Miss Trevelyan?

She was shaken from these ruminations by a cough at her elbow. Mrs. Fern stood looking down at her. "Has your man gone?" the puzzled woman asked. "You ain't meaning to stay here tonight, are you?"

"I'm not sure. Is there a hack and a driver I could hire to take me to Launceston?"

"Tonight?" Mrs. Fern asked wide-eyed. "You couldn't expect man or beast to be abroad on a night like this! Besides, it's Christmas eve!"

"Oh, dear. I had hoped—"

"Let me call Mr. Fern, dearie. He knows more about hiring out hacks than what I do. He's out in the kitchen, eating a piece of tomorrow's ham."

The innkeeper, Mr. Fern, a burly man with a bald head and a great walrus moustache, came from the kitchen, a look of curiosity clearly discernible in his face. "I wouldn't ask a driver to take you out tonight," he told her firmly. "Wouldn't be safe, ma'am."

"Do you think you can get someone for me tomorrow?" Evalyn asked.

Mr. Fern turned to the solitary man in the corner. "Sam'l?" he asked, "would you be able to drive a hack to Launceston in the morning?"

The man looked up from his tankard and shook his head. "Doubt it," he said shortly. "The snow ain't goin' to stop so soon. Not this'n."

The landlord shrugged. "If old Sam'l thinks not, you can lay odds you won't get out o' here tomorrow morning neither."

"Old Sam'l knows the weather, he does," Mrs. Fern agreed.

Evalyn shook her head, crestfallen. "I hope he may be wrong, this time," she said worriedly. "But in the meantime, do you have a room for me?"

"That we have, ma'am, with the house so empty. Don't

you fret. We'll have you snug in no time," Mr. Fern said kindly.

"That we will," agreed his spouse. "The best bedroom for you tonight. Mr. Fern will bring you a bit of ham and some greens, while I go up and start a nice fire and warm your sheets. Some food and a warm bed'll get you out of the dismals, you'll see."

Evalyn smiled weakly and resumed her seat. Mr. Fern filled a tankard, wordlessly placed it before old Sam'l, and went out to the kitchen. He returned a moment later with a platter heaped with several slices of ham, potatoes, and turnip greens, which he placed on a nearby table with a flourish. He held the chair for her, and Evalyn sat down gratefully. "It smells delicious," she said. "I suddenly feel quite hungry."

"We thought you might be, Mrs. Fern and me."

The innkeeper went off to the kitchen, and Evalyn began to eat. The ham was surprisingly well prepared. She had just begun her third slice when there came a sound of a carriage in the yard. An angry voice shouted, "Ostler! Ostler! Where the deuce is everybody?"

Mr. Fern hurried from the kitchen and out the door. "Everyone's gone home," she heard him explain. "It is Christmas eve, you know."

A confusion of footsteps and noise in the entryway made Evalyn aware that a number of people had arrived. There were several children's voices and the sound of a baby crying. "Merciful heavens! Ye'll not bring us in there!" said a woman's voice, distinctive for its Irish brogue. "I won't have my wee ones in a taproom. A private parlor, if ye please."

"The parlor's closed, ma'am. I ain't got no fire going in there tonight."

"Well, then, don't stand there gawkin'! Start one! And

when ye've done that, bring some more candles. Dark as a tomb in there, it is. And, Charlie boy, stop that! Take Mary into the parlor and sit her down. You, Sean, stop kicking the wall—the snow'll melt off y'r boots soon enough. Meggie, let Cathy help ye off with y'r cloak. Well, come along, then. The sooner we finish, the sooner we'll be home." The slam of a door stilled any further sounds.

Evalyn watched in amusement as the innkeeper hurried back and forth from the kitchen to the parlor bearing trays of loaded dishes. Mrs. Fern, returning from upstairs, was quickly impressed to assist. The two of them were too busy to do more than throw Evalyn a harried glance as they ran by. "Don't know what such a family's doing out on Christmas eve," Mrs. Fern whispered to Evalyn as she returned from her third trip to the parlor. "Those children should be home waiting for Father Christmas." And she ran off to the kitchen.

"Eating our whole Christmas dinner, too," grumbled her husband as he followed hastily behind her.

Evalyn, patiently waiting to be shown up to her bedroom, was surprised by the sound of sniffling coming from the doorway to the taproom. She looked round to see a little girl peeping in at her from the passageway. The child couldn't have been more than three or four years old, for she was still in short petticoats. Her red, curly hair was dishevelled, and her eyes and nose were running. A white tucker had been tied around her neck, and she wore only one shoe. Evalyn smiled at her. "Good evening," she said. The child sniffed forlornly but didn't move. "If you come here," Evalyn said invitingly, "I'll give you a bit of my biscuit. Would you like that?"

The child advanced toward her cautiously, her hands hidden behind her back. A few feet away, she stopped and eyed Evalyn with suspicion. Evalyn got up from her chair and held out her hand. The child backed away. Evalyn pulled out a handkerchief, knelt down and beckoned. The little girl advanced shyly. "There, now," Evalyn said soothingly, "no need to be afraid of me, you know. May I wipe your face with my nice handkerchief?"

The child nodded and toddled across the few feet still separating them. Evalyn wiped her eyes and nose. "You've been crying, haven't you?" she asked sympathetically. "Is it because you're hungry?"

The child shook her head. "No, ma'am," she said timidly, and brought her hands from behind her back. In one was a grimy doll whose elegant gown had been torn, revealing a missing leg underneath. In the other hand she clutched the severed limb. "Charlie did it," the child said with a quivering lip.

"Oh, that was too bad of Charlie, I'm sure," Evalyn said, taking the doll and the leg and looking them over carefully. "But we can make her well again."

"Can we?" the child asked dubiously.

Evalyn took her hand and led her to the table. She seated herself and lifted the child to her lap. She placed the wounded doll on the table, and the two of them examined it carefully. "If you ask your Mama to put some glue here and here," Evalyn explained, "this lovely lady will be good as new."

"Not her dress," the girl said knowingly.

"Yes, of course, you're right. The dress must be mended with a needle and thread."

"Needle and thread," the child repeated, nodding wisely. She leaned back against Evalyn, gave a shivering sigh to indicate that her crying was over, put her thumb in her mouth and sucked contentedly. Evalyn was about to distract her with the offer of a piece of biscuit, when she looked up and saw that she was being regarded by a woman in the doorway. The woman was full-formed, her buxom figure emphasized by the high-necked swansdown gown she wore. It fit her a bit too tightly and was badly rumpled and stained. Her head was swathed in a rose-colored turban which clashed with the ringlets of bright red hair that escaped from beneath it in youthful disarray. Her complexion was ruddy and marked with fine lines about the eyes and mouth, but despite the rather tasteless clothing and general untidiness, her eyes were merry and the smile that brightened her face gave Evalyn a distinct impression of beauty. "You must be thinking I've kidnapped your daughter, ma'am," Evalyn said.

"Not at all," the lady said in her soft Irish burr. "I was thinkin' that ye must have a gift of magic to have persuaded our little Meggie to go to ye like that. 'Tis a shy one, our Meggie. I've never seen her go to a stranger in all her born days."

"There was no magic, I assure you, ma'am. Just a little bit of biscuit and some sympathy," Evalyn said with a smile. She shifted the child to her shoulder, rose from her chair and brought the little girl to her mother. The lady put out her arms, but Meggie clung to Evalyn's neck.

"Will ye look at that, now!" exclaimed the lady. "She's taken a real fancy to ye, that's certain. Come here to me, Meggie. 'Tis enough time ye've disturbed this kind lady. Come to y'r mother, like the good girl ye are."

But Meggie still clung to Evalyn. She took her thumb from her mouth and whispered, "Tell Mama about Dolly."

"Oh, yes, indeed, Meggie," Evalyn said. "I'll tell her as soon as you go to her, and my hands are free to show her what to do."

Meggie held her arms to her mother, and Evalyn picked up the doll from the table. "There seems to have been an accident," she said, smiling at the red-headed Irishwoman. "Dolly needs a little glue here at the joint."

The woman thanked her and turned to go. At the door, she looked back. "I suppose ye have children of y'r own, to have such a way with 'em," she remarked.

"No, but children are my profession. I'm a governess."

"Are ye now? Well, ye must be a mighty good one. I wish I—"

At that moment, the parlor door slammed and a grey-haired gentleman appeared in the passageway, bearing a crying infant. He was tall and quite thin except for a rounded stomach which made a surprising protrusion in his otherwise lanky frame. "Oh, there you are, Mavis," he said irritably. "Why do you stand there dawdling, while I'm left alone to contend with the baby and the rest of this disreputable brood? Oh, I beg your pardon, ma'am. I didn't see you there." And he nodded embarrassedly to Evalyn.

"This lady was mindin' our Meggie. She's a governess, and a good one, too, if I'm a judge. Only thankin' her I was. Is the wee one still cryin'?" Mavis exchanged children with the gentleman and looked at the baby in concern. "He feels feverish to me, my dear," she said worriedly. "I'm thinkin' we'd best be on our way. The sooner I get him home, the better."

"It's folly to be setting out in this snow, Mavis. Let's put up here for the night and have done. We never should have left my mother's, as I warned you."

"Have done y'rself! 'Tis enough I've heard on that score. I'll not rest content until we're in our own home with our own nurse to tend to this sick babe. There's no one in y'r mother's house knows a thing about babies."

"But what if we're stuck in the ditch? Do you want to spend the night in a drafty coach?"

"Stuck in a ditch?" Mavis exclaimed. "Never've I known

ye to do such a thing. Ye'll not let that happen." She smiled up at her husband with a flirtatious glimmer. "Not such a skillful, artful, talented driver as y'rself."

Evalyn could see the warmth of his eyes, though he pretended to be angry. "Serves me right," he growled, "for marrying a red-headed, stubborn, willful Irish puss! All right then, let's get the children dressed again."

"If you wish," ventured Evalyn, "I'd be happy to help you get them ready."

"I must say, that's deuced kind of you, ma'am," said the gentleman with enthusiasm. "With six spoiled brats plaguing us, a bit of help would be much appreciated."

"Six? That's an impressive number," Evalyn said smiling.

"Impressive is not a word I'd use," Mavis laughed.

"We must seem utterly without manners," said the gentleman. "I am Hugh Caldwell, and this is my wife, Mavis."

"How do you do? I'm Evalyn Pennington. And I think we should get the children ready without further ado. The wind seems to have come up stronger than ever, so, if you are determined to set out tonight, you had better waste no more time."

Half an hour later, the children had been cleaned up and dressed, the baby fed and bundled up warmly, and the entire Caldwell clan stood ready to depart. Mavis, the baby in her arms, turned to Evalyn in gratitude. "Oh, my dear," she said earnestly, "I don't know how to thank ye. 'Tis a gem ye are, truly."

Mr. Caldwell nodded in agreement. "I would appreciate the direction of your employer, Miss Pennington. It would give me great pleasure to write to him and tell how helpful you've been."

Evalyn blushed in embarrassment. "Thank you, but you see I . . . I mean, that will not be necessary."

"But why not?" cried Mavis. "Sure and there's no harm in makin' sure your employers appreciate ye as ye deserve."

Evalyn lowered her eyes and shook her head. Mavis looked at her shrewdly. "Charlie," she said to the oldest boy, "take the children to the carriage and get them in." Then she handed the baby to her puzzled husband and took Evalyn's hand. "Something is not right with ye, I'm thinkin'," she said, looking at the governess's face. "I've been wonderin' why a governess is all by herself at an inn on Christmas eve. Ye've been kind to us. If there's some trouble ye're in, it would surely be a joy to us to do something for ye in return."

"Thank you, Mrs. Caldwell, but I'm in no trouble. I'm on my way to London to seek a post, that is all."

"To seek a post?" asked Mr. Caldwell. "Do you mean to say that you are not now employed?"

Evalyn nodded. Mavis stared. "I'll not believe it! What a bit o' luck for us! Ye'll come and work for us, then, if the size of our brood doesn't frighten ye. Right, Hugh?"

"By all means," said Hugh Caldwell firmly. "How long will it take you to get your things?"

"Oh, no," Evalyn objected breathlessly. "You cannot mean it. You don't know me well enough. I have not even . . ."

"What haven't you, Miss Pennington?" asked Mr. Caldwell.

"A . . . a character. You see, my last employer discharged me without giving me one."

"More fool, he," laughed Mavis, embracing her like a long-lost sister. "I had y'r measure the first moment I clapped eyes on ye. There's no letter I'll be needin'."

"Nor I," smiled her husband. "So get your things, before

the children upset the carriage. Unless, of course, you think you'll not relish six charges."

"On the contrary, it sounds like just what I'd relish. But did you not mention a nurse you have at home?"

"Yes, indeed," Mavis explained. "She's a dear old thing, and I'd be lost without her, but six are much too much for her. Sure, y're a Christmas miracle, my dear, so let's hear no more. Now, will ye get y're things?"

She embraced Evalyn fondly and pushed her toward the taproom. Evalyn picked up her cloak and portmanteau quickly. She looked around for the innkeeper and his wife, but they were not there. Old Sam'l still sat at the corner table sipping his ale. "Excuse me," Evalyn said to him. "Have you seen Mr. or Mrs. Fern?" He shook his head. "Will you tell them goodbye for me? I'm sorry I'll not be using the room, but I've left the money I owe them here on the table."

Sam'l nodded. Evalyn thanked him and ran out to the waiting coach.

· *Seventeen* ·

BEFORE BREAKFAST ON Christmas morning, Clarissa knocked on Philip's door. She had spent a sleepless night worrying about Sally's missing earrings and had decided that Philip should be told without further delay. Wellstock opened the door. "Is his lordship dressed, Wellstock?" she asked.

Philip's voice answered her from the dressing room. "I'm in proper enough attire to receive my sister," he said, coming in from the dressing room in his shirtsleeves. "You may go to Jamie, Wellstock. I can manage the rest myself."

Wellstock bowed and withdrew. Clarissa looked at her brother with concern. "You must have had a difficult night, too," she said with solicitude. "You look quite knocked up."

"A difficult night, *too*? If *you've* had trouble sleeping, it certainly doesn't show, my dear. You look as bewitching as always."

Clarissa snorted. "Don't try to flummer me, my lord. I have a mirror or two in my room. This wretched house party is making an old hag of me."

"What's wrong? I thought everything was proceeding famously."

"On the contrary. It's been a week full of major and minor crises—the sort of domestic contretemps that you never notice. But this one, I'm afraid, is too serious for me to handle on my own."

Philip felt a stab of alarm. "It's not—? There's no one seriously ill, is there?"

"No, no. Thank goodness, it's not quite as bad as that. I suppose I'm being overly dramatic to have made you think that. It's Sally. She reported to me last evening that her diamond earrings have been stolen."

With a relieved sigh, Philip took Clarissa's hand and led her to a chair near the fire. "Stolen? Rubbish! She's probably only misplaced them."

"That's what I thought at first," Clarissa said, sinking into the chair with a feeling of relief to be able to share this burden, "but I'm afraid Sally is right. She remembers quite clearly putting her earrings away in her jewel box, with her abigail looking on. It seems that this procedure is their way of making sure that Sally doesn't leave her jewels lying about carelessly, as she had been used to do. So the other day, as usual, Annette watched her lock her things away. And then, the next time they opened the box, the earrings were gone. I hate to admit it, my dear, but it does seem as though we have a thief in our midst."

"Unlikely. Most of the servants have been with us for years, and our guests are certainly above suspicion. Take my word, Clarissa, the blasted baubles will turn up before another day goes by."

Clarissa gave a hopeful sigh. "Do you really think so? I pray you may be right, but what if they don't?"

Philip gestured impatiently. "Then we'll buy Sally another pair and be done with the matter."

"But, Philip, we couldn't do that! We can't let a thief go undiscovered, can we?"

"I suppose not," Philip said with a sigh of resignation. The pair remained silent for a moment. Then Philip made a grimace of annoyance. "Blast that Trevelyan woman!" he growled. "She does have a way of cutting up one's peace."

"Yes, I'm afraid she does. Though watching you last night, I was almost convinced you had suddenly developed a *tendre* for her," Clarissa ventured with a coy glance at her brother from the corner of her eye.

"Don't be jingle-brained," her brother retorted curtly.

"Jingle-brained! Very pretty talking, I must say. I suppose you'll be telling me next that it was someone else who dangled at her shoe strings all evening!"

Philip darted a quick glance at his sister and grinned guiltily. "Only trying to be a good host, that's all," he said with obvious insincerity.

"What a whisker!" Clarissa declared roundly. "I didn't cut my eyeteeth yesterday, you know. You can't ignore the girl all week and then suddenly sit in her pocket all evening and explain your behavior away on the grounds of your obligations as a good host! You needn't explain yourself if you don't wish to, but I don't for a moment believe that this explanation is anything but a hum."

"You're right, of course," Philip admitted, "but since I don't wish to explain, let's get back to the subject of Sally's earrings. I agree that we'll have to investigate the matter, but can we wait until after Boxing Day? The household staff has been looking forward to the celebration, and I don't like to have them disturbed at this time of year."

"Neither do I. Rumors of a theft would be bound to spread, and everyone would be nervous and upset. I'm sure we can wait two or three days. And perhaps you are right," she added, rising, "that the earrings will turn up before we're forced to take action. Well, hurry and finish dressing. It's almost time for breakfast. I think we should all take Christmas breakfast together."

"Of course. I'll be ready in a few minutes." He took her arm and walked with her to the door.

She hesitated at the doorway. "I was only joking before, about you and Sally, you know. But Philip, is something troubling you?"

"Nothing at all. Why?"

"I don't know. I have the feeling that you're in the dismals and you're trying to cover up. . . ."

Philip leaned down and kissed her cheek. "Silly widgeon. Haven't you enough to worry you? If you must have something else to brood about, try to find signs of affliction in Gervaise. Truly, my dear, there's no need to trouble about me."

"Very well," she said, giving him a tired smile and patting his cheek. She was not at all convinced that all was well with him, for the dark shadows under his eyes belied his smile. But, realizing that he didn't want to discuss his private thoughts with her, she let the matter drop.

Philip, returning to his dressing room, turned back to her just before the door closed behind her. "Clarissa," he asked, "have you seen Miss Pennington this morning? Is she feeling any better today?"

"No, I haven't seen her. She hasn't yet come out of her room. She must still be asleep."

"Don't you think you should inquire?"

"Not yet. If she wishes to sleep late, I don't want to disturb her. I'll look in on her after breakfast, if she still hasn't put in an appearance."

Philip was about to remonstrate but changed his mind. "Well, do as you think best," he said with a shrug. "I'll see you at breakfast."

To Clarissa's delight, almost everyone had assembled in the breakfast room by ten for a repast that bid fair to rival her

Christmas dinner. She had provided for her guests a buffet that included eggs cooked in an assortment of styles, pickled salmon, a round of beef, two hams, an assortment of breads, biscuits and jellies, steaming pots of tea, coffee and chocolate, Hyland cream, gooseberry tarts, and even a dish of orange peel. This last was provided specially for Martha who forced herself every morning, Christmas or no, to drop the peel into a cup of boiling water and drink it, being convinced that this unappetizing brew had the power to dissolve what she called her "flegm." Since Christmas morning was made especially joyous by sharing with children the bounty of the day, the twins had been brought down by Mrs. Noakes and were seated at the head of the table, still in their nightshirts and tasselled caps. Piled before them were a number of parcels Father Christmas had brought and which they were excitedly opening in full view of the whole party.

While this was in progress, Hutton quietly came into the room and bent over Lady Steele, whispering that Miss Pennington's abigail was waiting outside to have a word with her. Clarissa nodded calmly but was struck with a feeling of apprehension. She got up as inconspicuously as she could and went out.

Nancy stood in the hall holding a letter and three small parcels, her face revealing her trepidation. She bobbed a quick curtsey and held out Evalyn's note. "What is this, Nancy?" Clarissa asked in surprise. "Is Miss Pennington still unwell?"

"Can't say, ma'am. She asked would ye read this 'ere note."

Clarissa took the note and tore it open. *My dear Clarissa,* Evalyn had written, *It gives much pain and embarrassment to have to say my goodbyes in this fashion. A personal matter has made it necessary for me to cut short this wonderful holiday and return immediately to my original plan for finding employment, which I had postponed when I accepted your kind invitation. Since I was convinced that you would use your persuasive powers to urge me against this course of action, and that this would probably cause some disturbance to the household at a time when nothing but merriment and joviality should prevail, I determined to leave quietly and without ceremony. The thought that most oppresses me is that you will think me rude and ungrateful because I left without a word to you. Please believe, most dear friend, that this is not the case. I shall never forget the many kindnesses you and your family have so generously bestowed on me, and the many happy hours I have spent at Gyllford Manor. Please convey to your family and your guests my thanks and warmest regards, and to Lord Reginald and Jamie my deep appreciation for their gallant attempt to rescue me from my difficulties at Carbery Hall. I would like to ask one last favor of you. Nancy, my abigail, has been a loyal, generous and hard-working girl, and it would make her very happy to continue in Lord Gyllford's employ. If a place can be found for her here, I will be, more than ever, your most grateful and devoted—Evalyn.*

Clarissa looked up from her letter with eyes filled with shock and concern. "I don't understand a word of this, Nancy. Is Miss Pennington really gone?"

Nancy bit her lip and nodded wordlessly.

"She left last night? In all this snow?"

"Yes'm."

"But why? I can't understand. What personal matter could have come to her attention at such a time? Had she received a letter or message from anyone?"

"Don't know, ma'am."

Clarissa perused the letter again, but it gave no clue. Her suspicion grew that whatever had happened to send Evalyn fleeing from the house had happened here. She looked at Nancy closely. "Did she quarrel with my nephew, Nancy? Don't be afraid to tell me the truth."

"With Mr. Everard?" asked Nancy in surprise at the question. "Not that I know of, my lady. But someone upset her, that's certain."

"Someone here, in this house?"

"I don't know, ma'am. She wouldn't tell me."

Clarissa sighed deeply. "Oh, dear, I'm at a complete loss as to what to do. Please sit down over there on that bench, Nancy. Lord Gyllford or I may want to speak to you in a moment or two." And she turned to go back to the breakfast room.

"Don't ye want these?" Nancy asked, holding out the parcels.

"What are they?"

"These are fer the twins, Miss Evalyn said. From Father Christmas, ye know. And this one is fer you. She made it for ye, all by 'erself. I'd find 'er working on it every spare minute."

Clarissa's eyes misted over, and the tears spilled over and rolled down her cheeks. "How like her to do such a thing," she said, brushing away the tears with the back of her hand. She took the parcels tenderly. "I can't bear to think she's gone."

She did not know precisely what, but it was clear to Clarissa that something had to be done. Where could Evalyn have gone in such a storm? And why? She returned to the breakfast room in a turmoil. The only explanation that had presented itself to her agitated mind had been the possibility that Evalyn and Jamie had quarrelled. Had Jamie changed his mind about marrying her? But no gentleman could cry off once a promise had been made! Had Evalyn realized (as Clarissa herself had already sensed and not let herself face) that she and Jamie were not suited? Or had Jamie's obvious neglect caused her to run away? Clarissa clutched the letter in her hand, wondering if she should take some time to reflect before coming to any decision about a course of action. She forced a smile and walked to the head of the table. "Here are two more presents," she said to the twins as she deposited the parcels before them.

"More gifts? These sons of mine shall be quite spoiled. Who sent them?" Martha asked.

"They are from Miss Pennington," Clarissa answered, sitting down at her place wearily.

Philip looked up from his plate. "Why didn't she bring them in herself? Is she still ill?" he asked tensely.

Clarissa glanced at Philip, then over at Jamie, who was wolfing down a mouthful of salmon, completely unconcerned. Her moment of hesitation, however, caught the attention of the others at the table, and she found herself being regarded curiously by seven pairs of eyes. "Well, I suppose I may as well tell you all now as later," she said with a sigh. "Evalyn's gone."

"Gone?" Philip echoed, getting to his feet so precipitously that his chair fell over. "What are you talking about?"

"Here, read this," she said and held out the letter. Philip reached across the table, snatched the letter, and strode to the window, while the unobtrusive Hutton stepped forward from his station behind the buffet and replaced his lordship's chair. Philip turned his back to the room, ignoring the faces staring at him curiously, and read the letter hastily. Then he shook his head in a puzzled manner and read it through more slowly and carefully.

Meanwhile, a babble of voices rose. Everyone in the room demanded of Clarissa some information. Had Evalyn left the house? When? How could she have departed in a snowstorm? Where or to whom had she gone?

"Please," said Clarissa, holding up her hands, "wait until Philip has finished reading her note. Perhaps he—or *someone* in this room"—and she glared at Jamie pointedly—"can make more sense of this than I can."

Jamie, completely puzzled by his aunt's look, asked in sincere confusion, "Why do you look at me so? *I* don't know where she's gone."

Clarissa blinked. Could her nephew be as innocent as he looked? She had been like a mother to the boy since his childhood. He had never lied to her. More confused than ever, she glanced at Philip, but he was still perusing the letter. "Well," she said, avoiding Jamie's eyes, "let's wait until Philip can join the discussion. Meanwhile, shall I open this package? It's a gift from Evalyn. The dear girl evidently fashioned it herself in her spare moments."

Edward stood up and bent over his wife's chair. "Don't you think we might excuse the twins, my dear? I'm sure they would rather be playing with their new toys in the schoolroom than listening to our discussion," he suggested discreetly.

"Oh, yes," agreed his wife. "Would you take them upstairs, Mrs. Noakes?"

"But we would like to hear what happened to Miss Evalyn," Freddie objected promptly, well aware that his father feared that the ensuing discussion might not be suitable for their little ears. Edward frowned at his outspoken son with severity, and the boy lowered his eyes. Mrs. Noakes quickly thrust a load of parcels into his arms and, after a smile and curtsey for the guests, hastily shepherded the boys from the room.

Clarissa opened the parcel and took out the little lacquered box. "Oh, how lovely," she exclaimed, holding it up for the others to see.

"Yes, it is," Martha said admiringly. "May I hold it?" She took the box and turned it lovingly in her hand. "It's so light. I think it's made of *papier-mâché*. I wish she had told me about it. I would have loved to learn the way of making it."

Sally, to whom this latest turn of events was quite a shock, shifted uncomfortably in her chair. Her plans were going all awry. Why had she not considered the possibility that Evalyn's enamelled box might be a gift for someone else?

"Open it," Gervaise urged. "Let's see what it looks like on the inside. I'm fascinated by all the things one can fashion from this interesting material. I hear that Prinny has a coat with *papier-mâché* buttons!"

Clarissa lifted the lid. "It's beautiful," she said, running her fingers over the satin. "She's lined it complete—why, what's this?" Her fingers had felt something hard and sharp beneath the lining. In another second the diamonds were in her hand. She stared at her hand in horror. "Good God!" she breathed. "Sally's diamonds!"

"How on earth did your diamonds get *there*?" Martha asked curiously.

"I have no idea," said Sally cautiously. "I'm as surprised as you are." She glanced at Philip, to see what his reaction was to this latest revelation, but he was staring out of the window, his face pale and his mouth set in a rigid line. He had obviously not heard a word of their conversation.

"Are you sure they are Sally's earrings?" Gervaise was asking. "Why would they be? Have Sally's been missing?"

Clarissa gave Gervaise a nervous glance. "They must be Sally's. Are they, my dear?" she asked. Sally nodded.

Clarissa's hand began to tremble, and she set the diamonds down on the table as if they burned her palm.

"Yes, they're mine," Sally said. "I reported to Clarissa yesterday that they had disappeared."

"Disappeared? You don't mean *stolen*?" asked Gervaise, shocked.

"What else?" Sally said shortly.

"You can't mean it," Reggie said with disapproval.

"I don't see what else it could have been. My maid saw me put them in my jewel case, and I haven't seen them since. Until this moment, that is."

Clarissa gasped. "You're not thinking . . . suggesting . . . that *Evalyn* stole them?"

"I'm not suggesting anything," Sally shrugged. "I'm as much in the dark as everyone else."

The entire assemblage was struck dumb. They stared at the diamonds in dismay. Philip, who had turned to hear Clarissa's outcry, glared at them all and bit back a retort. He must try to remain calm. He was too upset by Evalyn's letter to express his feelings now without giving himself away.

Edward was the first to speak. "The girl *has* run away," he suggested tentatively.

"I see what you mean," Sally said coolly. "The fact that she has run off seems to add substance to the suspicion that she *did* steal them."

A sound came from Philip's throat but went unnoticed in the hubbub Sally's words had aroused. "I don't believe it," Martha declared roundly.

"It'th a ridiculouth idea!" Reggie said firmly.

"If she were the thief," Gervaise asked reasonably, "why would she put the diamonds in Clarissa's gift box, only to give them—and herself—away?"

"Exactly what I was about to point out," Jamie said.

Edward cleared his throat. "I do not for a moment

suggest that Sally is right in her suspicions, but she does have a point. It is possible that Miss Pennington did indeed steal the gems and secrete them in the lining of the box. Then in her haste to leave, she simply forgot to remove them from their hiding place."

Clarissa groaned. "Oh, Edward, no!"

"Edward, that was dreadful of you," his wife snapped.

"There must be many other more plausible explanations than that!" Jamie said staunchly.

"That'th right!" Reggie said loudly, then muttered under his breath, "I wish I could think of one."

Philip, listening from the window in white-lipped fury, could restrain himself no longer. "I cannot believe," he said angrily, "that you can persist in discussing such an impossibility! How can anyone who has been more than five minutes in Miss Pennington's company doubt for a moment her honesty, her sincerity, her forthrightness? You, Edward, do you already forget how she cared for your son during his sickness? And Gervaise, did you not remark to me how impressed you were by her straightforwardness that night we discussed the enfranchisement of the working classes? There's not one of you to whom she has not been generous and helpful. Yet at the first wild, unsubstantiated and quite illogical theory that she may have been guilty of thievery— a thievery we don't even know took place!—you are, none of you, ready to stand up for her character!"

The room was silent. Everyone looked down at his hands. Then Gervaise looked up at his friend. "We all think the world of Miss Pennington, my boy. Yet in our defense, you must admit that she did run away."

"And a thievery *did* take place, did it not?" Sally put in, emboldened by Gervaise's remark to see what she could rescue of her original plan.

"Perhaps it did," Philip retorted curtly. "All we know is

that the diamonds were removed from your box and reappeared in this one. The circumstances, I grant, are strange, but they do not necessarily point to thievery. And at least you have your baubles back." He picked up the diamonds from the table, walked around to Sally and dropped them in her lap. "I shall do what I can to investigate the matter and solve this mystery, but I tell you all here and now that were I to find a witness who claimed to have seen Evalyn *with her hand in Sally's jewel box*, I would not believe she had stolen them! Nor, I think, should anyone with eyes in his head!"

"Hear, hear, Philip!" Clarissa cheered warmly. "I think you're absolutely right!"

"And so do I," Jamie said, smiling proudly at his father.

"Oh, you do, do you?" Philip growled at his son. "It's more than time to have heard something of the sort from you!"

Jamie looked at him in surprise. "What do you mean by that, sir? I don't understand you."

"Then I'll make myself plainer. Accompany me to the study, if you please, if our guests will excuse us."

"No, we won't," said Gervaise with asperity. "We want to know what is in that letter, dashed if we don't. I'm not cowed by your grand manner, my lord, even if everyone else is. Known you too long and too well, so it won't do you any good to get on your high ropes with me. If it weren't to make off with the gems, why *did* the girl take to her heels in weather like this?"

"I wish I could answer that, Gervaise, but I'm as perplexed as you. Perhaps my son will be able to cast some light on the matter. In the meantime, I hope you will all forgive me for getting on my 'high ropes,' as Gervaise puts it. This has been a sorry interruption of our holiday activities. Please try to continue them cheerfully and leave me to deal with these matters." And with an affectionate clap on Gervaise's shoulder, he quickly left the room. Jamie exchanged a puzzled shrug with his friend and followed his father out.

In the hallway, a tense and nervous Nancy stood waiting. "What is it, Nancy?" Philip asked her. "Did you want to see me about something?"

"No, me lord, but Lady Steele said I was to wait. She said ye might be wantin' to ask me some questions."

"As a matter of fact, I do. Did you see the box that Miss Pennington made for Lady Steele?"

"Yes, me lord. I saw it lots of times."

"Did you see what Miss Pennington put inside it?"

"Inside it? You mean the lining?"

"No. Something else."

"I didn't know there *was* anythin' inside it, except the lining."

"Well, there was," Philip said, his eyes fixed on her face. "Miss Trevelyan's diamond earrings were inside it."

Nancy gaped at him. "No, me lord, that can't be! How could they be in Miss *Pennington's* box?"

"That's what we'd like to ascertain," Jamie put in drily.

"What my son means," Philip said, "is that we don't understand either, but they surely were there."

"This ain't making any sense, me lord. I 'elped to wrap the box meself, and there wasn't anythin' inside it. And no one's touched that box but me, ever since Miss Pennington left. Until I give it to Lady Steele, that is."

"It certainly seems strange. Have you ever seen Miss Trevelyan's diamond earrings?"

"No, me lord, I ain't. Unless she was wearing 'em, o' course, but even then I wouldn't reco'nize 'em, not knowing the difference between a diamond and a piece of glass from that there chandelier."

"Have any of the servants ever spoken to you about diamonds, or seemed particularly interested in them?"

"No, me lord. Why would they? None of us'll live long enough to get to own one. And even if we did, what'd be the good? If we wore one, nobody'd believe it was real."

"That may be," said Jamie, "but diamonds can be sold for a good price, and money can be used by anybody."

Nancy looked at him shrewdly. "Are ye saying that Miss Trevelyan's diamonds was copped?"

"She thinks they were stolen, yes," Philip said.

"And then they showed up in Miss Pennington's box?" she asked incredulously.

"So it appears."

"Lord love me! Miss Trevelyan ain't thinking it was *me* that copped 'em, is she?"

"Your name wasn't mentioned," Philip assured her.

"Praise be for that!" she said, relieved. Then her eyes opened wide and she grew pale. "She surely wouldn't suspicion Miss *Evalyn*!" she asked, horrified. The two men didn't answer but just stood watching her. "Oh, me lord, not *you*! Miss Trevelyan, she ain't got eyes for anyone but her own self, but you . . . well, everyone below is always saying 'ow ye're up to the mark and nobody could tip you a rise. You can't believe such a thing! Why, anyone knowin' Miss Evalyn would swear she could no more do such a thing than cut her 'and off!"

Philip's tense face relaxed a trifle, and he patted the girl's shoulder. "Good girl, Nancy. I'm quite of the same mind. We'll talk no more of this diamond business now. But what I can't understand is how a plucky girl like you could have let your mistress go away in a snowstorm, without a word to us."

Nancy hung her head. "There wasn't nothing I could do.

She was plumb set on it. She was so 'eart broke, I couldn't argue."

"Heart broke? What do you mean?"

"Someone must've 'urt her some way. She wouldn't say 'ow."

Philip glared at his son, but the boy was looking at Nancy with completely innocent interest. He showed not a sign of guilt or misgiving.

"But how did she go, Nancy?" Jamie was asking. "She couldn't have *walked* in such weather."

"I can't say, me lord."

"Can't say, or won't?" Philip asked sternly.

Nancy kept her face lowered and her eyes on her shoes.

"Listen to me, girl, and listen carefully," Philip said to her warningly. "I know you think you're being loyal to Miss Pennington, but if she's lost or without shelter somewhere out there in that storm, you won't help her by keeping secrets. Now you sit down over there and think it over, while I have a little talk with my son. Come, Jamie."

With those grim words, he stalked off to the study, Jamie following at his heels. "Close the door and sit down," he said, between clenched teeth. Jamie looked at him perplexed. He had never seen his father so agitated. He was pacing in front of the fire in angry strides, his mouth set in a hard line.

"I don't think you need worry so about Miss Pennington," Jamie offered, sitting down gingerly on the edge of a wing chair. "She's quite able to take care of herself. She's really a redoubtable girl, you know."

"So you've told me repeatedly," his father said curtly. "You amaze me, Jamie. I find your lack of concern completely baffling."

"I'm not lacking in concern, sir. I'll feel much more

comfortable about Evalyn when I hear she's safe and sound."

"Safe and sound?" Philip asked in a voice heavy with sarcasm. "And how do you propose to get that news? By post, next spring, if the lady should honor you with a letter?"

"Well, I suppose that's one way," Jamie said, nonplussed. "Or I may hear about her from friends, or one way or another."

Philip groaned. "Does it occur to you that perhaps you should go to look for her, to make *sure* she's safe and sound?"

"Go to look for her?" asked Jamie, standing up in surprise. "In this snow? But why? If she chose to leave, I don't see what I can do about it."

"Confound it! What sort of a man are you?" Philip shouted, pushing Jamie back into the chair. "I never thought to hear my own son talk like a loose screw, and a cowardly one at that! Don't you feel any responsibility for her at all?"

"Responsibility? But why?"

"Why? *Why*? Need I tell you why? You brought her here, filled her with high expectations, and then you proceeded to ignore and humiliate her in every possible way! Finally, the poor girl could bear it no longer and ran away. And you have the effrontery to stand there and ask why you should feel responsible?"

"Hang it, sir, you're talking utter balderdash!" said Jamie, jumping up from his seat again. "I don't mean to be disrespectful, but your notions sound positively gothic! I know I brought her here, but I didn't think you'd expect me to dance attendance upon her, or entertain her! Nor do I think she expected any such thing!"

Philip stared at his son in amazement. "Gothic?" he

exclaimed. "Sit down, you fool! You think I'm behaving like a gothic father when I expect my son to treat the woman he is going to marry with some affection?"

Jamie gaped at his father stupidly. "Marry? *Me?*"

"Yes, you! How can you ask a girl to marry you when you haven't the least notion how to go on in such circumstances?" Philip ranted, too preoccupied with his outrage to comprehend his son's reactions.

"I think you must be foxed!" Jamie gasped. "What on earth made you think that Miss Pennington and I were to be *married*?"

Philip stopped his pacing and fixed his eyes on his son's bewildered face. "You told me so yourself," he said sharply. "You told me so the evening of the day you arrived home."

"One of us must be touched in his upper works!" Jamie exclaimed angrily, jumping to his feet a third time. "I never could have told you anything so preposterous!"

"I see nothing preposterous about it! I couldn't have misunderstood you. I remember it distinctly. You said . . . you said that you and Miss Pennington had an understanding . . . or some such phrase. Didn't you?"

Jamie shrugged. "I may have said something of the sort. Evalyn and I did have a kind of understanding. . . ."

"Aha! Then I didn't misunderstand." He glared at his son impatiently. "I told you to sit down!" he growled.

"I *won't* sit down! Not until we have this thing cleared up. If you think our understanding—Evalyn's and mine—had to do with marriage, you're out in your reckoning!"

"Well, what sort of understanding did you have?"

"It had to do with helping her to find a new post."

"A new *post*? What can you mean . . . ?" His breath caught in his throat. "You mean you never had any plans to *marry*?"

"Marry? Of course not! How could you *think* such a thing?"

Philip had the distinct sensation that the floor lurched under his feet. He put his hand to his forehead. "Pardon me, Jamie, but I'm beginning to feel too old for all this. Let's both sit down."

"I'm sorry about all this, father. If I'd known what trouble she would cause, I'd have left her on the Carberys' doorstep," Jamie said, returning to his chair.

"No, no," said Philip, sitting down opposite Jamie and leaning back wearily. "You could not have left her there. You've behaved quite well. I see that now. It's *I* who— Good Lord, what have I done?"

"Done?" Jamie asked bewildered. "I don't see how you can blame yourself for Evalyn's behavior."

But Philip understood at last. He had taken her in his arms and had seen her look up at him with that innocent face full of warmth and joy and trust, and he had thrust her aside. The recollection made him wince in pain.

"What is it, sir? What have *you* to do with this coil?" Jamie asked.

Philip shook his head. "I've been unbelievably stupid," he said in a constricted voice, "and caused all this hobble myself."

"Does it have something to do with the diamonds?" asked Jamie, utterly confused.

"Hang the diamonds! Of course not! I'll wager anything you like that Evalyn doesn't know a thing about them."

"Then what hobble are you speaking of?"

"The only hobble that concerns me—that she's run away." He got up and paced the room again. "Tell me, Jamie," he asked more quietly, "did Evalyn—Miss Pennington—understand why she was brought here? She could not have misinterpreted your intentions as I did, could she?"

"No, not possibly. I explained the whole plan to her quite carefully."

"Plan? Just what was this plan?"

"I asked you to invite her here so that she could spend the holidays with us, to permit Aunt Clarissa to get properly acquainted with her. . . ."

"But why? Doesn't that in itself sound like the plans of a bridegroom—to permit his family to become acquainted with his prospective bride?"

"I assure you that *that* aspect never occurred to either of us. Evalyn knew why I wanted Aunt Clarissa to know her. She had been discharged without recommendation, and I wanted my aunt to write one for her. In fact, we hoped that Aunt Clarissa would know of a household where Evalyn's services might be needed."

"I see. And that was *all* that was between you?"

"That was the whole of it."

"I . . . er . . . dislike to pry into your private affairs, Jamie, but I must know. Are you quite sure . . . without any doubt at all . . . that you are not . . . in love with Miss Pennington?"

Jamie laughed. "I'm dashed if you don't sound exactly like Reggie!"

"Like Reggie? What on earth do you mean?"

"Not two days past, he asked me the very same question about Marianne!"

"Marianne? How ridiculous! She's only a child. You couldn't be in love with her."

"Yes, so I told him. But he's in love with her himself, you see, so he . . ." His voice trailed off as an idea hit him with a shock. Could his father, who had seemed so impervious to women all these years, possibly have fallen in love with Evalyn? No, it wasn't possible. Not his father!

"Reggie?" Philip was asking. "In love with Marianne? You can't mean it!"

"Why not? You didn't think it strange for me to be in love with Evalyn, and she's a far less likely girl for either Reggie or me to be taken with."

"I don't see that at all. Marianne is only seventeen, a mere child. Whereas Evalyn—"

"Evalyn must be *years* older than I," Jamie declared, his eyes fixed on his father's face with a penetrating gleam.

"She's twenty-two," his father said with some asperity. "Exactly your age."

"Oh, *is* she?" Jamie asked innocently. "Well, perhaps she's not old, exactly, but she seems so to me. As I assured Reggie, I'm not in the petticoat line, but even if I were, Miss Pennington wouldn't be at all my style. Too serious by half."

"Rubbish! She has an irrepressible sense of humor."

"Does she, sir?" asked Jamie with a mischievous twinkle. "How clever of you to have observed it."

Philip shot a glance at his son, caught the look and reddened to his ears. "Never mind, jackanapes," he said with a rueful grin. "I'll brook no disrespectful quips about Miss Pennington or myself. A whisky-frisky, greenheaded, rope-ripe court-card like you cannot be expected to appreciate the qualities of a lady like Evalyn. I dread to think of the platter-faced, addle-brained fidget you'll eventually bring home to marry."

Jamie grinned broadly and jumped to his feet. "Well, whoever she is, sir, she couldn't be half the woman you've chosen," he said, wringing his father's hand with enthusiasm. "I must be a greenhead not to have noticed before that you and Miss Pennington are perfectly suited."

"Don't fly into the boughs too soon," Philip said, getting up from his chair and crossing to the wide window behind the desk. "Now that I understand the circumstances, I am painfully aware that it was my own stupidity that drove her from this house. She must be found! There will be time later to determine whether *she* thinks we're suited."

"You're right, of course," Jamie agreed, his smile fading. "I'll ride out immediately. If we're lucky, she'll not have got beyond Ashwater."

"Take a damper, boy!" said his father firmly. "Who asked you to go?"

"You did, not five minutes ago. The flattering names you called me are still ringing in my ears. A cowardly loose-screw, I think you said. And quite right, too."

Philip came quickly to Jamie and put his hands on the boy's shoulders. "Forgive me for that, Jamie. It's been bellows to mend with me ever since I laid eyes on the girl. I thought it was you who had driven her away, but of course, that isn't the case. So go back to our guests and forget what I said. I'd be much obliged if you would."

"Would you indeed?" said Jamie mockingly. "And what's to become of Miss Pennington, out there in God knows what kind of scrape? I refused to go before, because I thought it was none of my business, but that's not true any more. So I think I should set out at once, don't you?"

"Am I to understand by those remarks that you think your father too old and doddering to ride out in the snow?"

"Cut line! You did ask me before, did you not?"

"Only because I thought it was your responsibility. Now, I am happy to say, it is mine, and I intend to see to it. So if you'll excuse me, I'll get started." And he walked swiftly to the door. With his hand on the knob, he hesitated. Slowly, he turned back to his son. "Jamie," he said soberly, "this matter is too serious for hoaxing. Please be straight with me. Are you absolutely *sure* you're not in love with Evalyn yourself?"

"Oh, I love her!" Jamie replied with a wide grin. "I truly do. But only as a mother, I assure you, sir. Only as a mother!"

· Eighteen ·

NANCY HAD TAKEN to biting her nails again. She had not done it since she was a child, but sitting here in the hall waiting for his lordship to reappear had made her so nervous that she found herself chewing them. Three nails had already been badly reduced, and she was starting on a fourth when the study door opened and Lord Gyllford emerged. She jumped to her feet and made an awkward curtsey.

"Well, girl, have you thought it over? Who took Miss Pennington from the house last evening?" Philip asked curtly.

Nancy hung her head in misery. "Can't say, me lord. I promised," she mumbled.

"It's a bad promise, Nancy, but I'll not press you further. I think I can guess the answer to that question. I want you to get Joseph and that other girl—what's her name?—Miss Trevelyan's maid."

"Annette?"

"Yes. All three of you are to be in my study in half an hour. Meanwhile, where is Lady Steele? Is she still in the breakfast room?"

"No, me lord. She went to her room. I heard her say she had the headache and wanted to lie down."

Philip nodded and strode quickly to the stairs. "Remember, Nancy, all three of you in half an hour," he called over his shoulder and took the stairs two at a time.

Clarissa answered his knock in a feeble voice. He found her stretched out on her bed, a cold cloth across her eyes. "I told you I don't need you, Mathilda," she said querulously, without looking up. "I'll do very well if I'm left alone."

"If you mean that, my dear," Philip said teasingly, "I'll take my leave and disturb you no further."

"Philip!" Clarissa cried eagerly, sitting up and pulling the cloth from her eyes. She snatched at his sleeve and pulled him down beside her. "Don't you *dare* to leave! You know I didn't mean you! It's my wretched abigail. Mathilda insists on hovering over me whenever she suspects I'm in the least indisposed. It's enough to give one a fit of the dismals. But never mind that. I've been beside myself waiting for you to finish talking with Jamie. What did he say? Has he quarrelled with Evalyn? Did he give you any information at all? Tell me quickly."

Philip patted her soothingly on her shoulder. "He gave me all the information I needed. Prepare yourself for a shock, my dear. Jamie hasn't engaged to marry Evalyn at all."

Clarissa gaped at him. "What are you saying? They broke it off?"

"No, there never has been anything between them. It was all my fault, I'm afraid. I leapt to the wrong conclusion when he and I had that talk the night he arrived. I simply misunderstood what he told me."

Clarissa could not grasp his words. "You couldn't have misunderstood! Not on such a matter as that," she said, bewildered. "Besides, he wrote to me about it himself, before they arrived!"

"I remember the letter you speak of. Think back carefully, Clarissa. He only wrote to ask us to invite a young lady to spend the holidays with us, isn't that so?"

Clarissa frowned, trying to remember. "Yes, I suppose that's true. But even so—"

"There really was nothing in that letter to make us assume he wanted to marry her," Philip pointed out.

"I disagree completely!" Clarissa declared roundly. "How can you say so? A man can't bring a girl home for no purpose! Why else would he want her here?"

"As it turns out, his reason was quite altruistic and impersonal. He wanted you to become acquainted with her so that you would think well enough of her to find her a post."

"A post? What can you mean?"

Philip had to grin at his sister's utter confusion. "Our dear Jamie was being gallant," he explained. "Evalyn had been discharged without a character, and Jamie and Reg wanted to help her. You were to be the instrument of that help."

"I?"

"Of course. It's quite logical, really. You could not have recommended a *stranger* to one of your friends, but they felt sure that once you grew to know Evalyn, you would have no qualms about recommending her."

"I was to help her find a post as governess? Is that why they brought her here? Then why didn't the idiots *tell* us?"

"They did. But we had our minds so set on marriage plans and grandchildren and such, we didn't hear them."

"Oh, Philip," Clarissa moaned, putting her face in her hands, "it's all *my* fault. I was the one who put that nonsense into your head."

"I'm the one who interviewed Jamie when he arrived. And I'm the one who didn't listen to what he tried to tell me. Not that it signifies. There's no point in attaching blame."

Clarissa stood up and began to pace about the room, trying to adjust her mind to this new surprise. "Poor

Evalyn," she sighed. "She must have thought me completely buffleheaded. I never once discussed finding her a post." She stopped in front of Philip and put her hand to her forehead in confusion. "Philip, nothing as yet makes sense to me. If Jamie didn't drive her away, why did she leave?"

Philip looked down at his hands. "That's the most difficult part I have to tell you. Sit down here with me, will you?"

She looked at him worriedly and dropped down beside him on the edge of the bed. "Is it very awful? Oh, Philip, I don't think I can *bear* it if you're going to tell me she took the diamonds—or something equally dreadful."

Philip made an impatient gesture. "Can't anyone forget those blasted diamonds? I tell you Evalyn had nothing to do with them!"

"Then what is it you have to tell me?"

"Clarissa," he said hesitantly, "I'm very much afraid that it was I who drove her away."

"You? Rubbish! I'll never believe that. What could you have done?"

"You'll think me a sorry specimen, I'm afraid," he said, getting up and going to the window. He stared out, unseeing, at the snow and the leaden sky. "My behavior has been utterly reprehensible," he went on in a lowered voice. "I convinced myself that she was playing some sort of deep game—I scarcely know how to explain it to you. But I offended her—hurt her badly, I'm afraid, and I think that's why she left."

Clarissa looked at her brother, a puzzled crease between her brows. He was speaking so strangely—so unlike himself. "My dear," she suggested gently, "perhaps you had better start at the very beginning. This isn't making any sense to me at all."

He turned, a strange, self-mocking smile curling his

mouth. "It will all become clear when I tell you that I fell head-over-heels in love with her like the veriest schoolboy."

"In love—! Philip!"

"Shocking, isn't it? At my age? And with a girl who I thought was to become my son's wife! You can imagine my sense of guilt, and the torture I endured. I was furious with myself. The more I grew to know her, the less able I was to control my feelings. But more disturbing to me than anything else was *her* attitude. You know, I've never thought of myself as a coxcomb, Clarissa, yet I was convinced that she responded to my feelings."

Clarissa drew in her breath. She could hardly believe what she was hearing. Philip looked at her in quick understanding. "No, no, you must not think that anything passed between us that was not within the bounds of the strictest propriety. It was just . . . the warmth she seemed to exude when we spoke . . . or the way her mind and mine seemed attuned. I would have been a fool not to have noticed. Yet she had accepted *Jamie's* offer—or so I thought! I could not understand what her motives were. I even suspected her of playing a double game—like an adventuress—holding out for the biggest matrimonial prize!"

"An adventuress! Oh, Philip, no!"

"Was there ever a greater, more puffed-up coxcomb than I?" he asked, the self-mocking sneer more pronounced. "Can you bear to hear the rest?"

"I couldn't bear *not* to. Please go on."

He turned back to the window. "The day before yesterday—well, I cannot tell you what passed between us, but I suddenly realized that I had gone too far and . . . let me just say that I hurt her. I had determined to ignore her—to cut her if necessary—so that I wouldn't be tempted to any disloyalty to my son. I assumed, of course, that she would understand why I had done it. But how could she have understood, knowing nothing of the misconception that had misled me? I wonder what the poor girl thought of my behavior. Good God! What else can she have thought but that I had found her beneath my touch?"

Philip fell silent. Clarissa, too moved to say a word, watched him wide-eyed. Finally, Philip turned from the window. "Have I shocked you beyond words?" he asked with a rueful grimace.

Clarissa shook her head. "Do you care for her enough to . . . to think of *marriage*?"

"I daren't think of it. But I *dream* of nothing else," Philip answered in his tone of self-derision.

"Oh, my dear, how blind I've been," she sighed, her ready tears spilling over.

Philip came quickly to sit beside her. "I was afraid this would upset you," he said, taking out his handkerchief and wiping her eyes.

"I'm sorry to be such a watering-pot, but to think of you in love at last is quite overwhelming. How could it have happened without my noticing?" She smiled up at him, amusement shining through the tearful eyes. "When I think of how I've contrived, arranged and schemed! How I've trotted out every girl I could find to parade before your eyes! And then you, without any help from anyone, find for yourself the *perfect* girl!"

"But, Clarissa, I've made such a mull of it!"

"Yes, you have. So you must find her and make it right."

"I must find her, of course. I couldn't rest without knowing that she's somewhere safe and well. That's why I've told you all this, my dear. I mean to leave right away, if you think you can spare me from your Christmas dinner. And Boxing Day tomorrow, if need be."

"Heavens! For a moment I'd forgotten all about Christ-

mas and our guests and everything. Well, I can muddle
through the festivities without you, I expect, though your
absence will be awkward to explain."

"Just tell them the truth—that I've gone to find Evalyn."

"Very well, I suppose that will be best. But I cannot like
your going out in this storm. Do you think it wise?"

"I must go, Clarissa. I think I'd go mad if I had to sit
about here at home, worrying about her out there in this
storm—alone, perhaps without funds, in who knows what
sort of fix. . . ."

"Yes, of course you must go," she agreed, slipping an
arm about his waist and leaning her head on his shoulder.
"Oh, how happy we all shall be when you come back with
her! She'll make a wonderful wife for you, Philip. I won't
have a care left in the world!"

"Silly widgeon," Philip said fondly, "ten to one she
won't have me. After all, she's half my age!"

"Well, you're out there!" she assured him with a tremulous, sparkling smile. "You're the *perfect* age for a
husband—Evalyn told me *that* herself! Go and find her
quickly, and bring her back to us!"

Joseph, Annette, and Nancy waited in the study nervously,
not speaking. Each was reluctant to voice to the others the
fear that they would all find themselves without employment before the day was out. None of them could face with
equanimity this dire prospect. None of them had the faintest
idea of where to go or what to do if present employment
were to cease. Joseph had of course told Annette that he had
driven Miss Pennington into Ashwater. Annette's feeling of
loyalty toward the lady who had saved Joseph's life was as
strong as his, and she fully supported him in his action in
Miss Pennington's behalf. There was nothing any of them
would not have done for Miss Pennington. Whatever the

consequences, they, all of them, were agreed that they had done the right thing, and they would face whatever punishment was meted out. But they were far from joyful at the prospect.

Philip entered the room purposefully. Although he noticed the frightened expressions, he did not permit himself to soften his glare as he looked at each one of them in turn. "Well, which one of you is going to tell me what happened?" he asked sternly. "I want a complete and honest account, with no roundaboutation, if you please."

Nancy resorted to gazing at her feet. Annette made a movement of her hands indicating that she meant to make a complete denial of any wrongdoing. Joseph stayed her with a gesture. "Might as well make a clean breast of it, my lord," he shrugged. "You must've guessed it anyway, or you wouldn't have us here."

"I surmised that it was you who conveyed Miss Pennington to her destination. But I want to know the how and the where."

"I . . . er . . . borrowed the curricule, my lord. At the lady's request, it was. About six in the evening, yesterday. She asked me to take her to Ashwater."

"Ashwater? Why Ashwater? Did she tell you her plans?"

Nancy looked up and stuck out her jaw belligerently. "Don't tell 'im, Joseph. Miss Evalyn didn't want 'im to know, or she would've told 'im 'erself. You can sack us, me lord, but we ain't goin' to tell ye anythin' more. We ain't goin' to help you find 'er and turn her over to the magistrates."

Joseph and Annette turned to her in surprise. "What's this about magistrates?" Joseph asked, looking from Nancy to Lord Gyllford in perplexity.

"I don't know what you're talking about, girl," Philip said impatiently.

"Don't think ye can pull wool over me eyes so easy," Nancy declared bravely. "Why else would ye be lookin' for 'er, if not to turn 'er over? Ye're thinkin' she took them diamonds, ain't you!"

"Diamonds?" asked Joseph, completely confused. "What diamonds?"

"Damn it, I wish I had never heard the word diamonds!" Philip said in disgust. "Will you forget about the trumpery things? They have absolutely nothing to do with my desire to find Miss Pennington."

"Well, then, what do ye want to find 'er for?" Nancy asked challengingly.

Annette and Joseph listened to her with openmouthed dismay. Philip merely frowned.

"I'll overlook your impertinence, young woman, because of your loyalty to Miss Pennington, which I cannot help but admire. As for the answer to your question, I've already given you all the answer you're going to get. Must I explain again that Miss Pennington may be stranded somewhere in this storm, destitute and friendless? Don't you want her to have help if she needs it?"

Nancy's eyes wavered, and she twisted her fingers in indecision.

"There ain't any need to worry about her, my lord," Joseph put in. "She can't have left the Bull, not in weather like this."

"Is that where she went? To the Bull? What did she intend to do then?" Philip asked quickly.

Joseph looked at Nancy for guidance, but the girl was no longer so sure she should restrain Joseph from answering. She gave a helpless shrug. Joseph faced his employer squarely. "She was going to hire a hack for Launceston."

"Launceston? Whatever for?"

"The Exeter stage leaves from there," Joseph explained.

"Oh, I see. And the London stage from Exeter, I presume. I think that's all I need now. Unless, of course, there's anything else you can think of that will help me find her."

"No, no, my lord. There's nothing else I know," Joseph said.

Philip turned to Nancy. "Come here to me, girl," he said, a little more kindly. "Look at me closely—not at the floor. There. Now, Nancy, I want you to believe that I mean no harm to your mistress. You have my word. Do you believe me?"

Nancy glanced up at him, looked down quickly and nodded.

"Good, then. Now, I want you to think carefully. Did Miss Pennington tell you anything about her ultimate destination? Did she tell you where, or to whom, she was going?"

"No, me lord, nothin'. She never said nothing about anyone she knew away from 'ere."

"She never mentioned any relatives? Or anyone she might be acquainted with in London?"

"No, me lord."

"Very well then, I'll be off." He crossed to the door quickly, and then looked back at them. "I needn't remind you, I suppose, that this matter is not to be talked of among the staff."

"You can trust us, my lord," Joseph assured him. "We won't say a word."

"Good. Then you may go back to your duties," his lordship said abruptly.

"Our . . . duties . . . ?" Joseph asked in surprise. But his lordship was gone.

Annette threw her arms about Joseph's neck. "He didn't give us . . . how you say? . . . the sack!"

"It's a bloomin' miracle," Joseph said, staring at the door. "Twice, now, he's had cause to send us packing, and twice he's let the matter pass." He looked at the door and shook his head. "But I feel in my bones we'd best not try him a third time."

"I only 'ope," sighed Nancy worriedly, "that we ain't served Miss Evalyn a back-'anded turn."

Annette's brow puckered. "The diamonds you are thinking of, *non?* I too am not—how you say?—easy in my mind. There is something about the business I cannot like."

"What are you talking about? What is all this about diamonds?" Joseph demanded.

"Oh, *chérie*, I have not related to you the events. Ma'm'selle's earrings, they have disappeared."

"That's not all," Nancy added. "They showed up again—"

"This I did not know," said Annette, surprised. "Where?"

"In the box Miss Evalyn made for Lady Steele!"

Annette gaped. "How can this be?"

"The whole thing 'as me fair bamboozled. I was with Miss Evalyn when she wrapped the box, an' there was no diamonds in it. The box stayed with me 'til I give it to Lady Steele. Next thing I know, his lordship is asking me 'ow the diamonds got there!"

"It is of all things the most perplexing," said Annette thoughtfully. "I remember thinking that Ma'm'selle was up to something when she told me to watch her put those earrings away. She was most strange. But I cannot think what she intended."

Joseph looked at Annette intently. "Who discovered that the diamonds was copped?"

"Me, myself," Annette said.

"Did Miss Trevelyan accuse you?" he asked.

"No, she did not. I was much surprised. But she said it would be stupid of me to do it."

Joseph rubbed his chin speculatively. "When was it you discovered they were gone?"

"*Hier* . . . yesterday. When she came up to dress for dinner."

"Yesterday, eh? Did she have 'em the night before?"

"I did not think to look. She said she did not want to wear any jewels. This in itself is most strange."

"But why are ye asking these questions?" Nancy asked. "Do ye know something o' this?"

"I do recollect something that might—" He turned to Annette and said reproachfully, "I wish you'd told me about the diamonds before."

"I did not think of it. As long as I was not—how you say *soupçonné?*—in suspicion, the matter went from my head."

"But tell us quick," Nancy urged Joseph impatiently. "What is it that you know?"

"I don't know if what I saw is important or not. But I was in Miss Trevelyan's dressing room. Day before yesterday, it was. She'd gone out riding—remember, Annette, when you told me to come up to her room?"

Annette clapped her hands to her cheeks. "Oh, but yes! And she returned early and I had to go to her and left you in the dressing room. . . ."

Nancy looked from one to the other in disgust. "Don't tell me ye got yerselves in that same fix! What'd ye do? Climb out the window again?"

"Not me!" Joseph said with a snort. "You'll not catch me like that again! I crawled into the commode!"

"The commode?"

"It was the only place I could find to hide in! A tight squeeze it was, too. I couldn't even get the door closed. I was shaking so much I thought the bowl and pitcher on top would begin to rattle. Well, to get on with it, Miss Trevelyan comes in and goes to the dressing table, takes out the diamonds and looks at 'em in the light. Then she hides the key—I couldn't see proper where—and goes out. But I see before she goes out the door, that she drops the diamonds down her bosom. I thought it was a bit peculiar, but then she went out, and I was so happy to make me escape, I didn't think no more on it . . . 'til now, that is."

"*Mon dieu*, I see it all! From the first Ma'm'selle takes a dislike to Miss Evalyn. She put the earrings in Miss Evalyn's box. She sent me away that day, telling me she was tired. Tired, pooh! She hides the diamonds in her bosom, steals into Miss Evalyn's room and hides them there."

Nancy chewed an already well-bitten nail thoughtfully. "I would say you've gotten to the bottom of it except . . . "

"Except?"

"Except that something ain't right. If, as Joseph says, Miss Trevelyan took the diamonds in the afternoon, how is it that there was no diamonds in the box that night when Miss Evalyn and I wrapped it up?"

"You make too much the *logique* for me. I do not care for so much reasoning. I know Ma'm'selle has made this trouble, because I feel it here!" And she pointed to her heart with a passionate gesture.

"I ain't disagreeing with you," Nancy assured her. "It's the only thing what makes any sense at all."

Joseph sank into the nearest chair. "If you both feel that way, we're back in the soup again," he groaned.

"In the soup? *Je ne comprends pas*. Why?"

"Because I'll have to tell his lordship what I saw. And when he hears how I came to see it, well—" Joseph shrugged hopelessly.

"We should say nothing perhaps?" Annette suggested in

a tone that plainly indicated she hoped her suggestion would not be taken.

"I think we should tell 'em," Nancy said. "If we could clear Miss Evalyn's name, it'd surely be a satisfaction to me."

"And if Ma'm'selle had to pay for some of her mischief, it would be a satisfaction to me of the most enormous," Annette agreed with a wicked grin.

"I hope that satisfaction will keep you both warm when we're out in the snow," Joseph sighed and pushed himself to his feet. "Well, then, let's try to catch his lordship before he leaves the house."

Philip, dressed in his riding clothes, was almost out the door when they stopped him. "I'm sure that whatever it is you have to tell me can wait," he said to them, impatient to be off.

"I think you'll find it important, my lord," Joseph said. "I remembered something I think you'll want to know."

Philip stopped. "About Miss Pennington?" he asked.

"Well, not exactly." And Joseph hastily recounted what he had seen in Miss Trevelyan's dressing room. "And Nancy and Annette, here, are convinced that Miss Trevelyan, not being overly fond o' Miss Evalyn, did it herself, to get Miss Evalyn in a mess o' trouble."

"There's only one thing that don't fit," Nancy said in her unquenchably honest way. "I still don't see 'ow the diamonds got into the box when they wasn't there when Miss Evalyn and me wrapped it."

Philip clenched his teeth and his eyes grew hard. "They were there, Nancy. You and Miss Pennington just didn't know it. They had been slipped into the lining."

The three exchanged glances while Philip sought to control the furious anger welling inside him. His instincts urged him to burst in on Sally and give her the tongue lashing she richly deserved. But she wasn't worth the time—precious time that would keep him even longer from finding Evalyn. No, he'd leave the handling of Sally to his sister. He turned to Joseph. "I want you to tell the whole story to Lady Steele right away. She will know what to do."

"The whole story . . . ?" Joseph gasped.

"Yes, of course. Why not?" Philip asked impatiently.

"Well . . . you see, sir . . . she's bound to ask how I came to be hiding in the commode. . . ."

Philip's lips twitched. "Indeed she will. And when she learns of your behavior, she may well be much less lenient than I've been, is that it?"

Joseph nodded glumly.

"If she gave you the sack, it would be no more than you deserve. We cannot have our household staff carrying on in such a manner. And you had been warned before, after all." He looked at the three of them, miserably staring at the floor, and a laugh broke out of him. "Come now, cheer up. After all. Lady Steele doesn't know that you've been in this fix before. Besides, I think I've a solution to this hank. Annette, you give notice to Miss Treveylan right away, and tell Lady Steele to see that you and Joseph are married as soon as possible. Maybe that will restore some respectability to this disreputable household."

And with that he was out the door, leaving the three rascals dancing about the hallway in joyous abandon.

· *Nineteen* ·

PHILIP FOUND THE trip to Ashwater more than he bargained for. The northerly wind blew in his face with biting force, the swirling snowflakes almost blinding him. His horse could only pick his way slowly through the more than three feet of snow that had accumulated during the storm. Sometimes the drifts were so high that Philip had to guide the beast completely around them. The only comfort he could derive from the dreadful action of the elements was the certainty that Evalyn could not have left the inn at Ashwater in such weather. As the few miles separating them slowly lessened, his spirits rose despite the irritation caused by freezing ears and shivering limbs.

It had grown dark by the time he arrived at Ashwater. The lights of the Bull showed through the swirling snow like a welcoming beacon. He was overwhelmed with a boyish eagerness to dash into the inn and seize her in his arms without a moment's delay. But there was no sign of an ostler to care for his horse, and no answer to his call. He led the horse to the stable himself and reined in his impatience while he tended to the animal's needs. It was an endless half-hour later that he at last entered the taproom of the Bull.

The room was deserted. The fire was dying in the fireplace and no candles burned on the tables or the bar.

"Hello?" he called, somewhat dismayed. "Ho, innkeeper!"

A light appeared at the back of the room as a door opened and Mr. Fern emerged, blinking his eyes in surprise. "Who's there?" he asked, peering into the darkness.

"I'm here to see Miss Pennington," said Philip impatiently. "Please go up to her room and ask her to step down here to see me."

Mr. Fern had by this time come close enough to recognize who the unexpected traveler was. "Blimey, it's Lord Gyllford! Please, yer lordship, won't you sit down? It's been more'n six years since you last honored us like this! Please, sir, take this chair. I'll have the fire going in a trice. I never expected to see a soul tonight, I can tell you."

"Thank you," Philip said with forced politeness, "but I am most eager to see Miss Pennington. I'd be much obliged if you'd forego the amenities and take my message to her right away."

"I'd be glad to oblige, me lord, but there ain't nobody here by that name. I ain't seen a living soul this day, except for Mrs. Fern, o'course."

Philip couldn't believe his ears. "There must be some mistake. She arrived yesterday. Perhaps she kept to her room all day today."

"No, me lord, I mislike to contradict you, but there ain't a single guest in the house."

"Are you sure, man? I was told she was put down here last evening. Surely she can't have gone away from here in this storm."

"If you're meaning the young lady what had dinner here last night, she's gone."

"Gone! How can that be?"

A sudden flood of light turned both their heads to the source. Mrs. Fern entered with a large branch of lighted candles. "What're you doing, talking in the dark?" she asked, coming toward them. At the sight of Philip, she stopped and stared.

"Good evening, ma'am," Philip said absently. Mrs. Fern made an eager curtsey, her face growing pink at the honor of welcoming the greatest nobleman of the district.

"A most happy Christmas to you, me lord," she said in an awed whisper.

"His lordship's asking for the young lady what came here last night," the innkeeper told her. "I was just explaining that she up and left without a word."

"It's true, me lord," nodded the woman. "I was that surprised, I can tell you, when I'd found she'd gone. Though who she could've found to take her to Launceston through all that snow I can't imagine."

"She went to Launceston?" Philip asked tensely. "Are you sure?"

"Well, we couldn't say for sure where she went. I told her there was no one we knowed who'd be fool enough to go off on an errand like that," Mrs. Fern explained.

Philip sank into the chair the innkeeper still held for him. The sense of anticipation which had buoyed up his spirits on the ride now evaporated, and he was left benumbed in mind and body. He shook his head and tried to think purposefully. "Are you sure it is Miss Pennington of whom you speak?" he asked.

"There was only one young lady came here last night. Must've been her."

"A slim, dark-haired lady with grey eyes?"

"That's the one," the innkeeper said with assurance.

"And you have no idea whom she may have hired to drive her to Launceston?"

"No, me lord, none. Why, if Sam'l wouldn't take her, there's no one within miles who would!"

"Samuel?" asked his lordship. "Who is he? Was he here last evening?"

"Comes in every evening, does Sam'l. Wouldn't surprise me none if he come in tonight! A bang-up driver is Sam'l, old as he is, and knows all the roads hereabouts."

"Did he talk to Miss Pennington? Are you sure he didn't take her to Launceston after all? Perhaps she persuaded him."

"Couldn't have. He was still here after the lady was gone. And as for talking, it ain't likely. It's hard to get a word out o' him. Just sits and drinks his brew, with hardly a word to anyone."

"I see. Nevertheless, I should like to question him. You say he may come in tonight?"

"Wouldn't surprise me a bit, me lord."

"Even in this weather?"

"He only lives a few steps down the lane. If you're wishful to see him, I'll bundle up and get him for you."

"Thank you, but if you give me his direction, I'll go myself," Philip said rising.

"I'll not hear of it, me lord," said Mrs. Fern in motherly solicitude. "Your coat is damp, your hair is wet, and look at those boots—soaked through they are! You'll not stir from this inn, if I've anything to say. You'll sit here while I get the fire going. A rum toddy and a bit o' food's what you need now."

"Be still, woman," muttered her husband. "Watch how you talk to his lordship! But there's good sense in what she says, me lord."

"Yes, there is. Thank you, ma'am. Well, then, Mr. Fern, if you'll bring your friend Samuel to me, I shall be most grateful."

At Gyllford, the Christmas dinner was promising to be an awkward occasion. The snow would keep the neighbors who usually gathered for the occasion close to their own firesides, making the meal almost a family affair. Clarissa knew that Philip's absence would be sorely felt, and the mystery of the diamonds and Evalyn's disappearance would hang like a cloud over the evening's proceedings. But one shining bit of joyous news would help her to face the dinner with a light heart—Philip was in love and, with any luck, would be married soon. She knew she should not mention the business to a soul, but she longed to share the news with Gervaise. As Christmas afternoon wore on, she felt she must find him and tell him, or she would burst. Edward and Martha had gone to the nursery to play with the twins and their new Christmas toys; Reggie and Marianne were playing billiards with Sally and Jamie. Clarissa had a good idea where Gervaise was to be found.

She peeped into the library. There he was in a wing chair before the fire, a handkerchief spread over his face, fast asleep. With a sigh of frustration, she turned to let herself quietly out of the room, too shy to wake him up with such news. But just as she put her hand on the knob, he stirred.

"Hmm? Wha'? Who is it?" he mumbled, pulling his handkerchief from his face and blinking.

"I'm sorry to have disturbed you, Gervaise dear. But I'm glad you woke up. I . . . I've been dying to tell you something that I think will please you enormously."

Gervaise had been about to yawn, but the expression on her face caught his interest completely and brought him fully awake. "Well, then, no need to apologize. Sit here and tell me at once."

"I know I shouldn't be telling you about it as yet. It's all so indefinite. Besides, I'm sure Philip would not want me to reveal . . ." And her voice trailed off guiltily.

Gervaise looked at her askance. "If it is something which Philip would not want you to tell me, then by all means don't. It's not like you, Clarissa, to want to betray a confidence."

"Oh, pooh. Don't moralize at me, Gervaise. I've always confided in you, as you well know. It wouldn't be the first time I've told you something I shouldn't. It's probably very wrong of me to talk about this, but it is such good news, and you deserve to know it, if anyone does."

"Well, you've thoroughly aroused my curiosity. I would no more stop you now than I would forego the plum pudding tonight, though both indulgences will weigh heavily on my conscience. So proceed with your news, my girl, and don't keep me waiting any longer."

"Oh, Gervaise," Clarissa cried, released by his words from her guilt and flinging her arms about his neck, "Philip is in love! With any luck at all, he will soon be married!"

Gervaise, who had never, in the many years he had known her, taken Clarissa in his arms, was for a moment so stupefied that he let his arms remain limply in his lap. Then, as the awareness slowly came over him that his dream of many years was coming true—that it was truly Clarissa who had embraced him so impetuously—he put his arms around her and held her close. "Oh, my dear," he whispered, "is it really happening? Are you to be mine at last?"

Clarissa, suddenly becoming aware of the impropriety of her behavior, reluctantly withdrew from his embrace. Smiling shyly, she said, "I think so, Gervaise. If all goes well with Philip's romance, I see no reason why we can't be married . . ." She flicked a glance at his face, the color rising in her own, as she added, ". . . soon."

Before she could resist, she was swept into another embrace, and it was some minutes before a sense of the proprieties was awakened in either of them. Finally, Clarissa murmured, "Oh, Gervaise, no. Someone may come in. We must be careful not to set tongues wagging yet awhile. Philip is not yet able to give us any assurances. . . ."

Gervaise chuckled. "Miss Pennington is leading him a merry dance, eh?"

Clarissa stared. "Gervaise! How did you guess—?"

"I have eyes, m'dear, I have eyes. There's not much I miss. I've known for days that he was taken with her tail-over-top. And she with him, if I'm any judge of women. I hope you're pleased with his choice, for two people more suited to each other I never did see, despite the fact that she's so young."

"I'm more than pleased. I quite loved her like a sister before I ever dreamed she might turn out to be one."

"Then we've nothing to worry about," Gervaise chortled.

"Don't fly into the boughs too soon," Clarissa cautioned. "He's mishandled the whole matter—my fault, I'm afraid. I'll tell you the whole silly story one day. Now we must hope that he can find her and persuade her to forgive him."

"I refuse to be damped. Didn't Shakespeare say that love will find a way? Well, if he didn't he should have, for it will, nine times out of ten."

They left the library soon after, to find Nancy, Annette, and an under-footman waiting for Clarissa in the hallway. "Could we see ye alone, ma'am?" Nancy asked, with a sidelong glance at Gervaise.

Gervaise bowed to Clarissa. "I'm off to dress for dinner, my dear. Can't tell you how I'm looking forward to the Christmas goose. Your cook has a way with them that is positively mouthwatering." And off he went with a little dance in his step that brought a sparkle to Clarissa's eyes as she watched him go.

The tale unfolded by the servants needed much repetition and amplification before its full import was clear to Clarissa. So overjoyed was she at the solution to the mystery of the diamonds and the realization that no one she cared for was involved in a theft that her disapproval of Joseph's and Annette's transgression in using a guest room as a rendezvous was softened.

"You've all behaved in a most irregular and reprehensible manner," she told them at the end of the interview, "and I fully expect that I shall never find you involved in such goings-on again! However, you have been a help to us in the end, so I shall let bygones be bygones."

It was clear to Clarissa that something would have to be done about Sally and that the others would have to be told the truth, if only to clear the cloud of suspicion that hung over Evalyn. She looked at the trio standing ill at ease before her and said sternly, "I've been thinking that this is not quite the time to do anything about this matter. It is Christmas Day, after all. And tomorrow is Boxing Day, which I know you and the other servants have so been looking forward to. Nothing should disturb that day. Therefore, I would be obliged if nothing of this is said. I will take no action until the day after. In the meantime, I trust that I can rely on your discretion."

"Lord Gyllford already cautioned us, ma'am," Joseph said. "You can count on us to keep our lips shut."

The Christmas dinner turned out to be more delightful than Clarissa dared to expect. The evening started with Jamie's arrival at her bedroom door, stating his intention to escort his aunt to the drawing room. As they walked down the hallway, he asked if Philip had told her about their interview. She nodded and gave him an embarrassed apology. He teased her for being "goosish" and for thinking that he was ready to get himself "buckled" to any female. They laughed heartily over the whole silly pass. "But it shall all end well, when Father marries Miss Pennington in my place," Jamie said, expecting to give his aunt a pleasant shock. Her surprise, however, was only caused by his having guessed.

"How did you know?" she squeaked. "Did Philip tell you?"

"I guessed it, finally. I must have been a complete cawker not to have seen it before."

"I was worse!" Clarissa admitted. "I never guessed at all. Philip had to tell me himself!"

Their high spirits were evident from the moment they entered the drawing room, and Clarissa beamed at everyone so joyously and laughed at all the pleasantries so merrily that good will soon spread to everyone in the room. Only Sally felt uncomfortable. Not only was she bored to death with Philip absent, but Clarissa, who was spreading Christmas warmth everywhere in the room, seemed to turn cold every time she looked at Sally's face.

At the Bull the fire was crackling in the grate. Philip had surrendered his coat to the ministrations of Mrs. Fern and sat sipping his second toddy when Mr. Fern returned with Samuel. The taciturn old man stood before Philip and surveyed him with a complete lack of concern for Philip's elevated rank. Philip felt that the old, bird-like eyes were taking his measure, and he rose and shook Samuel's hand and thanked him for coming out on such a night.

"Tain't nothing," Sam'l said.

Philip urged him into a chair, and the innkeeper gave him a tankard of ale. "I understand that a young lady asked you last night to drive her to Launceston," Philip began.

The old man nodded.

"Did she find someone else to take her?"

"No, sir," Sam'l said.

"Can you be sure?" Philip asked him urgently. "How else could she have left here?"

"In a carriage. A private carriage."

"Come on, Sam'l," the innkeeper said in annoyance, "where'd she find a private carriage?"

"Came here last night, full o' little tykes. You gave 'em dinner, remember?" Sam'l said to the innkeeper in a tone of superiority. The old man's eyes gleamed with pleasure at having shown a better memory than the younger Mr. Fern.

"What's this?" asked Philip, leaning forward. "There was another party here last evening?"

"Well, yes," said Mrs. Fern. "A very big family, it was. They stopped here for a bite o' supper."

"But they bespoke the private parlor," Mr. Fern objected. "I don't think the young lady even saw 'em."

"She did, too," Sam'l said decisively. "Played with their little girl."

"Sam'l, you're an old fool. So what if she played with their brat," said the innkeeper. "She wouldn't go off with 'em. They were strangers. She was a lady. A lady wouldn't go off with strangers."

"Don't know if she was a lady," Sam'l said. "Don't know if they was strangers. She went off with them. Saw her."

"She went off in the carriage with this family?" Philip asked urgently. "Are you sure, man?"

Sam'l merely nodded. Philip turned to the innkeeper. "Did you get their name?"

"No, me lord, I never did. Did you, Mrs. Fern?"

"No. All I did was bring in a couple of trays to 'em."

"But *you* know it, don't you, old man?" Philip said to Sam'l with a smile. "You don't miss very much, do you?"

"Didn't get their name, but I could find 'em, right enough," the old man said to Philip with a twinkle.

"How?"

"Can't live too far from here, or they wouldn't've left so

late in all that snow. The mother had red hair. The father called 'er his Irish puss. Someone around 'ere 'll know a big family like that with a red-headed Irish mother." And he lifted his tankard and took a deep draft, as if to recover from the effort of that long speech.

Philip grinned. "I knew I could count on you, old man. Come then, let's go and find them."

The old man cocked his head and eyed Philip with an expression that mixed amusement with disdain. "You young'uns are all alike," he cackled, " 'specially when y're chasing a filly. Makes yer think-box stop working proper."

"Sam'l!" cautioned the innkeeper sharply. "Mind yer tongue."

Philip ignored the interruption. "Are you saying you don't want to help me find them?" he asked Sam'l bluntly.

"Not tonight I don't," Sam'l answered with equal bluntness. "Nor should *you* want to neither. We'd have to move about too slow in all this snow, and when you don't know where yer going, 'twould be plumb foolish. We'd never get there. Take the word of an old man, me lad, that y're stuck here 'til the snow stops, and that's a fact."

Philip went to the window and looked out. The lantern burning atop the post at the entrance to the inn showed the snow deepening steadily. In the light of the lantern he could see the large flakes swirling about in thick profusion. The sign of the Bull was completely whitened, and a high drift was already covering the lower half of the window from which he was looking. The old man was right, of course. It would be foolhardy to do anything but wait for the storm to pass. Even the gods seemed to be mocking him, for at that moment the force of the wind strengthened, its howl penetrating clearly through the panes and shaking them with unprecedented fury. When the gust died down, the snow-flakes in the light of the lantern appeared to be falling in even greater concentration than they had before. To Philip it seemed that they would never stop.

· Twenty ·

MR. CALDWELL WAS the owner of a rambling country house halfway between Ashwater and Hatherleigh which he had inherited, along with a more than modest competency, from a childless uncle. The news of his inheritance came to him in his twenty-fifth year, when he had been living in London, struggling to make ends meet as the owner of a badly situated bookshop and tail-over-top in love with a redheaded young Irishwoman employed as a milliner in a shop down the street. As soon as he learned of his good fortune, he sold the shop, married the redhead and carried her off to a house in Devonshire which neither of them had ever seen.

The house had a good number of bedrooms, and the happy couple promptly proceeded to fill them up. The first-born was Charles, followed in a year by Catherine. Then came Sean, Mary, and Meggie in quick succession. After Meggie was born, there was a three-year hiatus, but at last, to everyone's delight, another little boy was born. He was named Michael, but thus far he was called "baby." Baby was a delight to the entire family and to the cook, the nurse, and the neighbors as well. Only Meggie, her nose out of joint because she had been replaced as the youngest of the household, regarded the infant with growing chagrin. She wined and nagged and wept and pouted, but baby would not go away.

This was only one of the problems encountered by the new governess on her arrival, late on Christmas eve, at the Caldwell home. The house was loosely run and carelessly cleaned. The children were disciplined mainly by pleadings or scoldings from their loving Mama. Their father withdrew from household crises by riding off to the nearest public house. But the most severe problem facing Evalyn was the elderly woman affectionately called Nurse by everyone in the household. Nurse had taken one look at Evalyn and, contrary to the expectations of Mrs. Caldwell, had become as smitten by jealousy of the new governess as little Meggie was of the baby.

The four days following their arrival had not been easy ones for Evalyn. The baby's fever had risen alarmingly the first night, and Nurse would permit no one near the child but Mavis Caldwell and herself. She rejected out-of-hand any suggestion made by Evalyn for his care. Mavis, however, had instantly felt an affection for Evalyn, and as each day passed grew more and more to respect her good sense and rely on her judgment. By tactfully consulting Evalyn when Nurse was not present, Mavis managed to pull her baby through.

Evalyn was in some ways glad that her position was so difficult and challenging. It left her little time to brood over the pain that hovered like a cloud at the back of her mind. The night of her arrival, after she had helped to put the over-tired, quarrelsome children to bed, she had found herself alone in a tiny bedroom under the eaves. The room was dusty and smelled stale with disuse, and it measured only six paces from the doorway to the opposite wall. She had surveyed the cheerless little window set in a deep dormer, the stained Holland bedcover and the smoking fireplace, and a recollection of the room in which she had slept the night before overwhelmed her. Memories and misgivings attacked her, and the realization that she had buried her tracks, that she had irrevocably turned her back on Gyllford Manor, and that she would never again lay eyes on Philip Everard suddenly became too much for her to bear. For the second time in her life, she gave way to her emotions and wept until sleep finally came. At dawn, she had looked at her face in the little mirror on the wall at the foot of her bed. The worn silvering of the glass had emphasized the look of weariness and pallor of her face. She knew that self-pity, even more than lack of sleep, had given her face that hollow look. Then and there she had made a vow to busy her mind with her work and avoid any situation which would encourage idle reflection. Mavis Caldwell had been a godsend to her, and, in gratitude, Evalyn would give to the Caldwells all her waking thoughts and energies.

Now, four days later, Evalyn was beginning to feel that her efforts in the Caldwell establishment were having an effect. Charlie and Cathy, the oldest children, were starting to take seriously the course of study she had laid out for them. Sean and Mary were becoming less quarrelsome. And Meggie, who had adored Evalyn from the first moment at the inn, followed her about the house contentedly, the mended doll dangling from her left hand and her right thumb in her mouth.

The snow had stopped the day after Christmas, but the sun had not made an appearance until today. Evalyn, lifting her eyes from the history book she was reading to the children, looked out of the schoolroom window to see an unfamiliar brightness in the sky. "Oh, look!" she exclaimed. "The sun's come out!"

The children ran to the window. The sun sparkling on the unmarked snow dazzled their eyes. The sight was overpoweringly inviting. Evalyn did not need much persuasion that an hour or two of play in the snow would be more beneficial to children who had been cooped up in the house for four days than the best of history books. In less than a quarter of an hour, five pairs of galoshes had been donned, five pairs of mittens had been fetched, and five throats had been securely bound with mufflers. The children ran outside with squeals of delight, Evalyn following behind.

They chose the expanse of space at the back of the house as the scene for their play, and their laughter covered the sound of a horse riding up to the front door. It was not until Evalyn heard Mavis calling her name from the kitchen window that she became aware that a visitor had arrived at the house.

"There's someone here to see ye, Evalyn," Mavis called with an air of suppressed excitement. "Hurry inside! Charlie can take care of the children, can't ye, Charlie boy?"

Mavis shut the window before Evalyn could ask the identity of the visitor. Who it could be she could not imagine. The only possibility was that Mrs. Caldwell wanted to introduce her to a neighbor who had dropped in. Evalyn came in to find Mavis waiting for her. "Be quick, girl," she said breathlessly. "Here, ye'd best give me y'r cloak, I'm thinkin', and brush y'r hair back a bit, m'dear. Ye'll be wantin' to look y'r best." With that, she pushed Evalyn before her into the sitting room.

Mr. Caldwell stood at the fireplace, speaking with considerable deference to a gentleman seated with his back to the doorway. Mavis, entering behind Evalyn, clarioned eagerly, "Here she is!" And the visitor rose from his chair and turned. Evalyn, at the first glimpse of the tousled black hair shot with grey, began to tremble at the knees.

"Philip!" she gasped in unthinking gladness. Then her

hand flew to her mouth. "Oh . . . I m-mean, Lord Gyll-ford," she added awkwardly.

Philip, who had been waiting for this moment with mounting tension, felt a burst of laughter break through the knot of nerves that had been tightening his chest. "How do you do, Miss Pennington?" he asked with an amused gleam in his eye.

Evalyn, searching his face with an eagerness born of four nights of trying to recapture just that look in her mind's eye, felt a surge of emotion, but whether it was joy or dismay she could not tell. In this small room he seemed taller and more imposing than she remembered, and the look in his eyes was so warm and comforting that she would have liked nothing better than to cast herself in his arms and weep away the loneliness of the past four days. But the unexpectedness of his sudden appearance was quite as disturbing as it was miraculous. Why he had come was as much of a mystery as how he had managed it. "I never expected . . . that is, I cannot imagine how you f-found me!" she managed to say.

The smile faded from Philip's eyes. "I don't know why you imagined I would not!" he responded with some acerbity, his momentary amusement giving way to a feeling of resentment. He had waited for two days for the snow to cease, and it had taken two more days to find her. They had been dreadful, agonizing days. He had managed to endure them by dreaming of the moment of their reconciliation. But this scene was not being played at all as he had dreamed. He looked at her sternly. "Did you really think I . . . we . . . would let you run away—and in such a storm!—without attempting to assure ourselves of your safety?"

"I hoped my letter would relieve you of that obligation," Evalyn answered in distress.

"That hope was quite ill-judged," he said curtly. "All of us at Gyllford, the family, the staff, and the guests, have been concerned about your welfare."

"I'm very sorry to have c-caused so much trouble," Evalyn said in a voice which sounded suspiciously close to tears.

"And so you should be," Philip heard himself growl. He had heard the quiver in her voice, and he wanted nothing but to take her in his arms and soothe the hurt he knew they both suffered. But the vexation caused by the presence of two strangers watching them with rapt attention seemed to force him to react with a gruff coldness that was quite unlike him.

Evalyn heard only the bitterness of his tone, and the sound weakened the last of her self-control, already badly undermined by the shock of his presence. She turned her face away so that he might not see the tears which had begun to drip down her cheeks.

Mavis, who until this moment had only felt the excitement of entertaining a real Earl in her own sitting room, suddenly realized that her dear Evalyn was under attack. She rushed to the girl's side and put a protective arm around Evalyn's shoulder. "So that's the way ye talk to this darlin' girl, is it? No wonder she ran away from ye!" she accused. "Ye must've treated her like a little slavey, I'm thinkin', to make her run away from a situation in a home such as y'rs. Sure, 'n' a body has a right to leave her employer if she's a mind to. Besides, she's employed by us, now, she is, and I'll not have 'er bullied!"

Philip reddened under the unexpected attack. "Bullied!" he retorted angrily. "Do you think I've scoured this countryside through wind and snow for four agonizing days because I wished to find and berate a recalcitrant *employee*?"

Evalyn lifted her head and stared at Philip dumbfounded. Had he truly been searching for her ever since her absence had been discovered? Mr. Caldwell, observing this unexpected scene from his place at the fire, blinked at Philip in confusion. "Are you saying, Lord Gyllford, that Miss Pennington was *not* in your employ?"

"She certainly was not," Philip answered shortly.

"I see," said Mr. Caldwell, reddening. He crossed the room to his wife. "I think, my dear, that this is something which does not concern us. It seems to be a private matter. We had best leave the room to Miss Pennington and her . . . guest."

Mavis looked at her husband questioningly. Then a glimmer of understanding lit her eyes, and she glanced quickly from Evalyn to Philip and back again. Her eyebrows lifted. "Ooooh!" she said in a long breath. "Lord bless me soul! Aye, o' course, m'dear, we'll be goin'. There's . . . er . . . the tea things to see to, anyway." She smiled encouragingly at Evalyn, ignoring her husband's tug on her arm. "Please make y'rself at home, me lord," she said with another quick glance at Philip. She permitted her husband to lead her to the doorway, but there she stopped and turned again to his lordship, resisting Mr. Caldwell's persistent tug. "Sure'n' we hope, Lord Gyllford, that after you and Evalyn have . . . er . . . finished . . . that ye'll stay to tea." And her embarrassed husband pulled her from the room and shut the door.

Philip's eyes had not wavered from Evalyn's downcast face. Mavis's lengthy exit had given him time to regret the testiness which had so upset the usually calm Miss Pennington. For a long moment neither of them moved. Then Philip went to her and lifted her chin. "What a clodpole I am!" he said regretfully, as he wiped her cheeks with his handkerchief. "The last thing I wanted was to make you cry."

Evalyn forced a small smile. "You could not know I would behave so foolishly. Once I told you I never cried."

"So you did," Philip agreed gently and led her to the sofa, drawing her down beside him. "Only an ogre could cause the redoubtable Miss Pennington to cry. I should be horsewhipped for speaking to you so harshly. Please forgive me."

She shook her head. "No, there's nothing to forgive. It's I who . . . I never dreamed you would go to the trouble of finding me. I cannot fathom why you should have done so, or how you managed it."

"I've already explained the why. You underestimate the esteem in which you are held at Gyllford. As to the how, I encountered a very clever and observant old fellow at the Bull by the name of Samuel who had seen you leave in the carriage of a red-headed Irish lady with a large brood of children. Such a personage is bound to be noticed, and it was not long before we were able to ascertain her identity."

Evalyn lowered her head in shame. "I cannot apologize enough for causing you this trouble, my lord. Will you please tell Lady Steele and everyone at Gyllford how sorry I am to have created such a turmoil?"

"You must come back with me and tell them yourself."

She lifted her head and gave a baffled look. "Why do you ask me to come back, sir? There is no need for it, surely, now that you see me satisfactorily established."

"You're quite wrong," Philip said in a low voice. "There is a great need for it."

"I don't understand. What need?"

"My need," he said simply. Evalyn's pulse, which had quieted somewhat since he'd seated her on the sofa, started to race again. His meaning could not be what it seemed. She waited wordlessly, her eyes fixed on his, for him to explain himself.

He saw the confusion in her eyes and got to his feet. Now that the moment had come—the moment for which he had waited since Jamie's disclosure—his courage failed him. What was he doing, he asked himself, forcing his attentions on this lovely young woman half his age? She had just declared that she was satisfactorily established. She obviously wanted nothing further from him. He had convinced himself that she cared for him, but on what evidence? Merely on a look—the look on her face that day in the snow. On that flimsy foundation he had built his castle of dreams, and now the whole cloudy structure seemed to be evaporating.

He went to the fireplace and leaned on the mantel. What should he say to her now? Could he bring himself to leave her here in this place, to struggle to raise a large brood of children not her own? Even if she would not marry him, he had to find some way to take care of her, to help her to find a better life than she would find buried away here, an outsider in someone else's family. But he could think of no other way. "You say you are satisfactorily established here," he said in a constricted voice, his eyes on the fire in the grate. "Does that mean you find these surroundings more to your liking than at Gyllford?"

"How can you ask such a thing, my lord? The days I spent at Gyllford were the happiest in my life," she answered earnestly.

"Then why won't you come back?"

"You are more than kind to ask me, but you know I can not. My time there was an interlude, a time of . . . unreality. But sooner or later, reality must be faced. In this case sooner than we expected. But it has not turned out so badly. Even Clarissa could not have found me a better mistress than Mrs. Caldwell."

"Clarissa didn't intend to find you a mistress at all!" Philip muttered bitterly.

"Why, what do you mean?"

"We were a pair of fools, my sister and I," Philip said, turning from the fire and giving her a strained smile. "We thought Jamie had brought you home to make you his bride."

"His *bride*?" Evalyn asked in bewilderment. "*Me?* How could you have believed something so ridiculous?"

"Don't ask me to explain the whole silly coil that led us to jump to that conclusion, but the idea is not at all ridiculous. I only hope the girl Jamie eventually does marry is half so suitable."

"What nonsense," Evalyn said, brushing aside the idea with a wave of her hand. "We both know quite well how unsuitable I am."

Philip glowered at her. "If it is the 'difference in our stations' to which you are referring—a subject which I thought we had long since repudiated—I shall wring your neck!"

Evalyn gave a short laugh. "Well, wring away," she said challengingly, "for although *you* may have repudiated it, I never did. Besides, you must have seen that Jamie did not regard me in any light but as a sort of . . . maiden aunt."

"No, you're out there," Philip said with a sudden grin. "He regards you more as a mother."

"A mother? Whatever are you talking about?"

Philip's smile faded and he turned back to stare into the fire. "It was just a silly joke, I suppose. You see, when Jamie told me that you and he had no plans for marriage, I asked him if he'd mind if *I* married you."

Evalyn stared at him. "If *you* m-married me?" Her

cheeks paled and her eyes fell to her hands clenched in her lap. "Oh. Yes, I see. It *was* a silly joke."

Philip spun around. "No, no! I didn't mean it that way! It wasn't a joke then," he said, agonized. How could he explain what he'd meant? How had he gotten himself so hopelessly muddled? He strode over to the sofa, sat down, and grasped her hands. "Oh, Evalyn, I love you so, and I'm saying it so badly!"

Evalyn felt her heart lurch inside her. "Wh-what did you say?" she asked in a breathless whisper.

"My darling, please say you'll marry me. I wouldn't ask it of you if I thought that this course you've embarked upon would lead to a life of fulfillment or contentment. But to remain here, out of the way of society or the chance of change, raising the children of strangers—no matter how kind they are to you—seems to me to be a life of loneliness and drudgery. Surely a life with me—a man who loves you, who offers you the prospect of children of your own, even though he is twice your age—*must* be a preferable prospect!"

"Philip, you *fool*! How could you think that your *age* has any—? I wouldn't care if—! Oh, I don't know what I'm saying. Surely you must have guessed . . . have seen that I love you!" she said in a voice that wavered between laughter and tears.

For a moment he seemed not to have understood. Then the misery in his face vanished, and he pulled her to him and held her close. She buried her face in his shoulder and gave a shivery sigh. For a long while she held her breath, not wishing to miss a single one of the endearments he was murmuring into her hair. "Oh, my dear," she said at last, "you *know* you cannot marry me."

He released her and held her at arm's length. "I know nothing of the sort," he said with a grin. "You've said you love me, and there is no possible way you can cry off now. I intend to marry you as soon as I can arrange it. But at this moment, there is something else I'm going to do, something I've been wanting to do ever since that terrible day when I so foolishly interrupted myself." And taking her in his arms again, he kissed her with all the fervor which the long postponement had built up in him.

Some time later, he reluctantly released her. "And now, my girl, I think we had better face the Caldwells and tell them that I'm removing you from their midst as soon as you can gather your belongings."

"Oh, Philip, how can I? I have been with them only four days. How can I leave them so abruptly?"

"You can and you must, for I don't intend to be without you for another day!"

"But Mavis has begun to rely on me, and the children— such adorable little things they are—will be upset, and . . ."

Philip eyed her with a wicked gleam. "Surely Mrs. Caldwell cannot expect to have a countess serving as governess to her offspring, no matter how adorable they may be."

Evalyn looked at him aghast. "A countess! Oh, Philip, I couldn't—!"

Philip laughed and took her in his arms again. "I won't hear another one of your objections, my girl. You are going to be the most beautiful countess in all of Britain. You'll find it quite easy—much easier than being a governess— and I promise you shall enjoy it enormously." He kissed her so ardently that her objections were swept away with her breath. "Now, go and tell your Mavis that you are leaving within the hour, and that I shall send her the most good-natured and efficient governess I can find to replace you."

"Oh, Philip, what a wonderful idea," Evalyn said in happy breathlessness. "May I indeed tell her that?"

"Yes, my darling, of course. But you must in all honesty admit to her that I cannot promise to find one as redoubtable as the one she is about to lose."

New Year's day had come and gone, but the guests still lingered at Gyllford, enjoying lazy days near the fire, brisk walks through the winter landscape, and convivial evenings in the company of beloved friends. There was one exception: Sally Trevelyan who, upon learning from Clarissa that she had been observed removing the earrings from her jewel case herself, ordered Annette to pack her things immediately. Annette then announced that she was to be wed shortly to the very man who had inadvertently spied on her and would therefore be unable to accompany Ma'm'selle back to London.

Clarissa had made it clear to Sally that in all fairness to Miss Pennington—who she hoped would be returning to Gyllford shortly—she would have to tell the other guests the truth about the earrings. Therefore Sally was forced to take her leave of Gyllford without a single person present to wish her a good journey and no one in attendance except a coachman and footman who had been pressed reluctantly into her temporary service.

Evalyn and Philip returned to the warmest of receptions, and a spirit of rejoicing filled the house. Philip's announcement of their wedding plans was greeted with more delight than surprise. In this small, intimate circle of well-wishers, Evalyn was able to adjust to her new, elevated position with a minimum of awkwardness and embarrassment, and although Philip had to tease her from time to time about her tendency to remain "determinedly poor," she found it quite easy to bear being coddled, admired and adored.

A small family wedding was planned for the middle of January, and the Covingtons decided to remain for the occasion. Gervaise, who intended to follow Philip's example and lead Clarissa to the altar a fortnight thereafter, also stayed fixed at Gyllford. Reggie, who hoped to become so firmly entrenched in Marianne's affections that her come-out in June would have no adverse effect on their romance, seized the opportunity to remain at her side and also declared his intention of being present at both of the wedding ceremonies in the offing.

Thus it was that a bored and frustrated Jamie wandered through the house one January afternoon, looking for some companionship or activity. A look into the library revealed a contented-looking Clarissa bending over her Gervaise, who was showing her some pictures of the proper attire for the groom at a country wedding as illustrated in *The Gentleman's Magazine*. A search on the grounds revealed his father and Evalyn setting off for a walk, their arms encircling each other's waists. Edward and Martha were settled in the drawing room, he with a book and she with some embroidery destined for Marianne's trousseau. Finally, he found Reggie and Marianne sitting across from one another at the table in the breakfast room, gazing fixedly into each other's eyes, their hands stretched out toward each other and meeting in the center of the table in a loving clasp.

Jamie groaned. "Confound it," he said disgustedly, "this is getting worse and worse. Nothing but lovers wherever one looks! What am *I* to do, I ask you, while everyone in the house is behaving in this buffle-headed way? Do you two intend to spend the whole afternoon doing nothing but staring at each other like a couple of moonlings? Honestly, if I didn't have to stay for father's wedding, I'd take off for London this very afternoon! Do you know what I'm beginning to think? I hate to say this about my own home, but I think this place is becoming a worse bore than even the Carberys'!"

Marianne and Reggie had become accustomed to Jamie's tirades and had not really listened to a word he'd said. However, Marianne became aware of the silence that followed Jamie's outcry and felt that some response was expected. She sighed and—her eyes never leaving Reggie's face—offered her usual, all-purpose reply. "Oh, do you really think so?" she murmured softly.

Winter
Wonderland

· *Prologue* ·

BARNABY TRAHERNE, A tall, gawky nineteen-year-old, stood at the entrance of the ballroom of Lord Lydell's town house and stared inside in horror. The cacophony of loud voices and loud music was alarming enough, but the crush of people within was worse than anything he'd imagined. "I never should have come," he muttered in dismay.

Honoria, the Countess of Shallcross, who stood at his right, glanced up at her young brother-in-law worriedly. "Are you uneasy, my dear?" she asked kindly. "I know I would be, if this were *my* first ball."

On her other side, her husband, although twenty years older than Barnaby and with the experience of hundreds of balls behind him, did not look any happier than his brother. "What a crush!" he exclaimed in disgust. "I'd wager there are a hundred and fifty fools crowded into 'this room—a space designed to hold no more than sixty!"

"Then let's turn tail and go home," Barnaby urged, taking a backward step, quite ready to bolt.

Honoria grasped her husband's arm. "Perhaps, my love, the boy is right. We should go. His first ball should not be—"

But the butler was announcing their presence in a loud voice, and their hostess, Lady Lydell, was waving to them from the far side of the room.

"We *must* stay," the Earl reminded her. "We have social obligations. How can we consider making an escape when this misbegotten affair is in my honor?" He took a firm hold of his brother's arm and pulled him over the threshold. "Barnaby, try to look a little less alarmed. It's only a ball, after all."

But to the young Barnaby Traherne, who was truly, achingly, awkwardly, utterly shy, this was not "only" a ball. It was, in its way, a battlefield. He saw it as a test of his manhood, a test which, he belatedly realized, he was not yet prepared to face.

His brother, he knew, would not understand. It was hard for Lawrence Traherne, who'd lately come into his titles as the fourth Earl of Shallcross, to comprehend the feelings of a brother twenty years younger. Barnaby's father, the third Earl of Shallcross, had had four sons, of whom Barnaby was the youngest. Ten years separated him from his next-youngest brother, Harry. Because their mother had died shortly after Barnaby's first birthday, and the old Earl had been too bored with fatherhood to trouble himself with the newest baby, the brothers had taken it upon themselves to raise him. Though boisterous and domineering, they were also good-natured and kind, and they were delighted with this new responsibility. During all his formative years, Barnaby was cossetted and mollycoddled by three overprotective brothers and one motherly sister-in-law, Lawrence's wife Honoria.

During the years of his growing up, Barnaby had never been permitted to fight his own battles. One of the four was always on hand to defend him from any real or imagined attack. Even when he was a student at Oxford, one or another of his brothers managed to drop round often enough to keep a protective eye on him. The attention of his siblings was so pervasive that Barnaby's self-confidence could not properly develop. With so much custodial care, he was never permitted to stand up in his own defense, test his own courage, or even finish his own sentences. Shyness was the natural outcome. It was only recently that he'd begun to assert himself. Now, at nineteen, having won his degree and having returned from Oxford, it was finally time, he told himself, to fight his own battles.

This, however, was a battle he was not yet ready for. He should never have succumbed to Honoria's blandishments. She'd often tried to entice him to accompany them to the festivities being held in honor of the new Earl, but Barnaby had resisted her appeals with implacable resolve. "I'm not comfortable at social affairs," he told her. "I'm tongue-tied in the presence of elegant females, I'm an awkward dancer, and, furthermore, I don't own a decent set of evening clothes."

But yesterday, on the evening before the Lydell ball, he changed his mind. His brother Harry had spent the dinner hour bragging about the opera dancers and lightskirts with whom he'd been successful. The stories had filled young Barnaby with envy, for he himself had no experience of Womanhood. Moreover, it was a night when the air was fragrant and the moon cast a silver glow on all the world. What man could ignore the magnetic appeal of the female with such suggestive reminders all around him? Barnaby, feeling the blood of youth and health coursing through his veins, felt impelled to act. He admitted to his sister-in-law that he yearned to hold a pretty young woman in his arms. "So if you wish, Honoria," he said in blushing surrender, "I'll go with you to your ball tomorrow."

Honoria, delighted at this turn of events, set about at once to see that her brother-in-law was properly turned out. With an evening coat borrowed from Harry's wardrobe, trousers from Terence's, and a lace-trimmed neckcloth and striped satin waistcoat from the collection of the Earl himself, she and Lawrence's valet managed to outfit him. Barnaby, studying himself in the mirror, suspected that the waistcoat hung too loosely about his chest even after being taken in at the back, and that the sleeves of Harry's coat were a bit too short, but Honoria, looking him over with affectionate eyes, declared firmly that his appearance was perfectly satisfactory.

Now, however, standing here in the ballroom doorway and eyeing all those well-dressed men within, poor Barnaby was suddenly filled with misgivings. Moreover, the noise of the milling throng within was an assault on his senses. The nine musicians sawing away on their strings were no match for the chatter and laughter that reverberated through the room. Not only were one's ears assaulted but one's eyes. It was a scene of glinting, confusing movement: glasses clinked, jewels twinkled in the light of three enormous chandeliers, footmen maneuvered their way through the crowd carrying trays of canapes over their heads, and one hundred and fifty ladies and gentlemen jostled for space and attention. The turmoil made Barnaby wince. The impulse that had made him wish to attend this affair immediately vanished. All he wanted now was to shake himself loose from his brother's hold and break for the door. It had been stupid to come, he berated himself. He should never have agreed to—

But at that moment, his attention was caught by a scene at his left. He could not have missed it, for it took place on a staircase-landing in the far corner, a landing raised three steps above the level of the ballroom floor like the stage in a theater. On that raised landing, in the midst of a clutch of admirers, a young woman had just thrown her head back in laughter.

Barnaby blinked. His Adam's apple bobbed as he took in a gulp of air. The sound of that laughter was attractive enough all by itself—a light, musical laugh that tinkled above the noise with the crystalline clarity of a glass bell— but it was the *appearance* of the lady that held his attention once it was caught. She was the most beautiful creature he'd ever beheld. Tall and lithe, draped in green silk that clung to every curve of breast, hip and thigh, she took his breath away. Her skin gleamed, and her auburn hair glinted with gold in the light of the chandelier above her head. And at this moment, her throat, stretched taut by the angle of her head and pulsing with laughter, looked so lovely it caused a clench of pain in Barnaby's chest. He was smitten, as

only a very young man can be. "Who *is* she?" he croaked
as soon as he could manage his voice.

The Earl grinned broadly. "Why, that's Miranda Pardew!"
he chortled. "You've got taste, Barnaby, I'll say that for
you."

"Good God, she's lovely," Barnaby breathed.

"No argument there. She's a distant cousin of ours, you
know. Would you like to meet her?"

Honoria threw her husband a look of alarmed disapproval. "Meet her? Are you mad?" she demanded.

"Why?" the Earl asked his wife, befuddled. "Why
shouldn't he—?"

"Do you want the boy eaten alive? Miranda Pardew is
not the right sort for Barnaby. Not at all. Why, this is only
her second season, and she's already earned a reputation.
During her first, she jilted two men and caused a third to
take monastic vows. Is that the sort of girl you want to
introduce to our Barnaby?"

Barnaby, his eyes still fixed on the breathtaking creature,
hardly heard what his sister-in-law was saying. "Look at
her," he sighed, entranced. "She can smile with only her
eyes!"

Honoria rolled her eyes heavenward. "Listen to me,
Lawrence," she hissed in her husband's ear. "My friends
tell me that Miss Pardew has rejected more than a dozen
offers of marriage and set her cap for Sir Rodney Velacott.
He's the fellow, you know, who's bragged for years that
he'll never succumb to matrimony. The betting book at
White's has set odds of nine to one that 'the Magnificent
Miranda'—yes, that's what they call her!—will manage to
catch him. And Sir Rodney is standing right up there beside
her. Look at him in that circle of her admirers, looking smug!
With that fish to fry, Miranda Pardew will take no interest in
Barnaby! He should be meeting a sweet, quiet girl who'd
fawn on him, not a heartless flibbertigibbet who'll toss him
aside like an old shoe!"

"I only want him to dance with her," the Earl retorted,
"not marry her."

Honoria turned to her brother-in-law. "Barnaby, my dear," she said in what seemed to Barnaby to be real distress, "Miss Pardew is not the sort—"

But before she could finish, their hostess, having successfully made her way through the press, came up to them. Showering them with effusive greetings, she linked her arm to Honoria's and, without giving her a chance to object, bore her off to make the social rounds. Barnaby saw Honoria look over her shoulder worriedly, as if she wanted to warn him of something, but before she could make herself heard, she was swallowed up by the crowd.

His brother, however, showed no such distress. "Come, boy," he said, his grin reappearing as he took his brother's arm, "and let me introduce you to that charming creature who has you gawking. Don't pay any attention to Honoria's gossip."

Barnaby blinked at his brother in trepidation. "*Introduce* me?" he asked, so frightened at the prospect of having to speak to the dazzling creature that he almost stuttered.

"Of course. Don't gape at me like a frightened fish. I'll introduce you, and then you will ask her to dance."

"Dance?" Barnaby echoed. "But I don't—"

"Of course you do," his brother interrupted as he always did. "Nothing to it." And, dragging poor Barnaby behind him, he moved inexorably toward the platform where the ravishing young woman stood. "Miss Pardew," he bellowed as soon as they were in earshot, not at all concerned that he might be interrupting the young woman in the midst of an important flirtation, "how do ye do?"

The girl looked round, her smile fading and her expression becoming guarded—a look often seen in the eyes of mischievous young people in the presence of their elders. "Lord Shallcross, good evening," she said. If she was annoyed at the interruption, she did not reveal it by so much as a blink. "How kind of you, the guest of honor, to come out of your way to greet me."

"Not kind at all," his lordship replied, stepping up on the landing, breaking in on her circle of admirers and lifting her hand to his lips. "I feel it a family obligation to greet you. After all, you are a relation to me, did you know that?"

"Yes, I'd heard something of the sort," the girl acknowledged, her charming smile reappearing. "I do believe we're cousins, though quite distant."

The Earl nodded. "Your father was my second cousin once removed, if I calculate rightly."

Sir Rodney, who'd been standing behind the girl, moved closer to her. "A second cousin once removed, is he?" he muttered in Miranda's ear. "I only wish he'd remove himself further."

The lovely Miss Pardew could not quite restrain her giggle as she dropped Lord Shallcross a curtsey.

Lawrence chose to ignore Sir Rodney's obvious rudeness. "I'd like to make this young man known to you, my dear," he said to the lady pleasantly. "He is just out of Oxford and therefore somewhat tongue-tied. I believe he has a request to make of you." In his blunt, fatherly style, he pulled Barnaby up on the landing and pushed him toward the girl. "Go on, boy! Ask her!" he ordered. Then, bestowing a benign smile on both of them, he stepped down from the landing and walked off, abandoning poor Barnaby to his fate.

Barnaby felt himself redden to the ears as the girl looked him over with cool disdain, taking in his unkempt hair, ill-fitting coat and loose breeches in one disparaging glance. "What can you possibly wish to ask me, sir?"

Barnaby, more humiliated than he'd ever been in his life, could barely find his tongue. "I w-w-wondered, Miss P-Pardew," he managed, "if I might have the n-n-next dance."

"Next dance? What gall!" exclaimed one of the men surrounding the lady. "I should say not! Her dance card was filled more than an hour ago!"

"I can speak for myself, Charlie," the lady scolded, tapping the offending gentleman on his knuckles with her fan. Then she turned back to Barnaby. "Did no one ever tell you, young man, that asking a lady to dance at the very last moment can—in certain situations—be considered an insult?"

"An insult?" Barnaby was sincerely bewildered. "I don't see how—"

"Don't you? One asks one's maiden aunt to dance at the last moment. Or one's little sister. Or a wallflower one feels sorry for. Do I look like someone's maiden aunt? Or a wallflower?"

Barnaby, completely at a loss, shifted his weight from one foot to the other. "Well," he muttered miserably, "I didn't . . . I wasn't . . . I just . . ."

"You didn't. You weren't. You just," she mocked. "A man of few words, eh?"

The men around her laughed loudly. Never had Barnaby felt such a fool.

Sir Rodney put a proprietary arm about the young lady's waist. "What the lady means, you young idiot," he said with a pitying smile, "is that she is spoken for already. The next dance is mine."

"I'm s-sorry," Barnaby stammered, backing away awkwardly. "P-Perhaps some other—" His voice, like his self-esteem, faded away to nothing.

The girl seemed to enjoy his misery. "For a man of few words," she taunted, "you do keep tripping over them."

"Yes, m—" he began, but his sentence was cut off by a loss of balance; he'd backed to the edge of the landing and stumbled off the edge. He lurched backwards down the three steps, not quite falling but merely looking like a clumsy ass.

The girl looked down at him as he steadied himself, her brows arched in amusement. "You not only trip over your words, but your feet. What a delicious combination of gracelessness and gaucherie!"

There was another roar of laughter from the gentlemen, but Miss Pardew merely smiled. Nevertheless, Barnaby could see that she was enjoying herself. She seemed to find it amusing to turn a man into a fool. Barnaby was not so green that he didn't recognize her delight in flaunting her power over him, and in having Sir Rodney witness that power.

Barnaby blinked up at her, wondering how to end this torture. No longer did she seem beautiful or desirable. The only desire he felt was an urgent wish to be gone from her presence. "Excuse my p-presumption, ma'am," he said, making a quick but clumsy bow. "I obviously made a mistake. I wish you g-good evening."

But she was not yet through with him. "I would wish you good evening in return, sir, but it seems I've forgotten your name. Or did Lord Shallcross fail to give it to me? What *is* your name, fellow?"

Barnaby had the urge to tell her to take a damper. To cut line. To cease her gibble-gabble. His brothers would not hesitate to say those things. *Rudeness*, he wished he had the courage to retort, *is only weakness masquerading as strength.*

"Did you hear me, fellow?" she persisted. "What is your name?"

He stared up at her, tongue-tied. What did she want with his name anyway? To use it as the subject for her mirth after he was gone? *Never mind my name*, his mind said silently. *I only want to say that this meeting was a pleasure—if not in the arrival, at least in the departure.* But overwhelmed with shyness and humiliation as he was, he was incapable of defending himself in any way, of paying her in kind, or even of making that mild rejoinder. He could only answer helplessly, "My name is Bar—"

But she held up a restraining hand. "No. On second thought, don't tell me. Please don't give me your name." She flipped the upraised hand in a gesture of airy rejection. "I'd rather dismiss you *incognito*."

The onlookers roared at this riposte. And the lady, having reduced the poor fellow to quivering jelly, was now ready to return her attention to Sir Rodney, her main objective. She turned away at last, leaving Barnaby free to make his escape. As he pushed his way through the crowd, he could hear her tinkling laughter as it merged with the hoots of hilarity the others were expelling at his expense.

He got through the rest of the evening somehow, and later, at home, he sat down in front of the sitting room fire to think over the event. The evening had been a battle, just as he'd anticipated. And he'd lost it. He had to admit that. He'd lost it ignominiously.

He stared at the dying fire, experiencing the humiliation of defeat. But he didn't wallow in mortification for long. He was too young and too hardheaded, he decided, to let one defeat overwhelm him. There were many battles of the sexes still ahead of him. He would enter the fray again, and the next time he would be better prepared. *The war's not over yet*, he said to himself, squaring his shoulders. *Not by a long shot!*

· One ·

HONORIA, LADY SHALLCROSS, had a select circle of friends—like herself, refined, mature ladies of impeccable taste and breeding—who gathered in her drawing room weekly to do what ladies of such refinement are wont to do: drink tea and gossip. And one of their favorite subjects of gossip was Honoria's own brother-in-law, Barnaby Traherne. What made him interesting was the paradoxical fact that, although he was tall, handsomely featured, and reasonably well-to-do, none of the marriageable young ladies of the *ton* seemed inclined to set their caps for him.

The subject became almost heated one day when Honoria, pouring out the tea for the large-bosomed Lady Lydell, chanced to remark that this was Barnaby's thirtieth birthday.

"It's positively shocking," Lady Lydell observed, helping herself to a buttered scone, "that such a catch as Barnaby is, at his age, still a bachelor."

"I don't understand it," the white-haired Jane Ponsonby mused. "The girls should be pursuing him relentlessly. Why aren't they?"

"Because," Honoria replied in that tone of unalterable affection with which she always spoke of him, "he's shy."

This response brought forth a burst of satiric laughter. "Shy, indeed!" the sharp-tongued Molly Davenham,

Honoria's closest friend, exclaimed. "The man's as shy as a shark!"

Honoria stiffened. "Molly! How *can* you say such a thing?" she demanded furiously.

"I can say it because it's true." Molly stirred her tea with perfect calm. "A man with a stinging wit can't be called shy."

"And didn't he win a DSO for his bravery at Waterloo?" Jane Ponsonby asked. "Hardly the act of a shy man."

"But . . . but that doesn't mean—" Honoria sputtered.

"I heard, from my nephew in the Foreign Office," Lady Lydell cut in, "that your Barnaby is the only man there with the backbone to stand up to the Prime Minister. So how can he be shy?"

Honoria brushed back a lock of gray-streaked hair with fingers that shook with anger. "Nevertheless—"

"Never mind your neverthelesses," Molly Davenham said bluntly. "The fact is that every young lady I've tried to push in Barnaby's path was afraid of him."

"*Afraid* of him?" Honoria stared at her friend in disbelief. "What on earth can have made them afraid of him?"

"He's forbidding," Molly said, reaching for a cucumber sandwich, "and if you can't see that for yourself, I can't help you."

"Forbidding? *My* Barnaby, *forbidding*?" Honoria looked round the circle for support for her position, but there was none.

"I know what Molly means," Lady Lydell said thoughtfully, "although perhaps it's hard to describe just what it is that makes him forbidding. . . ."

It *was* hard to describe, but everyone who knew him agreed that there was something about Barnaby Traherne that put one off. He had a strong, lean face and a body that showed not an ounce of self-indulgence, qualities not necessarily daunting in themselves (in fact, most females found him quite attractive), but when combined with a certain glower in his expression, forbidding he became. His dark eyes, which glittered with saturnine intellectual acumen, had a way of cutting through a lady's pretensions; his manner of responding to most questions with brusque monosyllables quickly exhausted most ladies' efforts at conversation; and his icy witticisms easily discouraged the most persistent of flirts. And though his normal expression was only mildly thoughtful, the least annoyance caused it to give way to a frown so glowering that most observers backed out of range.

But Honoria, who had no children of her own and who'd helped raise Barnaby since he was ten, saw the man with a loving mother's eyes. "What nonsense!" she insisted sternly. "My Barnaby is as shy as a wallflower. You may take my word on it."

But none of the ladies took her word. They all had eyes and ears, and from the evidence of those most reliable of organs, Barnaby Traherne was anything but shy.

Honoria didn't pursue the subject, though she knew how wrong they were. There was much they didn't know about her Barnaby, but his story was not one which she wished to tell, even to these close friends. *If only you could have seen him as I did*, she sighed to herself as she sipped her tea, *eleven years ago, back in 1806, when he attended his first ball . . . that dreadful ball that altered his character forever. . . .*

Honoria remembered that ball better than she remembered her own wedding. It was one of those affairs given to honor her husband's coming into his titles. After a year of mourning for his father, Lawrence Traherne, the fourth Earl of Shallcross, was ready to celebrate his new position. It was a happy time, a time of celebration in the family, for not only had their year of mourning come to an end, but Terence, the second brother, had become father to a bouncing boy, and Barnaby, who'd been an excellent student despite his shyness, had won his Oxford degree with honors.

To celebrate, Lawrence had taken the whole family to London for a season of gaiety. Many of the *ton* held fêtes for the new Earl. During that season, Honoria had often tried to entice the shy young Barnaby to accompany them to the festivities being held in his brother's honor, but Barnaby had been too shy to go. This time, however, something had made him change his mind.

Honoria was delighted. She'd looked forward to this particular affair, for it was being given by her good friends, Lord and Lady Lydell. She remembered how excited she'd been as she'd climbed the stairs of the Lydell town house in Portman Square, her husband holding her right arm, and Barnaby, her left.

But as soon as they approached the ballroom doorway, Honoria was struck with misgivings. Perhaps she shouldn't have urged Barnaby to come. Honesty demanded she admit to herself that she'd not thought things through. She'd been too eager, too hasty. Barnaby would not be presented at his best. There had not been time to prepare him properly. He'd not been schooled in ballroom etiquette; he'd not been warned of the many social pitfalls; he'd not even been dressed to advantage. The boy's hair had not been cut, his borrowed coat now seemed a poor fit, and his breeches positively baggy when compared with the exquisite tailoring exhibited by the other guests. *This is all my fault*, she berated herself. *I should not have permitted him to attend his very first ball so ill-prepared.*

She could sense that poor Barnaby, too, was beset with doubts, though not from the flaws in his costume or the gaps in his education, for he was too naive to be aware of them, but from the shyness that was so much part of his character. But Lawrence pulled him into the ballroom before she could prevent it. And before they'd had a chance to adjust to the noise, Barnaby spotted Miranda Pardew!

Honoria, following his gaze, felt her heart sink. Right before her eyes, the boy became bewitched. She could not blame him; the laughing young woman attracted the eye of many of the gentlemen present. But of all the women in the room, this one was the last she would have chosen for her shy, inexperienced brother-in-law.

But her husband, with typical male ineptitude in these matters, would not heed her warnings. Before she could persuade him to change his intent, Lady Lydell came up to them, linked her arm to Honoria's and, without giving her a chance to object, bore her off to make the social rounds. As she moved away, the last words Honoria could hear were her husband's: "Come, boy," he was saying, "and let me introduce you to that charming creature who has you gawking."

Honoria had wanted to wring his neck. She kept looking back over her shoulder, wishing urgently that she could find a way to keep her husband from throwing Barnaby to the mercy of the room's most notorious flirt. But her hostess's strong grip was irresistible. She tried to signal her alarm to Lawrence by means of meaningful glances, but the Earl did not receive his lady's mental messages. He merely pushed the boy onward to what Honoria feared would be certain disaster.

Later, at home, after everyone in the household had gone to bed, Honoria learned how right her feelings had been. She came downstairs to find Barnaby brooding before the embers of the sitting room fire. With gentle prodding, she drew the story out of him. It moved her to tears. "Oh, my poor, sweet boy, how dreadful! That you should have had to experience such a set-down . . . and at your very first ball . . . it breaks my heart!"

But Barnaby was past self-pity. "Don't cry over the incident, Honoria," he said to her, his jaw set and his eyes dark with resolve. "It won't happen to me again. When next I set foot in society, I shall be fully prepared."

And so he was. No sign of shyness ever again appeared in his demeanor. He conquered that tendency so completely that now, eleven years later, none of the ladies drinking tea with Honoria would believe that the word *shy* could possibly apply to him.

Honoria looked up from her reverie to find Jane Ponsonby staring at her speculatively. "Well?" she was asking.

"Well, what?" Honoria blinked at her in confusion, not having heard a word.

"Well, do you think Barnaby would like her?"

"Like who?"

"Dash it, Honoria, haven't you heard *anything*?" Molly Davenham asked in disgust. "Your habit of drifting off is becoming positively distressing. Jane was speaking of her niece, Olivia. Do you think Barnaby might take to her?"

"Little Livy?" Honoria looked from one to the other in surprise. "But she's much too young, isn't she? A mere child."

"She's twenty-two," Jane Ponsonby declared, "and has been out three seasons."

"Has she really? How time does fly! But how did you come to think of her as suitable for Barnaby?"

"Because of what you said about him, insisting that the fellow is shy. So is Livy. If she weren't, she'd have been spoken for years ago, pretty thing that she is. Three seasons on the town and the chit still hangs back behind her mother's skirts. She's perfectly charming and talkative at home, but bring her to a ballroom, and she barely utters a word!"

"It might be a perfect pairing," Lady Lydell cooed, her eyes alight with a matchmaker's gleam.

Molly Davenham, however, was not a romantic. "I don't see how it can be done, with Barnaby so put-offish and Livy so shy."

"I do," said Honoria, already smiling dreamily at the prospect of a bride for her darling Barnaby. "I know just how to manage it."

"How?" asked the skeptical Molly.

"The family will all be meeting at Terence's place for Christmas. I'll simply bring Livy with me. At a quiet family gathering in the country, we can all relax and be ourselves. No one need worry about being shy."

The ladies all smiled at each other over their cups. Not even Molly could think of an objection. And as for Honoria, her heart actually sang in her chest. Olivia Ponsonby, little

Livy, was just the sort of girl Honoria had wished for Barnaby all those years ago at the Lydell ball: a girl who was sweet, modest, pretty and shy! Livy had come along eleven years late, but better late than never.

Honoria lifted her cup in a toast. "To sweet little Livy!" she said happily.

"To sweet little Livy," the others echoed.

"May she have success," Molly added wryly, "where braver girls have failed."

· Two ·

MIRANDA, LADY VELACOTT, looked most unladylike sitting on the dining room floor. She was swathed in an oversized apron and employed in wrapping pieces of china in sheets of old newspaper. It was an unusual occupation for a lady, but Miranda had long since grown accustomed to performing menial tasks. In a household that had once been run by a dozen servants but which had for a long time been reduced in staff to only three, she'd learned that her title did not protect her from having to engage in such unladylike but necessary tasks as bedmaking, laundering, mending, cooking and dusting.

A few feet away from Miranda, kneeling in front of two wooden crates into which she was carefully placing the wrapped dishes, was her Aunt Letty, a bony, spare, aristocratic old woman with small black eyes, a beak-like nose and a smooth helmet of iron-gray hair, all of which gave the impression of a silver-headed bird. Miranda, in her shapeless apron and with her curly auburn hair falling in neglected disarray around her shoulders, made a sharp contrast to her formally-clad, neatly-coiffed aunt.

The younger woman, her head lowered and her falling hair shading her face, was carefully keeping her back to her aunt. By hiding her face, Miranda hoped the sharp-eyed old woman would not notice that she was crying again. She couldn't seem to keep from dripping tears today. The sight of the familiar blue willow pattern on the Minton china reminded her of the many soothing cups of tea she'd taken in Letty's company during the past eleven years in this London house. Through those long years of her disastrous marriage, the companionship of this honest, blunt, sensible yet affectionate woman—who'd been like a mother to her after her parents died—was her one blessing, her bulwark against life's storms, the lifeline that kept her from drowning. The thought that this was their last day together was too hard to bear.

But Aunt Letty was indeed sharp-eyed. "You are not working, my dear," she said, eyeing her niece's back suspiciously. "Don't tell me you've turned on the waterworks again."

Miranda surreptitiously wiped her eyes. "No, of course I haven't," she said bravely. "I was only . . ." Her mind raced about, searching for an excuse for her idle hands. " . . . only noticing something in the newspaper here."

"Were you indeed?" Letty was too shrewd to be easily fooled. "And what on earth can interest you in a newspaper so old that it's good for nothing but wrapping?"

Miranda looked desperately at the printed sheet she had half-folded over a pretty saucer. "Advertisements," she said with false brightness. "Have you ever read these advertisements, my love? Did you know that ladies of quality actually use newspapers to find themselves household help? Here's a Lady Millington in Kent seeking 'a well-qualified butler with experience in supervision of household staff of more than two dozen.' Two dozen! Imagine! And here . . . a family in Norfolk by the name of Traherne seeks 'the assistance of a gentlewoman to supervise and educate three boys, ages five through twelve.' And this one, from a Mr. Drinkwater in Essex for 'a gentleman's gentleman, skilled at hairdress—' "

"Thank you, my dear, that's quite enough. You may find such reading interesting, but I do not. Besides, did you not insist that we pack these crates before I take my leave?"

"Sorry, Aunt," Miranda said, making a last brush at her cheek with the back of her hand and hurrying on with the wrapping, "but we have all afternoon. We'll finish in time."

A sound of wheels on the gravel drive outside the windows caught their attention. "Goodness me, Higgins can't have brought my carriage round so soon!" Aunt Letty exclaimed, raising herself to her feet with the stiff awkwardness of age. Once on her feet, however, she scurried to the window with the agility of a much younger woman and peered out. "Heavens, that's not my carriage! It's a drayman's cart! Those blasted Velacotts have sent their things!"

"Already?" Miranda felt her heart sink.

Aunt Letty frowned in irritation. "Isn't it just like your brother-in-law and his grasping little wife to take over the house a day early?"

Miranda rose and joined her at the window. "It's their right," she said, trying to keep her voice steady. "At least they gave me a year's mourning before moving in."

Letty snorted. "How very good of them."

They stood in the window, arms about each other's waists, listening to the November wind rattle the panes. The draymen down below ignored the wind as they busily carried furniture and boxes from the equipage and piled them up in the drive. Letty leaned closer to the window, her birdlike eyes glittering in disgust as she watched them. "I suppose this means that the Charles Velacotts themselves will be following shortly."

Miranda winced at the prospect. "Oh, dear, I suppose they will. I had hoped for one more night . . ."

Aunt Letty threw her niece a quick look of sympathy before turning away from the window and starting across the room. "Then I'd best send Higgins for the carriage and take myself off before they arrive."

"Yes, I suppose you sh-should," Miranda said, her voice choking on the tears she was trying desperately to control. "I know you don't wish to f-face them."

Letty, hearing the catch in Miranda's voice, stopped in her tracks. She'd made up her mind to keep her emotions in strict restraint during this final hour, but her strength failed her. She turned back to her niece, her eyes filling with the tears she'd promised herself not to shed. "Oh, my dearest," she cried, taking Miranda's hands in hers, "don't look so! Come with me to Cousin Hattie. We shall manage somehow."

Miranda shook her head. "We've been over this too many times to have to remind ourselves again how impossible it would be. You know there's no room for another female in your cousin's house."

Aunt Letty sighed helplessly. "Yes, I know. I keep assuring myself that you'll probably do better here in London than rusticating in Surrey in Hattie's tiny cottage with two old biddies. Here at least you'll have your old room, and all your things about you. . . ."

Miranda smiled ruefully. "Except that china. And my old Aunt."

"Perhaps you should keep the china after all," Aunt Letty suggested suddenly.

"No, I want you to have it. It belongs with you. It was you who brought it to this house when I married."

"As a gift to *you*," the aunt amended.

"Yes, but this house is mine no longer. If it remains here, my sister-in-law will think of it as her own. Belle has plenty of china. She doesn't need this."

"*Can* she claim it as her own?" Letty asked, her bird-like eyes flashing angrily. "Does everything in this house now belong to Charles? Even things you brought with you as a bride?"

Miranda shrugged. "I'm not certain. Mr. Baines said that Charles has ownership of the house and its contents. I didn't ask him about those 'contents' that Mama left to me. But there isn't very much. Just the Sheraton desk. And my bed, of course."

Aunt Letty looked over at the china piled on the floor and frowned. "Then I *will* take the china. I've no wish to add our lovely Minton to the other things Belle Velacott is taking away from you. But you'll have to send the crates to me later on. We shan't have time now to finish the packing."

Reluctantly, they started toward the door, both ladies throwing a last, longing look at the cups, saucers, butter plates and creamed-soup bowls still piled on the floor. "I never should have permitted you to wed him," the older woman suddenly burst out, tears rolling down her wizened cheeks again. "I should have told you what I felt the moment you announced your betrothal."

Miranda stopped and stared at her. "What did you feel?"

"That you were making a terrible mistake. I knew in my bones that Rodney Velacott was an irresponsible rake. I should have warned you. I should have threatened to break with you forever if you went ahead with the wedding. I was a coward."

Miranda almost laughed. "How can you be so silly? I would never have believed so ridiculous a threat. I didn't know much in those days, but I did know that you would stand by me no matter what happened. It was not your cowardice that ruined my life. It was my own vanity. Do you remember, Aunt Letty, what they used to call me?"

"Of course. The Magnificent Miranda."

"Yes, and I was stupid enough to believe them. What a silly young idiot I was. So pleased with myself. So foolishly arrogant. I'd caught the uncatchable Rodney Velacott, and I felt superior to every other girl I knew." She shook her head in bitter amazement at the memory of her younger self. "The Greeks had a word for it, you know. Pride. Hubris. The gods must have had a merry laugh at my expense as they took me down. I suppose I should be thankful they didn't make me blind, like poor King Oedipus."

"You may have been arrogant and foolish," her aunt said as they went up the stairs to collect her things, "but your crime was not so great as to deserve what followed. Why, you had not a single year of happiness with that man."

"No, but I had you to turn to." Miranda threw a tremulous smile at the older woman with heartfelt gratitude. "I thank the Lord for that."

Letty's belongings were already packed. Miranda's abigail and the one remaining housemaid had done the packing this morning, their last household chore before leaving to find other employment. (Miranda had written to Belle and Charles to ask if the maids and Higgins, the groom, could be retained on their household staff: *They have been employed here for years*, she'd written, *and not only are they familiar with the requirements of the house, they are very loyal, honest and deserving employees.* But Belle had written back that she would rather choose her own staff.) Higgins, the last remaining servant in Miranda's employ, would be leaving, too, after he conveyed Letty to her cousin in Surrey and brought back the carriage.

Higgins carried down Letty's things just as the draymen were bringing in the new owners' baggage. The entryway, the passageways and the stairs were scenes of complete confusion. Miranda and Letty could hardly manage a coherent goodbye. To postpone the parting as long as possible, Miranda went out with her aunt to the carriage. There they stood clinging together until Higgins coughed to remind them that the horses should not stand in the cold too long. But even he was tearful at this leave-taking.

Miranda stood there on the windy drive long after Letty's carriage disappeared into the dusk. Then she went in and, ignoring the draymen and the boxes and the disarray of her once-quiet domicile, climbed slowly up to her room, threw herself down on her bed and wept unconsolably. *It isn't fair*, she cried in childish self-pity. *It just isn't fair!*

She knew it was self-pity, but this once she was going to wallow in it. Life had been hellish for the past eleven years, and indeed it *wasn't* fair that her future held no prospects for improvement. How ironic life could be, she thought. She'd started out with such high hopes. She'd won the envy of all her friends when she'd married Rodney, who'd been so handsome, so very well-to-pass, and so determined a bachelor. Winning him had been a triumph for a young woman with no title and very modest means. But her feelings of triumph were short-lived. Within a month of her romantic honeymoon in Italy, after she'd moved into this very house glowing with happiness, she discovered that her new husband had a strong tendency toward drunkenness and lechery.

She'd not wept in those days. Her pride hadn't allowed it. She'd tried other kinds of cajolery: anger, sympathy, warmth, coldness, giving and withholding. But she'd not tried tears. Not at first. But when nothing else seemed to work, she'd even sunk to tears. All to no avail.

And tears are no avail now, she reminded herself, sitting up on her bed. It was all spilt milk. All the tears in the world would not change the past. She dashed them away, got up and went to her dressing table. If her brother-in-law and his wife should appear on the doorstep soon—as seemed likely—she was in no condition to receive them. She took off her apron, brushed the dust from her skirts and turned her attention to her unkempt hair. Hardly glancing at her reflection in the mirror (for her pale, gaunt face gave her little pleasure these days), she gathered her flyaway locks into one long, ropy coil, twisted it into a bun and began to pin it up to the back of her head.

She remembered how Rodney had disliked this way of doing up her hair. He'd always liked it hanging loose. Of course, after the glow of romance had worn thin, he rarely bothered to look at her. By the end of the first year, he was already accusing her of being nagging and burdensome. In fact, the more she indulged in pleas or scolds, the greater was his dislike of the married state. He began to come home at night badly foxed, and sometimes he did not come home at all. Still, she'd found it hard at first to believe that he'd taken a mistress. Later, of course, it was easy to believe. Over the years, he'd kept a succession of them.

She glanced at herself in the mirror. Her hair was neat enough, and her dress—a muslin roundgown with long sleeves and a high neck—was suitable for an evening at home. It had seen better days, but it would have to do. Rodney's brother and his wife would not expect her to greet them in formal attire. But she would make one concession to the occasion and wear her cameo. She took it out of her jewel-box, slipped it on a silver chain and hung it round her neck. It was a lovely piece—a miniature of a lady with a small diamond at her neck. Rodney had bought it for her on their honeymoon. It was not very valuable, Miranda supposed, but it was precious to her. It was her only reminder that she'd once been very, very happy.

But she'd not been at all happy since. Nor did she have any prospects of a change for the better. She wondered, as she stared at the pale, unfamiliar face in the dressing-table mirror, if she should have tried harder to change her life— to leave the man who'd so consistently humiliated her. But what could she have done? She had no parents to run to. Aunt Letty had no home of her own. Miranda had once thought of running off to become an actress on the stage, but it was a childish impulse; she had no talent for such an enterprise. Most women who tried it became, in the end, little better than lightskirts.

All those years, she'd felt quite hopeless. In a society in which divorce was almost unheard of, and where a wife had no rights, there was no way to free herself. Nevertheless, she felt inadequate. She'd failed in the one thing in which a woman was expected to succeed—as a wife. With this awareness of her failure, she had grown more withdrawn. She lost all interest in what had once been her major preoccupation: the pursuit of pleasure. She neither gave nor accepted invitations. She rarely went from home. She withdrew from society in shame.

Was it my fault? she asked her reflection in the mirror. *Was I not charming enough, or beautiful enough, or clever enough?* She knew she'd bored her husband. Her affection bored him. Her disapproval bored him. But then, everything bored him. He was so bored with his life that he could only find relief by gambling. Taking wild risks. Cards, horses or the market, it didn't matter which. All her attempts to reason with him failed. In an attempt to compensate for her husband's wild profligacy, she practiced economy in her home as much as possible, keeping the number of servants to a minimum, ceasing to buy anything but the most necessary items of clothes and household goods, hoarding the household money as best she could. But when, a year ago, her husband was killed—in a final irony, shot in a duel with a man he'd cuckolded—his man of business informed her that there was nothing left of his estate but debts. She had no dower, no jointure, nothing.

She shut her eyes, shuddering at the memory of the day they'd carried him home, everything hushed and secret to prevent the magistrates from learning of the illegal duel. And the poorly-attended funeral during which, numb from shock, she heard not a word of what was said to her. And the reading of the will, in which in the whole of the lengthy document her husband had not made one mention of her name.

She rose from her chair abruptly, for she heard the sounds of carriage wheels on the drive below. They were here! Charles and Belle Velacott had arrived. The moment she'd been dreading for the past year was now upon her. She had to go down, and smile, and make them welcome. There was no time now to dwell on the past.

It was just as well. Remembering the past was too disheartening. But then, contemplating the present was just as disheartening. Once, her hopes for her future had soared as high as the sky. Now reality had brought her down to this: bleak widowhood, impoverishment and the necessity of accepting the charity of Charles and Belle Velacott.

She could hear their voices at the doorway. It was time to go down. She took a deep breath, squared her shoulders and went from her room to face her new life.

How those who knew her before her marriage would laugh if they knew. The Magnificent Miranda, indeed. What a joke!

· Three ·

WITH A SMILE fixed on her face, Miranda reached the last turning on the stairs, but there she paused in surprise. The sight of the confusion in the entry hall below caused her to gasp. The hall was crowded with boxes, crates, pieces of furniture and bulging portmanteaux. Around this mountain of baggage scurried an army of servants that Charles and Belle had brought with them. Miranda counted at least two footmen, four maids, a dignified butler who seemed to be directing traffic, and several other persons whose functions she could not guess. *They must have had to rent a veritable caravan of carriages to transport them all!* Miranda thought.

In the midst of the confusion stood the new owners, Charles and Belle Velacott, happily surveying their new abode. Charles, tall and ruddy-faced, and still wearing his greatcoat (although it hung open to reveal his protuberent midsection), was giving orders to a coachman for the disposition of the horses. Belle, as small in stature as her husband was large, was gazing admiringly at the crystal chandelier over their heads. She was dressed to the nines in a velvet, fur-trimmed pelisse, and, in an apparent attempt to appear taller, carried on her head a high-crowned bonnet with the most enormous plumes Miranda had ever seen. The plumes bobbed about disconcertingly with every motion of the woman's head.

Suddenly Charles caught sight of his sister-in-law on the stairs. "Miranda, my dear," he bellowed, "*there* you are! We are a day early, as you can see. We were too eager to settle in to wait another day."

"Yes, Charles, I quite understand." Miranda ran down the remaining stairs and circled the impedimenta that stood between her and the new arrivals. "Good evening, Belle," she said, bestowing a formal peck on her sister-in-law's cheek. "I hope your trip down from Bedford was pleasant."

"As pleasant as travel with a train of four carriages can be," Belle replied, handing her fur-trimmed pelisse to one of the maids. "I'm glad the journey is over."

"You must be tired. Do go into the sitting room and rest yourselves, while I go and make some tea."

"No need for you to do that any more," Charles said grandly as he shrugged out of his greatcoat. "Our staff is quite ready to work." He signaled to the butler to see to the tea, threw his greatcoat to a footman, and led his wife and his sister-in-law into the sitting room, where one of the maids was already making a fire.

A few moments later, Miranda was enjoying the unusual luxury of being served her tea by a butler and two maids (who had so quickly settled in that they were already in uniform). She began to wonder if her alarm at the prospect of living with the Charles Velacotts had been premature. They were being very cordial. And she had to admit that it was very pleasant to be waited on like this, especially after all those years of caring for this large house almost single-handedly. Perhaps matters were not as desperate as she feared. She sat back in her chair, let the hot drink make its soothing way down her throat, and studied with new eyes the pair with whom she would now be living.

Charles Velacott, Rodney's younger brother and heir, looked older than his thirty-one years, but he had the handsome Velacott profile: aquiline nose, cleft chin and high forehead. Miranda acknowledged that she didn't really dislike him, despite his tendency toward pomposity. Nor did she resent his being Rodney's heir, for his inheritance had added little to his wealth. In truth, he owed his success to no one but himself. He'd gone to the West Indies as a young man and made a small fortune in the molasses trade. This he'd invested wisely, and he was now quite solidly wealthy. All he'd inherited from Rodney were huge debts and some badly-managed family properties which were heavily mortgaged. He'd dealt with the problem by simply selling off the inherited properties—all but this one—to pay the debts.

The Velacott London town house was the one property he'd kept because, as he'd told Miranda later, Belle wanted so much to live here. They would take a year to close up their country home and arrange the move. This, of course, Charles had every right to do. It was not his fault that the house had been Miranda's home for the past eleven years, and that she now had no place to call her own.

Miranda stirred her tea as she threw her brother-in-law a surreptitious glance from under lowered lids. Soothed by the warmth of the fire, the tea and the companionable silence, she was hopeful enough to admit that Charles, though pompous and self-important, was a good-natured, sober fellow, aware of his familial duty, though—and here was the rub!—often prevented by his wife from doing it generously. It was Belle who was the greater problem.

Miranda turned her glance to her sister-in-law, who sat opposite her in a wing chair, still wearing her ridiculous bonnet. The plumes waved every time the woman lifted her cup to her lips. There was no denying that Belle Velacott was a grasping sort who could make even an act of generosity seem vulgar. Miranda's recollection of their conversation after the reading of the will, several months ago, still chilled her blood.

The incident had occurred in this very room. They'd been gathered round the fire just as they were now. It was a few minutes after Mr. Baines, Rodney's solicitor, had departed. Miranda was trying very hard not to weep. "Poor dear Miranda," Charles had murmured, taking her hand in his, "do not add to your grief by believing we do not think of your plight. I quite agree with Mr. Baines that *something* is owed to my brother's widow."

"Though nothing is *legally* required of us," his wife had quickly pointed out.

"But Belle and I have already spoken of this," Charles went on, "and we've decided to offer you a home."

Belle had smiled at her smugly. "A rather generous offer, you must agree."

Miranda, too choked with grief, could not respond.

"A place in our household," Charles had gone on with more than his usual pomp. "A place in our household for the remainder of your lifetime."

"*If* you wish to have it," Belle had added. "You must not feel in the least coerced. And, of course, you do realize that this invitation does not extend to your Aunt Letty. One can only do so much."

Miranda had had to use all her control to keep from flying from the room in tears. The offer could not then—nor did it now—make her feel grateful. In her mind it had seemed rather like a prison sentence. Belle had made it quite plain that she did not really want to share her new home with a sister-in-law she hardly knew. On the few occasions they'd come together since Rodney's death, the woman had been just as she seemed at the reading of the will— smugly condescending. *And that's just how she seems now*, Miranda said to herself as she watched Belle looking about the room with the self-congratulating pride of ownership, her plumes waving.

All these months, the prospect of spending the rest of her life in the same house as Belle Velacott, without even the companionship of her beloved aunt to support her, had been most dismaying to Miranda. But perhaps she'd been wrong. Belle *had* offered her a home, after all. She deserved not to be too hastily judged.

Belle looked up at that moment. "Miranda, my dear, let's not waste time over tea. I do so wish to look over the house. Would you like to show me round?"

"Yes, very much," Miranda said, rising eagerly. "But won't you take off your bonnet first? You are at home now, you know."

They started in the drawing room, where Belle admired the marble mantelpiece and deplored the portrait hanging over it. "What an ugly thing!" she exclaimed. "It must go! I have a fine painting of my mother dandling me on her knee that will be perfect there. Remind me to tell Nash to take care of it, will you?"

They next surveyed the dining room, where Belle's eyes lit up at the sight of the pieces of china still on the floor beside the almost-filled crates. "What lovely china! Minton, isn't it? I shall have to display it in that armoire there."

"I'm sorry, Belle, but you can't," Miranda explained gently. "The china belongs to my aunt. I'm packing it to send out to her."

"Oh, I see," Belle said, disappointment and annoyance very clear in her tone and the set of her chin.

They proceeded through the library (where Belle criticized the placement of the furniture), the music room (where Belle disparaged Miranda's taste in draperies) and the other rooms on the first floor, and then up the stairs. Miranda led Belle straight to the two large, connecting bedrooms that would be hers and Charles's, and the mirrored dressing rooms that adjoined them. To Miranda's relief, Belle seemed quite pleased with their size and furnishings. It was not until Belle noticed a closed door that things went seriously awry. "And what is that?" she asked, pointing.

"That is my room," Miranda said. "Would you care to see it?"

"Of course," Belle responded in a tone that clearly implied, *That room is part of my house, too, isn't it?*

Miranda opened the door and stood aside to let her pass. Belle looked about the room with brows upraised. "Why, it's quite large!" she exclaimed in some surprise.

Miranda suddenly felt guilty, as if she'd somehow overstepped. "Yes, it is," she said defensively, "but not as large as the other two."

"And the windows . . . they face south, if I mistake it not."

"Well . . . yes, they do."

"I have always favored south-facing rooms," Belle declared sourly. Then her tone changed. "Oh!" she gasped. "*Look* at the *bed*!" She circled the high four-poster, fingering the carvings and eyeing the sheer hangings with a look of pure avarice.

"I believe it's Queen Anne," Miranda offered.

"It *is* Queen Anne," the new mistress of the house declared, her tone clearly accusing Miranda of stealing the best of the furnishings for herself.

"It was my mother's," Miranda said quietly. "It is one of the few things of value that I brought with me when I was wed."

"Oh, I see," Belle murmured, taken aback. She bit her lip, resentful and annoyed to learn that she was not mistress of *everything* in this house. "It seems a very fine piece."

"Thank you." Miranda wondered if she was expected to apologize for reserving for herself something of value. But she swallowed her irritation and tried to recapture the good feelings with which she'd started out on this tour. "Would you care to see the other rooms on this floor?" she asked pleasantly. "There's a little room down the hall that might do very well as a writing room for you. It has a lovely old desk inset with porcelain tiles, a Sheraton. I'm sure the room will please you—the windows also face south."

The desk, a large, eight-legged, ornate piece with solid gold pulls and magnificently-painted tiles, made a very distinct impression on Belle. "I suppose you'll now tell me," she said sarcastically as she ran her fingers over the polished surface, "that this was your mother's, too."

"I wasn't going to," Miranda retorted, stung by Belle's tone, "but as a matter of fact it was."

From Belle's snort, Miranda knew that the grasping little woman did not believe her. They proceeded on, but the feeling of warmth with which Miranda had begun the expedition was gone forever.

After the house had been thoroughly examined, and an impromptu buffet supper had been served in the dining room, Miranda excused herself and bid her new hosts good night. She needed to be alone to think over the day's events. She was still willing to try to find something about Belle to like, but the prospects were gloomy.

Half an hour later, she heard a tap on her door. Already in her nightdress, she only opened it a crack. In the corridor stood Nash, the butler. "I beg pardon for disturbing you at this hour, ma'am," he said, "but Mr. Velacott would like a word with you in the library before you retire."

"But I've already retired," she objected.

The butler bit his lip. "I believe," he said uncomfortably, "that Mr. Velacott feels that this matter shouldn't wait till morning."

"Very well. Tell him I'll be down as soon as I can dress."

In the library, Miranda found Charles pacing back and forth before the fire, looking very unhappy. His wife was nowhere in evidence. "Do sit down, my dear," he began, not ceasing his pacing. "I don't quite know how to tell you this."

"Just say it outright, whatever it is," Miranda said, sitting down at the edge of an armchair facing him. "I dislike roundaboutation."

"Well, then, without roundaboutation, here it is. My wife feels . . . that is, we *both*—she wants me to make it clear that I speak for both of us—*we* feel that your room is . . . well, it faces south, you see, and our bedrooms face west. Belle does love . . . that is, we *both* like a south-facing room . . ." His voice failed him, and he flicked her a look of sheer misery.

Miranda tried to make sense of this meandering speech. "Are you saying that Belle wants me to exchange my bedroom for hers?" she asked in disbelief. "But she can't be serious. In the first place, hers is much larger. And in the second, it adjoins yours. I can't take a bedroom adjoining yours."

"No, no, of course not. I did not explain properly." He took another quick turn across the room. "Damnation," he muttered to himself, "Belle should be doing this herself." He threw Miranda another shamefaced glance. "But she was very tired. It has been a long day."

"Yes, it certainly has. But you were saying . . . ?"

"Yes, about your room. She . . . we . . . are quite content with our bedrooms. We don't want your room as a bedroom but as a . . . a sitting room for Belle. Facing south, you see."

"A sitting room. Facing south. I see." Miranda swallowed hard. "And where would Belle . . . and you, of course . . . like me to sleep?"

"She says there's another south-facing room down the hall that would be very pleasant for you. She says you'll know which one she means. You thought it might be a nice writing room for her."

"Yes, I know the one. But, Charles, it is very small. I don't believe there's a wall wide enough to accommodate my bed."

"Belle's thought of that. She says that her bed is a good deal smaller than yours. She said to tell you she'd be willing to exchange her bed for yours."

"Would she, indeed?" Miranda rose from her chair. Her knees were trembling. "How very kind of her," she said between stiff lips. "Does she wish to make the exchange tonight, or may I sleep in my own bed for one more night?"

Charles's eyes dropped from her face. "Certainly you may stay where you are tonight," he muttered awkwardly. He turned to the fire and lowered his head till his forehead rested on the mantel. "Tomorrow will be soon enough to move things about."

"Then I bid you another good night, sir." And she strode quickly to the door.

"Miranda, I . . ." He looked up over his shoulder at her, his eyes more miserable than before. "I'm truly sorry. But there is one more thing. In your new room, Belle noticed—"

"I know. You don't have to say it. She wants the desk."

He reddened to the ears. "Well, you *will* have a bit more room without it."

"So I will," Miranda agreed, adding as she pulled the door closed behind her, "How considerate of Belle to think of that."

She was trembling with fury by the time she reached her room. *That blasted female!* she cursed in her mind. *She has everything in the world! Must she have my bed, too?*

She could not sleep. She prowled about her room for hours, like a tiger caged. In one short evening, Belle had proved herself selfish and manipulating. There was no other way to describe her. Was it to be Miranda's fate to spend the rest of her life in the same house with such a woman?

No! she told herself vehemently. There *had* to be another way she could live. She had to find a way to support herself, there was no other choice. She had to find work of some kind. Anything, any kind of humble life, would be better than to be in this humiliating, degrading position. She would be a barmaid in a tavern, a lady's maid, a cook . . . anything! There was work to be had in this world. Hadn't she seen, this very afternoon, a list of advertisements—?

She gasped, blinking into the darkness, as an idea took hold. Quickly she lit a candle, slipped out of her room and ran down the stairs to the dining room. Shaking with eagerness, she set the candle on the floor, knelt before the still-open packing crate and took out the last saucer she'd wrapped. She unwrapped it and spread the crumpled newspaper on the floor. According to the date at the top of the page, it was almost a month old, but she prayed she would not be too late. In the dim candlelight, she skimmed the column of advertisements. There it was, just as she remembered it: *Mrs. Terence Traherne of Wymondham, Norfolk, seeks the assistance of a gentlewoman to supervise the education of three boys, ages five through twelve.* She had never supervised the education of anyone, but she *was* a gentlewoman. Perhaps she might qualify!

She ripped the advertisement from the page and dashed back up the stairs to the room into which she was to be moved at daybreak. She set her candlestick on the Sheraton desk that Belle lusted after and propped the torn piece of paper up against it. Then she pulled a sheet of writing paper and a quill from a drawer, cut a point, dipped it in an inkwell and began to write: *To Mrs. Terence Traherne of Norfolk: Dear Madam, In response to your advertisement in the London Times of 15 October . . .*

· *Four* ·

THE HONORABLE BARNABY Traherne turned up the collar of his greatcoat and huddled deeper into the cushions of the stagecoach seat. *December,* he said to himself, shivering, *is not the time to travel north.* The wind rattled the loose-fitting windows and whistled in at the edges of the doors, making the inside of the carriage feel as cold as outdoors. He'd had to rise before five this morning, dress in the dark and hurry through the cold streets to the Swan With Two Necks Inn to catch the stage. *Perhaps I shouldn't have agreed to go to Terence's for Christmas,* he mused. *I could still have been comfortably asleep right now, and I could have spent the holidays lazing about in my flat right here in London.*

He glanced over at the one other passenger, a heavyset fellow with a florid complexion and a bulbous nose, who was busily chewing away on a large sugared bun and seemed undisturbed by the cold. At first Barnaby, who hated any sort of crush, had been glad there were no other passengers on the London-to-Norwich stage, but now he was sorry; two more passengers on each of the wide seats would have made the coach warmer. But there was still a stop to be made at Islington before the coach turned onto the North Road. Undoubtedly, a few more passengers would be picked up there.

He opened the newspaper he'd purchased at the Swan before departure but then resisted the compulsion to read it. He was on holiday, after all. He didn't want to trouble his mind with his usual foreign-office concerns: the unrest in Germany, Turkey's troubles with the Serbs, the workers' riots in Derbyshire, and all the rest. The world, in spite of its problems, would surely keep on turning on its axis without him.

He turned to the window and gazed out at the passing landscape, but it gave little pleasure. The sky hung heavy and dark over a gray December world, and to make things worse, a few flakes of snow drifted by his window. Snow! That was all he needed to solidify his regrets that he'd undertaken this journey. It would be seven o'clock at night—eleven hours from now—when the stage would reach Barnaby's destination, Wymondham. There he expected to be met by his brother's carriage, which would take him three miles west, probably another half hour of travel. It would be a long, tedious day before he reached his destination. If a heavy snowfall should develop, and the coach delayed, it would be the last straw!

To Barnaby's relief, the sprinkle of snowflakes dissipated by the time the coach pulled in to the innyard of the Queen's Head at Islington. The sonorous chimes of the bells in St. Mary's Church were ringing out the hour of eight. The yard of the Queen's Head was usually alive with activity at this hour, with ostlers and stableboys and porters dashing in and out among the waiting passengers. But this morning, Barnaby was surprised to see only one passenger waiting to board. The freezing weather had undoubtedly deterred most of the travelers. The lone passenger, a woman, was being cruelly battered by the wind. With her pelisse whipping about her and her skirts billowing, she had to hold on to her bonnet with one gloved hand while directing a porter where to stow her two large portmanteaux with the other.

Barnaby, having turned his attention to his newspaper, barely glanced at the woman as she climbed into the carriage and brushed by his knees to take a seat opposite him. But the other passenger lifted his hat. "Good morning, ma'am," he said in so obsequious a tone that Barnaby assumed the woman must be pretty, "Augustus Woodley, at your service."

Barnaby glanced over the top of his newspaper to see if his surmise was correct, but the woman was turned away from him, for she was nodding politely to Mr. Woodley in acknowledgement of his greeting. When she turned back, he got a glimpse of her face. At the sight of it, he felt a sharp tightening of his stomach even before his brain registered her identity. *Good God*, he thought, horrified, *it can't be! Not . . . Miranda Pardew!*

Instinctively, he hid himself behind his newspaper. He must be mistaken, he told himself. Miranda Pardew, or whatever her name was now, would not be taking a journey on a public conveyance, without a maid or companion. She could not travel like any ordinary housewife. Besides, his impression of this woman, quick as it was, was of a rather dowdy person of middle age. She seemed to be dressed somberly, her pelisse more serviceable than decorative and her gown a subdued grayish blue. As for her bonnet, it was not at all the high-crowned sort that women of fashion liked to wear. *No, no*, he assured himself, *it can't possibly be she.*

Slowly, he lowered the newspaper and squinted over it. Fortunately, the woman was engaged in searching through her reticule for something, enabling him to take a long look at her. Though not middle-aged, she was certainly past the flush of youth. Her skin was very pale, her eyes (which he had to admit were still beautiful, tilted upward in the corners and thickly fringed with dark lashes) seemed red-rimmed as if she'd been weeping, her lips were tightly pressed together, and her hair so primly pulled back from her face that it was completely hidden by her bonnet. One *might* call that face lovely, he admitted reluctantly, but it was no longer a face that would attract the eyes of half the men in a ballroom. Yet it *was* Miranda Pardew. There was no mistaking her.

As she fished a handkerchief from her reticule, he quickly ducked behind his paper. The act filled him with shame. What was he afraid of? It was unlikely that she would recognize him. They had met only once, and although she'd left an indelible mark on *him*, he had certainly not left a mark on *her*.

Nevertheless, he kept his eyes fixed on his newspaper for the next hour or so. During that time, Mr. Woodley tried repeatedly to engage the lady in conversation, but he received only murmured monosyllables for his pains. When they stopped at Epping to change horses and take a bite of luncheon, Barnaby watched Woodley follow the lady into the inn. She obviously tried to avoid him, but the fellow was persistent. Later, when Barnaby entered the taproom, he saw that Woodley had seated himself beside the lady at her table. Barnaby took a table near the window where he would not be in her direct line of vision but where he could observe them. As he ate his bread and ham and sipped at his mulled ale, he saw that Woodley's attentions were bringing a look of chagrin to the lady's face. Barnaby wondered why she didn't give the fellow a set-down. She'd certainly been very good at that in her youth. Had she lost the knack?

When they returned to the carriage, Miss Pardew (or whatever her name now was), the first to climb aboard, took a seat on the opposite side. It was a clear message to Mr. Woodley that she wished to avoid him, but he did not take the hint. Shoving himself up the coach steps ahead of Barnaby, he plopped down beside her, in the seat that Barnaby had occupied earlier. When Barnaby seated himself on the other side, the lady threw him a helpless glance, as if she were pleading with him to change seats. Nothing in that glance, however, showed even the tiniest bit of recognition. He looked back at her coldly and lifted his paper up between them. *If you need help ma'am,* he told her in his mind, *I'm the last man in the world who'll offer it to you.*

He knew he was not being gentlemanly, but she deserved no politeness from him. Miss Miranda Pardew was repugnant to him. When he was nineteen she'd treated him with merciless contempt, and even if she was now past her bloom and looking dowdy and plain, he didn't care. He remembered reading somewhere that one might forgive injuries but no one ever forgave contempt. How true. How very true.

He turned to the window and noticed, to his chagrin, that the snow had begun to fall again. And if this were not enough to raise his ire, he had to listen to Augustus Woodley's revolting attempts to gain the interest of Miss Pardew. The fellow kept up a barrage of asinine comments which did nothing to endear him to the woman he was trying to impress. "My, but you have tiny feet," he'd remark. Or, "Those are very fine-looking gloves. What do you call their color?"

These ploys were greeted with only a stony silence.

"It's getting a lot colder, ma'am," Woodley remarked several times. "Let me give you my muffler." Once he actually tried to wind it about her neck. She had to send him off.

Barnaby tried not to pay attention to the goings-on. But the lady's restraint surprised him. The girl he'd met at the ball would certainly not have kept her sharp tongue in check. She'd known quite well, back then, how to put a man in his place. Indeed, she seemed much changed in many ways. The slate-blue Kerseymere gown she was now wearing, with its prim white collar, straight skirt and simple gimp-cord trim, was a far cry from the clinging, enticing, soft green silk she'd worn the night of the ball. And her bonnet sported no feathers or ornamentation—it was modest in height and brim and was tied under her chin with the plainest of bows. She neither looked, dressed nor behaved like a belle of the *ton*. He couldn't help wondering if, perhaps, some sort of tragedy had befallen her.

While he was thus studying her, he noticed that the obnoxiously persistent Augustus Woodley had moved his leg to rest against Miss Pardew's thigh. The lady edged away. A few moments later, Mr. Woodley moved again. Miss Pardew edged away again. When the dunderpate moved a third time, and the lady, wedged tightly between him and the armrest, had no place to move, Barnaby had had enough. With an exclamation of disgust, he tossed his newspaper down, jumped to his feet and grabbed the fellow by the collar of his coat. "You don't seem comfortable, Woodley," he said, lifting the fellow bodily and throwing him over to the opposite seat. "I think you'll be happier sitting beside *me*." And he re-seated himself, picked up the newspaper and opened it to his place.

"Oh, I *say*!" Woodley cried in outrage when he regained his breath. "What do you think you're about?"

"I know what I'm about. And I know what you're about. So take my advice, fellow. Stay put and hold your tongue. We've had enough of your buffoonery."

Woodley opened his mouth to retort, caught a glimpse of Barnaby's glower that had intimidated so many others, reddened and retreated to his corner.

The lady threw Barnaby a look of melting gratitude. "Thank you, sir," she said softly, the corners of her lips turning up in a suggestion of a smile.

Barnaby did not smile back. He merely fixed his glower on her and, with cold deliberation, lifted up the newspaper between them. He could deliver a set-down, too.

How the lady took his set-down he didn't know, for he kept his eyes fixed on his newspaper. The journey proceeded in absolute silence. The only sounds were those of the carriage wheels, the horses' hooves and the whistling wind.

That was why, later that afternoon, on a deserted stretch of road between Barton Mills and Thetford, they all heard the clip-clop of other horses rapidly coming up from behind them. These sounds were followed by shouts, and the carriage rocked to an abrupt stop. Before they had time to interpret these signs, the door near Woodley was pulled open, and they found themselves staring into the black barrel of an ominously long pistol. Mr. Woodley started. The lady gasped. Barnaby let his newspaper drift to the floor.

A head appeared in the doorway, the eyes covered with a black mask. "Hands over yer heads, gents! And the lady, too. Quick now!" The voice had a low, frightening rasp.

All three did as they were told, but Barnaby was more irritated than frightened. "A damned *highwayman*!" he exclaimed in disgust. "Just what I needed."

· *Five* ·

THEY STEPPED DOWN from the carriage into an icy wind and a swirl of light snowflakes. The masked footpad, a large, broadly built fellow as tall as Barnaby, looked from one to the other and chose Mr. Woodley to fleece first. Without a word, and keeping one eye and the barrel of his gun aimed at the other two, he efficiently set about removing Mr. Woodley's valuables: his watch, chain and fobs, and his purse.

Barnaby used the time to look about. They were standing in a rutted roadway edged on both sides by woodland. There was no sign of human habitation. He noted that the highwayman was not alone, for two horses were tethered to a nearby tree. A quick glance toward the front of the coach revealed a second felon, also masked, but much shorter and slighter than his confederate. He was aiming a pistol at the coachman, who was hesitating to climb down from the box. "Move yer arse down 'ere," the footpad ordered. "I don't 'ave all day."

The coachman's arm made a swift movement downward. Barnaby saw his hand grasp the trace of the horse on the left and break it loose, thus unhooking the harness. Before the footpad realized what he was up to, the coachman had leaped to the horse's back, dug his heels into the horse's side and was galloping off, the harness dragging behind him. The horse on the right whinnied wildly, reared up, broke from his already-loosened trace and quickly followed. The footpad cursed, aimed his gun and fired, but the rider and both horses were already disappearing into the distance. The whole incident had taken but a few seconds.

The second highwayman cursed again, very loudly. The stir had drawn the eyes of the others, who were grouped at the side of the carriage. "Damn you, Japhet," the first highwayman shouted. "Whyn't ye watch—?"

But he got no further, for Barnaby had taken immediate advantage of his distraction and leaped forward, grasping the arm holding the gun. The tall highwayman dropped the gun, but not before a shot exploded into the air, causing the lady to scream. Barnaby and the highwayman toppled to the ground, rolling back and forth, first one on top and then the other. Barnaby was getting the better of the fight when the second highwayman, having reloaded, ran over and aimed his pistol at Barnaby's head. "Let 'im go or ye're a dead man," he said coldly.

Barnaby let go. Both men got to their feet. The highwayman retrieved his pistol and turned to his cohort. "It's all yer fault, ye blasted looby," he snarled as he reloaded. "Ye couldn' even 'andle the coachman."

"You ain't doin' so bloody well yerself," the one named Japhet retorted. "Seems t' me like you also lost one."

It was quite true. One of the three passengers was gone. During the melee, Augustus Woodley had managed to steal off. "Howsomever, old chubb," the taller footpad bragged, "I nimmed 'is goods afore 'e ran." And he waved Woodley's watch in the other fellow's face.

"Damn it, woman," Barnaby muttered to the lady, "you should have gone off with your admirer."

Miranda threw Barnaby a startled look and opened her mouth to make a reply, but before she could do so, the tall highwayman swung round to Barnaby. "Still yer clapper!" he snapped. "Not one word or one move more, or it'll be the worser fer ye. Keep yer weapon on 'im, Japhet, while I go through 'is pockets."

Barnaby's pockets produced the best of the loot. The highwayman gurgled with pleasure at the purse he found, heavy with guineas. And when he saw Barnaby's watch, gleaming with heavy gold and attached to a chain that bore a beautiful, jewel-studded fob (a gift from the Earl on the occasion of Barnaby's thirtieth birthday), he turned to Japhet with a shout of triumph. "Will ye clamp yer peepers on *this*?" he chortled.

Barnaby, cold, furious and humiliated, could bear no more. Grasping the fellow by the back of his collar, he pulled him around and landed him a facer on the side of his jaw. The miscreant staggered back, dizzied. Barnaby struck the fellow's arm a smart blow that sent the watch and chain flying from his hand. At the same moment, he made a lunge for the pistol. But the second felon, Japhet, shook himself into action and swung the butt of his pistol at Barnaby's head. Barnaby fell down, stunned.

He tried to lift his head, but the motion made the world spin round at so terrifying a speed he had to close his eyes. He dropped his head with a groan. When he opened his eyes again, he was staring into the barrel of Japhet's pistol. Off to the side the other footpad was digging about among the dead leaves and foliage at the edge of the road, evidently searching for the watch that Barnaby had made him drop. "Put the bullet in 'is noddle an' be done," he was saying, "so you can come over 'ere and 'elp me search."

Japhet cocked the pistol and aimed. Barnaby tensed. With a cry, the lady leaped upon the felon and knocked his arm aside. Though the report made Barnaby wince and the lady shriek, the bullet flew harmlessly into the air. The other footpad did not even look round. "I found it," he cried happily, holding up the watch.

Japhet, enraged by the woman's interference, pulled Miranda to her feet and lifted his hand to strike her across the face. She lifted her chin arrogantly. "Murderer!" she snapped. "Will you also strike a defenseless woman?"

"Finish 'em off, both of 'em," the tall highwayman instructed. "Then we won't 'ave to watch 'em whiles we go through the baggage."

"That would be a stupid thing to do," Barnaby said with deliberate nonchalance. It was a tone he'd learned to use in handling difficult negotiations in the foreign service.

"Stupid, eh? Ha! So you say," the tall highwayman sneered. "I'd say it too in yer place."

But Japhet, the other one, was caught by Barnaby's tone. "Why stupid?" he asked, his interest caught.

"The coachman managed to hold on to his horses, isn't that so?" Barnaby reasoned. "Sooner or later he'll return for his carriage. With his coach and his horses intact, he will have lost nothing belonging to him or to his employer. He'll probably be content to return to London without further ado. But if he finds two bodies lying here, he will certainly feel compelled to go for the magistrates."

The tall highwayman was not impressed. "So we'll bury yer bodies."

"In this frozen ground? It'll take hours."

" 'E's right," Japhet said, looking at his partner worriedly. "That coachy's a rum cove. 'E mought be back any time soon."

The tall footpad considered the situation for a moment. "Then just tie 'em up to that tree," he said at last, starting toward the back of the coach where the baggage was tied. "An' be certain sure that the tongue-paddler's hands is tied tight."

Japhet marched his prisoners to the tree indicated. Keeping a sharp eye on them, he backed over to his horse and removed a length of rope from a saddlebag. He made the lady tie Barnaby's hands behind him and then bound them both to the tree. After checking that all knots were tight, he went to help his cohort rifle through the baggage.

"That was a clever argument you used to save our lives," Miranda said to the man tied beside her. "You must indeed be a tongue-paddler."

"I can't say, ma'am," Barnaby answered coldly, "since I have no idea what a tongue-paddler is."

"It's a thief's word for lawyer."

"A thief's word, eh? I don't find it particularly reassuring to know that the woman to whom I'm tied is familiar with thieves' cant."

The lady gave a gurgling laugh. "I don't see why it should worry you. Even if I were a thief, you've nothing to fear. They've already taken all your valuables."

He glared at her over his shoulder. "I'm delighted that my losses provide you with a subject for amusement, ma'am. When you find yourself slowly freezing to death, I hope you're able to laugh at that."

"Freezing to death? But you said the coachman would be back soon."

"I said it to keep those felons from blowing out our brains. It's much more likely that the coachman is halfway back to London by this time. With the snow getting heavier, I'm certain he'll want to be back before it accumulates."

"Oh, dear," Miranda said worriedly, "I never thought—"

But she ceased speaking, for the two miscreants were coming toward them, their arms laden with loot. Japhet carried a load of assorted clothing, while his confederate lugged a wooden crate from which the top had been pried off. Inside were more than a dozen bottles of what Barnaby believed was Scotch whiskey. The thieves had got themselves a good haul.

The tall highwayman, who wanted to be certain he could not possibly be followed, approached his prisoners to make a last check on their bonds. It was then he discovered he'd overlooked something. "Well, well," he chortled, " 'ere's a rum bit I almost missed. The lady still 'as 'er reticule."

Japhet clucked his tongue. "Tch, tch, ol' chum. Gettin' a mite careless, eh? What else mought the lady 'ave on 'er person?"

"Let's see." He pulled off Miranda's gloves and examined her wrists and fingers. He made her remove her wedding ring. (*So she is wed*, Barnaby noted.) Then he removed her bonnet and the lace cap she wore under it, causing her hair to tumble down over her shoulders, but no clips or jewels were revealed among the auburn tresses. He finally pulled open her pelisse at the neck with so rough a jerk that he ripped out the hook. "Nothin' much else," he muttered, disappointed. "Just this pretty bauble hangin' round 'er neck." And he yanked her cameo from its chain.

"Please don't take that," Miranda pleaded. "Please. It isn't very valuable, but it's very dear to me."

"That's whut they all say," the highwayman sneered, looking over the piece appreciatively.

"I didn't say it about my watch," Barnaby pointed out.

"Wouldn't do ye much good if ye did. I knowed the minute I seed it that it was a fancy timepiece. I wouldn' take a cent less than twenny quid fer it from my fence."

"Only twenty guineas?" Barnaby snorted disparagingly. "You'd be a fool."

The highwayman peered at Barnaby intently with a gleam so calculating that it was apparent even behind his mask. " 'Ow much would it take fer me *not* to be a fool?" he asked.

"Give the lady back her bauble, and I'll tell you exactly what it's worth."

"Not a chance." He pocketed the cameo and walked toward his horse. "I'll ask the fence fer fifty quid, then. That'll be a good enough price fer me."

The two miscreants tied their loot on their horses' backs, jumped up into the saddles and rode off without a backward look. Soon the sound of their horses' hooves was swallowed up by the wind.

Barnaby stared straight ahead of him at the swirling snow, the flakes growing thicker and coming down heavier every minute, and silently cursed his fate. He could imagine nothing worse than being out in this freezing weather tied helplessly to a tree beside the last woman in the world he would have chosen for company.

A slight movement—the tiniest tremor—from the woman beside him made him turn his head in her direction. Flakes of snow were accumulating on her bare head. Her thick auburn hair was tumbled about her shoulders, hiding her face from his view. "I say," he asked, surprised, "are you crying?"

"No, no, of c-course not," she retorted in a choked voice. "Why should I be c-crying? I'm tied to a tree with a man who thought I should have run off with a lecherous toad, it's snowing, I'm likely to freeze to death in my bonds, my portmanteaux have been rifled and my clothes are lying tossed about on the ground, all my money has been taken from me, and I've even l-lost my l-lovely c-c-cameo. What on earth is there to c-cry about?"

"Crying is wasted effort," Barnaby responded calmly. "We should be using our energies to cut ourselves loose."

She drew in a trembling breath. "I would be happy to use my energies in that way. What do you suggest I do?"

"Try to wriggle closer to me. The less room we take, the looser the bonds. If we can loosen these ropes enough to allow you to move your hands, you might be able to reach into my coat pocket there on my right. There's a pocket knife in it."

"A knife?" Her voice took on a glimmer of hope. She began to inch closer to him. "How is it possible the knife escaped the notice of those thieves?"

"Carelessness. I think the tall fellow was so overjoyed at the weight of my purse that he looked no further."

She was quite close to him now. He could feel her pressing against his side. Her arm twisted against the ropes, giving her just enough slack to permit her hand to inch slowly up his leg to his coat pocket. The effort made her breathe heavily. "I can feel the opening," she said, "but I can't reach in. Can you lower yourself a bit?"

He managed to do so, but the ropes cut into his chest painfully. Her hand was in his pocket now, feeling about for the little knife. "Hurry, can't you?" he gasped. "I can't keep bent like this much longer."

"I'm doing the very best . . . There! I have it!"

But that was only the first step. The next problem was to pull out the knife's intricately-imbedded blade, a trick that required two hands. "You'll have to try to bring your other hand over," he told her.

The effort caused so much friction against the ropes that her wrist was rubbed raw. By the time she managed to open the little knife, it was getting dark. She sawed the rope closest to her hand with the little blade, but it was slow work.

While she labored, Barnaby had time to examine her face at close range. His earlier assessment of her appearance had been hasty, he decided. She was still quite lovely. Snowflakes glistened on her cheeks, emphasizing the translucence of her skin; they caught on her long lashes and bejeweled her marvelous, thick, red-tinged hair. And her throat! How well he remembered that voluptuously shapely throat. It was her throat that had first caught his eye all those years ago. And it was still the same. She was not so changed as he had first thought.

Her closeness stirred his blood. He could feel her breast pressed against his arm and her thigh against his leg. And her breath, warm and sweet-smelling, blew against his neck as she labored. It was enough to make any man weak in the knees. If only she were someone else . . . *anyone* else but Miranda Pardew. He could not let himself forget who she was, and what she'd done to him.

Once the first piece of rope was cut through, the rest went quickly. She unbound them from the tree and then set to work on the bonds that tied his wrists. "That took long enough," he said ungraciously when he was at last freed.

She threw him a look of astonishment. "What a very sullen fellow you are, to be sure," she remarked. "But I suppose I should understand. You've lost more even than I."

"You needn't make excuses for me, ma'am," he retorted, rubbing his wrists. "I am sullen by nature. But we have no time for bibble-babble. It's getting dark, I'm already chilled to the bone, as you too must be, and we have at least three miles to walk."

"To where, may I ask?"

"To a small inn we passed back there, a few moments before those footpads stopped us."

"You are admirably observant, sir," she said, "but shouldn't we rather go forward, in the direction in which we were headed?"

"No, for who knows how far we'd have to walk to find habitation. It's better to go toward certainty than doubt."

"Yes, I suppose you're right," she agreed. "Just give me a few moments to gather up what's left of my things."

"I won't give you a few moments. In the first place, it's growing too dark. In a little while, we won't even see the road. In the second place, I have no intention of lugging a portmanteau three miles through the snow."

She stiffened in offense. "I had no intention of asking you. I'll 'lug' it myself."

He grasped her cruelly by the arm and turned her toward the road. "No, you will not. You'll need all your strength and breath to manage the three miles—and it may be more, for all I know—in this wind and cold. Perhaps someone at the inn can be coerced into coming back for your things. Move along now, like a good girl."

She shook off his hold angrily. "May I at least have a moment to retrieve my bonnet?"

His answer was an impatient grunt. She picked up the mistreated headpiece from the ground where the highwayman had dropped it, brushed off the snow and set it on her head. Then she hurried down the road after him, rubbing her arm where he'd grasped it. "Sullen is too kind an adjective to describe you," she snapped as she caught up with him and fell into step beside him. "I've never before met such a rudesby as you. One would think that, sometime in the past, somewhere, somehow, I had done you an injury."

He did not bother to respond.

· Six ·

THEY HAD TO walk more than five miles, Barnaby esti-
mated, before they saw the lights of the inn flickering
through the snowflakes. It felt like twenty-five miles. His
feet were damp and icy-cold, his fingers frozen and his
ears numb. And the woman beside him was in an even
worse case. Her nose was red, her teeth chattered and
there were frozen tears on her cheeks, tears more likely
to have been brought on by the assault of the icy wind
than by self-pity. She was a game chit, he had to grant
her that, for she never made a word of complaint. He was
certain that her feet were colder than his, for she wore
only little leather half-boots—like a man's high-lows—
which were too short and too flimsy to protect against
the rapidly deepening snow. Despite his old, unchanging
dislike of her, he was unable to keep from feeling pity for
her plight. He could not supply her with protection for her
feet, but he'd twice offered to give her his greatcoat. Each
time she'd waved him off. "I will not be beholden to such a
rudesby," she'd said dismissively. And those were the only
words they exchanged during the long, cold march.

The lights of the inn made a welcome gleam in the
darkness, and when the travelers slogged into the courtyard, the actual sight of it was truly comforting. The inn
looked warm and inviting. Its snow-spattered sign, lit by

the guttering flame of a brass lantern and creaking as it swung in the wind, read *Deacon's Gate Inn*. It was small for a public house, with two picturesque bow windows and a thickly-thatched roof, quite like a cottage in a Mother Goose picture book. But the most welcome sight of all was the smoke billowing from the two chimneys at each side of the house; evidently there were some goodly fires burning within.

Barnaby pushed open the door and followed Miranda into the blessed warmth. As they stamped the snow from their shoes in the tiny vestibule, a middle-aged woman (with a head of wild, though faded, red hair pinned so carelessly atop her head that much of it was falling about her face) appeared in the doorway of what was probably a taproom. "Bless me sainted mither!" she exclaimed in a thick brogue. "What wind o' the de'il blew ye here in this storm?"

"Only shank's mare," Barnaby said shortly. "For God's sake, woman, save your questions and take the lady to a fire."

"Aye, sir. Yer lady does look frozen through." The woman promptly put a proprietary arm about Miranda's waist and led her into the taproom, a room only large enough to accommodate three tables. But the fireplace was huge, and an appropriately large fire crackled within it. Miranda knelt before the blaze and, pulling off her thin gloves, held her hands up to the warmth.

The woman studied the kneeling Miranda with a look of sympathy before removing her soaked bonnet and pelisse. Then she turned to another door in the far corner. "Hanlon, ye lazy sot, come out 'ere," she shouted. " 'Tis company we 'ave! They'll be wantin' a hot toddy, so shake yer leg, me man!"

A moment later, a man appeared carrying two mugs. Short and bald, his florid face exuded good humor. He greeted the lady at the fireplace and handed her a tankard. " 'Tis a specialty of the 'ouse," he explained, smiling broadly, "called a Lamb's Wool. The name's a mite unfittin', but it'll warm yer innards."

Miranda accepted the drink gratefully and took a swig at once. The innkeeper, meanwhile, crossed the room to Barnaby. " 'Ere, sir, let me 'ave that wet coat o' yourn. Just drink this down, an' you'll be feelin' better afore it's gone."

"A Lamb's Wool, eh?" Barnaby sniffed into the tankard suspiciously. "What's in it?"

"Cider an' home brew an' a bit o' the grape," the innkeeper said as he went off with the wet outergarments. "Nothin' at all t' trouble yer stomach."

Barnaby drank a draught and discovered that the innkeeper had the right of it. A delicious warmth spread through his body. Never had he tasted so satisfying a brew.

The innkeeper's wife came up to him and watched with a pleased grin as he drank. "Good, ain't it? No one's ever had a bad word fer my husband's Lamb's Wool. And now you'll be wantin' a hot supper, I'll be bound."

"Yes, indeed, Mrs. Hanlon—it is Mrs. Hanlon, is it not?— some supper will be most welcome. Anything you have on hand, so long as it's hot. And afterwards, of course, a place to sleep for the night."

"That goes wi'out sayin'. 'Tain't a night fer man 'r beast out there."

Barnaby, looking down at the woman's friendly, guileless face, felt dishonest for accepting her hospitality without telling her he could not pay for it. He decided that the only honorable thing to do was to be frank with her. Not wishing to involve Miranda in sordid money matters, he motioned to Mrs. Hanlon to follow him into the vestibule. "Before we proceed any further, Mrs. Hanlon," he confided in a low voice, "I think I'd better tell you that the Norfolk stage on which we were traveling was beset by highwaymen. We were robbed of every valuable we possessed. Thus, I've not a groat on my person with which to pay you. I won't be able to settle the bill until I pass this way again after the New Year. Do you think you can trust me until then?"

"Ha!" came a snort from behind him. Barnaby looked round to find the hitherto-beaming innkeeper standing in the doorway, but he now had no smile on his face. "*Trust* ye?" he exclaimed contemptuously. "Don't take us fer fools. We been ast fer trust afore. You ain't the first what claimed that highwaymen emptied yer pockets. But that don't mean I'll let ye try to empty ours!"

Barnaby was not accustomed to having his word doubted, but his diplomatic training had taught him that one doesn't win an argument by losing one's temper. "You do believe we were robbed, don't you? You can go to see the abandoned coach for yourself when the snow lets up," he pointed out reasonably. "It's only five miles up the road."

"Oh, we 'ave no doubt ye was robbed," Mrs. Hanlon said, throwing a glare at her husband. "That stretch o' road up north is a footpad's dream."

"Then you've dealt with their victims before?"

"And been cheated by 'em, too, givin' them trust," the innkeeper said scornfully. "At least the footpads, when they come," he added under his breath, "pay fer their shot in cash."

Barnaby did not miss the implications of that muttered remark. The innkeeper had had dealings with the footpads in the past. That was useful information for the future, when he returned to deal with the felons.

Meanwhile, the redheaded Mrs. Hanlon wheeled on her husband. "Hanlon, still yer clapper, and don' be a looby! Can't ye see that this here's a gen'leman? One look should tell ye 'e's the sort'll keep 'is word. An' there's naught to be done in any case. We can't put 'em out in the snow, now, can we?"

The innkeeper frowned, shook his head and stomped back to where he'd come from, muttering something about women being as suited to business as cats to water.

Mrs. Hanlon was not in the least perturbed. "Well, that's settled," she said cheerfully. "Ye'll pay in the New Year. With a bit extra, fer int'rest, which ye'll agree is on'y fair and proper."

Barnaby grinned. "You're a better businesswoman than your husband gives you credit for."

The woman winked at him. "Don' I know it!" Pleased with herself, she pushed back a lock of tumbled hair (which promptly fell back down) and led him back into the taproom. "Now then, sir, sit yerself down. I'll 'ave a supper fer ye in a trice. Do ye think yer missus'd like a bit o' mutton stew?"

Barnaby, having seated himself, blinked up at the woman. "My *missus*? Do you mean the lady there? She's not—"

"Come now, sir," Mrs. Hanlon laughed, patting him playfully on his shoulder, "I can sniff out a married couple easy as I can a spoilt fish."

"Can you, indeed? And just what is it about that lady and me that makes your nose conclude we're wed?"

"You ain't speakin' to one another. 'Tis on'y married folk who disregard one another that way."

"Perhaps all married people disregard one another," Barnaby pointed out dryly, "but not all people who disregard one another are married."

The logic eluded the innkeeper's wife. "I ain't followin' you, sir," she said, confused.

Miranda, who'd been listening, gave a small laugh. "What the gentleman means, Mrs. Hanlon," she explained, looking up from the fire, "is that disregarding one another is not restricted to married people. It's the same as saying that all fish swim, but not everyone who swims is a fish."

"Exactly!" Barnaby smiled across at her, pleased to be so well understood. "Or one could say that all artists draw, but not everyone who draws is an artist."

"Or . . ." Miranda's eyes brightened at what began to seem like a game. "All tailors sew, but not everyone who sews is a tailor."

Barnaby actually chuckled. "All doctors bleed you, but not everyone who bleeds you is a doctor."

"That's a good one," Miranda said appreciatively. "Let me think. Ah, yes. All murderers lie, but not everyone who lies is a murderer."

Mrs. Hanlon blinked in sudden understanding. "Oh, I see now. All candles burn, but not everythin' that burns is a candle."

"Yes, that's it!" Barnaby threw the woman a warm grin.

"Good for you," Miranda applauded. Warmed in body by the fire and in mood by the game, she wanted the camaraderie to continue. "All young girls flirt," she offered, "but not all flirts are young girls."

It was an unfortunate choice, for it suddenly reminded Barnaby of something he'd momentarily forgotten: who she was. His smile faded and he turned away. "That's enough," he said sourly. "The point's been made."

Miranda's eyebrows rose. The gentleman's abrupt change of tone was a surprise. What had she said to offend?

Mrs. Hanlon looked from one to the other curiously. "Are ye sure ye ain't married?"

"No, of course not," Miranda said, her mood destroyed.

"Heaven forbid!" Barnaby muttered.

Mrs. Hanlon could hardly believe them. "Well, ye surely fooled me. I ain't never yet seen a pair look more wedded than you." She glared at them in sudden disapproval. "All I can say is ye'd *better* be wed, for I 'ave on'y one bedroom upstairs. If ye can't share it, one of ye'll 'ave to spend the night down 'ere sleepin' on a bench."

Barnaby winced. "And we all know who *that* will be," he said in glum surrender to his fate.

Thus it was that, two hours later, he found himself uncomfortably laid out upon a narrow bench in a deserted taproom under a shabby comforter, his legs hanging over one carved armrest and his head propped on the other. Above him, snug under the eaves, Miss-Miranda-Pardew-that-was was contentedly ensconced in a featherbed, warm, cozy, and probably having happy dreams of all the men she'd destroyed in the past. Of all the irritations Barnaby had suffered this day, the fact that she was luxuriously, voluptuously asleep right over his head was by far the most irritating.

He tried in vain to find a position of comfort for his weary bones, but even the blanket folded in four thicknesses under him could not soften the rigidity of the hard oak bench. "It's perfect," he muttered to himself as he shifted awkwardly onto his side only to discover that there was no place for his damnably long legs. "Quite perfect. A perfect ending to this absolutely perfect day." He'd started out this morning with an instinctive conviction that he should never have left home. How right he'd been!

· Seven ·

MIRANDA WOKE THE next morning and looked round her tiny room in confusion. She had no idea of the time; the air was too gloomily dark to permit her to guess how far the morning had advanced. But as she reluctantly edged herself out from under the two comforters that had kept her warm during the night, she promised herself that, whatever the time, she would set out as soon as possible for Wymondham. It would not do to allow her new employer to believe she was unreliable. She had to get to the Traherne establishment before Mrs. Traherne lost patience.

She'd lain awake half the night worrying about how she was to get to her destination without funds, but the morning brought with it a feeling of optimism. Someone would give her a ride. The surly gentleman to whom she was tied yesterday was evidently going in the same direction. Perhaps she could prevail upon him to take her to her destination.

In one quick leap, she rose from the bed and, shivering, ran barefoot to the little dormer window of her low-ceilinged bedchamber and peeped out. To her dismay, she found that the snow was still falling. The whole world was buried in whiteness, and here and there the wind had blown the snow into huge drifts. The view smote her like a blow. There would be no traffic on the roads today. How could she possibly manage to reach the Traherne household under these trying circumstances? It might be *days* before the roads cleared. What would Mrs. Traherne think of her if she arrived at Wymondham several days after she was expected? Miranda's fear that she'd be given the sack— a fear that had haunted her in the dark of the night but had subsided in daylight—now returned in all its nighttime power. What a dreadful fix she was in! She'd cut her ties with the past so completely that they were past mending. If she were sacked, where on earth could she go?

Her spirits had only partially recovered when she came downstairs half an hour later. She found the surly gentleman standing before the bow window of the taproom, staring disconsolately out at the deepening white cover. He did not hear her approach. This gave her the opportunity to study him while he was unaware of her doing so. He was an attractive fellow, she noted, with a broad forehead, thick hair and a spare yet powerful frame. He had an air of refinement, and he'd shown both bravery and cleverness in his encounters with the footpads yesterday. All that was to the good, as was his momentary flash of charm during the brief little game they'd played with the innkeeper's wife last evening. But for the most part, he was sullen and insulting. For some reason, he'd taken her in dislike. She couldn't help wondering why. Perhaps she reminded him of someone he disliked. Perhaps he'd suffered a recent tragedy which affected his mood. Perhaps he was ill or in pain and too brave to speak of it. One should not judge too harshly, she reminded herself, when one lacks the relevant information.

She really knew nothing about the fellow. He seemed a gentleman, but did he have a profession or a trade? Was he riding toward home on the stage or away from it? Was he married? Did he have a houseful of children depending on him? Why, she didn't even know his name!

It would be helpful, she decided, to make friends with him, especially if she intended to ask him to assist her in getting to her destination. Moreover, if they were to be forced to spend days in a deserted country inn waiting for the snow to let up, the hours would pass more pleasantly if the company were congenial. Perhaps she should try again to win him over.

She stepped over the threshold, put on a bright smile and said, "Good morning," in the most pleasant voice she could muster.

He turned from the window, startled by her abrupt arrival. At this unexpected sight of her, something in his chest flipped over. Why did the sight of her move him? he wondered in dismay. But perhaps his perturbation was caused by his not having had time to prepare his defenses. Moreover, her appearance this morning was not what he'd anticipated. In the first place, her cheeks were still flushed from a warm sleep, making her look younger than she'd seemed yesterday. Then there was her hair, no longer covered by the matronly cap; it was brushed into shining smoothness and pulled back from her face into a tight knot at the nape of her neck, giving her an air of purity he found quite inconsistent with his impression of her character. Lastly, and most unexpected of all, was the look in her eyes—a look of glowing warmth and kindness. Miranda Pardew, *kind*? Impossible!

He gaped at her, unable for the moment to speak. In her severe blue muslin gown, trimmed only with a ruffle of white at the neck and at the edges of the long, narrow sleeves, she looked so proper and prim that she almost seemed to be someone else. That the voluptuous girl of the Lydell ball could be the same person as this straitlaced woman was hard to believe, though in both incarnations he had to admit she was lovely. Utterly lovely.

But as soon as those words registered in his consciousness, he was stricken with self-disgust. This woman represented everything he despised. How could he still find her lovely? *You must watch yourself*, a voice inside him warned, *or she'll make a fool of you again*. He must give her a set-down, and quickly, to be certain she was kept at a safe distance. He drew his eyebrows tightly together into his most forbidding frown. "Did you say good *morning*?" he asked disdainfully. "It's almost afternoon. I suppose ladies in your set are accustomed to sleep away half the day."

His tone put her instantly on the defensive. "But I'm usually quite an early riser, sir. It was just that the morning was so dark, and the featherbed so warm . . ." But she suddenly realized she had no need to apologize to him. "Not that my habits are any concern of yours," she added, lifting her chin.

"Mrs. Hanlon served breakfast three hours ago," he chastised, "and I had risen more than an hour before *that*. But it's not surprising I rose early. *My* bed was not conducive to late sleeping."

"I am sorry for your discomfort, sir, but you can't blame me for the inn's meager accommodations."

He merely shrugged and turned back to the window. "That tea tray on the table is for you," he informed her. "Mrs. Hanlon brought it in when she heard you stirring."

Miranda seated herself and reached for the teapot. She was discouraged by her failure to soften him but not defeated. "Would you like to join me?" she asked, determinedly cheerful. "The water is still hot."

"No, thank you."

She sipped her tea, calmly enduring the lengthy silence. After she'd poured herself a second cup, she tried again. "Do you think the snow will stop any time soon?"

"Soon? Huh!" he snorted. "If our good luck holds, we may expect to be imprisoned here till spring."

"If that's a sample of your sense of humor, sir," Miranda retorted, "I would not care for more of it. It lacks optimism."

"Then I would suggest, ma'am, that you go and exchange pleasantries with Mrs. Hanlon. She's as full of happy optimism as a puppy with a bone. She's gone to fix us luncheon. She promises ham and cold chicken and river trout and poached eggs and potatoes and custard pudding and, no doubt, several other tidbits I've forgotten. As if one could rouse an appetite after seeing the damnable depth of the snow on the road out there."

"I think it's very kind of her to feed us so lavishly. If she's gone to such trouble, we should try to do the meal justice."

"You must suit yourself, ma'am, but I would find it very hard to swallow a bite. This situation in which we're embroiled has taken away any semblance of appetite I might have had when I started out."

"I admit that our circumstances are discouraging, but it does no good to make matters worse by sulking."

"Sulking, am I?" He threw her another of his withering looks. "If you think, Miss Pardew, that you're likely to improve the situation by bandying about insulting epithets, you're far off the mark."

"Miss *Pardew*?" She stared at him in astonishment. "You called me Miss Pardew!"

He winced. *Damnation!* he cursed in his mind. *How did I let that slip?* If he wanted to keep her at a distance, he'd made a serious error. But he was a trained diplomat; he had some experience in rectifying blunders. He quickly adjusted his facial features to express bland surprise and asked calmly, "Did I? How strange. Is that your name?"

"You must know it is. At least, it was. I have not been Miss Pardew for many years."

"Ah. Your maiden name, then?"

"Yes. I am Lady . . . er, Mrs. Velacott, now."

So she did wed Sir Rodney, then, he thought. But she denied her title. He wondered why. Aloud, he only said, "How do you do?" and made a polite bow.

"You can't put me off with foolish amenities, sir. How did you know my name? Have we met before?"

"I suppose we must have, though I have no recollection of it."

"Then how can you explain—?"

He shrugged. "The name must have popped out from some deeply buried cache of memory."

"Astounding," she murmured, eyeing him suspiciously. "In fact, almost unbelievable."

"Yes," he agreed, turning away to pretend an interest in the bleak outdoor scene, "quite unbelievable."

"You've not yet told me *your* name, sir. Perhaps, if I learned it, I could determine where and when we met."

He had no intention of telling her his name. "What of your husband, ma'am?" he asked, ignoring her request. "Will he not be concerned about your absence?"

"My husband died a year ago. I am a widow."

"Oh. I see." He took a moment to let the information sink in. His reaction to the news was confused, his feelings unclear. Was he pleased? Relieved? Sorry for her? None of those reactions was appropriate, and all of them were dangerous. *Watch yourself*, the warning voice reminded him. But, too curious about the details of her life, he ignored it and plunged ahead. "Your children, then. Will they not be worried?"

"I have no children." She studied his back intently. "Now, sir, you know all about me. And I have yet to learn your name."

He turned round. In his head, he could hear her voice as it was a dozen years earlier. She'd asked him for his name then, too. But before he'd managed an answer, she'd waved him off. *I'd rather dismiss you incognito*, she'd taunted. He could give her that same "cut direct" right now, with almost the same devastating effect, and in almost the same words. Why not? Wasn't it said that revenge was sweet? *I think, Mrs. Velacott*, he could say with cold deliberation, *that I would rather remain incognito*. He took a breath and prepared to say it. "I . . . I . . ." he began. But something took over his tongue. "My name is Traherne," were the words that came out of his mouth.

He could not believe his own ears. He'd obeyed her request as meekly as a lamb. *God curse me for a damned jellyfish!* he berated himself furiously. What was the matter with him that in the presence of this woman he became a milksop, weak and unmanned?

But she, hearing the name, gazed up at him with a beaming smile. "Traherne?" she exclaimed excitedly. "Mr.

Terence Traherne? I can't tell you how delighted I am that it's you! Who better than you can explain to your wife why I am so delayed?"

Was the woman speaking gibberish? Barnaby wondered. He couldn't make sense of a word she'd said. "I only understood one thing in that speech, ma'am, and that is that you've misidentified me. I'm sorry to disappoint you, but I am not Terence. My name is Barnaby. Terence is my brother."

But if Miranda was disappointed, the feeling was momentary. After a brief blink, she turned her gaze back upon him with an expression of renewed delight. "Then you are Mrs. Traherne's brother-in-law. How wonderful for me! Her brother-in-law can as easily be my savior as her husband."

"Your . . . savior?"

"Yes, don't you see? With you to explain to your sister-in-law exactly what happened to delay us, I'm certain she will forgive my lateness. Oh, Mr. Traherne! What luck that we happened to be traveling together!"

"*Luck*?" He eyed her in disbelief, as if she were speaking in a completely foreign tongue. "Ah, yes," he said, his voice dripping with irony, "what luck, indeed."

· Eight ·

IN THE AFTERNOON, the snow stopped. It was the only good thing to happen that day. To Barnaby, it was otherwise the worst of days, full of irritations major and minor. First, there was the news that, of all people, Miranda Pardew (or Mrs. Velacott, as she apparently wished to be called) was heading for his brother's house. The prospect of having to spend his holidays in the same house as she was a major blow. Furthermore, she told him that she was to be employed by Delia, his sister-in-law, as a sort of governess. How Delia (whom he thought of as a perfectly sensible woman and an excellent mother) could have chosen this particular candidate to help raise her charming little boys was quite beyond him. Miranda Velacott was a sharp-tongued woman without an iota of sympathy for males; she would never have been Barnaby's choice as governess for his nephews. The youngest of them, little Jamie, was a quiet, sensitive sort (reminding Barnaby painfully of himself as a child) whose personality would not thrive under the tutelage of an overbearing, sardonic, cold female. Delia would soon learn what a mistake she'd made in her choice.

Added to his blighted expectations for his holiday and his concern for the well-being of his nephews was Barnaby's vexation at the prospect of having to spend another night on that hellish bench. If it were to be only one more night, he might not have been overly dismayed, but he feared he might be doomed to that deplorable wooden "bed" for a week or more. If the weather stayed cold, the roads could remain impassable well into the new year. That possibility was worse than anything else; it meant that he would be stuck here in this tiny, uncomfortable, Godforsaken inn with no one but Mrs. Velacott for company. This journey, he thought, was fast becoming a blasted disaster!

Miranda, however, was overjoyed at the cessation of the snow. Her spirit soared as the sky cleared. "Do you think Mr. Hanlon will be able to arrange a carriage for us tomorrow?" she asked Barnaby eagerly. "Do you think the road will be passable by then?"

He was unable to answer in the affirmative, but even that didn't dampen her mood. So long as she didn't let her thoughts dwell on the encounter with the highwaymen and the loss of all her worldly possessions (and there was no point in thinking about that, since it was spilt milk), she found herself surprisingly cheerful. She truly believed that her prospects were much improved since this morning; after all, the man with whom she was marooned was her employer's brother-in-law, who would not only take her to her destination but would also provide supporting proof of her explanation to Mrs. Traherne of her late arrival. If Mr. Barnaby Traherne weren't so grumpish, Miranda would have found this experience an interesting adventure.

During the long afternoon, while she sat at the fire warming her feet and he prowled restlessly round the room, she tried to converse with him, but he, when he deigned to answer her at all, responded only in monosyllables. Bored and frustrated, she finally sought out Mrs. Hanlon and prevailed upon her to unearth a deck of cards. Then she coaxed and cajoled Barnaby so relentlessly to play with her that he at last agreed. They sat down at one of the tables, and she proceeded to teach him a game of two-handed whist that she called Hearts (because, she explained, hearts were always trump). They played a full rubber, which she gleefully won. "If there's anything I despise," he growled as he pushed back his chair, "it's a gloating winner."

"Better that," she said with a throaty giggle, "than a grudging loser."

"I do not begrudge you the rubber. The whole matter is too insignificant to make me begrudge you your petty triumph."

"Petty it may be, but even in petty matters a triumph is better than a loss." She gathered up the cards and shuffled them expertly.

"You do that very well," he said, getting up from the chair. "Like an expert, in fact. Your skill at cards, coupled with your knowledge of thieves' cant, makes me wonder about you, ma'am. Can it be that beneath the prim and schoolteacherish costume hides the heart of a card-sharp?"

"Card-sharp? *I?*" She laughed heartily at the suggestion. "I hardly think so, Mr. Traherne. My knowledge of thieves' cant consists of that one word, tongue-paddler. I'm not certain how I came to learn it. I think my solicitor once referred to himself with that term. And as for my skill at cards, it was gained by spending long hours playing with my maiden aunt, who lived with me for the past decade. We passed many a lonely evening in this mildly entertaining fashion. To make it more exciting, we kept score with make-believe money. I believe, by the time we parted, that I owed her something in the neighborhood of forty-five thousand guineas."

Barnaby had to smile. She looked so innocent sitting there, the firelight on her face, her eyes misted with memory, that his suggestion seemed ludicrous. But so did her suggestion that she'd spent a decade of her life playing whist with a maiden aunt. She may not have been a card-sharp, but neither could she make him believe that she was a spinsterish stay-at-home. What really had happened in her life? he wondered.

But he had no intention of following this line of inquiry. He did not wish to become involved in her life. He had no interest in her history nor did he want any part of her future. He'd be damned if he'd permit her to charm him and entice him into any sort of web. He would not play fly to her spider.

He changed his expression from small smile to forbidding frown. "Card games are a sinful waste of time," he growled as he got to his feet.

Startled, she gaped up at him in sheer mystification. His shifts of mood confused her. This was not the first time he'd seemed to warm to her and then abruptly turned to ice. She cocked her head and studied him quizzically. "Card games *sinful*?" she teased. "What gammon! And as far as wasting time is concerned, what have we to do with our time here but waste it? Really, Mr. Traherne, you sometimes sound like a priggish Evangelical."

"Priggish?" He raised a disdainful eyebrow. "You are very quick to skewer me with insulting epithets, ma'am. I hope you're not so contemptuous of your pupils as you are of me."

Miranda lost her patience. "I am not in the least contemptuous!" she cried, getting to her feet. "Not of you and not of my pupils. I consider myself to be a good-natured, reasonably even-tempered woman. If anyone has been contemptuous, it is you!"

"Really? It was I, I suppose, who called *you* a prig."

"I did not call you a prig. I said you sounded priggish."

"Close enough as makes no difference."

"What I said was not nearly as contemptuous as your calling me a card-sharp . . . and . . . and, this morning, a sloth. And you just called into question my attitude toward my pupils. You, sir, have been offensive to me from the first."

"That, ma'am, is just the sort of wild exaggeration I might have expected from you."

"Dash it all, why should you expect *anything* from me? You don't know anything about me. We've never met before yesterday. I know you somehow heard my name, but I have no recollection of our paths having crossed. So why should you have any expectations regarding my behavior?"

"I expect *every* lady to behave like one," he said coldly.

She stiffened in offense. "If the truth be known, Mr. Toplofty Traherne, I've tried all day, in every way I know, to be pleasant and conciliating. But you've responded to every one of my attempts with rudeness and hostility. I can't imagine why you've taken me in such dislike, but I no longer care. In fact, I've had quite enough of you. I think you'd try the patience of a *saint*!" She strode to the door of the taproom with a great swish of skirts, her head high. "Good night, Mr. Traherne. Please tell Mrs. Hanlon that I'll take supper in my room."

Later that night, having given up any expectation of falling asleep on his excruciating bench, he stared up at the shadowed ceiling-beams and reviewed the words she'd thrown at him. She'd been quite right, of course. He'd behaved like a churl. But that was exactly how he wanted to behave. No one deserved it more than she. He ought to be quite pleased with himself, for the results were just what he wished. Then why, he asked himself, was he feeling like a cad?

She came down early to breakfast the next morning, but she did not respond to his greeting. Nor would she sit at the same table as he. She took a chair at another table with her back to him. Mrs. Hanlon, when she served their eggs and bacon, looked from one to the other with speculative amusement, but tactfully said nothing.

It was a brilliant morning, the sunlight dazzling on the snow. It was the sort of morning when even adults yearn to cavort in the drifts like little children. But neither Miranda nor Barnaby would let the glorious day interfere with their stubborn antagonism. As the morning advanced, and the silence between them grew more and more awkward, Barnaby actually considered offering her an apology— anything to end the deucedly appalling silence! But he quickly persuaded himself not to surrender. He was a man, he reminded himself, and she would not again turn him into a worm.

Miranda, too, was finding the silence oppressive. As she sat at a table, trying to find distraction in a game of solitaire, she wondered how she could break the silence without injuring her pride. But Mr. Traherne was a boor and a rudesby, she reminded herself, and his surly conversation would not be a great improvement over the silence.

Before either one of them was brought to the point of surrender, there was a sound of horses neighing and sleighbells jingling in the courtyard outside. They both ran to the window. A sleigh drawn by a pair of horses was drawing up beside the door. As they watched, a middle-aged man, well protected from the cold by huge boots, a high hat, mittens and a long muffler, jumped from the seat and slogged through the snow to the doorway. "Good God!" Barnaby shouted gleefully. "*Terence!*"

Miranda watched wide-eyed as the outer door was pushed open and the man from the sleigh stomped in. Barnaby Traherne was already in the vestibule when the fellow looked up from his boots. "Ah! *Barnaby*, old fellow!" he chortled in triumphant surprise. "So I've found you at last!"

The two men embraced, pounding each other's backs enthusiastically. "You *brick*!" Barnaby exclaimed. "How on earth did you—?"

"When your coach didn't arrive at Wymondham, we were all in a stew. Then Lawrence and Honoria arrived in their sleigh, which you'll agree was the perfect vehicle for this weather, so I decided to take it and go looking for you. When I discovered the stage half buried in snow, with no one about, no sign of horses, and baggage all strewn about willy-nilly, I was chilled to the marrow, I can tell you! I've been pounding on doors ever since. Damnation, boy, you're a sight for sore eyes!" And he embraced his brother again.

"It was a scurvy pair of highwaymen," Barnaby said in explanation. "They—"

"I thought as much," his brother cut in, nodding. "Thank the Lord you're safe. Everyone at home will fall on your neck, I promise you." He took off his beaver and shook the snow from it. "I say, Barnaby, you didn't by chance come across a stray female, did you? Delia was expecting a woman she'd hired to help with the boys."

Miranda, who could not avoid hearing every word, came up to the taproom doorway. "I'm the stray female, Mr. Traherne," she said, dropping a small curtsey. "Your brother and I were on the same coach."

"Mrs. Velacott, is it *you*? What luck!" Terence strode over to her and shook her hand effusively. "So you and my brother are already acquainted?"

Barnaby and Miranda exchanged glances. "Oh, more than merely acquainted," she said. "Your brother saved our lives."

"Did he, by Jove?" Terence grinned at his brother with fond admiration.

Barnaby threw Miranda a quizzical look. Her praise had surprised him. "Yes," he said to his brother, "but only after she saved mine. She leaped upon the brigand who was holding a gun to my head. And she didn't even know my name."

"Did you indeed, Mrs. Velacott? How very brave."

"Not nearly so brave as your brother, sir. He attacked armed highwaymen with nothing but his fists, not once but several times."

"Good God!" Terence exclaimed. "You seem to have had quite an adventure. You shall tell me all about it as we ride home in the sleigh. So get your things and come along. We mustn't keep Honoria and Delia and the boys in their state of alarm any longer than necessary."

By this time, Mr. and Mrs. Hanlon had come out from the kitchen. "They 'aven't any things t' get, sir," Mrs. Hanlon said, " 'cept their outer garments."

"That's right," Barnaby said, drawing his brother aside. "I say, Terence, can you pay our shot here? Those damned miscreants made off with all of my blunt."

The matter was no sooner said than done, and a few moments later Barnaby, clad in his greatcoat and hat, was climbing up on the seat of the sleigh while Terence assisted the cloaked Miranda up on the other side. Then he jumped up beside her and flicked his whip at the horses.

They waved goodbye to the Hanlons, who stood watching in the doorway, and the sleigh glided smoothly onto the snowy road. The horse's bells jingled, the sunlight glistened and a light wind blew sprays of tingling snowflakes on their cheeks. "Isn't this a glorious day?" Terence crowed loudly, his voice echoing cheerfully in the icy air. "I must apologize for crowding you, Mrs. Velacott," he added, "but since you say that you and my brother are so intimately acquainted, you won't feel awkward being crushed between us on the seat like this."

Not even this enchanting sleighride and Terence Traherne's robust good nature could make Miranda forget her resentment of Barnaby's rudeness. "I wouldn't say your brother and I are *intimately* acquainted," she said, throwing Barnaby a disdainful glance from under the hood of her pelisse, "but I *do* know your brother well enough to be familiar with all his moods and crotchets."

Barnaby met her glance with a scornful look of his own. "Perhaps we've passed mere acquaintanceship," he said dryly. "In fact, we may have reversed the whole process. If one thinks of saving a life as the ultimate act of intimacy, one could say we've gone from being intimate to being acquaintances to being total strangers."

"I say," Terence exclaimed, throwing his brother a puzzled look, "is something amiss between you two?"

"Nothing's amiss," Barnaby said.

"Nothing," Miranda echoed with an expression of bland innocence. "Nothing at all."

· *Nine* ·

IT WAS JUST growing dark when they arrived at the large, ramshackle manor house that the Terence Trahernes called home. It had been built for the first Earl of Shallcross in the sixteenth century, although the subsequent earls chose to inhabit a more elegant edifice in Surrey. Lawrence had given the property to Terence as a wedding gift. It was a box-like, brick-and-stone building whose third story consisted of a row of dormers behind which a number of huge chimneys reached up to the sky like blunt fingers.

Miranda had barely time to take it in, for her two sleigh companions leaped out of the equipage as soon as it drew up to the doorway and immediately helped her down. Without waiting for the others, Terence ran up the steps and brushed by the just-emerging butler. "I found him!" he shouted loudly to whoever was within. "He's *here!*"

The butler stopped Barnaby right on the stairs and threw his arms about him in a decidedly unbutlerish embrace. "Master Barnaby," he exclaimed, "we were that anxious about ye!"

"I'm fine, Cummings," Barnaby assured him. "Just fine. See to the lady, will you?"

The butler beamed at him, gave a last pat to his shoulder and then turned to lead Miranda up the stairs. They followed Barnaby over the threshold into a large, high-ceilinged hallway facing a wide stairway. Miranda had a quick impression of dark, cobwebby beams high above and worn carpets below, but she could not properly take in her surroundings, for a veritable mob of people filled the hall. They'd rushed in from all directions and were surrounding Barnaby with effusive demonstrations of welcome. The rafters rang with joyful greetings and relieved laughter. He was embraced with raucous affection by so many men and women that Miranda could not keep count of them. Nor could she recognize the surly fellow she'd come to know. Here among his family, he seemed like someone else entirely. Kissed and patted and embraced, he was actually blushing with shy pleasure! He permitted himself to be pummelled and pulled from one to the other with smiling good grace. Not only was he receiving this loving attention with becoming modesty, but what was more astonishing, he was showing equally warm affection to each of them as he returned their greetings.

Miranda, never having experienced anything like this exhibition of familial affection, felt a twinge of envy. She had to turn her eyes from the happy scene. It was then she noticed a pretty young woman standing apart in the shadows watching the excitement, just as she herself was doing. She wondered who this other outsider might be, and if she, too, was suffering pangs of envy. At that moment, however, a plump, kindly, elderly lady took the girl's arm, drew her into the circle and introduced her to Barnaby. Barnaby bowed and kissed her hand, and the girl blushed painfully, while all the others grinned and laughed.

Suddenly the crowd was distracted by loud shouts of "Uncle Barney! Uncle Barney!" from the stairs. Two robust young boys came racing down, followed by a distracted maid who had evidently failed to keep them in tow. They in turn were followed by an excited little toddler whose stubby legs could not manage the stairs with the ease of the older boys. Barnaby stepped out of the crowd that had encircled him and opened his arms. His two older nephews leaped into them and enveloped him in excited embraces.

Meanwhile, the little fellow, suddenly taking in the milling crowd in the hallway, hid himself behind the newel post, permitting himself only to peep out with one frightened eye. "Unca *Barney*," he hissed from his hiding place, "I'm *here*! Come an' hug *me*, too!"

Barnaby set the other boys on the floor and crossed over to the stairway. There he knelt down and took the little fellow in his arms. "Jamie, lad," he whispered in the child's ear, "I've missed you so!"

Miranda found herself oddly touched as she watched Barnaby swing the child up on his shoulders. She would never have guessed that the ill-mannered fellow with whom she'd passed the last three days was such an affectionate family man!

Meanwhile, the noisy arrival of his sons reminded Terence of Miranda's presence. Taking his two older boys by the hand, and motioning Barnaby to follow with Jamie, he approached the doorway where she was standing. "Mrs. Velacott," he said proudly, "I'd like you to meet your new charges." And while everyone turned and stared at her, Miranda stepped forward to face her future.

The two older boys, gazing up at her curiously, were strapping, well-built fellows, quite like their father. The little one, happily settled on his uncle's shoulder, was too preoccupied in nuzzling his uncle's ear to pay any attention to her. Terence made a sweeping gesture encompassing all of them. "This one," he indicated with a finger, "is George. He's twelve but likes to think he's fifteen. And the one with the dirty nose is Maurice—we call him Maury—who's ten. And the little fellow sitting on Barnaby's shoulder is James Lawrence Stephen Traherne, six years old, whom we call Jamie."

"George, Maury and Jamie," Miranda smiled, bowing to them, "how do you do?"

"Mrs. *Velacott*!" a ruddy-faced, middle-aged woman exclaimed, coming forward with an outstretched hand. "I didn't even know you'd come! Terence, you blockhead, why didn't you *tell* me?"

"Sorry, my dear. Too much excitement. Mrs. Velacott, this of course is my wife, Delia Traherne. And while I'm at it, I may as well make the others known to you. Standing behind Mrs. Traherne is my brother Harry. Next to him is his betrothed, Lady Isabel Folley. To my left, here, is my sister-in-law, Lady Honoria and, beside her, her husband, my eldest brother, Lawrence, the Earl of Shallcross. Finally, hiding behind them like a violet among the leaves, is their guest, Miss Olivia Ponsonby. Come out, Livy, and say hello to Mrs. Velacott, our new governess."

Miranda made her bow to his lordship and his lady, and then bowed to all the rest of them, trying hard to remember which name matched each face. She knew Barnaby and Terence, of course, and she would not mistake her new mistress, Mrs. Delia Traherne, whose ruddy, full cheeks and warm brown eyes made her seem friendly and open-hearted. The others would also be recognizable if she picked a distinctive characteristic for each as an identification. The Earl, for example, was the easiest to remember, for he had a remarkable head of wild white hair. She guessed him to be about fifty years old, but his hair made him look more like Barnaby's father than his brother. His wife, Honoria, a plump, pleasant-looking matron, had given a first impression of gentle warmth, but she was now staring at Miranda with the strangest kind of intensity. Miranda would have liked to ask the lady why, but she had to concentrate on the others if she was to identify them properly. Lady Honoria's guest, Olivia, was the youngest of the circle, certainly not more than twenty-two, and very lovely to look upon, with softly waving golden hair, soft skin and soft, frightened blue eyes. Harry, Barnaby's second brother, tall and robust, was quite like Terence in appearance. And his betrothed, Lady Isabel, was a dark-haired, proud woman with a stiff, regal bearing. *Yes*, Miranda assured herself, *I think I can remember all their names*.

The introductions made, Delia turned to her newly-arrived brother-in-law. "Barnaby, my love, you must be exhausted. Give your coat to Cummings, and let's all go to the drawing room and have tea. Mrs. Velacott, why don't you take the boys upstairs and get acquainted? I'll have tea sent up to you."

Miranda blinked for a moment, finding it necessary to adjust to a completely new way of behaving in society. *I am not a guest*, she reminded herself. *I'm a servant. I must learn to act the part.* "Yes, ma'am," she said, making a little bow. Then she turned to George and Maury. "Come, boys. You must show me the way. And Jamie," she added, reaching up for him, "do you think your 'Unca Barney' can spare you for a while?"

Barnaby, an expression of aghast surprise passing over his face, handed the reluctant child over. It seemed to Miranda that the man felt just as startled at seeing her in the role of servant as she did. She could feel his eyes on her all the way up the stairs.

When the children and their new governess disappeared, the other guests began to move toward the drawing room. Harry pulled Barnaby out of his trance and urged him across the hall. "Come on, boy, we want to hear about your adventures. Terence is frightening little Livy with the claim that the highwayman held a gun to your head. Is that true?"

The Earl and Honoria were the last to leave the hall. Both had remained staring up the stairway in a stunned silence. "Funny, Honoria," the Earl muttered, his brow knit, "but I could swear I've seen that woman before."

Honoria fixed him with a disgusted frown. "Don't you recognize her? That's Miranda Pardew!"

"What?" The Earl eyed his wife askance. "No! *Is* it? You don't mean the chit who made mincemeat of Barnaby all those years ago, do you?"

"The very same. Dash it all, Lawrence, what is she *doing* here? Governess, indeed! Her name's Velacott, isn't it? Shouldn't it be *Lady* Velacott? You don't suppose that idiot, Sir Rodney, has impoverished himself, do you?"

"How the devil would I know if he had?" the Earl responded curtly. "I don't keep up with town gossip. Haven't for years!"

"Well, I don't like it. I don't want that vixen interfering in our lives. I have such high hopes of this holiday. Livy is an angel, and Barnaby's bound to see it if he gets half a chance."

"Perhaps he'll see it, and perhaps he won't. But I don't see what Miranda Pardew has to do with it."

"I just don't like her being here, that's all. At this very critical time, too. I've a very bad feeling about this."

"Bad feeling or not, we'd better go in to tea before they come looking for us. Do you intend to say anything to Barnaby about the Pardew chit?"

"Tell him who she is, is that what you mean?" Honoria's pleasant face tightened into worried thoughtfulness. "No, I don't think so. If he hasn't recognized her, why should we stir the waters? Let's not say a word until we must. If God is kind, perhaps we won't have to."

"I imagine God has more important matters on His mind," her husband muttered, taking her arm.

They walked slowly toward the drawing room, Honoria emitting a sigh with every step. "That deuced Pardew woman!" she muttered under her breath. "She's a *curse*. What have I ever done to deserve it?"

· Ten ·

DELIA TRAHERNE BIT her lip worriedly as she mounted the stairway to the third floor where the children and the servants had their rooms. Now that her guests were dressing for dinner, she had time to interview the new governess, but she was not looking forward to the exchange. She had no talent for interviewing and instructing servants in general, and this interview in particular, she feared, would be an ordeal.

Delia was an unaffected, sensible woman who was content with her lot in life. She had a good-natured, lusty husband, three healthy sons and a comfortable if not luxurious life, and that was quite good enough for her. She did not mind the slightly run-down house, the shabby furnishings, the not-quite-adequate staff. Not afraid of hard work, she did not require servants to do things she could perfectly well do for herself. And one of the things she'd done for herself was raise her sons. If she hadn't been laid low with a severe case of pleurisy last fall, she never would have advertised for a governess. Now that she was better, she was beginning to wonder if she'd been hasty.

What had brought on these misgivings was her feeling that Mrs. Velacott in person did not appear as satisfactory a candidate as she'd seemed in her letter. There was something about her that was too . . . too—well, there was no other word she could think of—elegant.

But, Delia told herself, the woman had only been there for an afternoon. It was much too soon to make a judgment. She would not have been quite so uneasy if it hadn't been for two peculiar occurrences: a conversation she'd had with Honoria, and a remark made by Barnaby.

The first instance had occurred over tea. Honoria had taken her aside and, with the air of a conspirator, had whispered, "Did your new governess have any references?"

"References?" The question had given Delia her first twinge of discomfort. "No," she'd answered, "but that's not surprising. This is her very first position."

"I suppose it's all right, then," Honoria had murmured. "One has to start somewhere." Then she'd stirred her tea abstractedly. "Velacott," she'd added, half to herself. "I've heard that name. I once met a Sir Rodney Velacott, I believe. Do you think she might be related to him?"

"I have no idea," Delia had responded, "but I can ask her."

Honoria's eyes had lifted with a distinct look of alarm. "No, no, don't ask her. It's not . . . not at all important."

The second instance had occurred shortly afterward. Barnaby had stopped her on the stairs. "Don't you think, Delia," he'd remarked, "that a five-year-old is too young for a governess?"

"Too young?" she'd echoed stupidly.

"The older boys can handle a governess, I think, but don't you think Jamie would do better with his mother than with a . . . a stranger? When I was his age, I know I'd have preferred to have my mother guide me through my lessons."

Delia had believed, at the time, that she understood his motive. She'd patted his arm fondly, remembering how young he'd been when he'd lost his own mother. "Don't worry about Jamie," she'd reassured him. "He hasn't lost me. I'll always be there."

But now she needed reassurance herself. It was a worrisome coincidence that two people had already expressed concern about the new governess, and she'd only been there three hours!

She found Mrs. Velacott in the schoolroom with the boys. Jamie had taken her hand and, in his diffident manner, was showing her his toy soldiers. (He had hundreds of them, for all the Traherne brothers had contributed their own childhood treasures to the collection.) George and Maury, who had outgrown toy soldiers, were seated at the table, drawing. "Look, Mama," Maury said proudly as she entered, "we're making a map of the house for Mrs. Velacott, so she can find her way about!"

"What a very good idea," his mother said. "Did you boys think of it yourselves?"

"Well, Maury was trying to describe how the passage-ways connect," George explained, "and it occurred to me that a map might be clearer. I'm doing the first floor, and he's doing the second."

"An' I'm showing her my thojerth," Jamie said with his pronounced lisp. "*All* of them."

"Heavens!" his mother laughed, ruffling his hair. "Surely not every one! But you must give Mrs. Velacott to me for a while, Jamie boy, for I want to show her her bedroom. Do you think you can play with your 'thojerth' by yourself?"

"I'll keep an eye on him," George said importantly. "You ladies can go along."

Delia led Miranda a short distance down the hall. "Jamie's room is just next to yours, and the other two are across the hall," she explained as she opened the door.

"Yes, I know," Miranda said. "George already drew the sketch of the third floor for me."

"How very clever of him," Delia said proudly as Miranda stepped over the threshold and looked about her new abode. It was a small room (much smaller than the writing room Belle Velacott had offered her in the London house), with a low ceiling and a single dormer window. The furnishings were drab and spartan: a narrow bed, a dressing table and chair, a commode and a highboy—nothing as fine as a Queen Anne four-poster or a Sheraton inlaid-tile desk. But the bed had been freshly made, some Christmas greens had been set in a vase and the window cleaned to a sparkle in preparation for her arrival—all signs that Mrs. Traherne had tried to make her feel welcome. That was more than could be said for Belle Velacott.

"I hope this is satisfactory, Mrs. Velacott," Delia said, following her in.

"Yes, quite. But do call me Miranda. Mrs. Velacott is so very formal."

"Thank you, I'd like that. But only when we're private, of course. It wouldn't do for the children to hear such an informal address." She looked about her with some dissatisfaction. "I know this room isn't very spacious, but it's the only room near the boys. If you wish, we can go through some of the unused rooms downstairs after the holidays, and you can choose some pictures for the walls. And perhaps we can find a table to fit in the dormer, for you to use as a writing desk."

"That is very kind of you," Miranda murmured, trying hard to forget the luxurious surroundings of her past.

"Please sit down, Miranda," Delia said, indicating the bed. She herself perched on the dressing-table chair. "I'm sure there are many things we must ask each other."

"Yes, I suppose there are."

"For instance, do you understand your exact duties?"

"I think so. You outlined them in your last letter. Lessons in the morning, outdoor activity in the afternoon, weather permitting. George must be prepared for his entrance to school next year; I'm to tutor him in history, French and basic calculation. Maury must be helped with penmanship and spelling. And Jamie is to work on conquering his lisp and to start reading."

"Yes, that's it. And a bit of instruction in drawing would not be amiss, and some guidance in social deportment. I think, from this quick observation of you, that none of this will be beyond your capabilities."

"Thank you." She peered at Mrs. Traherne keenly. "But there is something else, isn't there?"

"Yes." There was an awkward pause. Delia's hands, resting in her lap, clenched. "To be honest, Miranda, although your letter was the most impressive of all I received, in person I find you . . ." She hesitated, not knowing quite how to go on.

Miranda looked up in alarm. "I am not what you expected? I have disappointed you, is that it? What is it, Mrs. Traherne? Am I too old?"

"Old? Oh, dear, no. What a ridiculous thought! You can't be much beyond twenty-five!"

"I am twenty-nine," Miranda admitted.

"I would not have found you too old at *forty-nine*, my dear. I myself am past forty but not yet too old to instruct my boys."

"Then what is it? Something improper in my appearance—?"

"You have a most appealing appearance, I assure you. But there *is* something about you that seems . . . well, unsuited to the position."

"Unsuited? How?"

"It's hard for me to put my finger on it. I'm not very good with words. But you look so . . . so . . . distinctive, and your carriage is so very proud . . . and even the gown you're wearing—it's quite well cut and of a very fine poplin, is it not?" She looked across at her new employee with a frank, direct gaze. "You're not running away from something, are you, Miranda? Using my household as a place to hide away from some problem in your life? *Playing* at being a governess, perhaps?"

Miranda's heart began to pound fearfully in her breast. What was Mrs. Traherne getting at? "My gown is four years old, ma'am, made for me in better days. I admit that I've seen better days. Does that disqualify me?"

"Only if it makes you dissatisfied with your position. If you have been used to elegance and luxury, how will you stand taking simple meals with the boys in the schoolroom? Or dining in the servants' hall? How will you bear taking orders from someone to whom you feel superior?"

Miranda gasped. "Oh, my Lord!" she said, horror-stricken. "Have I given the impression that I feel superior to you?"

"No, no," Delia said kindly, leaning forward and patting her knee. "Do not look so alarmed. It was only that your *yes, ma'ams* came so awkwardly to your tongue."

Miranda felt tears spring to her eyes. She got up from the bed and went to the little window, wiping at her cheeks surreptitiously. "It's true. What you say is very t-true! I am not accus . . . accustomed . . ." And to her shame, she burst into tears.

Delia jumped to her feet. "Oh, my *dear*," she exclaimed, coming up behind her new governess and putting an arm about her shoulder, "I never meant to upset you so. How you say *yes, ma'am* is . . . is such an unimportant little thing—"

"No, it's n-not a little thing," Miranda sobbed. "I am a s-servant. I m-must get used to it."

"Must you? You're obviously accustomed to servants of your own. Would it not be easier to forget this adventure and return to your old life?"

"You don't understand. This is not an *adventure* to me. I *can't* return!" She dashed the tears from her cheeks and turned to face her employer. "I'm not playing games, ma'am, truly I'm not. I have not a penny in the world. I *must* succeed at this!"

Delia, her motherly heart touched, pulled a handkerchief from her pocket and wiped the younger woman's cheeks. "Please, my dear, don't weep. I haven't any intention of discharging you if you truly mean to take your employment here seriously." She studied the other woman's tear-stained face with sympathetic concern. "You wrote that you are a widow. Was Sir Rodney Velacott your husband?"

Miranda's eyes widened. "Yes. How did you— ?"

"My sister-in-law Honoria wondered about it. The name is not commonplace, you know." Delia went thoughtfully back to her seat. If this peculiar relationship was to work— and she wanted it to work, for by this time she quite liked Miranda Velacott—it would be best to encourage complete honesty. "Then you should be called *Lady* Velacott, should you not?" she prodded.

"Yes." Miranda threw Delia a shamefaced glance and turned back to stare out the window. "I didn't wish to lie to you, Mrs. Traherne, but I just didn't think the title was suitable under the circumstances. My husband's property— what was left of it after his gambling debts were paid—went to his brother. I had to find a way to support myself. But who would hire a governess with a title? Can you imagine yourself saying, 'This is her ladyship, my governess'? So I simply dispensed with it. What need have I for it? The blasted title pays no bills, nor does it put a roof over my head. It is nothing but a burden to me."

"Yes, I see." Delia nodded, her mind made up. "So you still wish to be *Mrs*. Velacott, governess to my sons?"

Miranda, hearing the acceptance in Delia's voice, wheeled around. "Yes! Oh, yes!" She flew across to Delia's side and dropped down on her knees beside the chair. "I already adore your little boys," she said, taking one of Delia's hands in hers. "I will be the very best governess to them! And I'll learn to say my *yes, ma'ams* just the way I ought, I promise you!"

Delia smiled and squeezed her hand. "Heavens, woman, who cares for that? You may call me Delia, if you like. All I want is for you and the boys to be happy together." With a relieved sigh, she got up and went to the door. "I'm glad this is all settled, Miranda. Now that I understand you, I'm sure we shall deal famously together."

Miranda got to her feet. "I think I'm very fortunate in my choice of employer," she said gratefully. "Thank you, ma'am."

Delia looked over her shoulder and grinned. "That *ma'am* was very well done, but call me Delia. It's more comfortable."

Miranda smiled back. "Thank you, ma'am, but I have no intention of overstepping my place. I'll call you Delia, if you like, but only when we're private."

· Eleven ·

DINNER WAS A raucous family affair, as it always was
when the four brothers reunited. The food was abundant,
the atmosphere relaxed, the company noisily cheerful. The
ladies listened and laughed as the brothers threw taunts and
questions at each other. Delia and Honoria, accustomed to
the family patterns, smiled indulgently as the Earl, Terence
and Harry vied with each other for center stage. The three
older brothers still made it difficult for Barnaby to finish
a sentence, but Barnaby had learned, over the years, to get
his points across with a quick quip. He could now hold
his own.

Tonight the teasing began with a discussion of the Earl's
new sleigh. "Clever of you, Lawrence," Terence remarked,
"to buy yourself a sleigh. Barnaby wouldn't be sitting here
tonight if you hadn't."

"It cost a devilish long price, I can tell you," the Earl
bragged. "I ordered it from a sleigh-maker in Russia. The
Russians call it a *troika*, goodness knows why."

"Because they use three horses to pull it," Barnaby said.

"Listen to the boy," Harry taunted. "Showing off his
foreign-office erudition."

"Not having any yourself, you're jealous that the boy
has some erudition to show off," Lawrence rejoined in
Barnaby's defense. "But as far as *troika* is concerned, I

did perfectly well with only two horses."

"If I were the Earl, and well able to afford a stable full of horses," Terence said, to needle his elder brother, "I'd do as the Russians do and harness three."

"If I were the Earl—" Barnaby began.

"If you were the Earl," Harry cut him off, "you wouldn't buy a sleigh at all. You'd give the money to the poor and walk."

"And if you were the Earl," Barnaby rejoined, "you'd buy *two*."

Everyone, knowing Harry's tendency to extravagance, guffawed. Even his affianced bride, who hardly ever relaxed her dignity enough to smile, laughed heartily.

Conversation slowed when the lamb roast was brought to the table, smelling of rosemary and basil and other fragrant herbs. Honoria's earlier tension eased as she watched Barnaby making conversation with the quiet Olivia Ponsonby, seated at his left, and helping her to a slice of lamb. For Barnaby to show such attention to the girl was a hopeful sign. He seemed to *like* little Livy!

It gave Honoria particular satisfaction to see that all the brothers at the table this evening were paired with suitable females. This was the first time since she'd known them that this was true. Of course, the pairings were in various stages of maturity: she and Lawrence, now married for three decades, were an old couple; Delia and Terence were also well established in their fifteen-year marriage; Isabel Folley had managed to catch the elusive, forty-one-year-old bachelor, Harry, who looked happy enough in his newly forged chains; and, if all went well, Barnaby would discover in the sweet young Livy a promising partner for life. Honoria looked at the faces round the table, all smiling and aglow in the light of the branched candles at the center, and her heart filled with happy optimism. *By this time next year*, she said to herself hopefully, *all four brothers may be married men!*

She would not have been so optimistic if she'd heard what Barnaby had whispered to Delia just a few moments before. Barnaby, sitting to the right of his hostess, had leaned over and asked something that had been puzzling him. "I say, Delia, is Mrs. Velacott ill?"

"Mrs. Velacott? No, of course not. Why do you ask?"

"She isn't here at table."

"But Mrs. Velacott isn't a guest, you know, Barnaby," Delia'd whispered back. "A governess usually takes breakfast and luncheon with her charges and dines in the servants' hall after they've been put to bed, didn't you know that?"

Barnaby was startled. "No, I didn't. Is that how it's done? But, Delia, she's not . . . that is, a governess is not like a chambermaid, is she? Is it right to treat her so?"

Delia had scrutinized her youngest brother-in-law with shrewd amusement. "Can it be, Barnaby Traherne, that you're *taken* with the new governess?"

"Don't be silly," Barnaby had said quickly, his mouth tightening. "As a matter of fact, I don't like her at all. We got on so badly in the few days we were thrown together that I'm relieved to learn she's not to spend her evenings in our company. I was only curious about the . . . the proprieties."

"The proprieties, eh? I see. Well, I hope I've satisfied your curiosity. I must warn you, though, that Mrs. Velacott *will* be joining us for dinner the day after tomorrow. The boys always dine with us at Christmas Eve dinner, so she will, too."

Barnaby had pretended to indifference, shrugged and turned to smile at Miss Ponsonby at his other side. "Do have a slice of the lamb," he'd urged the young girl. "It's smothered in herbs and quite delicious."

Later, when the ladies excused themselves, and the four brothers gathered at the head of the table with their brandies, the Earl cleared his throat in an avuncular way that the others knew presaged a scolding. "See here, Barnaby Traherne," he said sternly, "I didn't wish to berate you in front of the ladies, but from what Terence told me of your encounter with the highwaymen, it seems to me you acted very rashly."

"Rashly?" Barnaby asked in sincere innocence.

"It seems you attacked the armed felons not once but twice! Attacking an armed man even once when one has no weapon seems rash to me."

"And to me," Terence added.

"And me," Harry also added.

"It wasn't rash," Barnaby said, looking from one to the other in disgust. "On both occasions I had an opening. I did exactly what you would have done in those circumstances."

"You flatter us," Harry said dryly. "I would have been shaking in my boots. And Terry would have run for cover at the first sign of an opening."

"Oh, very likely," Barnaby sneered. "Then it was not you who, before my admiring eyes, ran into a burning stable to save a horse? Or you, Terry, who dived into the lake at Shallcross to save me from drowning, and you couldn't even swim?"

"Just because they've been rash from time to time," the Earl said, "doesn't excuse you, boy! I expect better sense from you."

"Dash it all, Lawrence, I'm not a boy!" Barnaby snapped. "I'm quite old enough to know what I'm doing. And I'm here, alive and well. So let's have done with this nonsense."

"Nonsense?" the Earl said, glaring at his youngest brother in offense. "Since when do you speak to your elders in that tone?"

"Since I reached maturity," Barnaby retorted.

"The fellow's right," Harry said placatingly. "Let's be honest. If any one of us had been robbed of a gold watch and a fob to which we were sentimentally attached, we'd have put up a fight, just as Barnaby did."

"And you'd probably have beaten them," Barnaby said ruefully, "not failed miserably, as I did."

"They took your fob?" the Earl asked, suddenly sympathetic. "The one I had made for you?"

Barnaby nodded glumly.

Terence stared into his brandy-glass thoughtfully. "I think, Harry, that you and I ought to—"

"Yes!" Harry's eyes brightened. "We ought to ride out tomorrow and find those footpads."

"Right!" Terence grinned. "I've a new pistol I'm eager to try out. Those miscreants would make a most satisfactory target. With any luck, we can restore the fob to its rightful owner by Christmas."

"That is a very good idea," the Earl said approvingly, lifting his glass to them.

"*What?*" Barnaby glared at each of them in fury. "Do you think it is *still* necessary to fight my battles for me?"

Harry and Terence exchanged surprised glances. "Well, we *always*—" Harry began.

"We *like* to—" Terence muttered.

"After all," the Earl put in, "you *are* our baby brother—"

"*Damnation!*" Barnaby cursed, jumping to his feet. "Every time we get together we revert to our old ways! This must stop! I am past thirty and, I believe, completely competent to run my life. You will *not* call me baby, and you will *not* fight my battles! Is that clear?"

Under his furious glower, the Earl dropped his eyes. "We didn't mean to impugn your competence, Barnaby," he mumbled.

"We only wanted to help," Harry muttered.

"To show you what you mean to us," Terence said in meek apology.

"Affection, that's all it is," Harry added.

"That sort of affection could smother me to death," Barnaby said, refusing, for once, to surrender his anger. "I will take care of the highwaymen myself, in my own way at my own time. And if any one of you dares to interfere in this matter in any way, I'll show you how well this baby brother has learned to use his fists!"

The ladies, meanwhile, were having an entirely different sort of conversation. "Did you know, Honoria," Delia asked as soon as they'd seated themselves in the drawing room, "that Lady Isabel is quite talented on the pianoforte? Isabel, would you consent to play for us?"

Isabel nodded in gracious acquiescence, sat down at the instrument, spread her blue Persian silk skirt, closed her eyes and began to play. Her fingers moved expertly on the keys and her breast heaved with great emotion. Delia sat listening, enthralled, but Honoria had other things on her mind. She glanced over at Livy Ponsonby, who was sitting on a sofa, her hands folded in her lap and her eyes lowered. In her soft plum-colored jaconet gown and with her hair tied up on her head with silver ribbons that permitted bouncy blond ringlets to frame her face, Livy seemed as exquisite as a Sevres figurine. Honoria, disregarding the music, took a place beside Livy on the sofa. "Tell me, my dear," she whispered in the girl's ear, "what do you think of our Barnaby?"

A high color rose on Livy's cheeks. "What do I think of him?" she echoed timorously.

"Yes. You don't find him forbidding, do you? I've heard that some young ladies have described him so."

"Forbidding? Oh, no! No."

"Do you have *any* impression of him?" Honoria pressed.

The girl threw her an agonized look, like a young pupil who didn't know the location of India on the map. "I . . . I . . . think he is very kind."

"Kind?" Honoria's face clouded. "Kind" was not a word a romantic young female was likely to use to describe a man she was dreaming of.

"And good-natured," Livy added hastily.

"Yes?" Honoria urged, wanting more.

"And handsome," the girl offered, lowering her eyes and twisting a golden curl round a nervous finger. "Very handsome."

"Ah, yes." Honoria leaned back against the cushions and smiled placidly, satisfied at last. "He *is* handsome, isn't he?"

· *Twelve* ·

NOT LONG AFTER enduring the embarrassing questions Lady Shallcross had thrown at her, Livy Ponsonby pleaded exhaustion and retired to her room. In listless silence, she allowed her abigail to undress her. Then she excused the girl and fell weeping onto her bed. The day had been a long, horrid ordeal. To be forced to make conversation with strangers was a dreadful strain for someone as shy as she. *Dash it all, Mama*, she cried to herself, *why did you make me come?*

But she knew why. Her mother wanted her to make a good match. "You will never have a better chance," her mother had told her repeatedly in the week before she was sent from home. "Barnaby Traherne is a catch worthy of a Ponsonby. How lucky you are to have been invited! You have your aunt Jane to thank for that. You'll have a whole fortnight in which to attach him, and there'll be no other rival on the premises, either. You'll have the field all to yourself."

What her mother didn't say was that sending Livy off for a fortnight was also a way to separate her from the one man in the world with whom she was not shy: her Neddy. Ned Keswick loved her. Ned Keswick wanted to marry her, but her mother would not hear of such an "entanglement," for Ned was guilty of the very worst of sins: he was in trade.

"You are a fool, Livy," her mother had declared vehemently, "if you think Ned Keswick is a suitable husband. You are a Ponsonby, remember, not an East End nobody. You can win yourself a peer of the realm, if you set your mind to it. Yes, you can, even if you don't have a clever tongue. Don't look at me that way, Livy! I know whereof I speak. Cleverness isn't important for a girl. You're a beauty—everyone says so, not only your mother. Beauty is the only important quality a girl needs, and you have it. I won't have you throwing yourself away on that . . . that cotton merchant!"

The memory of these harangues brought on a fresh flood of tears. Ned Keswick was a dear. Positively a dear. And when he'd kissed her in the moonlight, that night less than a month ago after the Assembly dance, she thought she'd swoon in delight. He'd declared his love for her that very night, and in answer to his demands, she'd sworn to be true to him forever!

But now she'd met Barnaby Traherne, and she found herself utterly confused. Barnaby was awesomely handsome and charming, just as Mama had said he'd be, and he'd smiled at her very kindly at the table this evening. She liked him quite well. Was her mama right? she asked herself, sitting up in bed and wiping her eyes. Was her feeling for Neddy just a girlish infatuation? If Barnaby should take her in his arms in the moonlight, would she feel like swooning in delight?

And could she really win him? She'd heard rumors that other girls had found him formidable, even frightening. But he'd been very kind to her. Capturing him would certainly be, as Mama said, a feather in her cap. Why, all her friends would be green with envy!

But if she became betrothed to Barnaby, how could she explain herself to Neddy? He would accuse her of breaking her vow. He positively would! And he would have every right to hate her for it. She could not bear to have Neddy hate her!

The tears began to flow again, and she threw herself

down and buried her face in the pillows. All this was very bewildering. Making decisions had never been easy for her. This was not the first time she'd found life almost too much for her, but before when she was troubled, she'd been able to count on her mother to tell her what to do. Here, however, she had no one to guide her. It wasn't fair! Mama should never have forced her to come. *Oh, Mama*, she wept in lonely bitterness, *how could you have done this to me?*

On the floor above, Miranda, too, had retired early and then found that she could not sleep. Excited by the challenge of her new post, her mind made plan after plan of ways to tutor her charges. At last, convinced that sleep was still a long way off, she rose from her bed. Shivering from the cold, she wished she had the warm dressing-gown she'd packed in her now-lost portmanteau. But, having nothing else to put over her nightdress (generously given to her by one of the maids), she covered herself with her cloak. Then she lit a candle and made her way down the hall to the schoolroom.

The room was as the boys had left it: the table littered with picture-books and drawings, the floor covered with scattered toy soldiers. Evidently, the housemaids were too busy helping with the dinner downstairs to have had time to clean the schoolroom. Miranda threw back her cloak, pushed up the sleeves of the muslin nightdress and set to work herself, piling the papers and books on one side of the table and then bending down to pick up the toy soldiers. It wasn't the first time she'd done housemaid's work, she told herself ruefully, nor would it be the last.

A number of the little soldier-figures, she noticed, were grimy from sticky fingers. She laid them on the table, found a piece of cloth, sat down and set to work cleaning them. As she worked, she took a close look at the figures. They made a motley collection; some of them were roughly carved of wood, while others were carefully sculpted and cast in brass or fashioned from metal she could not identify, but all were colorfully painted, each detail of the uniforms carefully re-created. Some, from which the paint had faded or had been partially rubbed off, she set aside. Touching them up with fresh paint would make an enjoyable pastime for the boys on a rainy day, she decided.

Suddenly something made her look up. Standing in the doorway, studying her with a puzzled expression, was Barnaby Traherne. "Oh!" she said, startled.

"Good evening," he said, eyebrows raised questioningly.

She got to her feet, feeling awkward, like a housemaid caught trying on her mistress's jewels. "Good evening," she muttered, blushing as she drew her cloak around her.

"You needn't get up for me," he said, his eyes taking in her strange costume and her hair, which she'd plaited into one long braid. "You're not a housemaid, you know."

"Close enough as makes no difference, to use one of your own expressions," she said with a sudden smile.

He did not smile back. "I'm sure my sister-in-law does not intend for you to do the cleaning."

"I want to do it. I couldn't sleep, and this seems as good a way of tiring myself as any."

"I'm not sleepy, either," he said, stepping over the threshold. "May I help?"

"I'm sure your sister-in-law does not intend—"

He put up a hand to silence her. "You seem to enjoy throwing my words back in my face. Have your new duties had no effect on your saucy tongue, ma'am?"

She made a little housemaidish curtsey. "I do beg your pardon, sir. I shall try to remember my place and curb my tongue. Do sit down, if you truly wish to engage in so lowly an occupation—and can find yourself a polishing cloth."

"I'll take half of yours," he said, putting down his candle beside hers and ripping the cloth in half.

They sat down and began to work. "You couldn't have come up here with the purpose of helping me with this polishing," she said. "Was there something you wanted?"

"Well, yes," he admitted, throwing her a quick, embarrassed glance. "I didn't see you at dinner, and I couldn't help wondering whether . . . that is, Delia wondered . . ."

"Yes?"

"If your dinner was . . . er . . . satisfactory, down in the servants' hall."

"*Delia* wondered?"

"Yes," he lied.

"Why would you, or she, be concerned about such a thing?"

"Well . . ." He fixed his eyes on the soldier in his hand and polished away vigorously. " . . . you are not accustomed to dining with servants, are you?"

She stared at him in some surprise. He'd somehow sensed that she'd come down in the world, and he was evidently disturbed by the fact that she was required to dine with the servants. She could not help but be touched by his sympathy. "Of the many new experiences I must grow accustomed to," she assured him gently, "that one is the least difficult. But thank you—and Delia—for your concern. You may rest assured the servants' hall is cheerful, the staff friendly and the meals generous."

"Good," Barnaby said.

She peered at his bent head. "It was kind of you to ask."

"Hmmph," was his response.

They worked in silence for a while. "These soldiers are quite old," he remarked at last. "I used to play with them when I was a boy, and so did my brothers."

"Speaking of your brothers," she said thoughtfully, "you seem to be very attached to them. And to their families. That is quite astonishing to me. I had not thought of you as the affectionate sort."

"Hadn't you? Why not?"

She threw him a hesitant look across the table. "If I answer, you will only scold me for my saucy tongue."

"I promise not to. Tell me."

"Because . . . because you behaved so boorishly to me during our sojourn at the inn."

He lifted his head in offense. "I take umbrage at the word

boorish. I was in no way boorish."

"Oh? What word would you use?"

He thought for a moment. "Formal. I was trying to keep a formal distance."

"Why?" she asked bluntly. "I can see why you might feel a need to be formal here, where I am a servant and you are a guest. But why was there a need, at the inn, to be so distantly formal?"

He stared at her then, trying to formulate an answer. The question, he realized, was fortunate, because it reminded him of the *real* reason he'd kept his distance. He'd forgotten it again. She looked so lovely with the candlelight throwing a mellow glow on her cheeks and the curves of her throat, shining in her eyes and making a glinting treasure of her hair, that it was easy to forget himself. Sitting opposite her like this and speaking together with comfortable ease made her seem like an old acquaintance. If she hadn't asked the question, it would have slipped his mind completely that she was Miranda Pardew, the nemesis of his youth.

Of course, he wouldn't admit that aloud. He had to find an excuse for what she justifiably interpreted as boorishness. "We were strangers, after all," he hedged, "thrust together by circumstances, not our own wishes. It would not have been proper to . . . to . . ."

"To relax into friendship?" she suggested. "Would that have been improper?"

"I think so, yes."

"Then I suppose I am not as proper as you. Your standards are too exacting for me."

"Too exacting?" He threw down his cloth and rose. "You are implying that I am a prig. If memory serves, you said that once before."

Startled, her eyes flew up to his face. "I *never* said—! I didn't *at all* mean to—!"

"Never mind. Our standards of behavior *are* very different. You are bound to think of me as priggish, just as I am bound to think of you as . . . as . . ."

"Saucy?" she offered.

"Yes, I suppose that word will do as well as any."
He picked up his candle and went to the door. There he
paused. "The reason I came up here seeking you tonight,
Mrs. Velacott, was to offer my assistance if, in your new
position, you should run into any difficulties. Despite my
priggishness, that offer holds. Good night, ma'am."

Before Miranda could respond, he was gone, leaving
only a quickly disappearing circle of candlelight behind
him. She gaped at the empty doorway, dumbfounded. She
would never understand him. One moment he was sitting
opposite her, charming and friendly and apparently concerned for her welfare, and the next he was withdrawn,
cold and forbidding. Was it something she'd said? Had
her teasing him about being too proper touched some sort
of sensitive spot? He was a mystery.

With a sigh, she picked up her piece of cloth and resumed
polishing. She did not wish to trouble her mind about the
mystery of Barnaby Traherne. The strange Mr. Traherne
was not her concern. She tried to turn her mind back to
planning lessons for her three pupils, but her thoughts kept
returning to the man who'd just sat opposite her. What was
it about him that bothered her so much? she asked herself.
And, astoundingly, the answer popped into her head with
the shining clarity of true insight: what troubled her most
about him was her sense that, when he looked at her, he
was seeing someone else. Someone else entirely.

· *Thirteen* ·

BARNABY CAME DOWN to breakfast the next morning feeling out of sorts and dejected by the gloomy weather that would not go away. Though it was not snowing, the dark sky and icy wind persisted. It was a day in which no one was likely to venture out-of-doors. There would be no riding, no brisk walks, no outdoor games. There would be nothing to do all day but play billiards and cards, neither of which he particularly fancied.

He was not surprised that no one was yet at breakfast—it was a perfect day to stay late abed. Although Cummings offered to serve him his favorite shirred eggs or a bowlful of hot porridge (which, the butler said, "would sustain him mightily on such a dreadful morning"), he refused, not wishing to eat alone. Instead, he wandered off to the library. It was there he discovered someone even more unhappy than he: Livy Ponsonby, who stood at the window, crying.

He'd gone halfway across the floor to the bookshelves before he saw her. He stopped in his tracks in embarrassment. "Oh! I beg your pardon, Miss Ponsonby," he said, backing toward the door. "I didn't mean to intrude."

She took a quick glance round, colored, and then turned away again, lowering her head and brushing away her tears. "You d-don't intrude, sir," she managed, her light, girlish voice choked. "You have as much r-right here as I. More, in fact."

Something in her tone made Barnaby pause on the threshold. It seemed to him that the girl might actually desire a little companionship. "I'd hoped we had reached less formal terms than *sir* and *ma'am*," he said gently. "Can you not call me Barnaby?"

"But just now you c-called me M-Miss P-Ponsonby, didn't you?" she accused, throwing him a tearful little smile over her shoulder.

"I apologize for that. Olivia you shall be from this moment on."

She turned round to him. "Livy, please." She looked quite appealing in a figured-muslin morning dress with a neat white tucker and long sleeves puffed at the top. Her gold ringlets were pinned up at the top of her head in tousled charm, and her lips were swollen from her weeping. A man would be a churl not to wish to comfort her.

In this instance, Barnaby was no churl. "Livy, then," he said, smiling at her. He crossed the room to the window where she stood. "You were crying, Livy. Is something amiss?"

She shook her head. "I am a silly wetgoose. It was only . . . only . . ."

He took her elbow and guided her to an easy chair near the fire. "Only—?"

She lowered her lovely blue eyes. "Only that I was feeling lonely."

"Oh, is *that* all?" He perched on the hearth before her and grinned. "In an hour or less, the whole family will come tumbling down the stairs in various states of undress demanding their breakfasts, and the din will be so great you'll find yourself wishing to be lonely again."

She gave a hiccuping laugh and then, astoundingly, burst into tears again. "You don't understand," she wept. "You're such a jolly, c-close, af-f-fectionate family. Seeing you laugh and joke together as you do m-makes me miss m-mine."

"Oh, I *see*." Barnaby now fully understood her tears. The poor girl, being the only outsider in the midst of this close-knit clan, was feeling left out. "I can't say I blame you," he said, patting her hand sympathetically. "It's hard to be taken away from your family circle, especially at Christmastime."

"Yes," she admitted, wiping her eyes with an already-soaked handkerchief.

He pulled out his own handkerchief, lifted her chin and dabbed at her cheeks. "How many are there in your family?"

"Not so m-many as yours," she said, sniffing back a final sob and favoring him with a grateful, if tremulous, smile. "My mother, of course. And Papa. And my married sister, Charlotte, who always comes with her baby to spend Christmas with us, and my little sister Hetty." Her smile faded and she sighed pensively. "I've never traveled without Mama before. I m-miss her."

"Then tell me, Livy, what made you tear yourself away to come to us?"

"Mama insisted. She positively insisted."

"Did she? Why?"

"She said it was an honor that I could not refuse."

"An *honor*?"

"Oh, yes, indeed. Positively. Not many girls, Mama said, are invited to spend a fortnight with the family of someone as important—and as kind—as Lady Shallcross."

"I see." Barnaby couldn't help wondering if Honoria realized that the kindness she'd bestowed on the girl was the cause of loneliness and pain. "So, for this 'honor' you must miss Christmas at home with your mother and sisters. That *is* too bad. You have two sisters, you say?"

"Yes. I'm the middle one."

"No brothers?"

"No."

"How fortunate for you. Brothers can be a nuisance."

"Barnaby!" Livy clucked her tongue in reproof. "How *can* you say such a dreadful thing? You positively revel in each other's company, you *know* you do!"

"Yes, in truth, I do. Though my brothers can be irksome sometimes, I admit that I enjoy spending time in the family circle."

"Oh, yes. One's family circle is the very best place. Positively."

He chuckled, both amused and touched by her repetitive use of the word *positively* when her personality was not in the least positive. "Then, Livy, I shall see to it that you, too, enjoy this family circle," he said, rising and pulling her to her feet. In trying to cheer the girl, he found that he himself was feeling more cheerful. "From this moment on, you will share my brothers with me. I know that sharing my family will not be as satisfying as being with your own, but we shall make it the next best thing. Positively."

As Barnaby guided the girl to the door, intending to lift her spirits by encouraging her to take a hearty breakfast, he came face-to-face with Mrs. Velacott and her eldest charge, George. The boy's face lit at the sight of his uncle. "Good morning, Uncle Barney," he cried. "You'll never guess what we're doing."

"Then you must tell me," his uncle said, ruffling the boy's hair affectionately.

"We're studying history. We've come down to find a proper history book. Mrs. Velacott doesn't like the one I've been using." He glanced up at his governess, an expression of pride crossing his face. "She says it's too childish for me."

Barnaby eyed Miranda with raised eyebrows. "Starting lessons already? Two days before Christmas?"

"It seemed a good idea," Miranda said, feeling defensive. "The weather is not conducive to much else."

"I was not criticizing," Barnaby assured her. "Just surprised. I didn't expect you immerse yourself so promptly in your work."

"No?" she asked, lifting her chin belligerently. "Why not?"

Because I didn't think you a conscientious sort, he said to himself, but he would not make so disparaging a comment aloud—not now, in front of his nephew. So he only said, "No reason, ma'am." He stepped aside to let her by. "Are the younger boys doing lessons, too?"

"Oh, yes, indeed they are."

"Maury is writing a story in his notebook, and Jamie is practicing the letter A on his slate," George volunteered.

"Then you all are very busy, and I shouldn't keep you," Barnaby said, throwing Miranda a quizzical look before turning back to George and patting his shoulder approvingly. "But I must warn you, ma'am, that my brother's library is distressingly inadequate and idiosyncratic, despite the fact that he's managed to fill a wall of shelves. I believe the best you'll find here is Smollett's *History of England.* It might do for a while. When I return to London, I can send you something better, if you like."

"I would be very grateful, sir," Miranda said.

Barnaby nodded and, with his hand on Livy's elbow, led the girl off down the corridor.

Miranda stood gazing after them, feeling strangely irked. The man had not let go of the girl's arm during their entire conversation. Was he courting her? Miranda wondered. And what if he were? What difference could it make to her? "Come, George," she said, forcing herself to put the irritating Barnaby Traherne out of her mind, "let's find the Smollett. If his history is anything like his novels, reading it will be entertaining, even if not very accurate."

They returned to the schoolroom with three volumes of *A History of England from the Revolution to the Death of George II* by Tobias Smollett tucked under their arms. George, full of first-day enthusiasm, immediately took Volume I to the window seat and began to read, while Miranda placed the other two books on a shelf she'd cleared of toys for that purpose. Then she noticed that Jamie was not at the worktable. Instead, he was sitting on the floor in the corner, absently fingering one of his little soldiers and staring morosely into space. "Jamie," she asked, "have you finished your writing already?"

He turned his head away. "It'th on the table," he muttered.

She looked at the slate. It was covered with three rows of A's, surprisingly well executed for a first-time writer. "Why, this is excellent writing!" she exclaimed. "I'm very pleased."

"Mmmph," the child grunted, not looking up.

Puzzled at his strange reaction, she knelt down beside him. "Aren't you proud of yourself, Jamie? You should be."

"*Maury* should be proud."

"Maury?"

"He'th the one who did it."

"Maury did your work for you?"

"Yeth. Tho you can be proud of *him*, not me."

She got to her feet. "Maury, why—?"

Maury looked up from his work and shrugged. "He wasn't doing it right. You're not cross with me, are you? I just tried to help him."

"No, I'm not cross. But please let him do his own work in future. Come to the table, Jamie, and erase your slate. We'll start again. You can still be proud of—"

"No!" the child shouted, throwing his toy soldier across the room, getting to his feet and running to the door. "I can't do it. I won't be proud. I want Mama!" And, his underlip trembling, he ran out and slammed the door behind him.

Miranda stared at the door, aghast. What had she said or done that had caused this outburst? She'd been at work as governess barely an hour, and she'd already blundered. Being a governess, she realized with a sinking heart, was not going to be as easy as she'd anticipated.

· *Fourteen* ·

THE WEATHER FOR Miranda's second day as governess was quite different from the first. The air sparkled with sunshine made glistening by a brisk wind. The snowy landscape and the crisply fragrant air were too inviting for boys to be kept indoors. Besides, they had worked hard at their lessons all day yesterday. Even Jamie had returned to the table and, after much tender cajoling, had learned to read and write his name. Miranda decided they needed an outing. With Delia's permission, she instructed their nursemaid to dress them in warm jackets, boots, mittens and mufflers, and she took them outside for a couple of hours of play.

The ladies of the household, too, would probably have enjoyed an outing, but as soon as their leisurely breakfast had been consumed, they all agreed that they preferred to occupy themselves fashioning wreaths and mistletoe boughs with which to decorate the doorways, windows, bannisters and mantels. The gentlemen, on the other hand, were given an outdoor assignment: to fetch a suitable yule log from the home woods. Only Lawrence was unwilling to face the chilly outdoors. "I'm too old to chop trees and pull logs," he said, ensconcing himself in an easy chair before the sitting-room fire with a copy of *Waverly* on his lap, Sir Walter Scott being his favorite writer.

"Not too old, Your Lordship," his brother Harry taunted. "Just too high in the instep."

"Right," Terence agreed. "Taking advantage of your lord-ly privileges, if you ask me."

The Earl turned a page with calm deliberation. "There wouldn't be much use in lordly privileges," he said, waving them off, "if one didn't take advantage of them."

Terence, Harry and Barnaby, well protected from the cold with mufflers and wool caps, set off on their excursion with noisy enthusiasm. The task, even complicated by a great deal of snowball throwing and wrestling about in the drifts, was accomplished in less than an hour. It was not yet noon when they dragged the log to the kitchen door. Harry and Terence handed their axes to Barnaby, hoisted the six-foot-long tree trunk to their shoulders, and were just about to enter the doorway when Barnaby caught a glimpse of Jamie's red wool cap on the other side of the kitchen-garden shrubbery. "Go on ahead," he said to his brothers. "I'll be with you shortly."

He disposed of the axes and tramped round the shrub-bery. There he found his little nephew sitting cross-legged on a pile of snow, his chin resting on his mittened hands and his expression glum. Jamie's teary eyes were fixed on a scene across the field, where his two brothers and Mrs. Velacott were busily making a snowman. The sounds of their laughter tinkled in the air.

"Tell me, Jamie lad," Barnaby said, dropping down beside the boy, "how can you be looking so miserable when there is all this wonderful snow lying about?"

"They're makin' *my* thnowman," the boy said, pouting.

"What do you mean? Whom are you speaking of?"

"George an' Maury. They were buildin' a fort, an' I wath makin' a thnowman. An' then the head fell off." His underlip trembled, and he wiped his dripping nose with a soggy mitten. "An' then they came an' fixthed it, an' now *they're* makin' him an' I'm *not!*"

"I see. So it won't be your snowman any more."

"No, it won't." The boy unfolded his legs, threw himself upon his uncle and buried his head in Barnaby's lap. "I never get to make anythin' by mythelf," he whined.

"That *is* too bad," Barnaby said kindly, "but it seems to be the way of big brothers. Your father and your uncle Harry did the very same sort of thing to me, when I was your age." *And they still try to do it,* he added to himself.

The child looked up. "*Did* they? Honetht and truly?"

"They certainly did. It's the curse of being the youngest."

Jamie nodded wisely. "The curthe, yeth."

"But there's something you can do about it, you know."

"There ith?"

"Yes. You can fight back."

Jamie's eyes brightened. "I can?"

"Yes, you can. Come with me, and I'll show you how it's done."

They got up, Barnaby took hold of the boy's mittened hand, and they plodded across the field to the merrymakers. "I say, chaps, that's a very fine snowman," Barnaby said when they arrived.

The boys greeted him warmly, and Mrs. Velacott gave him a polite good-day. "Do you like the chest part, Uncle Barney?" Maury asked. "George thinks it ought to be fatter."

"I really couldn't say, Maury, because the snowman's not mine. Jamie says he's the one who started it, so wouldn't you say it's really his?"

Maury shrugged. "I s'pose so. Do you want the chest fatter, Jamie?"

Jamie motioned for his uncle to bend down, and with Barnaby kneeling, the two held a quick, whispered conference. Then Jamie turned back to his brothers. "No," he said firmly. "If I want him fatter, I'll do it mythelf."

"Oh, you will, will you?" objected George loudly. "That's showing a proper gratitude, I must say."

"Why should he show gratitude?" Barnaby asked.

"Why? Because he couldn't even get the head on."

"That's right," Maury agreed. "If we didn't help, he'd have a headless snowman."

"What if I *wanted* a headleth thnowman?" Jamie demanded, showing an unusual—and, to his uncle, a welcome—belligerence.

"You didn't want a headless snowman," George insisted. "You were bawling your eyes out about it."

"That's right, Jamie," Miranda said gently. "Your brothers were only helping. It isn't right to be sullen when you should be grateful."

Jamie, not knowing how to respond, turned his eyes up to Barnaby in confusion.

Barnaby glared at the governess. "Mrs. Velacott," he said stiffly, "may I speak to you in private for a moment? And while we're conferring, Jamie, you tell George and Maury just what *you* want to do to the snowman. It's up to you to decide how they may help, if you want their help at all."

He marched off across the field, Miranda obediently following. When they were out of hearing of the boys, Barnaby wheeled around. "Have you no feelings, ma'am?" he demanded angrily. "Didn't you see that child sitting all alone on a mound of snow, his snowman usurped by bigger and stronger powers and his joy in his creation destroyed?"

"Good heavens, Mr. Traherne," she said, surprised by his vehemence, "must we have such a to-do over a snowman?"

"It is not over a snowman, ma'am, but over a method of upbringing. The child needs some understanding, and some encouragement to defend himself."

"To defend himself from what?"

"From a pair of overbearing brothers."

"You are misinterpreting the situation, sir, not having seen it from the beginning. Jamie was *crying* for their help. George and Maury are quite generous with Jamie. Protective, even. I've noticed it often. Today, they were happily building their fort when the child's crying interrupted them. They quite cheerfully gave up their own activity to help him with his. But instead of thanking them, Jamie began to whine. I cannot encourage whining."

"Perhaps, ma'am, you might consider *why* the boy was whining. Has it not occurred to you that a child can be helped *too much*? That a headless snowman a boy builds *for himself* is a greater source of satisfaction than a better one someone else builds for him?"

Miranda stared at him, her expression suddenly thoughtful. "Yes, I *see*. Of course! What you're suggesting also explains something that happened yesterday. The child's self-confidence is being weakened by too much assistance from his brothers. I hadn't thought of that."

"No, of course you hadn't," Barnaby said with withering disdain. "What can a woman who has spent her life disporting herself in the ballrooms of London be expected to know about raising children?"

Miranda, who was already berating herself for not having understood what was now so obvious, did not need another abusive voice added to her own. Every muscle in her body tensed. "*Disporting* myself? What on earth are you talking about?" she demanded angrily. "What can you know about how I spent my life?"

"I know enough," he said. "Enough to be convinced that Jamie's mother has not been very wise in her choice of governess." And with that withering set-down, he turned about and stomped off to see what he could do to assist Jamie in asserting his rights to the snowman.

Miranda stared after him, her blood pumping through her veins in furious tumult. It was not fear of losing her position that caused this turmoil, for Delia had promised to give her support while she learned her job. It was Barnaby Traherne who upset her. Why was this man, who was so kind and affectionate to everyone else, so bitterly vituperative to her? True, he'd been wiser than she in the matter of Jamie, but she'd given him his due. She'd *admitted* her lack of insight. Was her error so great as to deserve that sort of reprimand? *Jamie's mother has not been very wise in her choice of governess*, indeed! Who was he to judge? How many children had *he* raised?

He may have been in the right this once, but that was no excuse to insult her. Confound the man, he invariably managed to raise her ire! It was getting so that, every time she saw him, she had an overpowering urge to box his ears.

· Fifteen ·

A FOOTMAN HAD been sent to the abandoned stagecoach and had recovered what was left of the baggage. For some reason, Barnaby's battered portmanteau had not been opened, so all the items of clothing he'd brought were restored to him. Miranda's things, on the other hand, had been rifled through and either stolen or scattered about. Most of her underthings were recovered, but only two of her gowns were returned to her. One was a shabby, gray-and-white-striped linsey-woolsey, suitable for the schoolroom but much too workaday for Christmas Eve dinner with the family.

Her only other dress, aside from the slate-blue kerseymere she'd worn every day since she left home, was a green ballgown made of lustring so luxurious that Miranda wondered why the highwaymen had not taken it. It was, in its opposite way, as inappropriate as the linsey-woolsey, for it had a shockingly low décolletage, a tendency to cling, a long train, and it was trimmed at the neck, sleeves and hem with gold-tasseled lace so exquisite that no one would believe a governess could afford it. A particularly daring guest might wear the gown, but a governess could not.

She was in a quandary. Tonight, Christmas Eve, was to be festive. She had not attended a festive occasion for years, so she felt unduly excited at the prospect of attending the dinner. She yearned to put off the blue muslin for one evening, but she had nothing else to wear but the ballgown. If she snipped off the tasseled lace, she wondered, and cut off the train, would the green lustring be passable? It might, she decided, if she covered her bare shoulders with a shawl.

Hurriedly, for she had very little time to spare, she made the adjustments to the gown. Then she removed her widow's cap and took down her hair. She'd worn it pulled severely back into a knot all these days, and well hidden under the cap, but tonight she would let it show. She brushed it up into the style she'd favored in her younger days; called *à la Grecque*, it required that the longer hair be caught up in the back and the shorter left free to curl round the face. Then she slipped into the gown, threw a dark green paisley shawl (the item she was most grateful the highwaymen had spared) over her shoulders and, without daring to look at herself in the mirror, ran out to gather the boys.

All three of the children were resplendent in manly coats, starched shirts and neatly folded neckcloths, their faces scrubbed and shining, and their hair pomaded into unrecognizable neatness. It was no wonder, for they'd been dressed this evening by no less a personage than Terence's own valet. She was about to exclaim over their appearance when George, taking his first glimpse of her, exclaimed, "Crikes!"

Maury stared for a moment, mouth agape, and then said, "Double crikes!"

"What does that mean?" Miranda asked, kneeling down to straighten Jamie's collar.

Jamie put his arms about her neck and whispered in her ear, "It meanth your hair is pretty."

"*Everything* is pretty," George said, beaming at her.

"Very, very pretty," Maury said, taking her hand.

"And so are the three of you. Handsome as can be in your fine coats and neckcloths. But we must remember that handsome is as handsome does. So please, Maury, don't slurp your soup. And George, make your bow to

Lady Shallcross first. Come along now, quickly. We don't want to be late."

Everyone had gathered in the drawing room for preprandial sherry. The fire crackled merrily, the wreath over the mantel looked appropriately festive, and the guests sparkled in holiday finery. Honoria, in purple velvet, sat close to the fire and sipped her drink, watching Barnaby from the corner of her eye. She was quite delighted at the attention he'd been paying to her shy little protégée, but tonight Livy looked particularly lovely, and Honoria wanted to see the effect on him. The girl was dressed in a soft, rose-colored evening gown of Florentine silk that seemed to reflect its color upon her cheeks. Her delicate features glowed in the candlelight and her golden curls made a halo round her face. If Barnaby was not completely smitten by this charmer, Honoria thought, she would have to give him up as a hopeless case.

But Barnaby did indeed seem to be admiring the girl. He was at this very moment handing her a glass of sherry and making some sort of flattering comment about her appearance, because the girl simpered and colored charmingly. As Honoria watched, however, Barnaby chanced to look across the room, and his entire expression changed. Honoria followed his glance. In the doorway stood Miranda Pardew, wearing a clinging green gown almost exactly like the one she'd worn at the Lydell ball so many years ago. *Good God!* Honoria thought. *She's almost as breathtaking as she was then, drat her!*

Barnaby must have thought so too, for the expression on his face was not unlike the one he'd had when he'd first laid eyes on her: wide-eyed adoration. Nor was he the only man in the room to react. Terence immediately crossed to her, saying, "Mrs. Velacott, you are a vision!"

Harry, who'd been seated next to Lady Isabel on one of the sofas, jumped to his feet to second the compliment, but a glance at his betrothed was enough to stay his tongue. He sank back down and said nothing.

The Earl, married too long not to know what his wife was thinking, merely exchanged a meaningful glance with Honoria. *She really* is *a vixen*, they said with their eyes.

Miranda, who recognized male admiration when she saw it, realized too late that she'd made too flamboyant an entrance for a proper governess. Her cheeks grew hot. "The *boys* are the vision," she said, gently urging them forward.

Honoria, swallowing her irritation, smiled and rose eagerly from her chair. "So they are," she said, holding out her arms to them. "Did you ever see three such handsome young gentlemen? Here, I'm going to place myself under the mistletoe, and you three must give me a kiss."

Delia and Isabel also rose and, amid much horrified squealing from the bashful Jamie and noisy laughter from the others, demanded their share of the boys' embraces. In the midst of this liveliness, Cummings came in to announce dinner. "Lawrence," Honoria ordered, "you must claim the honor of taking Livy in to dinner, since she looks so particularly lovely this evening. Livy, dear, take my husband's arm."

The Earl smiled obediently and started toward the girl's chair. As he passed his wife, he muttered sotto voce, "What are you up to?"

"I must talk to Barnaby," she whispered back. She then took it upon herself to direct the pairing-off of the rest of the group, assigning Harry to escort Delia, Terence to usher Isabel, and the three boys to see to their governess. "And you, Barnaby, may take *my* arm."

The parade passed into the dining room, but Honoria held Barnaby back. "Wait a moment," she murmured, taking him aside. "I want to talk to you."

Barnaby looked down at her with upraised brows. "You seem agitated, my dear. What's troubling you?"

"The governess, of course. Barnaby, my love, do you know who she is?"

"Yes, of course. Why do you ask?"

Honoria gasped in astonishment. "You *knew* she's . . . she's *Miranda Pardew*?"

"I knew who she was from the moment I set eyes on her on the stage. I suppose it was her appearance tonight that triggered your memory."

"Her appearance tonight, in that absolutely *shocking* gown, certainly *would* have triggered my memory, but Lawrence and I recognized her that first evening. I didn't know that you, also, knew her identity. Why didn't you say something to me?"

"What was there to say? Her identity is of no importance, is it?"

Honoria gazed up at him nonplussed. "But, Barnaby, doesn't it trouble you at all to find that . . . that *baggage* in the same house with you?"

"Not a bit. I admit to a certain curiosity about her reasons for taking a post as a governess—a post for which one would imagine she's eminently unsuited—and for dropping her title, but I am otherwise unaffected by her presence."

Those words were just what Honoria had prayed to hear. She expelled a deep breath of relief. But Miranda's presence still troubled her. "Do you think she's up to something havey-cavey?" she asked.

"If she is, I can't imagine what it could be. Why are you so distrustful of her?"

"I don't know. I never liked her. Why is she pretending to be a governess? And if she's not pretending, then what sort of governess brings her charges down to dine wearing a gown that would raise eyebrows in a ballroom?"

"Would it?" Barnaby asked innocently. "It seemed perfectly acceptable to me. Come, my dear, let's go in before the others begin to wonder what's keeping us." He took her arm and led her toward the dining room. "And as for our Miranda, what harm can she do? I wouldn't give her another thought, if I were you."

· Sixteen ·

EVERYONE BUT JAMIE heartily enjoyed Christmas Eve dinner. The boy, being petted, smiled at, teased and fondled by so many people all at once, became tongue-tied and uncomfortable. He kept his eyes fixed on his plate except when his parents or his governess or his uncle Barney spoke to him, and even they were rewarded with only brief, timid little answers. Poor Barnaby, seated between his bashful nephew and the bashful Livy, found himself having to work hard to draw out his dinner partners. Fortunately, Livy was by this time feeling more at home; she giggled frequently at Barnaby's quips and appeared to be enjoying herself.

After dinner, Terence, Delia and their guests gathered in the drawing room, where Lady Isabel played carols and everyone sang. Then Delia lit the Yule log with a bit of the charred remains of last year's log. Since the new log was covered with decorative greenery, it flared up in a great blaze that made everyone cheer. They settled themselves before the fire, the children stretched out on the floor, and listened to the Earl tell Christmas stories. Before they knew it, it was time to ready themselves to venture out for the midnight church service.

The older boys had been given permission to attend, but Jamie was ordered to go upstairs with his governess and get ready for bed. Unhappy at this decision, Jamie clung stubbornly to his mother's cloak and would not let go. Neither Miranda's coaxing nor Delia's firm orders would convince the child to release his hold. Finally, in disgust, Terence forcibly pulled him off. "Behave yourself, you imp," he snapped, and thrust him into Miranda's arms. "Wish us all Happy Christmas and say good night!"

But the boy, his trembling lips pressed firmly together and his eyes teary, would not say a word. He threw his father a look of heartfelt reproach and buried his face in his governess's shoulder. Miranda carried him up the stairs. The others either smiled in amusement or sighed in sympathy with the child as they wound their mufflers round their necks, drew on their gloves and started out to the sleigh. A young child exhibiting pique made a minor incident, requiring no further attention, they all believed. All except Barnaby.

Terence, ushering his guests out the door, noticed that his brother remained fixed in his place, peering up the stairway with knit brows. "Barnaby, old fellow, don't worry about Jamie. He'll cry himself to sleep and forget the whole thing by morning. Come along now. We're all waiting."

"Go without me, will you, Terence? I think I'd rather stay home tonight and . . . and read."

"Read?" Terence regarded his brother in puzzled disapproval. Reading was not a pastime the older man often engaged in, and he didn't understand its appeal. "Well, suit yourself," he said, shrugging, "though why anyone would wish to remain alone in the house on Christmas Eve with only a book for company is beyond my ken."

Barnaby waited until the sound of the sleigh bells died away. Then he went up the stairs two at a time. He found his nephew in his bedroom, sitting on Miranda's lap in a rocking chair near the window. Miranda was soothing the boy with soft, cooing words. "In a year or two," she was murmuring, "you'll be such a very big boy, quite old enough to—" She glanced up and saw Barnaby standing in the doorway. Her eyes at first gleamed with delight, but immediately afterward they became wary. "Look, Jamie, it's your uncle," she said, cocking her head curiously.

"Unca Barney!" the child clarioned, his tearful face brightening. "You didn't go!"

"No." Barnaby stepped over the threshold. "I stayed behind to be with you."

The boy jumped from Miranda's lap, ran across the room and clasped Barnaby's legs deliriously. "Did you thtay to tell me a thtory?"

Barnaby lifted him up in his arms. "Yes, if Mrs. Velacott will permit you to stay up just a wee bit longer."

"You'll thay yeth, won't you, Mithuth Velacott? Unca Barney tellth the betht thtorieth—Jack the Giant Killer . . . Thaint George an' the Dragon . . . King Arthur an' hith Knighth . . ."

"Of course I'll say yes," Miranda smiled, rising from the rocker, "if he doesn't tell all of them tonight."

Barnaby laughed. "I promise to tell only one," he said.

Miranda felt a little tremor in her chest. This usually sullen man so rarely smiled at her that the effect of his laugh was surprising—it warmed her through. "But Jamie," she said, trying not to be distracted from her responsibilities, "I think, first, you should get into your nightshirt."

The undressing was done with astounding dispatch. Then Barnaby sat down on the rocker with the child in his lap. Miranda started for the door. "Don't you want to thtay?" Jamie asked.

Miranda met Barnaby's eyes. "Oh, I don't think your uncle would like—"

"Do stay, Mrs. Velacott," Barnaby said, "unless you've something better to do."

"There'th nothing better than one of your thtorieth," the boy insisted.

"Then of course I *must* stay," Miranda agreed, and she perched on the edge of the boy's bed.

Jamie looked from one to the other happily. "Thith will be better than goin' to church. Go on, Unca Barney. Thtart."

Barnaby launched into an account of *The Marvelous*

Adventures of Sir Thomas Thumb, but before he'd concluded the second adventure, the child was fast asleep. Barnaby carried the boy to his bed and Miranda tucked the comforter around him. Then she blew out the candle, and they tiptoed from the room.

They walked together down the corridor. It was dimly lit by the candles in the wall sconces and quite chilly. Miranda pulled her shawl tightly round her shoulders. "It was good of you to stay," she said. "You made the boy's Christmas Eve a happy one."

"I enjoyed it myself. I remember too well what it was like being the youngest in a lively family. I like helping Jamie get through some of the torment." He threw Miranda an inscrutable look. "The boy seems to be growing quite attached to you."

"Yes, I think he is." They'd arrived at her door, but before going in, she peered at him curiously. "One would think you'd be pleased, sir, but something in your tone suggests otherwise."

He paused and faced her. "Why should I be pleased? I know quite well that you're only playing at being a governess. When the position bores you or becomes too onerous, you'll undoubtedly depart for something more entertaining, and the child will be left bereft."

A wave of irritation washed over her. "Dash it, Mr. Traherne, I'm tired of the groundless assumptions you make about me. You met me less than a week ago. What can you know of me to support the accusation that I am not serious about my post?"

"I know enough."

"Do you, indeed? And just what do you know?"

"I know, for one thing, that your identity is a lie. You are not Mrs. Velacott but *Lady* Velacott."

Her eyes fell guiltily. "Delia—Mrs. Traherne—told you, I suppose. If she did, then she also told you *why*—"

"She did *not* tell me. I knew it from the first."

She looked up at him again, her eyes flashing fire. "Now *you* are lying," she accused. "The first name you called me was Miss Pardew, not Lady Velacott."

"Nevertheless I knew. As I also know that you are reputed to have spent your youth in flirtations, to have devastated a number of men, and that you are more at home in ballrooms than in schoolrooms. In short, ma'am, hardly the sort suited to the care of children."

She felt choked with anger, not knowing how to argue against so closed a mind. "But this is all based on unsubstantiated rumors you must have heard more than a decade ago! How can you believe—?"

"I can believe them because they are *not* unsubstantiated. I myself can substantiate them."

"Are you saying you *knew* me in my youth?" She stared at him aghast, wondering which of her youthful excesses he'd observed that had evidently left such a dreadful impression on him. "But even if you did, what does it matter? It was all so long ago. Can you not grant the possibility that I'm changed?"

"Not so very changed," he said, his eyes measuring her from her face to the hands clutching her shawl over her revealing décolletage to the green shine of her gown which clung so enticingly to her breasts and hips and legs. Perhaps it was the gown, and the memories and feelings it invoked, that drove him to commit the final cruelty. His mouth curled upward in the disparaging sneer that had frightened away so many young women. "No, not so very changed. In fact, I heard you described quite recently as a baggage."

The blood drained from her face. *"Baggage?"* she croaked. White-lipped and trembling with rage, she wanted only to strike his cruel face. She swung up her hand to slap him, her shawl slipping unheeded from her shoulder. "You . . . you—!"

He caught her arm in midair. His blood began to bubble with an excitement he had no wish to control. With no real plan or intention in mind, he twisted her arm behind her and pulled her to him, feeling only a wicked pleasure in having her in his power, in being able to wreak a revenge for wounds that, he now realized, had never healed. Almost coldly, he took her chin in his free hand, tilted up her face and kissed her, the pressure of his lips hard and angry as a blow.

She struggled to free herself, striking his arm and shoulder with her free hand and twisting her head to wrench her mouth from his, but his grip was like a vise that only grew tighter with her resistance. After a while, she surrendered and lay limp in his hold.

From that moment, the nature of the embrace changed for him. As soon as she'd ceased her struggle, and he felt her softness against him, something melted in his chest. He lifted his head and eased the grip on her arm, his anger and lust for revenge somehow dissipated. He expected her to push him away, slap him, or scream, but she didn't move. She only peered at him with eyes wide and mouth slightly open, her lips trembling and her breath coming in gasps. *Let her go,* his mind told him. *Use your good sense and let her go.*

But he could not let her go. Acting purely on instinct, he let his hands move slowly up her arms, linger on her bare shoulders and then move to her throat, the throat that had so attracted him when he'd first laid eyes on her. He could feel the swelling curves of it under his fingers and the rapid, thrilling throb of her pulse underneath. He moved his hands to her chin and then, cupping her face with both hands, kissed her again, so tenderly that it elicited a soft moan from the depths of her.

The sound made him wild. His hands moved down again, quickly this time, and he took her in his arms, kissing her hungrily, with the starved passion of eleven years of waiting. But what surprised him more than his own impetuosity was her response. Her arms crept up around his neck, clutching him tightly, her lips clinging to his, as if she, too, had lost her head. He felt dizzy, shaken, more deeply stirred than he'd ever been by a woman's embrace. That realization horrified him. This was *Miranda Pardew,* the woman he despised!

Abruptly he pushed her away. She tottered back against

the wall, blinking at him, the picture of agonized confusion. Her eyes searched his face for some sort of explanation for what he knew was utterly crazed behavior.

But, furious with himself and as confused as she, he had no intention of attempting an explanation. He merely bent down, picked up her fallen shawl and thrust it at her. "I'm sorry," he muttered.

She used the shawl to wipe away a tear that had escaped from one of her startled, angry eyes. "You neither look nor sound sorry."

"Very well, then, I'm not sorry. Make of it what you will." And he turned on his heel and strode off down the corridor without a backward look.

· Seventeen ·

BARNABY WENT THROUGH the motions of Christmas Day, laughing and cavorting with his brothers and his nephews, playing Forfeits and Hunt the Slipper, drinking his share from the wassail bowl, and even making the dignified Lady Isabel giggle by kissing her ear under the mistletoe. But he did it all in a sort of fog. All day long, his mind played and replayed memories of the night before, like a simple tune one can't get out of one's head. Half distracted, he could still feel Miranda's lips on his mouth, the silken feel of her skin under his fingers, the softness of her body pressed against his. But the memories were not nostalgic; rather, they filled him with disgust. Disgust at his own weakness. Disgust at the realization that she still had the power to turn him into a blithering fool.

After an enormous Christmas dinner of goose and roast beef and smoking plum pudding and any number of other delicacies, the party divided into small groups and went off in separate directions: the children were taken wearily to bed; Lady Isabel and Harry strolled off with elaborate nonchalance to the small sitting room for a bit of lovers' privacy; Terence, Honoria, Lawrence and Livy sat down to a game of silver loo in the drawing room; and Delia set about helping the staff to clear the remains of the celebration and prepare for Boxing Day. That left Barnaby free to wander off by himself and try to clear his head. He went to the library, pulled a wing chair close to the fire and sat down to brood.

If this were a crisis in the Foreign Office, he told himself, he would know how to handle it. He would, first, clarify the nature of the problem. Then he'd list a number of alternate possibilities for a solution and evaluate them. Finally, after choosing the likeliest alternative, he'd proceed to get it done. This method was a useful, rational one, and, as far as he could tell, should work for personal problems as well as for professional ones.

Well then, he told himself, *let's get at it. What, exactly, is my problem?* But clarifying the problem was not easy. He mulled it over for several minutes, but the contradictory feelings that were tearing him apart—wild attraction and utter revulsion toward the same woman at the same time— were not easy to verbalize. The only honest statement he could contrive that clearly and accurately pinpointed the problem was: *I am falling in love with a woman I despise.* With this sentence, the illogic of his situation was immediately apparent. How could he find a logical solution for so ridiculous a problem?

It was obvious that the contrary feelings could not exist together; he had to rid himself of either the revulsion or the attraction. And since he'd lived with the revulsion for so long that it was now almost a part of him, it was the attraction that had to end. Separating himself from the source of that attraction seemed the easiest solution. Either Miranda had to leave this house, or he did. When he'd first learned that Miranda was to become governess in this house, he'd considered telling Delia what he thought of her, expecting that Delia would immediately sack the woman. But he hadn't done it. And now that Miranda was becoming a part of the household, and the boys were beginning to hold her in affection, it seemed a cruel thing to do. It would be easier on everyone if he simply took himself out of this house. All he had to do was invent an excuse for leaving and depart in the morning.

The plan was barely framing itself in his mind when the library door opened and Delia entered. She carefully closed it behind her, came up to the fire and seated herself on the hearth. "All right, my dear," she said, folding her hands in her lap and meeting his eyes with a level look in her own, "tell me what's troubling you?"

He shifted uncomfortably in his chair. "Why do you think anything's troubling me?"

"Come now, Barnaby, I've known you all your adult life. Do you think I can't tell when you're distracted?"

"I'm not distracted, exactly. Just . . . er . . . uncomfortable."

"Uncomfortable?"

"Yes, uncomfortable about telling you that I must cut my visit short."

Her eyebrows lifted in surprise. "How short?"

"I must go tomorrow."

"Good God! Why?" She peered at him worriedly. "Are you ill?"

"No, of course not. I simply must get home."

"But I don't understand. What must you do at home?"

"Er . . . nothing. Business."

She recognized evasion when she heard it. And her nature was too forthright to pretend she believed him. "What business can you have that came up so suddenly?" she asked bluntly. "You can't have had a message from London. No stage has yet come through."

He frowned, annoyed at himself for having launched on this course of lying without proper preparation. "It's something I knew about before I started." He looked down at his hands awkwardly. "I should have told you before, but I didn't wish to spoil the holiday."

"Barnaby, my boy, you are the worst liar in Christendom. I wish you would tell me the truth I shan't hold you back if you truly must leave, but I'd feel much better knowing the real reason. It isn't something I've done or neglected to do, is it?"

"No, of course it isn't. Don't even *think* anything so

foolish. You know you've always made me feel perfectly at home."

"Then what *is* it? It isn't having to play the gallant to little Livy, is it? I warned Honoria that you might not like being compelled to court the girl."

"Compelled to court Livy? To *court* her?" Barnaby looked over at his sister-in-law in sincere surprise. "Is *that* why she's here? So that I can court her?"

"Why did you *think* she's here? Really, Barnaby, you are unbelievably naive when it comes to female wiles. Honoria has been trying to marry you off for years! And all the ladies in her circle have aided and abetted her in that attempt. In fact, little Livy was the unanimous choice of all of them."

"You don't say!" Barnaby grinned, more amused at this news than annoyed. "Whatever made them think that a young chit out of the schoolroom, with nothing to say for herself except how much she misses her mama, would catch my fancy?"

"She not a chit out of the schoolroom. She's twenty-two! And she's soft-spoken and modest, as you are, with a gentle disposition, proper rearing and, above all, very lovely to look at. Quite the perfect girl for you, wouldn't you say?"

Barnaby stared at his sister-in-law openmouthed, for a completely new solution to his problem burst upon him. *Livy Ponsonby*, gentle and modest and pretty as a picture! Why couldn't he make himself fall in love with *her*? The best way to get over one love was to find oneself another, he knew that. Another girl could be the perfect antidote to his heartache. That solution would be much better than making an awkward departure, better than enduring a lonely ride back to London through the cold and snow, better than tearing himself from the warmth of his family circle. "I wonder, Delia," he said thoughtfully, "if Honoria hasn't done me a favor. Perhaps courting Livy is just what I should do."

"What?" Delia asked, startled. "You don't intend to leave here after all?"

"No. On second thought, my business in London can wait."

"Can it, indeed?" She eyed him suspiciously. "You're cutting it too rare and thick, Barnaby Traherne. Just what is going on in that head of yours?"

"Nothing that need worry you. You've persuaded me that it is more important for me to learn the ways of females than to take care of business. I'm thirty years old, after all. It's time I did a little courting. And Livy Ponsonby *is* a sweet, pretty little thing, just as you said she is."

"I don't believe a word of this," Delia declared, rising majestically, "but as long as you're not going away, I shan't press you further. But be warned, my dear, I shall get to the bottom of this enigma sooner or later."

"There is no enigma," he insisted, rising also, "but if it amuses you to imagine there is, go ahead." He preceded her to the door and held it open for her. "By the way, Delia," he said casually, "Mrs. Velacott tells me you know her real identity. Is that true?"

Delia paused in the doorway. "That she's *Lady* Velacott, you mean? Yes, she told me all about it."

"Doesn't her misrepresentation trouble you?"

"No, of course not. Why should it?"

He shrugged. "I don't know, quite. But if I were hiring someone to look after my boys, I would be leery of someone who lied."

"She had good reason for dropping her title. The woman is penniless, you know. Her deceased husband left her without a farthing. As she quite sensibly explained to me, a title has no value to an impoverished female. So she dropped it. It's not really a lie, under the circumstances, is it?"

Barnaby peered at her for a moment, his expression strangely arrested. "No, I suppose not," he mumbled after a long pause.

Delia cocked her head at him, her shrewd eyes suddenly alight. "I say, Barnaby, that's the second time you've shown an undue interest in our governess. Is there some significance in these inquiries?"

"Don't make this part of your enigma, my love," he answered flippantly. "I already told you I don't like her above half."

"So you did. But you didn't tell me why."

He shrugged and started off down the corridor away from her. "She isn't my sort, that's all," he said over his shoulder.

"Not like little Livy, is that what you mean?" she called after him.

"No. Not a bit like little Livy."

Delia gazed after him, her eyes twinkling speculatively. "But at least our Mrs. Velacott can speak of more interesting things than missing her mama," she said under her breath. "And I have a feeling that you, Barnaby Traherne, are even more aware of that than I."

· Eighteen ·

MIRANDA STOOD AT the schoolroom window, looking down at the snowy landscape beneath her. But it was not the appeal of nature that had attracted her eye. It was the sight of two figures cavorting in the snow. Ever since Boxing Day, for three mornings in a row, Barnaby Traherne had taken Livy Ponsonby walking. Sometimes they strolled sedately arm in arm, but at other times, as now, they capered about like children, throwing snowballs at each other or tumbling about in the drifts. It was a sight Miranda found completely odious.

She turned away and fixed her eyes on her three charges, now bent over their slates, busily occupied with their lessons. A little while ago, she'd had to break up a fight (the usual tussle between Maury, who'd been teasing Jamie, and George, who'd charged in to defend his baby brother with clenched fists), but now all was calm. George was wrestling with a problem in long division, Maury with multiplication, and Jamie with listing "-AT" words—*b*at, *c*at, *h*at, and so on—laboriously on his slate. Their boyish absorption in their tasks made the governess smile. Each of them had an unconscious habit—a small gesture that revealed the intensity of his concentration: George pulled at his left earlobe, Maury twisted a lock of his hair, and as for Jamie, the tip of his tongue stuck out of the corner of his mouth and wiggled with every stroke of his chalk.

She walked slowly round the table looking over their shoulders, but none of her charges seemed, at the moment, to require her help. Then she wandered over to the bookshelf, looking for something to do, but the books were all neatly arranged. So, quite against her will, she found herself drawn back to the window and the view outside. The couple below were now chasing Miss Ponsonby's bonnet, which had blown off. As Miranda watched, Barnaby caught it and placed it back on the girl's head. The act was tenderly performed; he even tied the ribbons himself. For one horrible moment, Miranda feared he was going to lift the girl's chin and kiss her!

But he did not. He merely took her arm in his, and they strolled back toward the house.

Miranda sank down on the window seat, her heart beating rapidly and her emotions in turmoil. She couldn't understand why the scene below had such a powerful effect on her. Barnaby Traherne's doings were of no concern to her!

She couldn't help wondering, however, if he'd ever kissed Miss Ponsonby. But even if he had, it could not have been in the same way he'd kissed her. Miranda was not a green girl; she knew that the kiss they'd exchanged the other night was quite out of the ordinary. The memory of it still had the power to set her trembling.

The trouble was that she couldn't understand Barnaby Traherne's behavior. It was plain that he'd taken her in dislike, probably because he'd seen her in her youth indulging in some flagrant flirtation. That much was easy to fathom. But that abominable kiss had thrown everything askew. Perhaps he'd begun it as an act of dislike—more of an assault than a kiss, really—but he certainly hadn't ended it that way. She'd felt the tremor in his arms, the urgency in his embrace, the passion and hunger that had shaken them both. What had he meant by such an act? *Make of it what you will*, he'd said, but she couldn't make any sense of it at all.

She couldn't make much sense of her own feelings, either. Barnaby was sullen and insulting to her, yet, knowing this, she still was drawn to him. His way with Jamie endeared him to her, and she found his demeanor within his family circle warm and charming. The contradictions in her feelings were epitomized by her reactions to that kiss, at first so infuriating and later so . . . so overwhelming. At first, she'd wanted nothing more than to strike him down and stamp on his limp and prostrate body, but later, when he'd shown that unexpected tenderness and then such shattering passion, her whole body had responded. She would have clung to him forever, if he'd continued to hold her so.

But he hadn't continued. He'd made another of his abrupt mood changes. Cold and distant, he'd stalked away, leaving her shaken and confused. And shaken and confused she remained.

In the last analysis, however, the matter was not so confusing. If one faced it honestly, it was quite simple. She could state the problem in fewer than ten words: *I'm in love with a man who despises me.*

And now he was pursuing Livy Ponsonby. Surely he couldn't be serious. His character was too complex and too subtle to find the naive Livy interesting. Yet, on second thought, Miranda couldn't blame him for taking her up. Livy, besides being a beauty, had the more significant advantage of being quiet, sweet and virtuous. She was not wasting her youth in wild behavior and meaningless flirtations. Barnaby would not be able to accuse *her* of being a liar and a flirt.

Very well, she said, addressing him in her mind, *if that's the sort of namby-pamby female who pleases you, I wish you well of her. Go ahead and woo her, with my blessing.*

Miranda peered out of the window again, but the two of them were gone. There was nothing to see now but the impressions of their movements in the snow. Footprints, male and female, side by side. The molded remains of a scene of blossoming romance. How picturesque. How romantic. How utterly revolting.

· Nineteen ·

DELIA, COMING CHEERFULLY down the stairs after a very satisfactory visit to the schoolroom (during which George cogently explained to her the causes of the War of the Roses, Maury exhibited a proud proficiency in multiplying double digits, and Jamie wrote half the alphabet for her in capital letters on his slate), was startled to discover her dignified sister-in-law, Honoria, down on one knee outside the closed library door, her eye to the keyhole. "Heavens, Honoria," she exclaimed, "are you *eavesdropping*?"

"Sssh!" Honoria hissed, waving a hand at her in a gesture of restraint and not even bothering to look up. "I think he's going to *offer* for her!"

"Who? *Barnaby?*" Delia hurried to the doorway, her cheery mood dissipating. "Good God! You don't mean it!"

"Hush, I said! Do you want them to hear us?" Honoria tottered to her feet and drew Delia down the hall so they would be out of hearing of the pair inside the library. "I'm so excited I can hardly *breathe*!"

"Why?" Delia asked suspiciously, not wanting to be taken in by Honoria's histrionic fervor. "What makes you think—?"

Honoria clasped her hands at her breast, her eyes shining. "He's taken her in there, just the two of them," she whispered gleefully, "and he's teaching her to play *Hearts*!"

"Well, what of that? There's nothing especially meaningful in two people playing a simple card game."

"Yes, but I don't remember Barnaby ever doing such a thing before. And there's something about him today. Something edgy. Why, at breakfast this morning, he dropped the jam jar."

"Then that settles it," Delia said dryly. "Dropping the jam jar is all the proof one needs."

That remark did succeed in deflating Honoria's high spirits. Her smile transformed itself into a glare. "What sort of proof do you need, for heaven's sake?" she retorted. "It's as plain as pikestaff he's pursuing her."

"If you'd seen through the keyhole that he was down on his knee before her, I might have taken you seriously. But frankly, Honoria, I don't believe he can be such a fool as that."

Honoria's whole body stiffened. "Why, whatever can you mean? Don't you *want* him to marry?"

"Yes, of course I do. But not your little Livy."

"Why not? What's wrong with her?"

"Nothing's wrong with her. But nothing's right with her, either."

"*Everything*'s right with her!" Honoria exclaimed, ready to defend the girl to the death. Having convinced herself that Livy was the ideal partner for her dearest Barnaby, she would not give up that dream merely on Delia's say-so. "She's well-bred and pretty and kind and shy . . ."

Delia expelled a grunt of disgust. "I don't know why you think Barnaby needs a shy, retiring flower of a female."

"Because he's so shy himself," Honoria declared without hesitation. It was the same argument she'd used with her friends in London, so it came easily to her tongue. "He's not attracted to those over-animated, domineering sorts."

"Barnaby is *not* shy, Honoria. You must stop believing that he is. He hasn't been shy since early manhood. And an animated woman is probably the only sort who'll keep him interested."

Honoria blinked at her younger sister-in-law, her confidence shaken. "How can you sound so sure, Delia? Has he said anything to you on the subject?"

"No, not much. But I have good instincts in these matters. And my instincts tell me that he'd grow bored with the likes of Livy Ponsonby in a very short time. I think he'd do much better with someone like . . . well, like my governess."

"Your *governess*!" Honoria eyes popped, her face reddened, and her voice rose to a squeak. "Your governess would be the very *worst* choice for him. Do you know who she *is*?"

"What sort of question is that? Of course I know who she is. She's Mrs. Velacott. Or *Lady* Velacott, if her dropped title is what's bothering you."

"That's *not* what's bothering me. She's *Miranda Pardew*!"

"Heavens," Delia said, puzzled. "You say that as if you were saying Lucrezia Borgia. Who's Miranda Pardew?"

"Miranda Pardew, I'll have you know," Honoria ranted, "is the woman who made mincemeat of poor Barnaby at his very first ball. I blame her, and her alone, for his avoidance of females and for his bleak and miserable bachelor existence."

Delia stared at her sister-in-law, her breath arrested in her throat. "Good God," she gasped after a moment, "is that *true*? My governess is the same woman who offended Barnaby all those years ago?"

"As true as I'm standing here. She is one woman, believe me, whom I shall never forget!"

"Aha," Delia crowed as if in triumph, "I *thought* there was something havey-cavey about his interest in her."

"See here, Delia Traherne, if you're speaking of Barnaby, you can be certain that he *has* no interest in her! The woman is nothing but a . . . a . . . *flibbertigibbet*."

"She may well have been, for all I know," Delia acknowledged. "But it was long ago, wasn't it? Even Lucrezia Borgia turned out to be praiseworthy in the latter part of her life."

"What has Lucrezia Borgia to do with this?" Honoria snapped disgustedly.

"Never mind." Delia eyed Honoria with a speculative gleam. "When, exactly, did this infamous set-down business occur?"

"I don't remember *exactly* when. Ten or eleven years ago. Barnaby was nineteen."

"And he remembers the incident, I suppose."

"All too well. He recognized her at once. She, of course, has no recollection of the incident or the devastation she caused, the heartless creature."

"I shouldn't think she would. One can't be expected to remember *all* the foolish acts of one's youth." Delia rubbed her chin thoughtfully for a moment, and then, as a wicked smile suffused her face, she grasped her sister-in-law's arm. "Honoria, my love, come with me into the sitting room. I'll have Cummings bring us some soothing tea, we'll put our feet up, and you'll tell me every detail of this fascinating story."

Honoria, although quite suspicious and full of objections to everything Delia said and was not saying, allowed herself be led away. "I don't understand you, Delia. Why on earth do you wish to hear those unpleasant details?"

"Because I'm beginning to understand the enigma of Barnaby's heart. I think, my dear, that we may have stumbled upon the one woman who'd be a perfect match for our Barnaby. With a bit of good fortune, we may marry him off after all." She squeezed Honoria's arm affectionately before giving a final blow to her sister-in-law's hopes. "But *not*," she added, laughing, "to your little Livy."

· *Twenty* ·

IN THE LIBRARY, completely unaware of the scheming going on in his behalf right outside the door, Barnaby sat at a small card table in front of one of the windows dealing cards to Livy Ponsonby, who sat opposite him. They'd been playing long enough for him to realize that Livy did not play cards with the same zest for winning that Miranda had exhibited when he'd played with her at the inn. At that time, he'd found Miranda's chortling triumph quite annoying, but he now reluctantly recognized that her enthusiasm had added to the game a vivacity that was absent here, with Livy showing such good-natured indifference to the outcome. "Are you sure you'd enjoy playing another rubber?" he asked, searching her face for signs of boredom.

She threw him one of her sweet, sincere smiles. "Yes, of course," she said. "Positively."

The game proceeded quietly, the only sounds being the occasional snap of sparks from the fireplace and the occasional groan from Barnaby when his luck was bad. Livy didn't say a word. Barnaby glanced up at her from time to time, wondering what the girl was thinking. Was it wise, he wondered, to pursue a girl who never made her thoughts or feelings known?

Playing Hearts with Livy did not occupy his full attention, so his mind roamed about at will. This afternoon he was preoccupied with the question of offering for her. Honoria had hinted quite broadly at breakfast that she was expecting to hear the happy news within the next few days. Honoria was right about the importance of prompt action. If he truly intended to offer for the girl, he ought to do it soon. There were only a few days left before this fortnight's visit came to an end. The matter would have to be broached before Lawrence and Honoria took Livy back to her mama. Positively.

But somehow he couldn't seem to bring himself to the sticking point. Although he was sincerely taken with the girl—she had a lovely face and form, a most pleasing voice, the modest demeanor that he believed enhanced a woman's appeal and, at times, a look in her large, shockingly blue eyes of surprised fright that never failed to touch him and make him feel protective toward her—he felt, in her company, that something important was missing. The trouble was that he couldn't figure out what that something was.

As these thoughts were circling round in his mind, the library door opened and Miranda came in, heading for the bookcases. A moment passed before she saw them. When she did, she stopped dead in her tracks. Her cheeks reddened painfully. "I'm so sorry!" she gasped. "I didn't know—"

Barnaby peered at her in some surprise. He had not seen her since Christmas Eve, when she was wearing her green gown and her hair was gloriously tumbled about her face. She was now wearing her blue muslin with the white ruffle, and her hair was covered with her widow's cap. She hardly looked like the strumpet he'd conjured up in his memory. "That's quite all right," he assured her politely. "You are only interrupting a card game. Livy, my dear, it was Mrs. Velacott who taught me to play this game."

"Did she really?" Livy gave the governess a warm smile.

"Yes, I did," Miranda said, speaking rapidly to mask her embarrassment. "I'm glad to discover, Mr. Traherne, that you still remember it. But let me not interrupt." She backed awkwardly to the door. "I'll come back later."

"That's not necessary," Barnaby said, rising. "Please do what you came to do."

As she hesitated in the doorway, he stared at her with what he knew was undue intensity. He'd scrupulously avoided her since Christmas Eve, five whole days ago. When he wanted to see his nephews—which he liked to do daily—he sent the butler up to get them. Miranda tactfully had not accompanied them on those occasions. Now he could not tear his eyes away. It was as if they'd been starved for the sight of her. But this sort of thinking, he knew, was contrary to the rules he'd set for himself. Such thoughts were dangerous. "Were you looking for something, ma'am?" he asked, his tone formal and distant.

"Yes," she said, stepping back into the room. "The last volume of Smollett's *History*. We took only three volumes upstairs the other day, but today I learned there are four."

"There are indeed. Come in, ma'am, please. I'll help you search for it."

Before she could object, he crossed to the shelves nearest the window and began to look. She went to the opposite side. Since the books were shelved in no discernable order, it was necessary to read the title of each one. Many minutes passed in silence. Finally, squatting down and peering through the tomes on the lowest shelf, Barnaby came upon it. "Here it is, sandwiched between John Wesley's *Primitive Physic* and Madame D'Arblay's *Journal*," he announced.

Miranda ran quickly to his side to get it, arriving and bending down for it just as he was rising. He didn't see her, for though the Smollett's was in his hand, his eyes were still on the other books on the shelf. The top of his head struck her chin with a loud clunk. She cried out and tottered back. "Damnation!" he swore, dropping the book and reaching for her with quick instinct to keep her from falling over. "I'm so sorry!" he muttered. "Are you hurt?"

But before the words had left his lips, he realized he was holding her round the waist. For a fraction of a second their eyes met. Then he dropped his hold on her with the alacrity with which one drops a hot coal.

"N-No, don't b-be alarmed," she stammered. "I'm all right."

He nodded and handed her the book. She took it, made a quick curtsey and fled from the room.

"I don't think she was hurt," Livy said calmly from her place at the card table.

He looked round in surprise. He'd forgotten she was there. Embarrassed, and with his feelings in turmoil, he returned to the card table. "Where were we?" he asked absently.

"Perhaps we ought to start this game again," she suggested, her manner so placid and sweet that it was obvious she'd seen nothing untoward in what had just passed.

He fixed his eyes on her as his racing pulse quieted itself. There was something soothing in Livy's company. Being wedded to her would be calm and reasonable and eminently sane. He would never feel the turmoil, the tension, the downright agony that he invariably experienced when Miranda was anywhere near. He needed protection against the disquieting feelings that Miranda always generated. Livy could be that protection. If he had a brain in his head, he would propose marriage to this girl. Right now.

Livy looked across at him with her big blue eyes. "Is it my turn to deal?"

"Your turn? Yes, I believe it is your turn. Livy, my sweet, will you marry me?"

It was done. Said and done. His chest heaved with a large, relieved breath. He smiled over at the girl for whom he'd just offered, confident that he'd made both of them very happy.

But Livy, her mouth slightly open, was staring at him with her shocked, fearful, helpless look. "Wh-what did you s-say?" she asked.

"I'm sorry, my dear," he said contritely, realizing that he'd not shown an iota of romance in his proposal. "I was thoughtlessly abrupt. But you must have known what my intentions were. Surely I've shown you how much I care for you. I'm asking you to marry me."

Her eyes opened even wider. "Oh!" she breathed. Her response was unquestionably more frightened than happy.

He reached for her hand. "May I take that as a 'yes'?"

The little hand trembled under his, and her eyes fell from his face, her long lashes brushing her cheeks. They sat, silent and unmoving, for a long moment. Then she wriggled her hand free, stood up and looked down at him. "Yes," she breathed. "Th-thank you."

"Do you mean it?" he asked, getting to his feet and smiling down at her. "Positively?"

She didn't laugh, nor did she meet his eyes. She merely nodded. "M-Mama will be so g-glad," she said, and then she, too, fled from the room.

Barnaby gazed after her in bewilderment. For the second time in less than five minutes, a woman had fled from him. "Barnaby, my boy," he muttered dryly under his breath, "how do you account for this magical effect you have on the ladies?"

· Twenty-one ·

BARNABY, UNCERTAIN OF the meaning of Livy's response, said nothing to anyone that afternoon about being betrothed. And Livy, hiding away in her room, had neither the opportunity nor the inclination to make any announcement. But in the mysterious way that such news has of disseminating itself, the whole household was buzzing with it within an hour. Honoria heard about it from her abigail when the girl was brushing her hair, preparing to dress it for dinner. Honoria let out a little scream. "How did you *hear* it?" she cried, clasping her hands together at her breast. "Are you *sure*?"

"Everyone's whisperin' about it," the girl said. "Even Mr. Cummings won't deny it, an' he ain't one to permit us t' spread gossip."

That was enough for Honoria. Pulling her dressing gown tightly around her ungirdled waist, and with her long gray hair hanging unplaited down her back, she ran first to the Earl to tell him the news and then down the hall to Barnaby's room. "Dearest!" she exclaimed as soon as he opened his door, "I'm so delighted I could weep!" And she threw herself into his arms.

He patted her affectionately on her back as he led her to the nearest chair. "Calm yourself, my dear," he warned. "I'm not yet certain that Livy is happy about this."

"Of *course* she's happy. How can you think otherwise? Why, she told me herself that she finds you the kindest, most good-natured and handsomest man alive!"

Barnaby was not taken in by his sister-in-law's hyperbole. "I suspect, my love, that it was you put those words in her mouth. Nevertheless, you must promise me not to say a word of this betrothal until Livy herself affirms it."

Livy did affirm it that very evening at dinner. She made a shy announcement during the serving of the second course. And when the whole family reacted with boisterous delight (rising to their feet, surrounding the pair, pounding Barnaby on his back, kissing the blushing Livy and loudly toasting the couple's health), Barnaby was relieved to see that Livy did at last look happy.

A short while later, upstairs in the schoolroom, Miranda sat on the window seat staring out at a pale winter moon. The boys were not there, having been invited to join in the celebration of their uncle's betrothal, but Miranda had declined to go with them. "It's a celebration for the family," she'd explained as she sent them off in the care of the butler, "not for the staff."

She remained in the schoolroom alone, not noticing that the fire had died. She'd not even lit a candle to dispel the darkness. She merely sat gazing out at the sky. It was a sad-looking moon, she thought, coldly bluish white in color and fuzzy in outline because of a layer of clouds that partially obscured it. It barely gave light to the snow. *Pathetic*, she muttered. *Like me.*

Indeed, she *was* pathetic, sitting there in the corner of the window recess with her feet curled up under her and her arms crossed over her chest, shivering with cold and letting a veritable flood of tears drip down her cheeks. It was pathetic to weep over the betrothal of a man who had shown his dislike of her from the first moment they'd met. How could she have been so foolish as to permit herself to fall in love with him? Anyone with a grain of sense could have foretold that she would end up in tears.

She'd not used good sense in this matter. She'd let a kiss blind her to the facts. Barnaby Traherne had kissed her, and she'd made herself believe it was a meaningful act. But evidently it had meant nothing to him, for he was now betrothed to the insipid Miss Ponsonby. Of course, if Miss Ponsonby's kisses had the power to drive the memory of that other, extraordinary kiss from his mind, perhaps "little Livy" was not as insipid as she seemed!

Miranda tried to stop weeping by turning her mind to other matters, like her future. But how bleak her future suddenly appeared to be. Her prospects now seemed to have turned as cold and unexciting as that fuzzy moon. Thinking about Barnaby had given her days a little spice, the stimulus that comes from speculation. Each day a sense of expectation—the possibility of surprise—hovered in the air. With Barnaby lurking about to watch her handling of Jamie, to criticize her, to assault her in the corridor, there had been a zest to her days. Now that zest was gone, and nothing seemed likely to take its place. All she could look forward to now was his leaving. When he was gone, she could set her mind on forgetting him. The rest of the days of her life might not be eventful, but they might eventually be free of pain. That, at least, was something to look forward to.

And there was always memory. She could, in future, content herself with reviewing her few happy memories, as she used to do when her husband's behavior was at its worst. She used to finger her little cameo and remember that happiest month in her life when they were traveling on honeymoon in Italy. A pathetic kind of consolation, admittedly, but better than nothing.

Instinctively she uncrossed her arms, her fingers feeling for the cameo that had always hung round her neck on a silver chain. Nothing was there. She'd forgotten—the highwaymen had taken it. Even that innocuous solace was denied her.

A fresh flood of tears was about to flow when a knock at the door stopped them. Miranda brushed her cheeks free of wetness. "Come in," she said hoarsely.

"Miranda?" The door opened. Delia, her face eerily lit by the candle she carried, peered into the darkness. "Are you here?"

Miranda unfolded herself from the seat. "Yes, here I am."

Delia stepped over the threshold. "What are you doing sitting in the dark?" She went to the bookcase, took down another candle from the top shelf and lit it with her own.

Miranda blinked in the sudden light. "I was only . . . looking out at the moon. Did you wish to see me?"

"Yes. Miranda, my dear, why didn't you come down when we sent for you?"

"I'm sorry. I thought it was a family affair."

"Yes, so the boys explained." Delia set the two candles on the low schoolroom table and sat down at it. "But you must have understood that we wanted to include you."

Miranda did not answer. She remained standing in the shadows, trying to compose herself.

"I am not scolding," Delia assured her, looking over at the shadowy figure with a knit brow. "Was there any reason why you decided to stay up here alone?"

"I only . . . I thought . . . that is, if I may be honest, Delia, Mr. Barnaby Traherne has no liking for me. My presence at his celebration would not have added to his pleasure."

Delia did not deny the truth of that. "Do you know *why* Barnaby has no liking for you?" she asked in her forthright style.

"No, not really. But one doesn't have to have reasons for taking someone in dislike. Sometimes it's purely instinctive. I don't much like him, either."

"Don't you?" She cocked her head, trying to get a better look at Miranda's face, but the light of two candles was not enough to penetrate the shadows. "Do sit down, Miranda. You seem like a ghost standing there before the window, with the moonlight outlining you with eerie light."

Miranda laughed mirthlessly and came forward. "Shouldn't you be downstairs?" she asked as she sat down on one of the low chairs.

"I won't stay long enough to be missed." She looked across the table at the younger woman, noting the red-rimmed eyes. She believed she knew why Miranda had been crying. "You're wrong about Barnaby, you know," she said bluntly.

"Wrong? In what way?"

"In what you just said—that his dislike of you is instinctive. That dislike has nothing to do with instinct. I've learned he has quite specific reasons for his dislike."

Miranda immediately stiffened. "If you are referring to his disagreements with me about handling Jamie," she said defensively, "I believe those differences have been settled. Besides, he disliked me long before that."

"Yes, he did. Since his nineteenth year, I'm told."

"What?" Miranda's eyebrows rose in astonishment. "What on earth are you talking about? You know we met on the stagecoach, less than a fortnight ago."

"No. That's not so. I'm told you met at the Lydell ball eleven years ago."

"The Lydell ball? Eleven *years*—?" She gaped at Delia openmouthed, the words not making sense. She did have a vague memory of a ball at the Lydells' during the season before her betrothal. And, yes, she did remember that Rodney was there, and Fred Covington and Lord Yarmouth and a few other of her swains. But she had no recollection of Barnaby, not the slightest. "I would have remembered," she muttered, blinking into the candle flame in an effort to bring it all back. "A man like Barnaby, tall and handsome and distinguished . . . I would have remembered . . ."

"He was scarcely distinguished," Delia said gently. "Not at nineteen."

"No, I suppose not . . . but even so . . ."

"It was his first ball, Honoria tells me. He was gawky, and very shy."

Hearing those words, something flashed into Miranda's memory: she recalled standing on a sort of platform . . . a circle of admirers milling about . . . Rodney whispering the most charming of pleasantries into her ear . . . then, an interruption . . . the Earl of Shallcross—Yes! Lawrence Traherne, the very Earl now staying in this house!—thrusting a gawky, clumsy fool at her; a stuttering, ill-clad *fool* with a bad haircut . . . Oh, God! Was that *Barnaby*? Whom she teased and tormented and tossed aside, just to impress Rodney with her power over men!

"No," she groaned at this vision of her younger self, "*no!*" And she dropped her head in her arms on the table in shame.

"So you *do* remember the incident," Delia said.

"Yes, I remember. Now I remember. Oh, Delia, I could *die!*"

"That would be a rather severe punishment for the crime, wouldn't it?"

"No!" came the muffled cry from the buried head.

"Come now, Miranda," Delia scoffed, "it was a set-down, not a murder."

Miranda lifted her head. "It was the sorriest, most flagrant example of arrogant vanity imaginable! If you had been there, you'd have hated me."

"Nonsense. And what difference does it make that I might have disliked you then? You are obviously not the same person. I like you *now*. Give yourself credit for having improved your character."

"No, I can't take credit. The trials of life improved my character, not I."

Delia pushed back her chair and rose. "If you're determined to flagellate yourself over your long-past depravity, Miranda Velacott, I'm not going to stay here and watch you do it." She picked up one of the candles and started toward the door. "Good night, my dear."

"But Delia, wait! If it was not to berate me for that depravity, why did you tell me this now?"

Delia, her hand on the doorknob, turned a level gaze on the woman slumped over the table. "Because I wanted you to see on how slight a basis Barnaby built his dislike."

"Slight?" Miranda sat erect in stern objection to Delia's belittlement of her crime. "It's not slight at all! What I did was unforgiveable."

"Heavens, woman, you sound as nonsensical as Honoria. You struck him with words, not sticks and stones."

Miranda shook her head. "Contempt can sometimes be more brutal than physical injuries, isn't that so?"

"Sometimes, perhaps, but in this case, contempt may be too strong a word. It seems to me—and I made this point to Honoria as strongly as I could—that the entire incident has been overblown. Much too overblown. And for far too long."

"Whether overblown or not, Delia, I suppose it's foolish to worry about it at this late date," Miranda sighed. She stood up, turned to the window and gazed out at the bleak, eerily lit landscape. "It cannot matter to Barnaby now. Not any more."

"If you think that," Delia remarked as she threw open the door and strode out of the room, "you're not nearly as astute a young woman as I think you are."

Miranda wheeled about. "Delia? What do you mean by that?" She ran across the room to the doorway. "Are you suggesting that he—? That I—? *Delia!*"

But the corridor was deserted. Delia was gone.

· Twenty-two ·

IT WAS MUCH later than his usual bedtime when the nursemaid undressed Jamie and tucked him in. But the boy was not sleepy. He lay awake waiting for someone to come in and give him a good-night embrace. Usually his mother did it, and sometimes Mrs. Velacott, but when he was really lucky, it was both. His mother's embrace was the best, of course, but Mrs. Velacott rated a close second. He could tell that the new governess really liked him, and that gave him a warm feeling inside. Besides, she had soft hands, softer even than Mama's, and the smoothest cheeks, and she always smelled like cinnamon candy. He wished that she or Mama would come. It was hard to fall asleep without a hug.

Tonight, however, a long time passed and no one came. He got up from his bed, wrapped his comforter around him to protect him from the cold and, after feeling his way to the door (for he was not permitted to light a candle on his own), went out the door and down the corridor to the schoolroom.

The room was very dimly lit by a guttering candle on the table, but he could see someone sitting on the window seat. "Mithuth Velacott?" he asked.

She turned round in surprise, wiping her cheek with the back of her hand. "J-Jamie? Why are you still awake?"

He waddled over to her, his comforter dragging behind him. "You didn't come to thay good night."

"Oh, that's right. I'm sorry. Come, give me your hand and I'll tuck you in properly."

He came closer and peered at her. "Were you crying, ma'am?"

"No, of course n—" She paused and thought better of her answer. "Well, yes, I was."

"Why?"

"Because I . . . I . . ." She looked down at his worried little face. His child-like affection touched her heart. "No good reason, really," she said, kneeling down and wrapping his comforter closely round his neck. "I was missing my . . . my cameo, that's all."

"What'th a cameo?"

"It's only a little trifle I used to wear round my neck."

The boy thought the answer strange. Why would one cry over a trifle? Unless . . . "Wath it like a good luck charm?" he asked.

"Yes, exactly like a good luck charm," she said, smiling at him proudly. "You are very understanding." She rose and took his hand.

"Did you mithplathe it? I can thtay and help you find it. I'm not a bit thleepy."

"I didn't misplace it, though I thank you for your offer to help."

"Then what happened to it?" he persisted as she led him from the room.

They went hand in hand down the corridor. "The highwaymen—the ones your uncle Barney told you about—they took it," she explained. "I'm afraid it's gone for good."

"That'th a shame," he said. "Unlucky."

The boy's concern for his governess's luck lasted all night and into the next day. It was a windy, overcast day, not conducive to outdoor games, so he and his brothers were forced to play indoors during what Mrs. Velacott called their morning "recess," an hour of unsupervised play. That was when Jamie told them about Mrs. Velacott's loss.

"Wouldn't it be thplendid if we could find the highwaymen?" he asked, his eyes shining.

"Splendid," Maury said in sarcastic agreement. "Except how would we find them?"

"It might not be too hard," George said thoughtfully. "The coach was attacked a few miles south of Wymondham. The thieves must have a hideaway somewhere nearby."

"Yeth!" the little fellow said excitedly. "We'd find 'em thouth of Wymondham. And then we could fight 'em an' thlit their throatth and get her lucky piethe back for her!"

"Yes, slit their throats! Good!" George smiled with pleasure, imagining the bloody scene. "We could fight them with our swords and demand their loot before hacking them to bits."

"Righto!" laughed Maury, pulling out his toy sword and flourishing it in the air before lunging at his older brother. "Take that, you varlet! Mrs. Velacott's cameo or your life!"

The boys skirmished about, brandishing their swords and making drama of the imagined confrontation. Jamie watched, wide-eyed. "Let'th do it!" he cried when both boys fell down on the floor, exhausted.

"Do what?" George asked.

"Fight the highwaymen with our thwordth and get the good luck piethe back."

"We just did," Maury said.

"No! For *real*!"

George got up and patted his little brother's head. "We will, Jamie, someday. When we're older," he said kindly.

"When? Thoon?"

George shrugged. "Next month."

Maury laughed, but Jamie took him seriously. "Nextht month? Do you promith? All three of uth?"

"No, you're too little," Maury teased. "George and I will fight the highwaymen, and when we bring back the cameo, you can give it to Mrs. Velacott and take all the credit."

Jamie glared at him. "It'th alwayth you and George. You never let me do anything mythelf."

"That's enough, Jamie. Don't start whining," George said, dismissing the subject. "Come on, Maury, let's play spillikins."

But Jamie wouldn't let it go. "I don't care what you do! Getting the good luck back wath *my* idea! I'll do it mythelf, thee if I don't!" And he stomped out of the room.

An hour later, when their lessons were resumed, Miranda asked where the child had gone. "Sulking in his room, probably," George said.

But he was not in his room. Miranda, after searching through every room on the third floor, grew alarmed. She sent the two older boys to seek out all the child's favorite haunts in the house, but they couldn't find him. "I'd wager the little bufflehead has gone looking for the highwaymen," Maury told the governess in disgust.

"The highwaymen? What do you mean?"

"He wants to be a hero and bring you back your missing cameo," George explained.

Miranda paled. "Do you mean to suggest he might have gone *outside*?"

George was not at all perturbed. "There's no need to fall into a taking, ma'am," he said reassuringly. "Jamie knows the way to the road. And the direction to Wymondham. When his feet get cold, he'll turn round and come home; you have my word."

But Miranda could not be so complacent. She set the two boys to their schoolwork, ran to her room for her cloak and bonnet and flew down the back stairs and out the kitchen door, making for the road. She was beside herself with alarm. Jamie had as much as a two-hour start. Even if she ran the entire three miles to Wymondham, she might not catch up with him. And if the child had got that far, there was no way of knowing where he might go from there.

She felt almost hysterical as she slogged through the snow toward the road, tying the ribbons of her bonnet as she stumbled along. The brim of her bonnet hid the sight of a man who was approaching, and she blundered into him. "Oh!" she gasped, startled.

"Damnation, woman, watch where you go!" came Barnaby's irritated voice.

She glanced up at him. "I beg your pardon," she said hastily, trying to pass him without further conversation.

He noticed her perturbation. "Wait a moment, ma'am," he ordered, holding her by the arms, his eyes searching her face. "What's amiss?"

"I must go!" She tried to shake off his hold. "Jamie's run off."

"Jamie?" He frowned down at her. "Don't be foolish. He wouldn't do such a thing."

"Please, let me go! I haven't time to explain. He's had a two-hour start. He may be more than halfway to Wymondham by this time."

"If this is true, ma'am, then there's a better way to catch up with him than shank's mare. Come with me to the stable. We'll take the sleigh."

A little while later, they were gliding swiftly along the road behind a pair of frisky horses, Barnaby holding the reins and Miranda peering anxiously at the passing landscape for a sign of Jamie's red knit cap and blue muffler. "It's all my fault," she moaned after a quarter-hour had passed with no sign of the child. "I told him about my cameo. He thinks it's my lucky piece. He's gone to find the highwaymen and get it back for me."

Barnaby grinned. "Good for him. Plucky little chap."

"How can you smile?" Miranda demanded. "What if we don't find him?"

"We'll find him. He's bound to follow the road."

"We can't be certain of that."

"No, but it's likely. He'd find the road easier going than the fields."

"But if he's already made it to Wymondham—"

"He hasn't. His legs are too short to make such good time. I doubt if he's much further along than— Wait! Look there! What's that ahead?"

She saw only a blur at first, but there was something red in it. As they drew closer, they could make him out. He was trudging along with weary determination, his muffler blowing out behind him and a toy sword hanging from a belt strapped about his waist.

"Oh, thank God!" Miranda whispered hoarsely.

Barnaby slowed the horses, and she leaped from the sleigh and ran to the child. "*Jamie*," she cried, kneeling beside him and embracing him, "you naughty imp! How *could* you frighten me so?"

"Mithuth Velacott!" His face lit up with joyful relief. "Have you come to take me home?"

"Yes, of course we've come to take you home. Your uncle Barney's brought the sleigh."

"I'm tho glad. My feet are *frothen*."

"I'm sure they are. Come along, then. We have a lap robe in the sleigh."

He took her hand. "I haven't yet got your good luck piethe back," he said, shamefaced.

"Don't trouble yourself about it," she said as she helped him up to the seat. "Finding you is all the good luck I need for one day."

They bundled him up in the lap robe. "I hope, Jamie, that you won't play such a trick as this again," his uncle lectured sternly. "You're not yet old enough to travel about on these roads alone."

"But I had to find the highwaymen, you thee," the child explained.

"No, you had not! Finding the highwaymen is my job."

"Yourth? Why?"

"Because it was I who was attacked by them. I want to fight my own battles, just as you want to fight yours."

The child looked up at his uncle adoringly. "*Are* you going to fight the highwaymen, then?"

"Yes, I am."

"And you'll bring Mithuth Velacott'th good luck piethe back to her?"

"Yes, I will."

"Will you mind, Mithuth Velacott, if Unca Barney geth your cameo inthtead of me?"

Barnaby looked over at her. "Will you mind, ma'am?"

Miranda, feeling her color rise, dropped her eyes. "I won't mind," she said to the boy.

Jamie snuggled up against his uncle contentedly. "Good, then, Unca Barney," he said, "I'll leave it to you." Snug and warm, and with his heavy responsibility lifted from his shoulders, he promptly fell asleep.

Barnaby held the horses to a relaxed pace. Now that the boy was found, there was no reason to hurry. Miranda threw a sidelong glance at him. "I hope, Mr. Traherne, that you don't really believe I was serious about the cameo. I would not wish you to do battle with the highwaymen for any reason at all, much less for the sake of such a trifle."

"My battle with the highwaymen will not be over a trifle," he assured her.

"That isn't the response I wished for," she said, frowning.

"You wished I'd say there would not be a battle at all, is that it?"

"Yes. The matter of the highwaymen is best forgotten."

"That, ma'am, is too womanish a point of view. For a man, it is not 'best' to forget when one has been robbed and assaulted."

"You must have vengeance, is that it?"

"I'd prefer to think of it as righting a wrong."

She looked over at him, taking in the manly grace of his posture, the relaxed ease of his hands on the reins, the breadth of his shoulders under the capes of his greatcoat, the strength of his profile under his high beaver hat. "You've changed a great deal since the Lydell ball," she said on a sudden impulse.

His head came round abruptly, his eyes ablaze with surprise and anger. She met his gaze without wavering. After a moment, he turned back to the horses. "I've not changed as much as you think," he said carefully. "I like to believe that, even at nineteen, I was not lacking in courage. I would have wanted to do battle with the highwaymen even then."

"Yes, I suppose you would." She lowered her eyes to the hands folded in her lap. "But in those days, I wouldn't have recognized courage," she admitted. "Not courage, nor sensitivity, nor true manliness, nor any worthwhile quality. I was a very poor judge of character back then—a silly chit, unable to see clearly."

He threw her a quick, questioning glance, wondering if he'd fully understood what she'd just said. Was she actually *apologizing* to him for what happened at the ball? And how was it that she so suddenly remembered an incident that she'd not had an inkling of a few days before? "What do you mean," he asked, temporizing to give himself time to think, "when you say you were unable to see clearly?"

"My judgment was impaired by an unwarranted and shameful vanity."

He heard the tremor in her voice. It touched him to the core. She *was* apologizing, and in a generous, self-deprecating, heartfelt way. "I don't know that your vanity was unwarranted," he said softly. "You were the loveliest, most breathtaking woman my nineteen-year-old eyes had ever seen."

Her eyes flew to his, wide with surprise. His quiet compliment, belated though it was, took her breath away. But a moment later, her awareness of the painful present reasserted itself. She smiled a wry, regretful smile. "Then *I'm* the one who's greatly changed, it seems."

He didn't answer. He didn't trust his voice. Her apology had caught him completely off guard. Her words had stirred a depth of feeling in him he didn't know he was capable of. He had to clench his fingers tightly on the reins so that she wouldn't see they were trembling.

He didn't understand her or himself. What had stirred her memory? And what was she trying to say in that oddly-worded apology? If she was truly sincere, how could he maintain the anger and resentment he'd built up against her? That resentment was the constant that had guided all his decisions since he first saw her on the coach. Even his betrothal had been instigated by his determination to keep

Miranda Pardew Velacott at a distance. A revised view of her could seriously jeopardize his life! He had to *think* before he could let himself warm toward her. And there was no time now for thinking, for the horses were already turning into the drive.

The stable man came running out as they drove up to the front door. Barnaby threw him the reins. "Keep the horses walking," he instructed as he lifted the sleeping child in his arms. "I shall be taking them out again in half an hour."

"*Barnaby!* You're not going to look for the highwaymen, are you?" Miranda asked in alarm.

She'd called him Barnaby. His heart leaped up to his throat at the sound. But the emotion frightened him. *Good God*, his mind said to him in disgust, *one brief expression of regret from her lips, and you're putty in her hands!* He had to take himself firmly in control, or he'd find himself kissing her again with the same insane passion he'd felt earlier. That kiss had been disturbing enough before, but this time it would be unthinkable. He was now betrothed to another. Such an incident could not be permitted to happen again. Not now. Not ever.

He turned to look at her, making his whole face rigid with disapproval. "Where I'm going, *Mrs. Velacott,* is none of your affair," he said with chilling finality. He shifted the boy to his shoulder and climbed down. Then he walked round to her side and, with formal propriety, offered his hand to help her down.

She could only gape at him, aghast. He'd done it *again*! Without rhyme or reason, he'd switched his mood from warmth to ice. One moment he was reminiscing about how lovely she'd once been, and the next he was calling her "Mrs. Velacott" in that disparaging way, a clear set-down to retaliate for her calling him by his given name! And telling her without roundaboutation to mind her own business! If she lived a thousand years, she'd never learn to understand him.

Angrily thrusting his hand aside, she climbed down from the sleigh without his help. "I'll take the boy," she said, making her voice as cold as his. "You're evidently in a hurry."

She took the boy in her arms, turned on her heel and stalked into the house without a backward look. *The man really is a churl!* she said to herself furiously. She'd tried to apologize. She'd tried her very best. If he chose to spurn her attempt at reconciliation, too bad for him. As far as she was concerned, he was not worth another thought. Or another tear.

· Twenty-three ·

THAT AFTERNOON WAS as good a time as any, Barnaby decided, to take care of the unfinished business of the highwaymen. His state of mind would benefit more from engaging in the perilous but straightforward adventure of tracking down the thieves than from remaining safely in an easy chair in the library brooding over this latest emotional upheaval. To solve the riddle of his confused feelings about Miranda would require maturity, mental clarity and serenity. To solve the problem of the highwaymen would require nothing more than a pistol.

Of course, he didn't have a pistol. But Terence surely had some weapons in this house. And Lawrence often brought a gun with him when he traveled. Barnaby, after a moment's thought, decided to ask Lawrence first. If he asked Terence, he'd lose precious time convincing the fellow not to come along. This was one adventure Barnaby was determined to engage in alone.

He found the Earl napping in his room. He shook the poor man heartlessly. "Wake up, Lawrence. Do you hear me? I need a pistol. Did you bring one?"

The Earl blinked. "Pistol?" he asked sleepily. "Yes, but . . . what for?"

"Where have you hidden it?" Barnaby persisted.

"In the second drawer of the dressing table. But why—?"

Barnaby strode across the room and found it. "Thank you, Lawrence. I shall restore it to you shortly."

"Wait just a moment!" the Earl ordered, now fully awake. "You can't have it till you tell me what it's for."

"I'll tell you all about it when I return, I promise."

Lawrence sat up and peered at his brother nervously. "It's those deuced highwaymen, isn't it? You're determined to wreak your revenge. Barnaby, I won't have it."

"It's not revenge," Barnaby assured him, his manner affably casual. "It's a purely materialistic act. I'm after the watch fob. I must have it back." He threw his brother a wide grin. "I'm sentimentally attached to it, since it was a gift from a beloved relative."

"Rubbish. I'll order another from my jeweler as soon as I return to Shallcross."

"I don't want another. It won't be the same." With a cheery wave, he started to the door.

Before reaching it, however, it flew open, and Honoria fluttered in, the wide skirt and sleeves of her dressing gown wafting on the air in her wake. "Lawrence, dearest, have you taken my wide-toothed comb? I can't seem to— Oh, *Barnaby! Here* you are!"

Barnaby surreptitiously hid the pistol behind him, out of Honoria's view. "Yes, here I am."

"Yes," Lawrence muttered irritably, "here he is, indeed. Perhaps you can talk sense to him."

"I always talk sense to him," Honoria retorted, completely missing her husband's point. "Barnaby, you are a rudesby. Why did you skip luncheon without a word to anyone? We all missed you. Livy didn't know what to do with herself. Where have you been hiding?"

"Nowhere in particular. I was out riding. But I can't stay here chatting. I must be off, so if you'll excuse me . . ."

"But Barnaby, you mustn't take off again," his sister-in-law cried in loud objection. "You *can't*."

"That's just what I've been telling him," the Earl growled.

Barnaby edged toward the door. "Why can't I?"

"You can't offer for a girl and then leave her constantly to her own devices," Honoria scolded. "It's rude and unkind."

Barnaby shrugged. "Can't be helped, my dear." He kissed her cheek and whisked himself out the door. But after taking a step down the corridor and hiding the pistol in an inner pocket of his coat, he turned back. "By the way, Honoria," he said from the doorway, "there's something I must ask you. Why on earth did you remind Mrs. Velacott about the Lydell ball?"

Honoria's eyebrows rose. "I *never* did! What makes you think—?"

"She suddenly indicated that she remembers what happened between us that evening. She actually apologized to me for it."

"*Did* she, indeed!" Honoria muttered tartly, not at all impressed. "Good of her, I must say."

"It *was* rather good of her, actually. She seemed truly to be ashamed of her younger self. I was quite . . . touched."

"Were you really?" Honoria peered at him through narrowed eyes. She had not forgotten Delia's comments about the governess. Could Delia be right? Was Miranda Pardew, of all women in the world, the proper partner for her beloved Barnaby? Was it possible that, underneath all the resentment, he actually harbored a *tendre* for the woman who'd spurned him?

"It seems strange, doesn't it," Barnaby was saying, "that, out of the blue, a woman would suddenly remember an eleven-year-old incident that could not have meant anything to her at the time?"

Honoria gave a troubled sigh. "If the answer to that question is important to you, my love, speak to Delia about it."

"Delia? Why Delia?"

"Well, you see, she . . . I . . . she has more . . . ah . . . insight into these matters than I." Honoria dropped her eyes from her brother-in-law's face and fingered the sleeves of her dressing gown uneasily, expecting him to demand to know why she'd discussed this matter with Delia at all. "You said you were in a hurry, didn't you, Barnaby? So why don't you save your questions for a more propitious time?"

Barnaby started to protest but changed his mind. He merely nodded and accepted the opportunity to take himself off.

After he'd gone, Honoria sank down on the side of her husband's bed, her eyes fixed on the door Barnaby had just closed behind him. "Do you think I made a mistake, Lawrence, pushing little Livy on him?"

"You didn't push," Lawrence protested. "You merely brought the girl here. Barnaby's the one who made the offer. But you do have a way of confusing me, my dear. I thought you were overjoyed over the boy's betrothal. Why are you suddenly apprehensive about it?"

Honoria eyed him for a moment, reluctant to admit her doubts about the girl she'd thrust under Barnaby's nose. "Something Delia said," she said at last. "She thinks Livy Ponsonby's a dead bore."

"Hmmm." The Earl scratched his nose and lowered his head but said nothing more.

"Lawrence!" Honoria knew him well enough to recognize the full meaning of the gesture. "*You* think so, *too*! Why didn't you *say* something to me?"

"Because, my dear, matchmaking is not in my line. You are the expert in affairs of the heart. When have I ever questioned your judgment in these matters?"

"Perhaps you *should* have questioned it. How shall you feel if I've made a dreadful mistake this time?"

"Naturally, I should be most distressed to see Barnaby unhappy. But, Honoria, it's time we both learned a lesson from all this. Barnaby has asked, time and again, that we permit him to manage his own life. I think, if we truly let him be, he will do very well for himself."

"Even if he's entangled in a mistaken betrothal?"

"Especially in that regard. For several years now, it's been obvious to me that Barnaby is better able to take care of himself than any of the rest of us. So leave the fellow free to make his own mistakes—and to correct them, too. That, mark my words, is the very best thing you can do for him."

· Twenty-four ·

THE SLEIGH SLID to a quiet stop in the small courtyard of the Deacon's Gate Inn, and Barnaby hopped down from the seat. The inn looked less inviting in the late-afternoon shadows than it had on the night, almost a fortnight ago, when its lights had glimmered out at him through the heavy snow. That night its appearance had signified much-needed warmth and comfort. Now it meant only a challenge.

Barnaby threw open the door, strode into the taproom with the sureness of familiarity, and took a seat at one of the three tables. Only one table was occupied, and that by a lone drinker, an elderly man bent over his tankard. He would not be in the way, Barnaby decided.

Barnaby did not have long to wait before Mrs. Hanlon approached. "Welcome, sir," she greeted in her cheery brogue, "an' what can I—?"

Barnaby got to his feet and smiled down at her.

The woman's face brightened in pleased surprise. "Why, it's Mr. Traherne, as I live an' breathe! What're ye doin' back 'ere again?"

Barnaby was glad it was Mrs. Hanlon rather than her husband. She would be easier to deal with. "I came to have a word with you, Mrs. Hanlon," he said quietly. "Will you kindly sit down with me?"

Mrs. Hanlon's face clouded, as if she suspected what was

to come, but she slid into a chair opposite him. "Are ye certain it's me ye want an' not me 'usband?"

"Yes, quite certain. Let's get right down to it, shall we? I remember, when we were last here, Mrs. Hanlon, hearing your husband say that the footpads always paid their shot in cash."

The woman mouth tightened. "Did 'e?"

"He did. One may assume from those words that the footpads have called at this taproom from time to time."

"I wouldn' assume that a-tall," she equivocated.

"I would. In fact, I'd wager a small fortune on it." He took out a handful of gold guineas and stacked them on the table before him. "I'd wager this small fortune that you know their hideaway."

Mrs. Hanlon eyed the gold pieces longingly. "Knowin' is one thing, an' tellin's another."

"Knowing without telling won't earn you a farthing, I'm afraid."

She shook her head. "You know what 'appens to anyone what blabs on 'em. Tellin's too dangerous, even fer a lovely pile o' gold like that."

"But your name will never pass my lips. My word on it. And they can't connect me with this place, for they have no idea I ever stayed here. They would guess I kept going north."

"That's true." She remained silent for a moment, considering the problem, her eyes fixed on the guineas. "There's a little tavern 'bout two miles west, on Deacon's Road, wi' three or four rooms upstairs. The rooms ain't available, 'cause they're permanently spoke fer, if ye take my meanin' "

"You mean they live there."

She shrugged. "It's a filthy 'ole, called the Blue Fox. Not near a main road, see, so the patrons 're on'y locals."

"A safe hideway, then."

She dropped her eyes. "So far."

He slid the pile of coins toward her, but kept his hand over them. "It's a *pair* we're speaking of, isn't it? One tall and broad, the other small in both height and breadth, named Japhet?"

She looked up at him in fright. "Y' ain't goin' t' ask me fer names, now! It wasn't part o' the bargain."

"No, no. But I must be certain I'm chasing the right pair. If my description matches what you know, simply nod."

She nodded.

He released the coins and rose. "Thank you, Mrs. Hanlon. I stand in your debt."

She was counting out the coins with greedy fingers. "No, I wouldn' say that, sir. This is 'andsome payment, I'd say. Very 'andsome indeed."

"Then, ma'am, perhaps you'll agree to do one more thing for me. If two brawny fellows come asking questions about my whereabouts—both as tall as I but a good bit broader—I'd be obliged if you'd deny ever having seen me."

She cocked her head at him suspiciously. "An' who might these brawny fellows be? Bow Street Runners?"

"No, not runners, but just as persistently annoying. They're my deuced brothers."

· Twenty-five ·

AT THE MANOR house it was not yet time to dress for dinner. Harry and his betrothed sat together in the small sitting room in a comfortable—and for a couple on the brink of matrimony, perfectly respectable—embrace, the man's arm lightly holding her round the waist and the lady's head resting on his broad shoulder. They were passing the time by discussing plans for their wedding, set for the opening of the London Season in spring. Lady Isabel's parents, who were very well to pass, were planning an elaborate affair for their only child, with four hundred invited guests. Harry, not at all shy, had no objection to the plans, but he loved to tease his bride-to-be by pretending to be appalled by the ostentation of large weddings and by constantly urging her to elope. "We could do it tonight," he was whispering into her ear. "I could wait under your window with the sleigh, you could slide down a rope-ladder made of Delia's best sheets—"

"Oh, *Harry*," his betrothed objected, laughing and pretending to push him away in punishment, "what a ridiculous notion! If you think I would consider dashing off to Gretna, catching my death in the cold and snow, and ruining my reputation in the bargain, you are much mistaken."

"Reputation!" Harry sneered. "How can your reputation compare to the sheer romance of running—?"

But before he could finish, the door burst open. "Harry," cried Terence from the doorway, "I think he's gone and done it!"

Harry dropped his hold on his betrothed and moved a discreet distance away. "Did no one teach you to knock, you blockhead?" was his greeting. "Isabel and I were planning an elopement."

"Sorry, Isabel," Terence said, "but this can't wait. I tell you, Harry, Barnaby's *done* it!"

"Done what? *Eloped*?"

"Harry, really!" Lady Isabel scolded. "You should know better. Livy Ponsonby would never—"

Terence smacked the heel of his hand against his forehead in impatience. "Will you *listen*? He's gone after the highwaymen!"

That made Harry snap to attention. He jumped up from the sofa in alarm. "Barnaby? All by himself?"

"Yes, just as he said he would."

"Damn the boy! How could he—?"

"Let's not stand here and discuss it, you slowtop. Let's go after him."

"Right!" Harry turned to his openmouthed betrothed. "You will excuse me, won't you, my love? I'll be back before morning, I promise."

"But Harry—!"

Before she could begin to enumerate her objections to this hasty action, the butler appeared in the doorway. "Madam sent me to tell you you're wanted in the drawing room, Mr. Traherne," he said to Terence. "At once."

Terence shook his head. "Not now, Cummings. Tell her I've gone off to help Barnaby. She'll understand."

"I'm afraid not, sir. This is urgent."

"Urgent? What can possibly be more urgent—?"

"Visitors," the butler said succinctly. "Lady Ponsonby and a young man. They both appear to be extremely upset, and Miss Ponsonby is having a fit of hysterics."

This did indeed sound urgent. Harry and Terence exchanged looks. "I suppose we ought—" Harry muttered.

"Of course we ought," Lady Isabel said with the decisiveness her rearing had bred in her and which had won her everything she'd ever wanted, including Harry Traherne. "Lead the way, Cummings," she ordered, sweeping to the door. "Lead the way."

In the drawing room, they were met with an ominous silence, except for the hiccuping sobs issuing from the chest of little Livy, who was huddled in an easy chair, her head buried in one of its wings. Sitting opposite her, erect and stern-faced, but dabbing at her eyes with a wet handkerchief, was a deep-bosomed matron who was apparently Lady Ponsonby, the weeping girl's mother. Standing at the window, his back stiff and his arms crossed over his chest, was a handsome, redheaded fellow who appeared to be in his mid-twenties. And leaning on the mantel, looking over the scene with a frown on her face but a strange, almost amused, glint in her eyes, was Delia Traherne.

Delia greeted her husband with a look that said, *Thank goodness you're here. Now you can take over.* Aloud, however, she merely made the introductions. "Lady Ponsonby, Mr. Ned Keswick, I'd like you to meet Lady Isabel Folley, my husband Terence Traherne and his brother Harry. Terence, dear," she added in a voice that was sugary-sweet, "we seem to be embroiled in a rather huge misunderstanding. Mr. Keswick and her ladyship are at odds on a point that is of concern to all of us. But perhaps I should say no more until Barnaby joins us."

"I could not find him, ma'am," the butler said from the doorway, where he'd lingered in hopes of catching some hint of the nature of the crisis. "Mr. Barnaby Traherne has apparently taken the sleigh and ridden out."

"I see." Delia expelled a sigh of disappointment. "Well, thank you, Cummings, you may go."

As soon as the door closed, Terence stepped forward. "May I be told about this 'point of concern' on which the gentleman and her ladyship are at odds?"

Delia nodded. "Mr. Keswick claims that Livy is *betrothed* to him."

"Betrothed?" Terence peered at his wife, trying to judge if this were some sort of joke.

But to Lady Ponsonby, it was no joke. She stiffened. "I unequivocally deny that claim," she said in a voice both quivery and firm. "Mr. Keswick is mistaken. How can there be a betrothal which is neither agreed to nor acknowledged by the girl's parents?"

"The *girl* acknowledged it," the young man shouted from his place at the window. "She accepted me, and she's of age."

"Now, just a moment, here," Harry interjected. "A girl can break a pledge of that sort, if she wishes. So that ends that."

"She never broke her pledge. Never!" The young man strode over to Livy's chair. "For heaven's sake, *tell* them, Livy! Pull yourself together! I'm here now. I'll protect you from your mother and anyone else who tries to bully you."

Livy's only response was an increase in the volume of her sobs.

"You're doing the bullying, you cad!" cried Lady Ponsonby.

"So, my dear," Delia said to Terence, "you see how matters stand."

Terence nodded. "Your Ladyship, Mr. Keswick, will you excuse the members of my family for a moment? I think we need some private conversation to determine how to proceed."

The four—Delia, Isabel, Terence and Harry—huddled together in the corridor. "What a fix!" Harry exclaimed. "Can't the girl be made to speak and explain herself?"

"She's been weeping ever since her mother arrived," Delia said, "and when her redheaded swain made his appearance, she became utterly incoherent."

"Are you saying they did not arrive together?" Isabel asked.

"They came in separate equipages."

"That means the roads are open to the south," Terence remarked.

"Of what relevance is that?" his wife demanded impatiently.

"None at all." Terence rubbed his chin, trying to make sense of this muddle. He couldn't help wondering how much his beloved brother would be hurt by this latest revelation. "Poor Barnaby." He sighed.

"Do you call him poor Barnaby because he has a rival," Delia asked dryly, "or because he's chosen such a watering-pot for a bride?"

Terence gave a short laugh. "Yes, on both counts."

"What has the Earl to say about this contretemps?" Isabel inquired.

"I haven't told him." Delia looked up at her husband worriedly. "Honoria may take this very much to heart. Perhaps we should wait until Barnaby gets here before we bring them into it."

Harry and Terence glanced at each other again. "Barnaby may not get back very soon," Harry said, attempting to break the news to his sister-in-law gently.

Delia looked from one brother to the other. "What do you mean? *How* soon is not very soon?"

"Perhaps," Terence muttered, "not until morning."

"*Morning*! Where on earth has he gone?"

Isabel cast a disparaging look at both the brothers. "What these hulking cawkers are too cowardly to tell you, Delia, is that Barnaby has gone after the highwaymen, and that *they* intend to go after Barnaby."

"Good God!" Delia threw her hands up in disgust. "Men!"

Terence put his hands on her shoulders. "It won't be so bad, my love. Give everyone dinner and send them off to bed. We'll fetch Barnaby back, and by morning we'll be able to settle the whole matter."

"Hmmm," Delia said, thinking over the possibilities. "I suppose that's all I *can* do. But if these new arrivals are to join us for dinner, I shall have to tell Lawrence and Honoria what's occurred."

"Tell them, then," said Terence, relieved to be free to make his escape and leave this mix-up behind. "Come, Harry, let's be off."

"Just fetch the fellow," Delia ordered, "and let the high-waymen *be*! If I discover that you've become embroiled in a shooting match with those miscreants, I warn you, Terence Traherne, that when I next lay eyes on you, I'll shoot you myself!"

· Twenty-six ·

THE BLUE FOX tavern was tucked away in a grove of trees, so far off the road that Barnaby drove right past it. It was dark by the time he found it, but not so dark that he couldn't see how squalid it was. Its sign hung crookedly from only one hinge, its courtyard was littered with debris that even the snow could not cover, its windows were so filthy that Barnaby could not see through them to the inside, and one of them was boarded up with such careless workmanship that not one of the roughly hewn slats lined up with its neighbor. It was through one of the gaps between those slats that Barnaby was able to get a glimpse of the scene within.

He'd hidden the sleigh in the trees and tethered the horses well out of sight of anyone entering or leaving the tavern. Now, his eye to the gap in the window-boarding, he was trying to discover what—and whom—he might be facing. Inside he could see a small, smoky taproom furnished with one long table and benches along its length. Half a dozen ill-clad patrons sprawled upon them. They were being served by a buxom barmaid in a dirty apron and beribboned cap, who evidently was not averse to being fondled by one and all. Barnaby studied the men at the table carefully, but he could not identify any of them. One smallish fellow, whose back was to the window, looked like Japhet, but the tall highwayman could have been any one of the others.

Calculating that, even if he were wrong about the identity of the small man, the risk of error was not great, he decided to proceed on the assumption that the fellow was Japhet. He lowered his hat over his forehead so that the brim shadowed his face, opened the door of the tavern and stepped inside. He found himself in a small vestibule lit by two candles burning in wall sconces. He blew them both out. Then he positioned himself just behind the doorway to the taproom and waited for the barmaid to walk by.

He did not have to wait long. As she sauntered by the doorway, carrying a lightly-loaded tray, he reached out, seized her arm and pulled her into the vestibule, catching the tray with his free hand. While she gasped in angry surprise, he set the tray on the floor. " 'Oo the devil are ye?" the girl demanded, trying to make him out in the shadowy hallway.

He stepped behind her, and holding her arms against her sides with one arm, he covered her mouth with his other hand. "Hush, me darlin', hush," he whispered in her ear in a soft Irish brogue. "There's a yellowboy for ye if ye keep your voice down an' do me a tiny favor. Hush, now, an' I'll let ye go." Slowly he released his hold on her mouth and waved a gold coin before her eyes.

She tried to get a glimpse of him but could not turn in his hold. "Who are ye? An' what do ye want o' me?"

"I want ye to go inside and tell Japhet there's a friend of his out here has a surprise for him."

"Whyn't ye tell 'im yersel'? 'E's right inside."

Barnaby smiled to himself. The risk had paid off. "I said it's a surprise," he whispered into the girl's ear. "Isn't it worth a gold piece to ye to play the game my way?"

"I s'pose so," she said dubiously, but as soon as he loosed his hold, she made a lunge for the coin.

He held it up out of her reach. "Now, me darlin', ye do know what ye're to say, don't ye?"

She took a close look at him, but his appearance meant

nothing to her. "I'm to say a friend o' his is waitin' outside wi' a surprise fer 'im."

"Yes. Exactly so." He gave her the coin, which she immediately tested with her teeth. Then he turned her about and pushed her toward the taproom door. "Hurry, now," he said, "like the sweet lamb ye are."

As soon as she crossed the threshold, he whisked himself outside to watch her through the gap in the window-boarding. He saw her come up to Japhet and tell him something. Then she pointed to the vestibule. He looked in that direction, shrugged and shook his head. She showed him the coin, tossed it up in the air triumphantly, caught it, pocketed it and sauntered off. *Come on*, Barnaby urged him silently. *No man of sense would give a barmaid a gold coin for nothing. Someone outside must have something of value for you. Come and see what a lovely surprise awaits you!*

As if his mind had received the message, Japhet got slowly to his feet and started toward the vestibule. Barnaby moved to the doorway and flattened himself against the outside wall just to the right of it. In a moment, the door opened and Japhet stepped outside. "Molly, you lying slut," he shouted, "there's nobody—"

"Yes, there is," said Barnaby, grabbing the little man's neck in the crook of his elbow and holding the pistol to his head. "Now, if you don't want a bullet in your noggin, you'll do what I say without a word."

"But who—?"

Barnaby tightened his hold and let his prisoner hear him cock the pistol. "I said without a word. Nod if you understand me."

Japhet nodded tensely.

"Good. Now, fellow, lie facedown on the ground, arms spread."

Japhet followed the order. Barnaby uncocked the pistol, stuck it in the waistband of his breeches, knelt down with his knee in the footpad's back, and took out two small lengths of rope, with which he first tied Japhet's hands tightly behind him and then bound his ankles. Then he dragged him to his feet. "Now, Japhet, tell me your partner's name."

"I . . . I ain't got no partner."

"The one who robbed the stagecoach with you about a fortnight ago. It must have been your last job, for there hasn't been much traffic since. His name, please."

"I don't know whut yer talkin' about. Ye mus' be mistakin' me."

Barnaby pulled out the pistol and held it to the miscreant's head again. "You evidently have a desire to die young. One more chance. His name, please."

"T-Timothy Cosh."

"You call him Tim, do you?"

"Sometimes. Mostly we call 'im Coshy."

"Good. Now, I'm going to help you to the tavern door, which you so carelessly left open, and you're going to call him. Loudly. Coshy, you'll say, there's something out here that you must see."

Japhet, shaking with fright, did what he was bid. Nervousness affected his voice, so the shout had to be done twice. When it was done, Barnaby pushed him down on the ground again and swiftly tied his mouth with a large handkerchief. Then he placed himself against the wall again, his pistol at the ready.

When Timothy Cosh stepped over the threshold, he didn't see a thing at first. When he saw Japhet trussed up and lying shivering on the ground, he gasped. In three quick steps, he came to his partner and knelt down. "Damn it, Japhet, what—?"

Then he heard the door close behind him and swung around. He found himself facing the barrel of a very deadly-looking pistol. "Oh, hell!" he cursed. "Who—?"

"Don't you remember me?" Barnaby asked. "You once relieved me of my very favorite gold watch."

Timothy Cosh groaned. "I remember. You was the bloke wi' the 'andy fists."

"That's right. Raise your hands, if you please. I want to see what you have in your pockets."

"I don't 'ave me pistol on me."

This proved to be true. "Now, Coshy, let me tell you what I have in mind. I'm going to allow you to go back inside and upstairs to the place you inhabit. There you will collect everything you stole from the stage that day and bring it all down in a sack. Meanwhile, I'll be holding this pistol against your partner's temple. If you don't come back by the time I count to one hundred, poor Japhet's brains will be spilled out all over the snow."

Japhet made little mewling sounds in his throat, and he wriggled his body around in hysterical fear.

"Japhet seems to understand me," Barnaby said to the other man. "Do you?"

"Yes, but I don't 'ave the loot no more. It's all in the 'ands o' me fence."

"No, it isn't. No fence could have come up from London through all that snow. Not yet."

"I ain't got nothin' left, I swear!" Coshy insisted. But his confederate on the ground groaned and wriggled with more hysteria than before.

"Of course, I can shoot you both right now—you first, Coshy—and go upstairs and see for myself."

"A'right, a'right, I'll go," the tall fellow muttered.

"I knew you would. But before you do, let me point out that if it should occur to you to bring a pistol down with you, or to enlist the assistance of any of your confederates inside, I shall have the pistol cocked. Even if someone shoots me in the back, my finger will be able to squeeze the trigger before I fall. So if you wish to see your friend alive when you return, you will refrain from any activity other than that which I've requested. Remember, you have only to the count of one hundred."

A most pathetic, pleading whimper issued from Japhet's throat. His partner looked down at him. "Stop whinin', ye numbskull. I ain't never let ye down afore, an' I won't do it now." With that, he turned and trudged back into the tavern and shut the door.

Barnaby wasted no time. He grasped the fallen Japhet

under the arms and dragged him across the small clearing and into the line of trees. There he took a place behind a tree and waited.

He didn't bother to count, but it seemed longer than two minutes before the door opened again. The tall highwayman stood silhouetted in the doorway, carrying a sack. He looked around the deserted clearing, bemused.

"Come out," Barnaby shouted. "I'm still here."

Timothy Cosh stepped over the threshold and out into the clearing. "Ye don't 'ave much trust in me, do ye?" he asked.

"Should I? Come into the center of the clearing and toss the sack over this way."

"Where's Japhet?"

"He's here, safe and well. Toss it!"

Coshy heaved it over, his reluctance apparent in every move he made.

"Good. Now, spread out your arms and lie facedown on the ground."

"What fer?"

"Do it!"

The footpad got down. Barnaby waited for several minutes. There was no sound but a weak whimpering from Japhet. Finally, with his pistol poised, Barnaby stepped cautiously out from the protection of the trees and crossed the clearing to the prostrate Coshy. He was only a foot away from him when he thought he detected movement at the corner of the building on his right. Quickly he dropped down on his knees, one of them planted right on Coshy's back, and fired at the corner. A groaning cry (telling him he'd made his mark) coincided with a red flash of light, and a bullet whizzed by his ear. "Damn you, Cosh, you can't even be straight with your partner!" Barnaby swore, hastily trying to reload his pistol while keeping all his weight on the footpad's back.

"*Fire*, ye looby," Cosh shouted to someone at the tavern, "afore he reloads!"

There was another flash, this time from the other side, but the shot was wild. Cosh, no fool, knowing that Barnaby was still trying to reload, took the opportunity to try to wrench himself free. Heaving himself up, he dislodged Barnaby from his back and rolled over, reaching for a gun he'd hidden in his belt. But before he could pull it out, Barnaby, from his prone position, kicked his booted foot into the miscreant's chin and rolled over, swinging the butt of the pistol against Cosh's forehead. The man fell back unconscious.

Another shot rang out, this time from the left side of the tavern. Barnaby, shielding himself with the body of the unconscious highwayman, tried again to reload. But at that moment, he heard a burst of shots behind him, and two horsemen came galloping into the clearing and up to the tavern, shouting and shooting and making enough noise to wake the dead. They frightened every man who still lurked in or around the tavern. As Barnaby watched, three men ran from the place, one pulling a wounded man behind him, and disappeared into the trees. Meanwhile, the two horsemen pulled their horses to, wheeled about and rode toward him. By the time they reached him, Barnaby was on his feet and grinning. "You blasted gudgeons," he greeted his brothers, "can't you ever keep your noses out of my business?"

"We only came in at the finish," Harry chortled, leaping from the saddle and clapping Barnaby on the back.

"You seem to have done very well on your own," Terence grinned, sliding down and shaking his hand.

"Then why did you find it necessary to come after me?" Barnaby demanded.

"To bring you home. You're needed there, and at once," Terence informed him. "Emergency."

"Emergency!" Barnaby glared at him. "What rubbish!"

"It's not rubbish," Harry said. "There *is* an emergency."

"Truly?" Barnaby's face took on a look of alarm. "Not Jamie. Is he ill?"

"No, no. Nobody's ill. It's nothing like that," Terence assured him.

"Then what sort of emergency is it?"

"Delia will tell you all about it. So take yourself off, if you please."

"Dash it, Terence, you can see that I can't go right now. There are details to finish up. First, I must cart this fellow and his cohort, whom I have lying tied up in the woods, to the magistrate in Wymondham. Then, after I remove a certain watch and a cameo from that sack of loot over there, I intend to drop the rest into the nearest church poor box."

"Very commendable," Harry said.

"I suppose," Terence suggested tentatively, "that it would demean your triumph if we offered to assist in the finishing up."

"Assist?" Barnaby eyed him with suspicion.

"I could deal with the felons for you," Harry offered.

"And I can find the church poor box," Terence said. "In that way, Barnaby—with your permission, of course—we could free you to go through the sack for your treasures and take yourself home."

Barnaby shrugged his agreement, and the three cheerfully set about the "finishing up." After they'd trussed up the pair of highwaymen and sorted through the loot, they agreed that Harry would transport the footpads in the sleigh, with Terence and Barnaby making their separate ways home on horseback. Barnaby was the first to mount. He looked down from the horse at the two devoted brothers smiling proudly up at him. "Dash it all," he said with a happy sigh, "it's been a ripping adventure. The first one of this sort you permitted me to execute on my own."

"You don't have to thank us," Harry taunted. "We were glad to do it."

Barnaby shook his head. "Impossible. You're both impossible." He spurred his horse and started off. "But next time," he threw back over his shoulder, "if you don't want a pair of bloody noses, you'd better wait for me at home."

· Twenty-seven ·

MIRANDA HAD HAD a difficult time getting her charges to go to sleep. Rumors that their uncle had ridden off to capture the highwaymen were circulating throughout the house, and the boys had begged to be allowed to stay awake for his return. She'd had to tell them six fairy tales and invent a new, utterly fantastical adventure of Robin Hood before she was able to settle them down for the night.

She, too, would not be able to shut her eyes this night, she realized. The day had been too disturbing, what with Jamie's running away, and her set-to with his uncle. And now this rumor of his going off to find the highwaymen. She wondered how much she was to blame. If she only hadn't mentioned the blasted cameo!

Then, to add to her distress, she'd heard the rumor concerning the new arrivals, Lady Ponsonby and a redheaded young man. What if the rumors were true that the fellow was Livy's betrothed? What sort of scrape had Livy fallen into? And would Barnaby be badly hurt by it?

There was no point in trying to sleep. She would only lie in bed and toss about, worrying about Barnaby Traherne, although he, on his part, would not be wasting a thought on her. Nevertheless, going to bed would only lead to a wallow in painful and useless self-pity. So, instead of retiring, she decided to go down to the kitchen and make herself a pot of tea. There was nothing like tea to settle one's nerves.

She expected the kitchen to be deserted by this time, for the entire household had retired early, but she found Lady Shallcross's abigail there before her. The girl, in her nightclothes, and with her hair tied all over with rags, was setting a tea tray for her mistress, her pretty, bow-shaped mouth distorted by a sullen frown. "Everythin's at sixes and sevens today," the girl complained. "Her ladyship's sore distressed—not as I blame her with all that's happenin'—but she waked me from a sound sleep, askin' for some tea. So what am I to do, I ask you, with my hair in rags an' my eyes half shut? Can I bring her tea lookin' like this?"

"I'm still dressed," Miranda said. "Let me take it to her."

The girl's surly expression cleared at once. "Oh, *would* ye, Mrs. Velacott? I'd be ever so grateful."

Miranda, the tea tray in hand, tapped at Honoria's bedroom door. "Come in, come in," came a querulous voice from within.

She found Honoria lying on her bed with eyes shut, pressing a wet cloth to her forehead. "Lady Shallcross!" she exclaimed. "Are you ill?"

Honoria's eyes flew open. "Mrs. Velacott? Is that you?"

"Yes, ma'am. I've brought you your tea."

"But my Betty should not have asked you to take on her task," Honoria said, throwing off the cloth and sitting up. "It's a dreadful imposition."

"Not at all. I was happy to do it. Will you take your tea in bed, Your Ladyship, or shall I set it up for you here on this little table near the fire?"

Honoria tossed off her covers and climbed down from the bed. "On the table, please, if you will consent to join me. There are some teacups on the mantel."

Miranda shook her head. "It's not necessary to give me tea, Lady Shallcross. I—"

"Please," Honoria begged, hastily pulling another chair over to the table. "I have been wishing to speak to you all day."

Both women, eyeing each other uneasily, took seats across from each other at the little table. No words were exchanged while Miranda poured the tea, but then, with her teacup in hand, Honoria looked across at her visitor and frowned. "I never liked you, you know. Never. Even *before* the Lydell ball."

Miranda blinked at her, feeling as if she'd been slapped, but she recovered her composure in a moment. "No, of course you didn't," she said bluntly. "I don't blame you, ma'am, not a bit. I was a dreadful, vain, self-centered, foolish creature."

"Yes, you were," Honoria agreed. "My word for you was flibbertigibbet."

Miranda smiled. "I can think of many worse words for me." She stirred her tea thoughtfully, her smile fading. "I don't remember much about the Lydell ball," she admitted, "but I remember enough to realize that what I did was quite unforgivable. In your place, I would not like me, either."

Honoria was touched by the apology. "Very few things in this life are unforgivable," she said generously, her eyes searching the younger woman's face. Miranda Pardew was still lovely, she admitted to herself. And her frankness was refreshing. And she was certainly easier to talk to than the tongue-tied Livy Ponsonby. Honoria sighed deeply. "In regard to the Lydell ball," she confessed, "Delia says I've made much too much of an insignificant incident."

"Oh, no, I don't agree. If your brother-in-law was greatly affected by it, how can it be insignificant?"

"Yes, that's *just* how I feel! How generous of you to grant that!" She set her cup down on the table and stirred her tea reflectively. "But in a sense, Delia may be right. Perhaps the effect on Barnaby was, in the end, a beneficial one. Everyone seems to be convinced that he's not at all shy any more. And he's turned out to be a fine and successful man, a really *good* man, wouldn't you say so?"

Miranda dropped her eyes. "He certainly seems so to me."

"Does he? Truly?" Honoria peered closely at the young woman opposite her. She hoped that Miranda would say more. If there was anything she liked to hear, it was praise for her beloved Barnaby.

"Oh, yes," Miranda said, her lips curling into a reflective smile as the many qualities that had endeared Barnaby to her flew into her mind. "He's so clever and quick-witted and . . ." She stared into the fire with unseeing eyes, her heart swelling with fondness and a strange sort of pride. " . . . and very brave, of course. Fearless, almost . . ."

Honoria beamed. "And handsome, wouldn't you say?"

"Handsome, of course. And so devoted to his family, and . . ."

"And . . ." Honoria prodded.

"And spontaneous . . . impulsive, I mean . . ."

That surprised Honoria. "Impulsive? My Barnaby?"

"Yes. At least, he seems so to me."

"Does he? In what way?"

"Well, for instance, he once . . ." Blushing, she quickly picked up her cup and took a sip, berating herself for going too far. "No, never mind," she murmured in embarrassment.

"No, please, Miranda," Honoria urged, "don't be shy with me. He once what?"

Miranda glanced up at her and quickly looked down again. "He once . . . very impulsively— Oh, dear, I don't know why I'm telling you this!"

"Please go on, my dear. You can't imagine how much this talk means to me."

"He . . . kissed me."

"You don't say! When did he do that?"

"Just a few days ago. But you mustn't think . . . it was not . . . you mustn't make too much of it. As soon as he'd done it, he thought better of it. I only mention it to show his . . . his . . ."

"His spontaneity. I quite understand." Honoria smiled, wondering what Delia might make of that information. But it wouldn't do to press Miranda on the matter now. She was still red-cheeked over having mentioned the incident. "So you think him impulsive. And what else?"

"What else?" Miranda echoed, still too embarrassed to think clearly.

"Some young women call him forbidding. Would you describe him so?"

"Forbidding?" Miranda recovered herself with a start. Why had she been so loose of tongue with this woman who claimed to dislike her? And why had she revealed so much? But Honoria's warm and motherly manner made it difficult not to open up to her. "Yes, I'd say he's forbidding sometimes. He has a frown that can chill one's blood."

Honoria, remembering a similar conversation with Livy, was enchanted with Miranda's very different, very honest responses. "Then you wouldn't call him kind?"

"No, I wouldn't say he was kind," Miranda said with a rueful smile. "At least, he's not very kind to me."

"Oh? Isn't he?"

"No, not at all. But then, who can blame him? At first, at the inn, I believed him to be the worst of rudesbys. But now that I know the circumstances, I understand why he's often unkind."

"Oh, but that is really too bad." Honoria threw Miranda a darting glance. "Delia will be disappointed."

"*Delia*? Really? Why?"

"She believes that you and Barnaby would be well suited."

Miranda's eyes widened. "She *does*? How very astounding!"

"Isn't it? In truth, when she said it, I was convinced she was quite mad. But lately, I've not been so certain."

Miranda's breath caught in her throat, and she felt her fingers begin to tremble. "Lady Shallcross! You're not suggesting, are you, that you, *too*—?" She put a shaking hand to her forehead. "But you said you never liked me."

"Not until now." Honoria gazed with new eyes at the woman she'd so long disliked. All Miranda's comments

had been honest and modest and very satisfying. Honoria
had not enjoyed a conversation so much in years. *Good
God*, she thought, *Delia is right about the girl after all.*
Miranda Pardew might have been a flibbertigibbet, but
Miranda Velacott was someone else entirely. This one—
she had to admit—was a delight.

"But you . . . you *can't* like me!" Miranda was saying.

"Why not? If you can change, so can I. Besides, I don't
have to like you. Barnaby has to."

"What are you saying?" Miranda, already shaken not only
by Honoria's unexpected kindness but by these astounding
revelations, felt her eyes fill up with the tears she'd suppressed all day long. Barnaby's icy words—the rude barbs
he'd thrown at her this very afternoon—now rang in her
ears in painful counterpoint to his sister-in-law's warmth.
"But I've already told you," she said, her voice choked,
"Barnaby hates me."

Honoria nodded sadly. "Yes, I suppose he does. And I
suppose you dislike him, too."

"I?" She stared across the table into Honoria's soft, kind
eyes. "Dislike him? No, I w-wouldn't say *that*, ma'am."
The tears began to spill down her cheeks, and overwhelmed
with emotion, she dropped her head in her arms right there
on the table. "I l-love him!"

Honoria clutched her hands to her breast, astonished and
touched to the heart. The anger and resentment that had
built up for years seemed to fall away. Tenderly, with
a heart aching with regret, she reached over and gently
smoothed Miranda's lovely hair. "Oh, my poor dear!" she
murmured.

Miranda looked up. "You are very k-kind," she whispered. "I'm so ashamed. I shouldn't have revealed—"

"Of course you should. I'm glad you told me." She pulled
a handkerchief from her sleeve and wiped the younger
woman's cheeks. "I only wish I could offer more than this
handkerchief to dry your tears."

"You have. You can't know how much! I've had no one
to open my heart to for a long, long time."

"Oh, my dear!" Honoria held the handkerchief to her own eyes. "It has just occurred to me that you could have been the daughter I always dreamed of!"

It was true, Honoria realized with a shock. Miranda Pardew Velacott, of all the women in the world, was just the sort of woman that Barnaby—and she herself—could love. Her throat choked with the painful knowledge that she'd closed her mind for too long . . . and that all her actions in regard to Barnaby's prospects for wedlock had been nothing but dreadful blunders.

· *Twenty-eight* ·

BARNABY RODE THROUGH through the night toward his brother's manor house, feeling as elated as any soldier after a battle won. Though the cold wind nipped at his nose and froze his fingers, and though the horse had to pick his way carefully through the snow and could not be made to gallop, Barnaby's spirits soared. He even sang for a while, an old Scottish air that Honoria used to sing to him when he was a child. Every once in a while, he'd put his hand in his pocket and finger the trophies that he'd won for himself this night: the watch and fob, and Miranda's cameo. The felons had broken the chain on which the cameo had hung, but he could fix it. Every time his fingers touched the little trinket, he smiled to himself. He couldn't wait to see her face when he dropped it into her lap.

But as he drew closer to the house, his spirits waned, and a depression, as chilling as the night air, enveloped him. At first he didn't recognize the cause, but after thinking about it for a while, he knew what it was. He was riding home to Livy Ponsonby, not Miranda.

Here in the icy darkness the truth became blindingly clear. The prospect of bringing Miranda back her cameo brought him a singing joy; the prospect of bringing himself to Livy brought a smothering gloom.

Not that these feelings made any sense. The fact was that Livy had accepted him; Miranda never would. Besides, he was convinced that Livy was everything a bride should be: pretty and gentle and agreeable and sweet. On the other hand, she was also tongue-tied and conventional and unsurprising and dull. Miranda was just the opposite: shocking, argumentative, insulting, dangerous and . . . and more exciting than any woman he'd ever met. That was the crux of it, he realized. Livy was—he had to admit it— tiresome. And Miranda was . . . dazzling.

That was the word. Every encounter he'd had with her dazzled him. Riding with her in the carriage, tied with her to the tree, playing cards with her at the inn, arguing with her about Jamie—every one of those moments had set his blood dancing in his veins. And kissing her had been . . . well, even "dazzling" was an inadequate word for *that*.

He'd loved her since he was a boy of nineteen, he knew that now. Some part of his mind had held on to his boyhood infatuation with an unshakable tenacity, becoming with time an unacknowledged conviction that she was the only woman he would ever truly love. And though she had not responded to him when he was young, she was different now. She had even, he believed, occasionally shown a liking for him. There had been warmth in her eyes from time to time, but each time he'd seen it, he'd stupidly cut her down. Even when he'd kissed her and—had he imagined it?—she'd melted in his arms, he'd pushed her away. Why on earth had he done it?

He tried to reconstruct his thinking from the time he'd rediscovered her in the carriage. The incident at the Lydell ball was the problem, of course. He'd kept it in his mind every time he saw her, a stubborn memory that had stood between them, as thick and impenetrable as a wall. He'd used it as a shield to protect himself from pain. How stupid! Didn't he know he was no longer a vulnerable boy? He'd long since learned how to handle hurt. What was he afraid of? True, Miranda was a challenge to his manhood, but he didn't meet the other challenges of his life so fearfully. No one could say that Barnaby Traherne lacked courage. Why had he turned cowardly with Miranda?

Instead of making a mature attempt to win her, he'd thought only of taking revenge, of giving her a set-down to equal the one she'd given him. In seeking an idiotic revenge for a minor insult, he'd made a major blunder. He'd lost his chance.

He put his hand in his pocket and fingered the little cameo once more. He pictured the chain hanging round her marvelous throat and the cameo lying between the curves of her breasts. The image made him dizzy with desire. That settled it. He could not—would not!—give up the girl he'd wanted for so long, not without a fight. After all, he was not yet wed. The holiday was not yet over. There was still time.

· Twenty-nine ·

MIRANDA AWOKE THE next morning with a feeling of bubbling anticipation. She could not account for it, but it was quite real. She drew back the curtains and discovered a day that matched her mood. The snow sparkled in the brightest sunlight she'd seen since her arrival, and the sky reflected back that sparkle with a crystalline-blue gleam. In the distance, she could see a wagon moving along the road, indicating that traffic was returning to normal. And somewhere nearby, a hardy winter bird was chirping excitedly, the chirp an embodiment in sound of what she herself was feeling inside.

But neither the bird nor the sky nor the glinting snow could account for her sense of tingling excitement. Of course, her conversation with Lady Shallcross last night could have something to do with it. Lady Shallcross had indicated that both she and Delia believed Miranda to be a more suitable wife to Barnaby than Livy Ponsonby. That *anyone* could wish to pair her with Barnaby Traherne was the outside of enough, but that the two women closest to Barnaby wished it quite took her breath away.

But of course, if one thought more carefully about it, the idea was ridiculous. Barnaby would never learn to like her. Besides, he was betrothed. It would be best to put such thoughts out of her mind.

She dressed quickly, for she had a great deal to do to get ready for the day's studies, but when she hurriedly threw open her door, she heard a strange rattle. Something was hanging on her outer doorknob. She looked down curiously and discovered—hanging by its chain, with a little note pinned to it—her cameo!

Her heart leaped into her throat. He'd recovered it! Barnaby himself! Staring down at the bauble, she felt like Elaine of Astolat, or even Queen Guinevere herself. Barnaby had been her knight on a quest. He'd tracked the dragon to its lair and recovered his lady's talisman! Now that it was over, and the knight was apparently unhurt, the idea of the quest delighted her. *And oh*, she thought, *how thrilled the boys will be to hear about it!*

With eager fingers, she unpinned the note and opened it, and her eyes flew over the words. *It is customary,* he'd written, *for the recoverer of a treasure to receive a reward. I shall be coming, in due course, to claim one. I hope you can think of something suitable, but if you can't, I have one or two suggestions.*

She clutched the trinket to her bosom, her spirit soaring. Even the note had the quality of knightly romance: the triumphant knight coming to claim his prize. Could it be that her feelings on awakening had been prophetic—that this was going to be a very exciting day?

But no, she warned herself. Barnaby was no knight and she was no prize. His recovery of her cameo was a gesture. It was a kind and generous gesture, of course, but nothing more. She should not make too much of it. Later, when the boys took their recess, she would go downstairs, thank him nicely and make an end of it.

But he was asking for a reward. What did he mean? He knew she had nothing to give him. Was he joking? But even if he were, she wanted to give him something tangible as a symbol of her gratitude. Would her finest, lace-edged handkerchief be acceptable? It was a modest reward, but it would have to do.

With these sobering thoughts, she was able to bring her spirits back down to earth. She had work to do.

On the floor below, at that very moment, all Barnaby's brothers, both his sisters-in-law, and Lady Isabel, were gathered in his bedroom. They surrounded the bed where he was soundly asleep. "Wake up, you gudgeon," Harry shouted into the sleeper's ear.

Barnaby sat up with a start. "What—?"

"Congratulations!" they all shouted, bending over him and embracing him all at once. Then they admitted Cummings into the room. The butler carried a tray holding glasses and a bottle of champagne. The Earl accepted the honor of opening the bottle, and the bubbling liquid was poured. Toasts were drunk until they ran out of words and drink.

Then Terence insisted that the hero make a speech. Barnaby, dizzy from the abrupt awakening and the early-morning imbibing, got up on his bed on two wobbly legs. "Ladies and gentlemen," he said, grinning sheepishly, "although I thank you for your good wishes, I hope you all will acknowledge that if you'd left me to my own devices before this, I'd have been a hero long ago." And with that, amid much laughter and applause, he fell forward on his face.

Delia, whose feet were always on the ground, took this opportunity to bring the roisterers back to earth. "Enough of this gaiety," she said sternly, urging them out of the room. "It's time to return to reality. You all must go down to the breakfast room, to entertain our visitors. Livy and her guests must be wondering what's become of us. Meanwhile, I shall inform Sir Hero about what awaits him down below."

By the time a sobered Barnaby had dressed and presented himself in the breakfast room, all signs of gaiety were gone. The large, round family breakfast table was surrounded by gloomy faces. Livy, still red-eyed, was no longer weeping, but she looked as if she might burst into tears again at a moment's notice. Her mother stood over her, with a hand on her shoulder, as if she didn't trust the girl out of her clutches. Ned Keswick, looking white about the mouth, as if his teeth had been clenched all night, stood leaning on the mantel, his eyes fixed on the girl he'd come to claim.

Barnaby regarded all of them. "Good morning," he said cheerfully. "I don't think there's a need for such long faces. This problem, if I understand it rightly, will not be difficult to solve."

"Oh, it won't, won't it?" Mr. Keswick snapped. "And how would you solve it if you were me, and you'd found out your betrothed had given her promise to another?"

Lady Ponsonby sidled across the room and took Barnaby's arm. "Please excuse this embarrassing scene, dear boy," she cooed, a smile on her face that was as false as it was inappropriate. "Mr. Keswick has no claim, I assure you. My dearest girl was swayed by a stroll in the moonlight, and she made promises to that fellow that she did not mean. She hadn't yet met you! She feels quite differently now and has a sincere desire to be your bride."

"That, ma'am, is a deuced lie!" Mr. Keswick exclaimed. "You are forcing the girl into a betrothal she does not want."

"But why would Lady Ponsonby *do* that?" the Earl asked in honest confusion. "Why force a girl to wed against her wishes?"

"Because she thinks your brother is a better catch than I!" Keswick said bitterly. "He's a Traherne of Shallcross, and I am in trade. It doesn't matter that my father's cotton mill will someday make it possible for me to provide more luxuries for her than a duke could. I'm in trade, and that makes me scum!"

"You're n-not scum!" little Livy muttered. They were the first words she'd spoken since her mother's arrival.

"Now, now, my sweet," her mother twittered nervously, "you must let me do the talking if you want to get out of this fix."

"I don't see that there's any fix at all," Barnaby said, removing his arm from Lady Ponsonby's grip. He strode over to the chair where Livy sat and knelt down beside her. "Livy, my dear, that afternoon in the library when I made you an offer, you looked as if you wanted to burst into tears. Do you remember that?"

Livy kept her head lowered and her eyes veiled, but she nodded.

"Was it Mr. Keswick you were thinking of then?"

She nodded again.

"Are you in love with Mr. Keswick?"

"Livy—!" her mother said warningly.

Barnaby threw Lady Ponsonby one of his daunting frowns. "I think it would be better, ma'am, if you said nothing more. Now, Livy, before you answer me, let me tell you—and your mother—that I am far from rich, that I am the fourth son of an earl with three very healthy brothers, so that the likelihood of my ever winning a title is so remote as to be unthinkable, and that professionally I am a mere public servant. Mr. Keswick, on the other hand, is young, handsome and, I gather, will one day be rich enough to buy himself a title. Am I right, Mr. Keswick?"

Redheaded Ned blinked at him in some surprise. "I think you put that very well."

"Now, then, Livy, let me ask you again. Are you in love with Mr. Keswick?"

A tense silence filled the room as every eye was fixed on Livy's bent head. She turned slowly in her chair. "I think I . . . love you *both!*" she stammered. "P-positively."

There was a universal groan. Barnaby winced. But for Mr. Keswick, this was the last straw. "Balderdash!" he exploded, and striding across the room, he pushed Barnaby aside, pulled Livy to her feet and took her in his arms. "You goose," he said firmly, "you do *not* love us both!" And he planted a very businesslike kiss on her mouth.

Livy did not struggle, nor did anyone in the room make a move to stop this flagrantly vulgar act. It was many moments before Ned Keswick let her go. When he did, Livy turned to Barnaby, her eyes shining. "I do love you both," she said, "but I . . . think I . . . love my Neddy more."

"Aha! That's my girl!" Ned crowed. He lifted her up in his arms and swung her round in triumph. "Now you and

I are going straight to Gretna." Without another word, and with only the merest nod to his swooning mother-in-law-to-be, he carried Livy from the room—and from the house.

Delia called out for Cummings to come running, and she went quickly to Lady Ponsonby's side. "Now, now, Your Ladyship, please don't take on," she soothed gently, helping the defeated woman to a chair and holding a glass of water to her pale lips. "Here, take a sip, do! As soon as you feel able to stand, we'll help you upstairs. A bit of a rest, and you'll find yourself perfectly well restored."

"Restored?" the woman cried. "How can you say so? My daughter is eloping with a *tradesman*!"

"That tradesman," Delia said, taking her under one arm while Cummings took the other, and walking her to the door, "seems a very admirable specimen to me. A more dashing, romantic fellow has never crossed this threshold. In fact," she added, throwing Terence a glinting glance over her shoulder, "if I were a free woman, I might have tried to win him for myself."

All the other members of Barnaby's family, fearful that the incident had made him unhappy, tried to hide their concern by busily attacking their breakfasts. Barnaby, watching them, wanted to laugh aloud, but he put on as somber an expression as possible, went over to Honoria and took her hand. "I hope, dearest, that you're not too deeply overset by this turnabout," he said, patting her shoulder affectionately.

"I? Certainly not," she assured him, searching his face in a vain attempt to read his emotions. "It is *you*—! How unfair that you should have to bear another . . . another . . ."

"Another set-down? Yes, can you believe such deuced bad luck?" But the twinkle in his eye belied his words. He leaned down and kissed his sister-in-law's cheek. "But I expect I'll learn to bear my loss." He sauntered to the door with a decidedly cheerful step. "I'm sure I'll learn to bear it passably well. In time."

· Thirty ·

HE WENT WHISTLING down the hall, his step as light as his heart. He felt as if a terrible weight had been lifted from his chest. He was free to pursue his dream, and to that end, he intended to go upstairs and face Miranda Pardew. But as he rounded the newel post and put a foot on the first step, he came face-to-face with her. "Oh! Mi— Mrs. Velacott!" he stammered. *Confound it,* he swore to himself, *whenever I come upon her unexpectedly, I'm a bubble-brained nineteen-year-old again!*

"Mr. Traherne," she greeted him, sounding a little breathless, "I was just coming to look for you."

"And I you." He laughed.

"About the reward," they said together.

She stood a step above him, so that they were face-to-face, eye-to-eye. "I do thank you," she said, dropping her eyes from the intensity of his stare. "I don't know what happened, but I do know that tracking down the robbers and confronting them couldn't have been easy."

"It was an adventure I very much enjoyed. But much too much ado has been made of it, so let's not dwell on the details."

"Very well, if you don't wish to speak of it now. But the boys are agog. You must come up and tell them about it."

"I will. Later. Right now, I'm more interested in what you've decided should be my reward."

She put her hand in her pocket and drew out a small, neatly folded, lacy handkerchief. "I haven't anything of real value, as you know," she said, holding it out to him, "but I hope that this will serve."

He looked up from her offering to where the cameo lay between the swells of her breasts and up to her shapely throat, her slightly-pointed chin, the full lips that were beginning to tremble under his scrutiny, and to her lovely, speaking eyes that at this moment would not tell him anything. And he shook his head. "A handkerchief," he said in a low voice, "is not quite what I had in mind."

"Then, what—?"

"I think you can guess," he said, and grinning boyishly, he pulled her to him and kissed her, eagerly, hungrily, but cleanly, without guilt or fear of being hurt by it. He felt her stiffen in resistance, but after a moment she swayed in his arms and seemed to melt, and he heard a little moan deep in her throat. *Oh, God, she does love me,* his heart sang.

But at that moment, she pushed him away with such force that he tottered back down the step. It reminded him of tripping down the rise of that platform at the Lydell ball. She was *playing* with him again! He was eleven years older and making the same fool of himself. And the pain of it was every bit as strong as ever!

He looked up at her, stung. But she didn't look in the least triumphant. She was backing up the stairs, rubbing away his kiss from her mouth with the back of her hand, her eyes wide with a pain as great as his. "That was cruel!" she said hoarsely. "Cruel and beastly! Lady Shallcross says you are kind, but I don't believe you capable of kindness." And she turned and ran up the stairs.

He didn't understand her. "Miranda, wait!" he croaked, stumbling after her. "I didn't mean to—" He caught up with her at the landing and grasped her arms. "Confound it, Miranda, how can you think me beastly?" he asked, gasping for breath. "I only thought . . . for a reward . . ."

"All right, then, you've had your reward! Let me go!"

"But you don't understand. I haven't yet—"

"Oh, haven't you? Well, it's all the reward you're going to get! Let your little Livy reward you!" She pulled off the cameo, breaking the chain, and threw it at him. "Here! If you must be rewarded for it that way, I don't want it!"

He gaped after her as she ran round to the second flight and disappeared from his view, and a sense of what had hurt her broke upon him. *Lord*, he thought, *I am a fool*. He'd done it backwards. He should have explained his feelings to her first and *then* kissed her. How could he have expected her to understand all the cowardly vacillations that had tormented him since he'd seen her on the stagecoach?

But I shall not be a coward again, he swore, and he dashed up the second flight, taking the steps three at a time. He almost caught up with her on the third flight, but she was too fleet for him and had almost reached the next landing. He reached up, caught her ankle and pulled her down. She twisted herself around and beat at his chest with her fists, tears coursing down her cheeks. "Let me up!" she muttered through clenched teeth. "Haven't you humiliated me enough?"

Holding her fast with his body, he caught her fists in his hands. "Damnation, Miranda, will you listen to me? You don't understand—"

"Yes, I do. It's revenge. You're obsessed with revenge. You had to take revenge on the footpads, and you have to have your revenge on me, for what I did to you eleven years ago."

"Miranda, please," he pleaded, trying to keep her from wriggling out of his hold. "It's not—! Won't you—?"

"Don't you see that you've already succeeded? I've been quite adequately set down. I'm crying. I'm humiliated. I'm hurt. So we're even. Let me up!"

"I'm not trying to get even. I love you! I'm trying to *win* you, don't you understand?"

She stopped wriggling. "I don't know what you're talking about. You're betrothed, aren't you?"

"No, I'm not. Livy has run off with another. A redheaded Midas called Keswick."

"Oh?" She blinked at him, arrested, her lips parted in a kind of suspended animation.

"And let me tell you, ma'am, that when he kissed Livy, *she* didn't push him away. She leaped into his arms and let him carry her off to Gretna."

"Did she?" She wriggled one hand free and wiped her cheeks with the back of it. "I'm . . . sorry."

"Don't be sorry. I only offered for her because I was afraid of you."

"Afraid of me? Why?"

"Because I felt such a fool for loving you all these years. Because you're still so beautiful. Because I was sure you'd rebuff me again."

She gulped back what was left of her tears. "You certainly don't appear to be afraid today. Kissing me on the stairs like a lecher with a kitchen maid! And holding me down on these uncomfortable stairs in this humiliating way. Let me up!"

"Very well, I will if you wish it. But then, will you agree to give me another chance? Please, Miranda, let me begin again. From the very beginning. So that we may meet properly this time."

She did not answer, but he got up and helped her to her feet. "Miss Miranda Pardew?" he asked, making a slight bow. "I was wondering if I might have this dance."

Her lips turned up in the slightest of smiles. "But my dance card is filled, sir. Don't you know that it's only maiden aunts and wallflowers who don't have their cards filled by this time? Do I look like a wallflower to you?"

"Oh, I know your card is filled, ma'am. But I hoped that, when you understood that my heart is bursting with the desire for you to dance with me, you would ignore your other partners and, in pity if for no other reason, choose me."

"That is a most touching invitation, sir, but I don't know even know your name."

"Does it matter? We can dance together *incognito*."

She slipped her hand in his. "Then lead the way, sir. I am yours, at least for the duration of one dance."

He led her down the stairs and through the hallway to the library, not saying a word. When he'd closed the door, he turned to face her. "Listen, Miss Pardew. Do you hear the music? It's a waltz." He slipped his arm about her waist. "Do you waltz, ma'am?"

"A waltz is rather daring for an inexperienced young man like yourself, isn't it?"

"When you know me better, you'll discover that underneath this rather cowardly, sheepish exterior, I *can* be rather daring," he said, sweeping her round the room in time to the music in his head.

When they'd grown so dizzy that the room spun around, they stopped dancing, but they clung to each other to steady themselves. "Is the dance over?" she asked in a whisper.

"I want it to go on forever, but it's not for me to say." He peered down into her face intently. "*Is* it over?"

She shook her head, threw her arms about his neck and drew his head down to hers. The kiss was long, and deep, and told him everything he needed to know—they'd come through the miasma of misunderstandings and confused emotions that had surrounded them for far too long, and had found each other at last.

The kiss might have gone on endlessly, but the library door flew open. "I say, Barnaby," said the Earl from the threshold, "Honoria has been looking for— Oh!"

Barnaby lifted his head. "Looking for me?"

"Well, er . . . I don't suppose it was very urgent," the Earl muttered in embarrassment.

Just then, Harry appeared in the doorway. "How about a game of billiards, old fellow? Isabel is busy with her hair, and I— Oh, am I interrupting something?"

As if on cue, Terence put his head in the door. "Barnaby, are you in here? Delia said to tell you that Lady Ponsonby is taking her leave and— Oh, I say! What's going on here?"

Barnaby, refusing to release the blushing Miranda from his hold, looked over at his three brothers crowded in the doorway and fixed them with one of his famous glowers. "I might have known the three of you would find a way to interfere. What is going on here is a private matter. I'm trying to make an *offer* to this young lady."

"An offer?" the Earl asked, his face lighting up.

"I say!" exclaimed Terence, awestruck.

"Oh, capital!" Harry chuckled. "That's famous news!"

"Thank you for your approval," Barnaby said dryly, "but I would be obliged if you'd all turn round and make yourselves scarce. Unless, of course, you think it necessary to do *this* for me, too!"

"No, no," said Harry, whisking himself out.

"Wouldn't think of interfering," Terence murmured, following his brother out the door.

"Seems to me," said the Earl, backing to the door and cackling with delight, "that you're doing quite splendidly all on your own. Just as I always said you would."

· *Epilogue* ·

A YEAR LATER, rosy-cheeked from the cold and brimming with good spirits, Mr. and Mrs. Barnaby Traherne came into their town house on Henrietta Street from a Christmas frolic given by Molly Davenham. Barnaby took his wife's cloak from her shoulders, shook the snow from it and handed it, with his greatcoat, to the butler. Taking the fellow aside, he asked in an undervoice, "Is the job done, Merwin?"

"Yes, sir. Everything's in place," the butler whispered back. Then he threw Barnaby a half-smile and a wink and discreetly withdrew.

Miranda, crossing the foyer to the stairway, turned round. "Did you say something, dearest?"

Barnaby returned to her in three quick strides. "Just dismissing Merwin," he said, pulling her into his arms. "I've been waiting for hours to be alone with my bride."

She slipped her arms about his neck. "Scarcely a bride, my love. By this time next month, we shall be wed a whole year."

"A whole year!" He shook his head in disbelief. "I continue to feel as if we're still on our honeymoon." He kissed her mouth, his hand caressing her throat, the throat whose sensuous curves never failed to clench his innards. "Did you see how the Prime Minister devoured you with his eyes?" he murmured, his lips against hers. "I wanted to call the damned fellow out!"

Miranda giggled. "He was no worse than Celia Carew. The little minx flirted with you shamelessly."

"Did she indeed? I never noticed."

He let her go and, with arms about each other's waist, they started for the stairs. "Molly Davenham remarked to me that marriage has changed you drastically," Miranda said, throwing her husband a laughing glance.

"Drastically?" Barnaby's brows rose in surprise. "In what way?"

"She said you were no longer—" But she stopped in midsentence, for they were passing the sitting room doorway, and she had a fleeting impression that something within had been moved. For a moment, she thought she glimpsed a familiar piece of furniture: her old Sheraton desk. But of course, it couldn't be . . .

"No longer what?" Barnaby was asking.

She shook off her momentary lapse and grinned up at him. "Forbidding. She says you used to be forbidding."

"Nonsense," he retorted complacently, urging her up the stairs. "I was never forbidding. How can a fellow who suffered from a near-fatal case of shyness be called forbidding?"

They'd reached the top of the stairs. He dropped his hold on her, crossed the hallway and threw open their bedroom door. His eyes swiftly took in the scene before him. Merwin had done very well; the floral arrangement on the night table was perfect, and all the candles were lit.

Miranda came up behind him and blinked. For a moment she didn't breathe. Then she gasped, "My *bed*!" She crossed the threshold like one dazed and gaped at the huge four-poster ensconced against the far wall. "It's Mama's Queen Anne bed! How did you—?" She turned to her husband and threw herself into his arms. "*Barnaby*! How could you have known?"

Barnaby beamed down at her glowing face. "Your Aunt Letty told me about it, and about your desk, too. It's downstairs in the sitting room."

Miranda put a trembling hand to her forehead. "No, no, all this is quite impossible. How could you have talked to Aunt Letty? And how could you have persuaded Belle Velacott to give the pieces up? I'm dreaming."

"You're wide awake, my love, I promise you. Once your aunt told me the story, I had very little difficulty in persuading the Velacotts to return your property. In fact, they were so delighted to be invited to our anniversary ball, they were almost eager to part with the furniture."

"Anniversary *ball*? Wait a moment, please. You're going much too fast for me. First, when and where did you speak to Aunt Letty?"

"I went to see her last week."

"You went to see her?"

He nodded. "To invite her to our anniversary ball. You do want her here for that occasion, don't you?"

She gazed up at him with eyes that were beginning to brim with tears. "Are we going to have a *ball*? But I thought you disliked them."

"With you at my side, my dearest, I've discovered that they are quite enjoyable affairs. Don't you *want* to have a ball to celebrate our first year?"

"Oh, Barnaby!" She drew him down beside her on her newly-restored bed and, clutching him tightly round the waist, nuzzled his neck. "An anniversary ball is exactly what I want."

"Good, then. It's done. We shall have the grandest of balls and invite absolutely everyone. All my brothers. All their wives. Your aunt Letty. The Velacotts. Everyone in the world we've ever known. It shall be the most talked-about crush of the Season. There are only two requests I have to make of you in regard to it."

"Oh? And what are they?" she murmured contentedly.

"First, that you wear your green gown."

"Done. What else?"

He put his cheek against her hair and breathed in the fragrance of her. "That *this* time, my dearest, you give me the opportunity to sign your blasted dance card before it's filled."

CLASSIC WINTER ROMANCE TO READ BY THE FIRE